RELIEF VALVE

The PLUMBER'S MATE MYSTERIES TWO

JL MERROW

D1096851

RIPTIDE
PUBLISHING

Riptide Publishing
PO Box 1537
Burnsville, NC 28714
www.riptidepublishing.com

Relief Valve

Cover art: Christine Coffee, coffeecreatescovers.com
Editor: Carole-ann Galloway
Layout: L.C. Chase, lcchase.com/design.htm

ISBN: 978-1-62649-722-1

Second edition
February, 2018

Also available in ebook:
ISBN: 978-1-62649-721-4

RELIEF VALVE

THE PLUMBER'S MATE MYSTERIES TWO

JL MERROW

RIPTIDE
PUBLISHING

For my mother, who didn't so much encourage me in a love of reading as lead me into a labyrinth of books and leave me to find my own way out. She's still waiting for me to emerge.

With thanks to the many lovely people who helped me with this book: Jo, Tricia, Kristin, Pender, Lou, Blaine, Jennifer, and Susan. Plus, as always, the guys from Verulam Writers' Circle—who, I would like to stress, are nothing at all like the Literati!

TABLE OF
CONTENTS

PROLOGUE

All right, so Phil and me were having a bit of a barney. It happens, especially when your significant other has a habit of behaving like a pigheaded git. And yeah, so maybe we'd got a bit loud, considering this was a polite soiree at the Old Deanery in St. Leonards, not Saturday night at the local Wetherspoons pub. People were starting to stare at us as if they thought maybe we'd been laid on as entertainment for the evening.

Then their heads all snapped round away from us like the crowd at Wimbledon after Murray's returned a serve.

I twisted around to see what they were gawping at now—well, you would, wouldn't you?—and stared, helpless, as my big sister crumpled at the knees. The glass she'd been holding dropped from her hand and hit the carpet, bouncing and rolling. Must be quality crystal, not supermarket tat, I thought, as Cherry joined it on the floor. Daft what you think about, times like that. The noise in the room, which a moment ago had been all party-jolly, chattering voices and ear-wincing laughter, quietened down, then swelled again, shriller this time, like someone was mucking about with the volume control on the telly.

Cherry wasn't moving—well, she was, but it was the wrong sort of moving. Twitching and convulsing.

Not getting up.

I started towards her.

CHAPTER ONE

It had all started a week or two previous, when the phone rang. (And if you haven't got déjà vu at this point, where have you been?) It was the landline, not my mobile, which meant it wasn't work, or a mate, or . . . Come to think of it, why did I still have a landline?

"Aren't you going to answer that?" Phil asked, secure in the knowledge that with the ten-ton furry cushion that was Arthur snugly asleep on his lap, he was excused errands for the foreseeable future. "Put the kettle on while you're up."

Serve him right if he got pins and needles in his dick. "It'll only be some bloody telemarketer from a call centre in India. It'll stop ringing in a minute when one of the other six lines they're calling picks up."

We listened as the ringing carried on. Even Merlin paused in batting at something under the armchair and twitched a furry ear.

"Might be important."

"Fine, fine, I'm going." I heaved myself up from his side—I'd been comfortable there—and plodded over to the house phone, overdoing it a bit to make a point. "Yeah?"

"Tom? It's me. Cherry." Not a telemarketer, then. My sister. Right: family. That's why I still had a landline. I hoped they appreciated how they were costing me fourteen quid a month plus call charges. She sounded worried—at least, as far as I could tell from the unfamiliar voice on the phone.

To say my sister never calls would be—well, not an understatement, obviously, because that'd just be daft. I suppose the word I'm looking for is *accurate*. Until now, that was. I hadn't even been sure she had my number, but then it wasn't exactly a state secret. Mum had probably divulged it without any need for excessive fingernail-pulling or waterboarding.

"Cherry? What is it, love?" I cringed a bit at the endearment that had just slipped out. Put it down to consoling one too many housewives after a domestic disaster.

"Mrs. Morangie's died."

"Who?" I wasn't winding her up. I genuinely didn't have a clue.

"Don't be wilfully obtuse. Mrs. *Morangie.*" She huffed. "Mrs. Next-door."

I managed to tamp down my irritation. But seriously, who uses the phrase *wilfully obtuse* on the phone to close family members? "Which one? You mean from Mum and Dad's, right? Not yours." I was fairly sure there were people living in the houses either side of Cherry's, and that they hadn't all moved out in horror when she'd moved in. Maybe she even cared if they lived or died. But I couldn't think of a single reason why she'd be calling up to let me know one of them had popped off to the Neighbourhood Watch meeting in the sky.

Her *tsk* crackled down the phone line in a burst of static. "Auntie Lol," she said as if it pained her.

"*Ohhh.* Oh. She died? How? I got a card from her at Christmas, same as usual," I added, feeling a bit lost. That'd only been a few weeks ago. I mean, yeah, people died, but Auntie Lol was well young, relatively speaking. Younger than my mum and dad, anyhow. Although, to be fair, so were most people. "And hang on a mo, since when has she been Mrs. Morangie?" I'd addressed the envelope to Ms. Fernside, same as always.

"Since she married *Mr.* Morangie, perhaps? I thought you knew she got married. It was while you were still living at home."

Actually, as I recalled, it'd been while I was mostly living in hospital having bits of metal screwed into my pelvis. It was a lot less fun than it sounded. "Yeah, but it's not like it lasted. Didn't they get divorced years ago? But what happened, anyway? You never said. To Auntie Lol, I mean. Was it an accident?"

"If you'd let me get a word in edgewise . . ." Cherry's voice trailed off. When she spoke again, it was softer. "Well, she killed herself."

"What?" I sat down hard on the sofa. From his position on Phil's lap, Arthur opened his eyes a crack and flicked his tail at me. No respect for the recently bereaved, our Arthur.

As Cherry spoke again, I felt a large, warm hand massage my shoulder. Going out on a limb and assuming Arthur hadn't suddenly acquired opposable thumbs and, more to the point, a heart, I deduced it was Phil's. "I don't know all the details, but apparently she had cancer. I suppose she didn't want to go through chemo or surgery or whatever. At any rate, she's supposed to have told her doctor she'd had trouble sleeping since the diagnosis, and then sat down one evening with a bottle of sherry and took all the pills he gave her at once."

"Fuck."

"Charming. Well, anyway, I'm named as executor of her will, so there are some practical things we need to sort out."

She's not *actually* a heartless bitch, my sister. Well, not totally. She just didn't know Auntie Lol like I did. Which begged a bit of a question, now I came to think about it. "How come you're executor, anyway?"

"The law degree? It was all sorted out years ago. Anyway, we need to meet. Tomorrow morning? Around eleven? You can come to my office."

That'd be nice for me. I mentally ran over my schedule while Merlin physically ran over my feet and started clawing his way up my legs. "Can't. Got a washing machine at ten, and every time I go round to hers, she's always got another nineteen jobs that'll *only take a minute, honest*. I'll be lucky to get away much before twelve." I patted a sleek, furry head as Merlin nuzzled into my thigh. I appreciated the affection but not the line of cat snot he'd probably left in his wake.

"I suppose it'll have to be lunch, then. One o'clock, Carluccio's?"

"Or we could just meet up for a sarnie in the park."

"In January?"

"Okay, so maybe it's not peak picnic season, but fresh air is fresh air. And dodging those gangs of Canada geese that always try and mug you for your lunch will keep you on your toes. Can't be good for you, working in an office all day."

"Don't be daft. I'll see you at Carluccio's. Oh, and Tom? Don't say anything to Mum and Dad about this, will you?"

"Why not?"

"Mum and Mrs. Morangie were quite close friends at one time. I, well, I haven't told her she's dead yet. So don't say anything. I don't want Mum upset."

I supposed it was good she was worried about *someone's* feelings. "Fine. Mum's the word, that all right?"

"Very funny." She hung up.

"So who's Auntie Lol?" Phil asked, his hand still on my shoulder. It was nice, but I felt a bit uncomfortable, to be honest. We hadn't exactly been together all that long—then again, how many dates do you have to go on before you get to the emotional-support part of the relationship?

Now I came to think about it, I wasn't really sure how many actual dates we'd been on anyway. Do sneaky house searches and near-death experiences count?

Probably, if you're going out with a private investigator.

"Well, we're not actually related. I just called her Auntie Lol."

"I take it that's short for something?"

"Laura." I gave an awkward little shrug with the shoulder he wasn't holding on to. "I used to have a problem with my *r*'s when I was a kid."

"Don't worry. There's nothing wrong with your arse these days." His hand squeezed my shoulder, then slipped away. I expected it to slip all the way down to said arse, but it didn't. I wasn't sure if I was relieved or sorry.

"Har har. She used to live next door to my mum and dad back when I was at school. She babysat me sometimes, and I'd go round to play with her cats."

Phil smirked. "Lolcats?"

"I can't believe you actually said that." I smiled a bit, though, remembering. "She had a ginger one called Sooty, and a fluffy black one called Sweep. Dad's allergic, so we never had any pets." Which, obviously, was the most important part of the story.

"You seem a bit more upset about her than I'd expect, if she was just some old neighbour."

"You know it's dead sexy when you go all Sherlock on me? She used to look after me a lot when I was a kid. Mum was always keen to get me out of the house while Richard and Cherry were studying for exams or Dad had had a bad day at work. Auntie Lol always seemed really pleased to have me. She didn't have any kids; she lived on her own. She used to keep toffees in an old tea caddy and chocolate biscuits in a glass jar," I remembered. And she'd thought my knack of being able to find stuff was the best thing since sliced bread. "She was the first person I ever came out to. As gay, I mean, not the finding-stuff thing."

"Yeah? How'd she take it?"

"Well, put it this way. She moved up to Scotland a few years later to go and live with her girlfriend, so either she took it totally in her stride, or she was so permanently traumatised it turned her queer. Sod it. I wonder what's happened to the girlfriend? If she's still around, this must be well rough on her."

"Yeah." Phil had experience in the bereavement area. His husband—sorry, civil partner—died a few years ago.

"Auntie Lol topped herself," I told him, so he'd know it was even rougher than he thought. "She was dying of cancer already, though. She never said."

"Jesus." Phil let out a long breath, stared at the wall for a moment, then turned and pulled me close. Not expecting it, I got caught off-balance and narrowly missed elbowing Arthur in the eye. Arthur *mrowed* in a low, affronted tone, then stalked off Phil's lap for somewhere he wouldn't get hit by flying body parts.

"Oi, warn a bloke, would you?" The sofa creaked as I struggled into a more comfortable position. "Not that I don't appreciate it, mind," I added when Phil showed signs of relaxing his grip on me.

"You stayed in touch, then?" Phil's thumb rubbed my side soothingly.

"Well, cards and stuff. Letters at Christmas."

"What do you expect, then? *Happy Birthday, I'm terminally ill, many happy returns*?"

I stiffened. And not in a good way. "Oi, this is my surrogate auntie you're talking about. Have a bit of respect."

"Sorry."

He sounded it too, so I relaxed back into the curve of his arm. "Nah, I don't know. Just … I'd have thought she'd have said *something*."

"Probably didn't want you worrying about her. It wasn't like you could've done much, all the way down here."

"I could have gone to see her."

"Sometimes it's better to remember people like they were in their best days. Not when they're halfway out the door." He gave me a sharp look. "I remember my grandparents, and the last years weren't pretty."

"S'pose that's what she was trying to avoid."

"Yeah. Better to go on your own terms, that's what I reckon. Was she getting on a bit?"

"No. That's the thing. She always seemed way younger than my mum. She had all this curly blonde hair—still rocking the eighties perm, I guess—and she used to take me down the park and play football with me and stuff. Mum never liked going down the park with me. Can't blame her, really."

"Too full of yobs from the council estate?"

I really wasn't feeling up to reliving the memory of my first dead body right now. "Something like that."

Phil sort of *hmphed*. "Yeah, I remember your mum. Council estate yobs really weren't her thing, were they? I suppose they still aren't."

I pulled away and stared at him for a moment. "Are you calling my mum stuck-up?"

"I'm saying she's got class, you wanker. God, you're touchy sometimes. Come here." He pulled me back against his side, his hand drifting down as if by accident to rest on my arse.

"Yeah, well. Runs in the family, doesn't it?" I said with a cheeky grin.

Phil rolled his eyes. "You, classy? Don't push it. So you're seeing your sister tomorrow? She's the barrister, right?"

"Yeah. Carluccio's." Was he angling for an invite? I thought I'd better come up with a way of distracting him just in case, so I swung my leg over Phil's recently vacated lap and started proving I could be a lot more fun than Arthur.

Classy? No. Creative? Yes.

CHAPTER TWO

Carluccio's, in St. Christopher Place, was modern, bright, and ear-splittingly noisy. It was market day in St. Albans, so the place was stuffed to bursting with yummy mummies showing off the latest toddler-and-buggy combos and picking at green salads and glasses of fizzy water. The place smelled more of rice cakes than of garlic.

I was on time—I swear I was—but my sister was already there, sitting at a table near the back with her phone out, checking her emails so as not to waste a second of her very valuable time. All right, for all I could tell, she might have been playing Angry Birds, but I know what my money was on. Cherry hadn't changed much. Still the same mousy-brown hair, wrenched back in an uncompromising ponytail. She didn't wear makeup, never had, and dressed a bit frumpy, in a middle-aged, middle-class, Church of England sort of way. She looked up and frowned when she saw me. "*There* you are." I swear her accent had got posher.

Or maybe I'd just got more common.

I squeezed past a couple of off-road baby buggies, picking up a light dusting of Hertfordshire mud in the process, and sat down opposite her. "All right, Sis?"

"You'd better choose quickly," she said by way of fond sisterly greeting, thrusting a menu at me. "I've got a meeting at two thirty."

I gave it a glance and shrugged. "I'll just have a spaghetti carbonara." I twisted round in my seat and managed to catch the waitress's eye.

Cherry went for the chicken salad with prunes. I asked for a Diet Coke, and she ordered a glass of fizzy water.

"So, how've you been, then?" I asked to be polite as we waited for our food.

Cherry ate *polite* for breakfast. "We didn't see you at Mum and Dad's for Christmas. Again." It sounded like her court voice. *And I put it to you, m'lud, that the defendant wilfully and culpably spurned his mother's roast turkey and all the trimmings (cries of horror from the gallery).*

I looked down briefly to check I wasn't actually sitting in the dock in handcuffs. "Yeah, well . . . I had stuff on, that's all." Stuff like avoiding soggy veg and stodgy conversation. And hoping a certain private investigator would turn up for a cosy Christmas dinner but not actually asking him until it was way too late for anyone to change their plans.

"Stuff? What stuff? You're single and childless—how much *stuff* could there be?" *It seems clear to me, m'lud, and I'm sure the jury will agree, that the defendant's alibi is flimsy at best.*

"I've got cats, all right? I can't just abandon them. Pets are for Christmas too, not just for life. And, well . . . I'm with someone now." Not that Phil had actually shown his face round mine until Boxing Day.

"A man?"

"Er, yeah? Since when has it ever not been a man?"

"Oh, I don't know. People change, you know." At least she wasn't sounding like she was wearing a horsehair wig anymore. "So who's this one, then? Not that awful one with the dog?"

I sighed. *One time* I'd taken Gary round to Mum and Dad's for Christmas, a few years ago when he'd been suffering from a particularly traumatic recent breakup. Not that they aren't all traumatic for Gary, poor sod. Since then, the whole bloody family seems to have it fixed in their heads that me and him are an item. "Told you, Gary's just a mate. And what's wrong with him, anyway?"

"What's right with him? Honestly, when he told that story about King's Cross Station toilets, poor Mum didn't know where to look!"

Okay, maybe she had a point there. Cherry, mind, had known where to look. It was at Gary. With daggers. "The bloke I'm with is called Phil," I told her, secure in the knowledge that, unlike Gary, it wouldn't ring any bells. Catch my sister taking an interest in my life. "Phil Morrison. He's a private investig—"

"Phil Morrison?" She cut me off sharply. "Not the Phil Morrison who pushed you under a car when you were seventeen?"

"What? No! He didn't push me. I ran. By accident. And how the bloody hell do you remember him after all this time? You don't even remember my birthday!"

"I remember your birthday. We just don't exchange cards. Anyway, there were some interesting legal ramifications, that's all. I was very into tort at the time."

Anyone else, I'd have said something like, *Taut abs?* But I wasn't sure I was feeling up to one of Cherry's patented withering looks.

Not that she let me get a word in edgewise, anyway. "What on earth are you doing with him? I thought you hated each other. *You* certainly ought to hate him. We could have sued, you know, but Dad thought they weren't worth it, living on the council estate."

I bristled on Phil's behalf. "Yeah, well—it's like you said. People change. He's a decent bloke now."

Her eyes narrowed. I could practically hear a little voice in her head going, *Hearsay! The jury will disregard that last statement.* "So how long's this been going on?"

"Couple of months," I said, as casually as I could. "We met— met again, I mean—back in November, over the murder in Brock's Hollow."

"Oh my God. I knew I'd seen his name somewhere recently. It was in the papers. He was the one who got shot, wasn't he?"

Um. Maybe there were one or two things I'd forgotten to mention in my not-quite-weekly-all-right-more-like-monthly phone calls to Mum. I rubbed my arm. "Can't believe everything you read in the papers, you know."

Especially seeing as Phil and I might just have made a concerted effort to keep my name out of all the stories about the murder. Whoever said "all publicity is good publicity" clearly didn't work in the kind of business where women on their own, the elderly, and the infirm had to invite him and his big bag of tools into their homes on a daily basis.

She ignored my unsubtle hint for sympathy. "You were involved in that as well? Why?"

"Phil was asked to investigate by Melanie Porter's family. You know, the girl who died. She was engaged to someone we were both at school with—Graham Carter. Remember him?"

"Don't be daft, of course I don't. Although I recognise the name from the papers. But how did you get involved?"

I looked over at the window currently being smeared with orange goo by a solemn-faced toddler in a high chair while Mum nattered gaily to her chums. "The police. They asked me to help find her." The police, now, they've always been great about keeping my name out of the news. Probably so no one knows just how bloody desperate they were, calling in a so-called psychic.

"Oh. You're still doing that, then." It was said flatly. Like, say, the sort of voice you'd use to say, *No, m'lud, the defendant has* not *ceased his hobby of torturing and dismembering little fluffy kittens.*

"Yeah, well, not everyone changes. Take it you're still single, then?" I couldn't imagine Cherry with a bloke. She had *spinster of this parish* stamped right through her like a stick of Brighton rock.

And now she was blushing. "Not exactly, no."

"Bloody hell, have you got a boyfriend?" I was tempted to check out the window just to make sure there weren't any airborne porkers flitting past. "Good thing you didn't take me up on the park suggestion. You could knock me over with a feather—all those Canada geese would have bloody flattened me."

"God, you sound about twelve. Yes, actually, I have met someone." Her chin rose, defiant. "*He* went to Christmas dinner at Mum and Dad's. Thank you." She turned briefly to the waitress, who was just putting our plates down in front of us.

"Cheers, love," I added with a smile. The waitress dimpled and swept away with a swish of curvy hips. "So go on, tell us all about him. Found yourself a bit of rough, have you? Tell you what, I'd have come to Christmas dinner just to see that, if I'd known."

"Don't be ridiculous. He's a canon of the Church of England."

I wasn't too sure what sort of place a canon occupied in the church hierarchy, but the way she said it, you'd have thought this bloke had Jesus himself looking nervously over his shoulder.

"Is he a loose cannon?"

"Very funny. His name's Gregory. Gregory Titmus."

"Rings a faint bell . . ." Unlike my mate Gary, who's always been loud and proud about both his camp and his campanology. "You sure he's not gay?"

She tutted. "Not you as well. Honestly, just because someone's reached their forties without getting married . . . People will keep jumping to conclusions."

Uh-oh. I remembered Cherry was due to hit the big four-oh in a few months. "Nah, that's not it. Honest. Actually, I dunno where I got the idea from."

"Well, Gregory's always been open about his support for gay clergy," she said dubiously, cutting up a piece of chicken into its component molecules.

I nodded encouragingly. "Yeah, that'll be it. I've probably seen his name in *Pink News* or something. Being supportive."

She gave me a hard look.

"What? No, seriously, that's probably it. What, were you worried I might have met him at a gay club or something? Now who's jumping to conclusions? Anyway, I don't even go to any gay clubs."

"I wasn't jumping to conclusions! Stop putting words into my mouth." She frowned at a prune as she prodded it with her fork. "Maybe if you *did* go to gay clubs, you'd meet someone a bit better than Phil Morrison."

"Let it go, Sis, let it go." I forked up some spaghetti and gave it a twirl. "Anyway, I thought we were here to talk about Auntie Lol."

Cherry sighed. "Don't you think it's time you started calling her by her proper name? I assume you can pronounce *Laura* these days?"

"Bit late now, innit?" I took a swig of Coke, silently toasting Auntie Lol.

"I'd have thought you of all people would have some respect for the dead."

I jabbed at a rogue piece of bacon. "What's so bloody respectful about changing someone's name after they're gone? And anyway, what do you mean, me *of all people*?"

"You've spent enough time with them. The dead, that is." I swear I could see the prunes on her plate shrivelling up further under the force of her glare.

"Oh, for— You make it sound like every time I step out the door, I'm knee-deep in corpses! Anyway, you're a fine one to talk, Miss Spends-Her-Days-with-Criminals."

"I don't *associate* with them. I just defend them."

"Yeah, well, I don't exactly go down the pub with the dead either." I paused. "I mean, I would, but they're shit at buying their round. And they're always losing fingers and stuff, and it puts you right off your peanuts, finding bits—"

"*Anyway*," Cherry interrupted me. "The bequest is a bit, well, strange."

"Strange? What sort of strange?" God, she hadn't left me a collection of dodgy sex toys, had she? Yeah, I knew Auntie Lol had a girlfriend, but I was quite happy staying in the delusion that the closest they ever got was a cup of tea and a cuddle. It was like thinking of your parents having sex. Worse. Your *grandparents* having sex.

"Well, you know what she was like. She never could see the harm in encouraging you."

"Encouraging me to do what?"

There was a slice of lemon in Cherry's glass of fizzy water. It was currently curling up and cringing at the sourness of her expression. "You know. Your *thing*."

Oh. That. I carefully kept my face blank. "Sorry, don't follow."

"Yes, you do. Your *finding-things* thing." She pronounced every syllable with the sort of distaste you'd expect if she'd just discovered a cockroach performing unspeakable acts with a maggot in her salad. Then she sighed. "I always thought you'd grow out of that."

"Well, I'm only twenty-nine. There's still hope. So are you going to tell me about this bequest, or what?"

She huffed. "It's so silly. You have to go to her old house in Mill Hill and look for it."

"Hang on, Mill Hill?" That was north London. "Auntie Lol lived in Scotland. Near Edinburgh. And before that, St. Albans."

"Yes, but after she married Mr. Morangie, she lived in Mill Hill with him, remember? And their son. Until she left him."

"What? Auntie Lol had a kid? No way. She never mentioned that when she wrote. Nah. Must be some mix-up." She'd always been so, well, motherly to me. I felt a bit weird about it, to tell the truth.

Not to mention guilty. Yeah, we'd kept in touch, but I hadn't really made any effort to see her after she'd married. She'd visited me in hospital a few times back when I was seventeen—on her own, so I wasn't sure now if it was before or after she'd married—but after that, I hadn't seen her again. To be fair, I'd been a bit busy relearning how to walk and sorting out my life.

"He was her stepson. I don't really know much about him."

I frowned. "S'pose he stayed with his dad, then." It still felt funny to think of Auntie Lol leaving him behind. "What's the deal with the house, then? If it was hers, how come she was the one who left?" Somehow I didn't reckon Cherry would have said it was *her* house if it'd been the husband who'd owned it. Who still owned it? This was getting confusing. "Or, you know, how come it didn't get sold when they split up?"

"I don't know, do I? You're the one she stayed in touch with."

"So who owns the house now? The husband, right?"

"No." Cherry glared at me. "Actually, you might own half of it."

"What?"

"That's what's so annoying. As far as I can see, she really didn't have anyone else to leave anything to."

"No? What about the girlfriend?"

"They split up a while ago." Huh. Just another thing she hadn't mentioned. I was beginning to wonder just how well I really knew Auntie Lol. "And she didn't have any other family. But we don't have the full version of her will—that's what you have to find. For all anyone knows, she could have left you anything or everything. Including half of the house."

"Hang on, though. That's not how it works. You can't inherit half a house." Hadn't Phil said something about the other half of his flat just going to him automatically when the Mysterious Mark popped his squeaky-clean little clogs? "Doesn't it all go to whoever's the joint tenant or something?"

"*If* they're joint tenants. But they weren't. They were tenants in common."

"'Scuse me while my head explodes." I guzzled the last of my Diet Coke—wasn't caffeine supposed to be good for headaches? "So you're saying I *might* co-own a house with some old bloke who used to be married to Auntie Lol? Or it might all be some April Fool's joke from beyond the grave?" Actually, I kind of liked the idea of Auntie Lol looking down from heaven and laughing herself silly.

"I told you it was annoying." She speared the last bit of salad with a vicious jab of her fork. "And I really don't think she thought it all through. What if her ex-husband doesn't want you to go rummaging through his home?"

"Oi. I don't rummage."

"Sniffing like a bloodhound, then."

"Don't sniff either. Course, I have been known to bury the odd bone in the back garden—"

"Very funny." It was a good thing Cherry had already finished her lunch. The prunes would have shrivelled up into currants at that tone of hers.

"What happens now?"

"*Now*, we have to speak to Mr. Morangie. And hope he isn't going to be difficult about things."

"Is he even still living there? Or, hang on, *could* he sell up without her, with this common-tenants thing? Or—"

"Yes, and yes. Well, theoretically. Although I can't imagine who'd want to buy his half of the tenancy in common, and of course he wouldn't have been able to buy a comparable house with the proceeds. He was better off staying in the property, as long as she was happy for him to do so."

"Could she have kicked him out, then?" Seemed a bit unfair if the house was half his.

"Well, she'd have had to go to court and try to force a sale. It's what I'd have done, though."

"Yeah, but court's like a home from home for you. Not everyone wants to get into all that legal stuff if they don't have to."

Cherry frowned. "It still seems odd she never tried. I suppose she mustn't have needed the money."

"Maybe she was worried about legal fees, thought she'd end up worse off than she'd started. Or maybe she just didn't want all the stress. Anyway, so what you're saying is, Mr. M.'s still living there, and we've got to go and pay him a visit, right? When's the funeral, anyway?

I know it'll be up in Scotland, but I'd like to go. Pay my last respects, that sort of thing."

"Oh."

I had a bad feeling about that *oh*. "Oh, what?"

"Well, it was a few days ago."

"A few days ago? And you didn't think I might want to know about it? For fuck's sake! Even if I couldn't have gone, I'd have wanted to send flowers. Did *anyone* know? Or did you just tell them to bury her in the first hole in the ground they could find and not bother with a service or, you know, any sodding mourners?"

"*I* didn't tell them anything. Mr. Morangie arranged it all with a local undertaker, up in West Lothian. She was cremated. No flowers."

"Was that what she said she wanted?" Auntie Lol had loved flowers. She'd had a garden full of them back when she'd lived in St. Albans, and she used to let me pick bunches and take them back home to Mum.

"She didn't leave any instructions about the funeral, so her husband did what he thought best, I suppose."

"He wasn't her husband. He was just some git she married and then thought better of it. I can't believe you didn't tell me about it in time."

Cherry stared at me. "Well, if I'd known you were going to get upset about it . . ."

"I'm not upset." All right, maybe that was a lie. "Right. So when am I supposed to be going over to his place for this *rummage*, then? You coming too? Fancy a good rummage, do you?"

"You're so *bloody* childish, sometimes. I'll set something up. All right?" She pulled out her purse and peeled off a couple of twenty pound notes that looked like she'd ironed them this morning. Nah, what was I thinking? She probably had all her money dry-cleaned. "That should take care of lunch. I'll call you when I've arranged things with Mr. Morangie, but it may be a while. Some of us have work to do."

Whereas the rest of us, apparently, just mucked about with a set of tools from Toys "R" Us, tinkering with taps. I watched her clump off in her sensible black shoes and sighed.

"Would you like anything else? Coffee? Dessert?" The waitress with the hips smiled kindly as she started to clear the plates.

"Just the bill, thanks, love."

"Sure? The chocolate-and-hazelnut panettone's on special." The dimples were out in force again. "And it's not like *you* need to worry about your figure."

I had to smile. "Sounds great, but I've got to get back to work. Maybe I'll come in for it some other time."

"I'll look out for you." She balanced the plates with practised ease and swept off, swishing back with the bill a lot quicker than I was expecting.

Cherry's forty quid covered it easy and then some. "Keep the change. Have a panettone on me." I winked at the waitress.

"I wish. That stuff goes straight to my hips." She slapped herself on the bum, then dithered a moment, fiddling with the plateful of money. "None of my business, but you could do way better."

"Come again?"

"That woman you were with. She didn't look like your sort at all."

I sighed and pushed back my chair. "Don't I know it. Cheers, love."

"You have a good afternoon." She smiled at me again and wiggled her way back through the tables.

I glanced at the receipt before shoving it in my pocket. It had a phone number scribbled on it in felt-tip, and the name *Angie* with a little heart instead of the dot on the *i*. I smiled and shook my head.

On the way out, I passed one of the mummies turning a suitcase-size handbag out onto the table looking for something, so, being a helpful sort, I paused to listen in. *There.* I reached into the recesses of a nappy bag, hoping to God I wouldn't come across any dirties, and pulled out a mobile phone. "Here you go, love," I said, handing it to a baffled mum.

"Oh my God! How the hell did it get in there? Georgie, did you put Mummy's phone in your bag? He must have thought it was one of his toys," she excused him, turning back to me. "Um, thanks," she added.

"No problem," I said with a smile and a cheery wave at a pesto-smeared Georgie, who sent back a rabbit-in-the-headlights look. He knew he'd been caught bang to rights.

Thought it was a toy, my arse. My *thing*, as Cherry put it, only works for stuff that's been deliberately hidden. The only reason I'd been able to find that phone was because Georgie had known he was being a little sod when he put it there.

On the way back to the van, I took a detour through the market to pick up a couple of bits for tea. Darren was there on his stall—well, technically, he was on a box behind his stall—and he greeted me with a cheery, "All right, short arse?"

I never know what to say when he brings out the short jokes. Him being all of four foot six himself. So I went with, "Can't complain. How's the fruit-and-veg business going? Making a killing on dodgy kumquats?"

Before you ask, I do actually know what a kumquat is, and it's not just from watching *MasterChef*. They sell all sorts in the greengrocers down my way, and they're pretty good at telling you what to do with the weird stuff.

In the cooking sense, I mean.

Darren leered at me. "Nothing dodgy about my kumquats. Ask Gary. There you go, love, that'll be a pahnd," he added to the old dear he'd just handed a paper bag full of mixed veg. He waited patiently as she stowed it securely in one of those wheeled tartan trolley things, then counted out a pound's worth of change. "You enjoy those parsnips, and if the old man don't like 'em, you tell him to come talk to me about it."

"Oh, I will, dearie." She dimpled and doddered off with a spring in her orthopaedically booted step.

"I'm seeing Gary tomorrow—you coming along?" I tried not to make it sound like a loaded question. Ever since him and Gary got together, Darren's had a habit of turning up when I meet Gary for a drink. Which, don't get me wrong, he's an all right bloke, but sometimes you just want a natter with your mate without significant others muscling in.

"Nah. Thought I'd let you and him enjoy a girls' night out without me." He grinned. "Gary's got something to tell you."

"Yeah?" If that was the case, I was surprised I didn't know already. Not one for keeping secrets, Gary isn't, even when they're his own. "What's that about, then?"

Darren tapped the side of his nose. "Have to wait and see, won't you? Right, you buying, or you going to shift your arse and let my customers through?"

I grabbed some onions and red peppers. "Pahnd?" Everything's a pahnd on Darren's stall. Unless it's the end of the day, when it's two fer a pahnd.

"On the 'ouse. Mind how you go, then."

"Cheers, Darren."

CHAPTER THREE

I met Gary in our usual place, Thursday night, the Devil's Dyke pub in Brock's Hollow. It's a proper old-fashioned country pub, with horse brasses on the walls and signs on the low ceiling beams warning you to *Duck or grouse*. Harry, the landlady, was having a break, perched on a barstool with her border collie, Flossie, at her feet and a cup of tea by her elbow. Which was no reflection on the quality of the beer in the place, nor on Harry's ability to take her drink. She's a head taller than me and fights at around twice my weight—or at least, she used to; these days she only dusts off her boxing skills on the rare occasions when the customers get rowdy.

I was a bit late getting to the pub—Mrs. G.'s downstairs loo had turned out to be a total bastard—and Gary looked like he was well into his third vodka martini by the time I stuck my head in the door and spotted him at the back of the room.

Gary managed to simultaneously wave a welcome and roll his eyes at my timekeeping. At least, I hoped it was my timekeeping he had the problem with, although to be honest, I'd had my doubts about the shirt I was wearing when I'd put it on. I made a buying-a-pint gesture, followed by a can-I-get-you-one-too gesture, and Gary replied with his version of a cheers-mate gesture, which consisted of pointing to his martini glass, clapping his hands to his heart, and blowing me a kiss.

Next time, I decided, I'd just go over and ask, and sod the bloody sign language.

There was a new member of the harem behind the bar. She looked all of fourteen, but I knew Harry wasn't daft enough to risk her licence by employing someone under age. Even someone as pretty as this girl, who was tiny, bubbly and had a My Little Unicorn tattooed on her shoulder.

"All right, love? Pint of bitter, please."

She smiled wide enough to show off her tongue piercing. "Hopfest, London Porter, or Mr. Squirrel?" She had a strong West Country accent.

I pursed my lips. "Go on, then, hit me with the squirrel. You're new here, aren't you? I'm Tom."

"Marianne. It's my first day, so be gentle with me. You're with Gary? He's lovely, he is."

I nodded, then looked at her sideways. "Well, I'm with him, but I'm not *with* him. He's a mate. Vodka martini for him, when you've finished pulling that pint. Cheers, love."

I paid her, then carried the drinks over to Gary's table and slumped down next to him to take the weight off. Julian, Gary's Saint Bernard, looked up briefly, wagged his tail once and shifted so he could start drooling on my leg instead of one belonging to his cuddly campanologist owner. He's always been free with his favours, Julian has. Whoever it was who said pets resemble their owners had Gary and Julian bang to rights.

Gary took his drink from me with grabby hands. "*Finally*. Darling, I've been waiting *eons* for you. Poor Julian has aged around a decade in dog years. And what on earth are you wearing?"

I looked down at myself. "Clothes?"

Gary's got one of those faces that are somehow way more expressive than your average. Like he's a caricature of himself or something. Right now he was looking at me like I'd just turned up straight from a stint in a cesspit. "For want of a more descriptive term, perhaps. Where did you get that shirt? Oxfam?"

"Oi. It was quite expensive, actually. What's wrong with it?"

Gary shuddered. "What's right with it? Darling, it's *shiny*, and not in a good, Jake Shears sort of way. And broad stripes went out while you were still in nappies. Which I'd have thought were probably a better look on you."

My shoulders slumped. "I thought Phil might like it. He's always complaining about my old shirts." Actually, that was a bit of an exaggeration, but there had been one or two pointed suggestions that I might want to get changed before we went out for a drink.

"Trust me, my dear, if he sees you in this monstrosity, he'll never say another word about your customary pocket-lumberjack look."

"Pocket . . .? You and that bloke of yours are going to give me a complex, you know. Talking of which, he said you've got something to tell me. So come on, out with it, what've you done?"

Gary beamed, a happy teddy bear. "Guess! No, don't bother, you'll never guess. Darren has asked me to be his husband! Isn't it marvellous?"

"Bit sudden, innit? You've only known him a couple of weeks!"

"Months, actually." Now he was a grumpy bear. "Longer than you've been with thingummy."

No, Gary hadn't forgotten Phil's name. He was just a card-carrying member of the Tom Can Do Better Club. I nearly choked on my pint at the thought of Gary having something in common with my big sister. "That's different. I've known Phil since we were at school. And neither of us have got down on one knee."

"Sweetie, you don't have to tell me about your sex life. Or lack of one. We're supposed to be talking about *me*." He leaned forward, the glint of the born party planner in his eye. "I was thinking of a June wedding, because it should be sunny but not too hot—nothing worse than shiny red faces and sweat stains in a wedding photo. But it's such a nightmare working out what to wear. Not that I'd want your opinion, based on today's fiasco. Anyway, you're both invited, assuming he's still around by then. If not, I'm sure we can find you somebody just as photogenic to pair up with. Darren knows *lots* of people."

And most of them carnally, seeing as they all seemed to be hangovers from his old porn-star days. "Phil's still going to be around," I said with a lot more conviction than I actually felt. If I didn't nip this fixing-me-up thing in the bud, Gary and Darren were likely to end up discussing it in front of Phil, and that was a self-fulfilling prophecy I could do without.

"Of course he will be, dear." Gary sucked the olive off the end of his cocktail stick with an obscene slurping sound. "If you want him to be."

"Why wouldn't I? The bloke saved my life, remember?" I lifted my pint and drank to that memory.

"It doesn't count if he was the one to endanger it in the first place, *remember*? But let's not talk of depressing subjects."

I leaned back in my seat and crossed an ankle over my leg. "I'll assume you mean my little moment of mortal peril, not my boyfriend. So what do you want to talk about?" Over at the bar, Marianne was getting chatted up by a bloke in paint-stained jeans and tatts who hadn't yet noticed Harry's watchful eye on him. I reckoned Marianne was in safe hands there.

"Well, you've had my big news. Surely something noteworthy must have happened to you since we last met? Apart from your fit of insanity while shopping."

"Saw my sister."

Gary shuddered. "I bet she didn't ask after me."

"Not as such, no. And there's the possibility I've inherited half a house, but it might be nothing." Gary perked up at that, and even Julian pricked up an ear as I told them about Auntie Lol.

"It *all* sounds very Gothic. The wife who ran away; the mysterious legacy—even the funeral undertaken—pun not intended—in indecent haste."

"Too bloody right about that last bit. I still can't believe Cherry didn't tell me about it. Just because she'd never kept in touch with Auntie Lol."

"Maybe she was jealous, darling? After *all*, she's doing the work, and you're the one with the juicy bequest."

"The *possibly* juicy bequest. Dunno what it is yet, do I?"

"I know. This is so exciting. Have you thought what you'll do with the money? You could go travelling, move out of Fleetville, buy a whole new wardrobe—"

"Oi. Stop going on about the bloody clothes. And I like living in Fleetville. It's handy for the shops and it's not full of pretentious tossers like most of the villages round here." I drained my pint glass a bit pointedly. "And it's your round, seeing as I haven't actually come into any money yet."

Gary heaved a long-suffering sigh and stood up. "Same again? Look after Julian for me, then. Daddy will be back soon, yes he *will*." The last bit was to the dog, thank God.

The following night, the landline rang again. Phil was cuddling up to Arthur on my sofa again, watching *CSI*. It seemed a strange choice of relaxation for a detective, but whatever, so I took the phone into the kitchen.

It was Cherry, obviously.

"Hi, Sis. Two calls in one week? I hope nobody else has died." I wasn't joking.

"Gregory wants to meet you. Seeing as he missed out on doing so at Christmas." Her tone made it quite clear what dear old Sis thought of that. "And your . . . partner."

"Phil's not my partner," I protested, with a half-guilty glance in the direction of the living room. "It's not like we've gone and got married or anything. We're just going out together."

She *tsk*ed. "All right, your *boyfriend*. Whatever. Anyway, he's asked me to invite you round for drinks. Both of you."

"Right. Fine. When and where? Your place?" I was fairly sure I knew where that was. "You're still in Pluck's End, right?" It was a village out towards Berkhamsted—one of those ones with no shops in the high street, only restaurants. Plus a Waitrose tucked discreetly out of sight near the station so all the bankers and lawyers could get a ready meal and a bottle of plonk on the way back to their tastefully decorated homes.

"I am, but you'll be coming to Gregory's place. My house is a bit of a state right now. I'm having some work done."

"Extension?" I leaned back on the counter and wondered how many times bigger than my little place Cherry's house was already.

"New bathroom, actually."

"What, and you didn't call me? I'm wounded." That, and sincerely bloody relieved I wouldn't have to work for her. Knowing my sister, she'd have been a right pain about it, and she'd have expected a hefty friends-and-family discount as well.

There was a pause. "I . . . I didn't know you did bathrooms."

"I'm a plumber, what the bloody hell do you think I do? Make jam?" Merlin padded into the kitchen at that point and gave me a significant look, as if to say, *Make jam? What a waste of valuable can-opening time.*

"I don't know! I thought you just did drains and taps and things."

"What, like I just went out and bought a copy of *Plumbing for Dummies* and an ad in the Yellow Pages?" I was seriously miffed. "Just because I haven't got a bloody law degree from Oxbridge and more letters after my name than are in it doesn't mean I'm just playing at this."

"Fine. Next time I need some work done, I'll call you. Happy now?"

Not really. "So where is Greg's place, then?" I paced around the kitchen. The bin needed emptying again. I swear the rubbish breeds in there.

"Gregory. He lives in St. Leonards, in the Old Deanery in Cathedral Close."

"Doesn't the old dean mind? Or does he like cosying up to the canons?"

"There's no need to be facetious."

"You know, I looked that word up the other day. Comes from a French word for *witty*. I was amazed. I always thought it meant *full of shit*. And you need to lighten up a bit. So is there a New Deanery?"

"The dean lives in the Old Rectory. As if you cared."

"What about the rector?"

"Does it matter?"

"Well, I'd have thought it would to him." I reckoned a change of subject might be in order if I didn't want Cherry hanging up on me. Which was tempting, now I came to think about it, but . . . No. "So how did you meet him, then? Greg, I mean, not the rector." St. Leonards wasn't that far from Pluck's End, but it was in the opposite direction from St. Albans, where Cherry worked.

"*Gregory*. We, er, had an interest in common. Anyway, can we *please* get this sorted? Gregory suggested Saturday evening, if that's all right? Around half past eight?"

"I'll have to check with Phil, but yeah, should be okay."

We said our goodbyes. I wondered what the common interest was, and why she was being cagey about it. I couldn't really remember Cherry having any interests, apart from her career. I grinned. Maybe they were both heavily into the fetish scene? I couldn't see it, somehow.

What else would Cherry find too embarrassing to mention? Maybe they'd met at a pole-dancing class or a Justin Bieber concert.

Strong arms slipped around me from behind, and I leaned back into a nicely solid chest. "What are you smiling about? And what are you supposed to be checking with me?" Phil's breath warmed my neck and tickled my ear.

It took a moment for what he'd asked to register. "Oh, that was Cherry. My sister."

"Yeah, I'd worked that out."

"She's invited us over to the biblical boyfriend's gaff. Fancy a cup of tea with the vicar?"

"I can think of things I fancy more." His hardening dick prodded me in the back, just in case I didn't catch his drift. "When?"

"Saturday. Unless you're planning on staking out any more dogging sites?"

"That case is over, thank God. I've seen enough bare bums sticking out of car windows to last me a lifetime. No, the only plans I had involved you and that sofa."

"What, you wanted to watch *Britain's Got Talent* together?"

"I'll show you Britain's got talent." Phil nipped at my neck, just the right side of painful, and slid his hand down to my dick, which perked up nicely at the attention.

After that, I got a bit distracted from the question of my sister's love life.

CHAPTER FOUR

aturday night, I opened the door to Phil, who was all wrapped up like a posh Christmas present in his cream cashmere sweater and tan leather jacket. Oh, and something else, which hit me like a bit of lead piping to the stomach. "You're wearing that to meet my sister?"

"What?" he said, presumably on the off chance I'd missed his guilty glance down to his ring finger. Which was still prominently adorned with his wedding ring. Civil partnership ring, what-the-hell-ever. Point was, he was going around flaunting a token of his commitment to someone who wasn't me.

"She'll think you've got some wife stashed away somewhere you're cheating on with me, and you can't even be arsed to hide it."

"Plenty of widowers wear rings."

"Not when they're out with the new bloke, they don't." It was a bit of a bone of contention between us, that ring. Phil reckoned it made him seem more trustworthy, for the benefit of potential clients and people he was trying to worm stuff out of. At least, that's what he said. Thing was, I was beginning to wonder if that was a load of bollocks, and he just liked to remember the man who'd given it to him. Even if they had split up by the time the bloke had died. "Come on, you really want to get into all the explanations at a first meeting?"

That did the trick. Phil never liked talking about the Mysterious Mark. He slipped off the ring and put it carefully in his breast pocket. "Happy now?" he demanded, sticking his denuded finger in my face.

It had a clear mark and, even in the middle of winter, a bit of a tan line where the ring had been. Bloody fantastic. "As a sodding lark."

Don't know what my face was saying, but apparently it spoke volumes to Phil. His granite expression softened to half-set putty.

"She won't notice. You'd be amazed at how observant most people aren't. Come here."

"What, on the doorstep and scandalize the neighbours? You can come in for a minute." I tugged on his arm, and he stepped inside, shutting the door behind him. Ice-cold hands rested on my waist for a moment, dropping down to my arse just as I began to shiver. Phil pulled me in tight. I kissed refrigerated lips, tasting mint, and my body melted into his. Parts of me started to get a bit more interested than was a good idea, seeing as we were supposed to be off to see my big sis around five minutes ago. God, he was gorgeous. Tall, broad, solid as a particularly finely sculpted rock. Speaking of rocks, there was a part of me doing a bloody good impersonation of one. I ground it against his hip, just to make sure he'd noticed.

Oh, he'd noticed all right. His kiss turned aggressive, hungry, and his grip on my arse tightened. Sod it. I wrestled myself out of his eager mitts and dropped to my knees, thankful beyond measure he wasn't wearing his jeans with the button fly. Total cockblocker, those jeans. I undid his smart-casual-meet-the-family chinos in a jiffy and had him in my mouth before he could blink. God, he tasted good. Salty and male, with a hint of expensive shower gel. He was big enough to give my jaw muscles a proper workout too. I sucked hard and glanced up to see how he was taking it.

Yep, I'd definitely got rid of the granite expression. Phil's eyes were screwed up, his jaw tense. His hands were scrabbling at the wall behind him. I added just a hint of teeth.

"Jesus," he gasped out, his voice hoarse.

I shoved the hand that wasn't playing with his balls down the front of my jeans, moaning a bit myself as I grabbed hold of the red-hot poker in my pants.

Phil was trying to thrust now. Or maybe trying not to. Whichever, it meant little jerky motions towards my throat that made my jaw ache and my balls tighten. My wanking hand went into overdrive. I wished I'd stopped to undo my flies, but it was too late now. I couldn't have stopped even if Cherry had turned up on the doorstep with the archbishop of bloody Canterbury. The stretch in my lips, the weight of Phil's cock on my tongue, all combined with my furious jerking off, and I exploded in ecstasy. My lips went slack around Phil's dick as he banged away in earnest at the roof of my mouth, coming seconds later in a bitter, salty flood that I swallowed down like I'd been starving for a month.

"Jesus," Phil said again. He was leaning against my wall, looking like it was the only thing holding him up right now.

I sat back on my heels and wiped my mouth. "Nah, it's Tom, actually."

"Prick." But his look was fond as he ran his hand through my hair.

Sod *fond*. I jerked my head back out of reach. "Oi! Don't mess it up. We're going out, remember?"

Phil laughed. "You really think you're going anywhere looking like that?"

I frowned. "I thought you liked this shirt."

"I've got nothing against the shirt. Just depends if you want your sister and the vicar to know exactly why we're late tonight."

I looked down and noticed for the first time a thin trail of spunk that must have dribbled out of the corner of my mouth. Then I remembered I'd just come in my pants. "Shit. I'm going to need a bloody shower." I scrambled to my feet. The cooling mess in my underwear started making its presence felt. Unpleasantly.

Phil was still smiling. "Nah, sponge bath'll do it. Want some help?"

I won't say I wasn't tempted, but . . . "Yeah, right. Like we need anything else to delay us. Just wait here, all right? I'll be five minutes." I made to go upstairs, then changed my mind and doubled back to kiss him, open-mouthed and dirty.

Then I legged it up those stairs and grabbed a wet flannel, hoping like hell I had another decent pair of jeans that were clean and dry.

It was a bit of a drive out to St. Leonards, out past Berkhamsted. It was less than twenty miles as the crow flies, but it was all winding country lanes, which slowed us down a bit, and then we had to find Greg's place. It'd have been a lot simpler if Phil had turned on his bloody satnav, but far as I could tell, he only used it for work, if ever. Bit of a problem with people telling him what to do, was my diagnosis.

St. Leonards was one of those places that must have been pretty important when the cathedral was built around eight hundred years ago, or else they wouldn't have bothered, but to say it had fallen into a bit of a decline since then was like saying the Russian government was just a little bit anti-gay. It was a nice enough market town, but sleepy. Even compared to St. Albans. The sort of place you moved to when you retired, assuming, of course, you'd retired from the sort of job that left you with a pension several times the size of most peoples' salaries.

We eventually got to ye olde cobbled streets of Cathedral Close only around fifteen minutes later than Cherry had told us to be there. Which was probably still ten minutes earlier than she'd been expecting me.

The Old Deanery was signposted, luckily. It was a big old (obviously) pile with a wide, well-stomped-down gravel drive which you reached via a crumbling gateway. The gate itself, a wooden barred thing gone green with age, looked like it was permanently open. Actually, it looked like it'd disintegrate into a heap of dust and woodworm if you tried to shut it. The house itself seemed to be all windows, and they were the old-fashioned sash type.

"Carbon footprint of this place must be the size of Las Vegas," I said as we got out of the car and headed for the front door. It was large, blue, and apparently too posh to have a letterbox in it—that was set discreetly to one side, right next to an honest-to-God notice directing tradesmen to use the rear entrance. I grinned. "Think we ought to do what it says?"

"What, right here on the doorstep? I think the neighbours might complain." We both glanced up at the bulk of St. Leonards Cathedral, looming darkly over us from around a hundred yards away.

"Probably get struck by lightning," I agreed. I pushed the antique doorbell, one of those Victorian ones with *Press* written on it in fancy font, presumably for the benefit of those who couldn't work it out without instructions. It jangled sonorously.

"They don't make 'em like that anymore, do they?" Phil muttered as we shuffled our feet on the Old Dean's doorstep.

"Yeah, they do. You can get them online. There's this site: Snobs' Knobs and Posh Knockers, it's called."

"Oh yeah? I've never been that into knockers, personally. Knobs, on the other hand . . ." Phil smirked.

"As if I hadn't noticed. I don't smell of spunk, do I?"

"If the Rev gets down on his knees and sniffs your crotch, I think you'll have more to worry about than the way you smell."

Git. "I meant my breath. I washed and changed, remember?" I huffed out a breath in Phil's face. He grimaced and stepped back. "Shit, I do, don't I?"

"No, but I think those bloody mouthwash fumes just took the skin off my face. How many bottles did you gargle with?"

"One capful, just like it said on the label." Okay, maybe two, to be on the safe side.

The door opened, and another dark figure loomed over us, this one from considerably nearer. Next to him, I was relieved to see my sister.

Gregory was . . . not quite what I'd expected. Tall, dressed all in black, with dark, curly hair that was rapidly receding around a widow's peak, he looked more demonic than canonical. He had sharply arched black eyebrows over brown eyes with a devilish glint. I didn't have to look far for evidence of his evil powers: one look at Sis showed he'd managed to transform her from hard-nosed barrister to simpering schoolgirl. She was hanging off his arm like it was the only thing holding her back from a terminal fit of the vapours.

"Ah, you're Cherry's baby brother?" He reached out unusually large hands to enfold mine in a dry, meaty grip. I'm usually a bit careful when I shake hands with people. In my line of work, you develop a strong grip. But I wouldn't have liked to bet on my chances in an arm-wrestling match with the Hand of God here. "Delighted to meet you. And this is your . . .?"

"Phil," Phil said bluntly, while I was still struggling to work out exactly which noun I should finish that sentence with for him.

Gregory nodded, as if he thought everyone should have a Phil of their own. "Excellent!" Phil's turn to be treated to the hearty ecclesiastical welcome. "Well, come on, come in." Slab-like hands waved us past him and shepherded us through the hall and into a large reception room—it was too big and, to be honest, uncosy to be a living room or anything like that. A log fire flickered half-heartedly at the far end, but it seemed to have given up on trying to heat the rest of the room. The grim brown carpet was that industrial-grade sort of stuff that's only marginally softer than concrete, and the walls were bland magnolia interrupted only by muddy landscapes and the odd ecclesiastical mug shot.

"Sherry, Cherry?" He said it with an absolutely straight face. "And for the menfolk? Whiskey? Something stronger?" Stronger than whiskey? What was he peddling here—neat ethanol? I gave him a sharp look, which he fielded as if he'd been standing there on mid-off in his cricket whites all afternoon, just waiting for it. "I'm recently returned from a retreat in Bratislava," he said as if it explained everything. "Slivovitz?"

I reckoned Cherry probably had the *We're-not-Polish* bit covered, so I went with, "I thought the Lord didn't let no spirits in?"

Gregory guffawed. Seriously. I'd always wondered what a guffaw would sound like, and now I felt a gentle pang of nostalgia for my lost ignorance. Cherry giggled and clutched at his arm. I edged back a little closer to Phil's solid, cashmere-clad shoulder, worried Gregory might clap me on the back with one of those dustbin lids he had for hands and swat me like a fly.

"What the bloody hell are you lot on?" Phil muttered in my ear.

I blinked for a moment, then remembered what I'd said. "It's a song. You know. 'I'll never get to heaven—'"

"Could have told you that."

"Shut up. We used to sing it in the minibus on Sunday School trips." Back before I'd left under something of a cloud, which, sod's law, someone was bound to mention any moment now.

"Bloody Sunday School. How did you ever end up a plumber?"

"Just lucky that way," I said firmly. I wasn't going to get into the old story of how come I didn't have any A levels. From the stony look on Phil's face, he was filling in the blanks for himself already.

I thought Gregory had tactfully turned away from our little tiff, but when he turned back, he was holding a couple of shot glasses filled to the brim with clear, yellow liquid. I hoped he wasn't taking the piss. Or handing it to us, for that matter.

"This'll put hair on your chests. Distilled by monks, so you can rest assured it has the official seal of approval from On High. *Na zdravie!*" Gregory downed the contents of his shot glass in one.

"Bottoms up," I muttered and took a cautious sip. I managed not to turn bright red and cough up a lung, but it was a close-run thing. Forget growing hairs on chests, I could use this stuff to clear drains. Phil, I saw out of the corner of my somewhat watering eye, had tossed his shot down in one just like the Extremely Reverend Greg. His face was blank of all expression, but I noticed his ears had gone a bit pink.

Bloody hell. Did canons and private eyes really get into pissing contests? Didn't their cassocks get in the way? The clergymen, I meant. If Phil liked to go around in a cassock in his free time, clearly we weren't yet at the stage of the relationship where he'd feel comfortable mentioning it to me.

"Nice stuff," I lied a bit hoarsely and looked around for something else to talk about before he decided it was time for round two already. "Is your dog all right?" There was a border collie poking its nose around the far door to look at us nervously, showing no signs of plucking up the courage to come and be sociable. Usually, dogs are all over me, probably because I smell of cat.

(All right, I smell of what my mate Gary calls *eau de plumber* a lot of the time too, which, if you haven't had the pleasure, is, I'm reliably informed, a sort of rancid putty aroma. It comes from the chemical sealants I use. But I'd had a shower and changed—twice, now I came to think about it—since work, so today, it was all cat.)

"Oh, he's fine, fine. Why don't you go over and say hello?" Greg's eyes sparkled a bit manically. "I promise he won't bite."

Seeing as how I wasn't born yesterday, I already had my suspicions even as I crossed the room. The fact that Fido didn't turn a hair at my approach only confirmed it. He didn't stir when I reached down to pet him gingerly on the head. The dog's soft black fur was cool to the touch, the skin beneath unnaturally rigid and unyielding, and there was a dry, dusty smell about him, more old bones than Bonios.

"Not very lively, is he?" I threw back over my shoulder. "You want to mix a bit of Red Bull in with his Pedigree Chum."

The Obnoxiously Reverend Greg was practically pissing himself laughing. Even Cherry indulged herself with a worryingly girlish giggle.

"Gregory's a keen taxidermist," she explained, composing herself.

"Well, I wouldn't like to think poor old Fido had been done by a half-hearted one," I managed. "That could get messy—internal organs left in, that sort of thing."

"His name was Buster, actually. Or so I believe." Gregory had recovered from his fit of mirth.

"Stuff a lot of dogs, do you?" Phil put in. He was looking even less full of the joys of life than old Fido, sorry, Buster.

"Good heavens, no. I prefer to work on smaller creatures, actually. The delicate work is more challenging. But come, come! You must meet the rest of the family."

I had a brief vision of a household of stuffed Gregories, some male, some female, but all with glassy dark eyes and unfeasibly large hands, and I couldn't hold off a shiver.

"Feeling the chill?" Greg asked solicitously. I shivered again as his hand pressed into my back. "It's this old Gothic pile. Absolute nightmare to heat, I'm afraid. Still, it's what the family prefers."

He'd shepherded me into the next room, which, thank God, contained no human figures whatsoever. What it did hold was about a dozen little furry creatures—no, more than that, I realised, looking around. There was a red squirrel on the windowsill, squaring up to a grey one. A tortoiseshell cat sat beneath, looking up at them both. I thought of Arthur and Merlin and vowed to have their furry little bodies cremated whenever they shuffled off this mortal coil, rather than let weirdoes with too much time and sawdust on their hands get hold of them.

"Come and meet Mrs. Tiggywinkle," Cherry urged in my shell-shocked ear. She ushered me over to where a hedgehog snuffled silently around the bottom of the floor-length curtains. "Isn't she adorable?" Cherry actually crouched down, picked the thing up, and shoved it in my face.

"Oi! Careful. Those things have fleas," I protested, backing off.

Behind me, Phil sounded amused. "That one won't. Unless Gregory stuffed them as well."

"Alas, that's a little beyond my skill." Gregory was beaming at me over Cherry's shoulder.

"I thought all things were possible if you had faith?" Phil's voice was right in my ear now, so I stopped backing up before I ended up tripping over his expensive loafers and falling, damsel-like, into his arms. Thank God I'd brought him with me, though. He could distract them while I ran away.

"'Thou shalt not put the Lord thy God to the test,'" the Augustly Reverend Greg reminded us all.

"That's Leviticus, isn't it?" Phil challenged.

And he went on at me about having gone to Sunday School?

"Deuteronomy, actually." Greg's expression changed somehow. The line of his eyebrows had softened, and they didn't look quite so demonic. It would have been reassuring if it hadn't been so bloody unnerving. "Our Lord, you'll find, was much less fond of Leviticus."

I waited for Phil to come back with *I see your Leviticus, and I raise you Genesis, Exodus, and all the prophets*, but he just sort of grunted.

"I hear you're a *private eye*." Greg rolled the words around his tongue with relish. "It strikes me that must bring you into contact with the worst excesses of human nature."

"Pays the bills," Phil said shortly.

"Oh, don't mistake me—I admire you for it. It's not everyone who can, as it were, gaze into a cesspit and remain unmoved. I suppose a great many of your cases involve affairs of the heart?"

"There's always people who want to know if their husband or wife is cheating on them," Phil admitted.

"And are they? Generally speaking, I mean. I've always thought one must have a sixth sense about the person one lives with. So to speak." Greg leaned in towards Phil, his eyes getting that alarming glint in them again.

Phil didn't seem fazed by it. "And there's no smoke without fire? It varies. Some people are just paranoid, and sometimes the 'other woman' turns out to be a gambling problem."

"And how do they tend to take the news? I imagine there must be a certain degree of relief when one knows the worst . . .?"

I could see this was going to be a long discussion, and if I wasn't careful I was going to be stuck there with the legions of the stuffed for the duration.

Desperate times called for desperate measures. Actually, looking at my glass, I reckoned it was more like a desperate triple measure, but I girded my stomach, took a deep breath, and tossed it down. I just about managed not to collapse in a choking fit, although there was probably a bit of steam coming out of my ears. "I'll, er . . ." I cleared my throat, held up my empty glass, and then legged it back to the other room, giving Buster a sympathetic pat on the way.

I was staring at the arrangement of bottles and decanters, wondering what was safe to touch—I'd have killed for a Coke and probably at least mugged someone for a Pepsi—when Cherry came up behind me. "You're being a bit rude," she muttered in my ear. "You could at least admire the skill that goes into Gregory's art."

"I don't bloody believe this," I whispered back. "You go on at me about chumming around with corpses, and your boyfriend has a whole bloody houseful!"

She stared at me. "They're *animals*, for goodness sake." Not *for God's sake*, I noticed. Apparently you couldn't say that sort of stuff while you were actively hobnobbing with one of his main men on Earth. "Not people."

"Are you sure the Rev knows that? He called them family."

"It's a joke. You've heard about those?"

I was momentarily speechless. She was accusing *me* of not having a sense of humour? "Pot, much?" I managed feebly.

She blanked me. "If that's some druggie reference—"

"Come off it! Since when have I ever done drugs?"

"Well, I don't know *what* you got up to. You dropped out of school—"

"I got hit by a four-by-four!"

"—and then the next thing I know, I've got Mum on the phone telling me you're not even going to bother with an education. It wasn't easy for her, you know." She picked up a bottle of something I was fairly sure was sherry, and tugged at the cork.

"Right, because it was such a bloody walk in the park for me. Anyway, Dad was fine about me taking up plumbing."

Cherry was still struggling with the sherry bottle, frown lines forming on her forehead. "Yes, but that's different."

"What?"

She stared at me blankly. "What?"

"What you said— Forget it, just give that here." I took the sherry bottle and opened it with a quick twist of the wrist. "There you go."

"Thank you." She poured herself a generous measure, then waved the bottle in my direction. "You?"

"Nah, 's okay. Actually, any chance of a soft drink?"

"There's probably some fruit juice in the fridge. You're driving, are you?"

"Nah, Phil is. I'm just not really into all this poncey stuff. More of a beer drinker, you know?"

I probably imagined her lip curling. Wait, what was I thinking? No way did I imagine that. "I'll see what I can find in the kitchen."

"No half-stuffed animals, I hope. Unless it's a turkey for tomorrow's dinner. In which case, feel free to invite me. And Phil, obviously." I followed her through the hallway to the kitchen, which was decorated in hideous 1970s' style, all Formica tops and cupboard doors in shades of grunge. No pet cemetery in here, though, thank God, or at least his representative on Earth.

"Gregory's having lunch with the bishop tomorrow," Cherry told the fridge. "I don't think you'd really fit in."

"I dunno. Bloke goes around in a purple frock all day, doesn't he? We might have more in common than you think."

Cherry pulled out an opened carton of orange juice, frowned at it, sniffed it, and handed it over. "Here. I think it's still in date."

I *tsked*. "Your Greg needs someone to look after him, doesn't he?" I took the tumbler she handed me and poured in some juice, then tasted it carefully. "Seems okay. Ta."

"It's Gregory. You're welcome. Right, well, we'd better get back to the others." She didn't make a move, though, so neither did I. After a moment, she spoke again. "Is it serious, you and this Phil?"

"Maybe." I put my glass down on the counter and folded my arms. "What about you and Greg? Ory," I added, as her forehead wrinkled up. "You never did say how you met."

Sis had gone a bit pink. "Oh, the usual sort of way. Now come on, they'll be wondering where we've got to." She scurried out of that kitchen like it'd just made an improper suggestion to her. After a moment, I picked up my glass and followed her.

We got back to the "family" room to find it empty of anyone except, well, the family. Cherry looked a bit put out at Greg disappearing like that. I just hoped he hadn't taken Phil off to his workshop to get busy with the skinning knives and sawdust.

"Think we should send out a search party?" I asked, wandering aimlessly around the room with my orange juice. I peered at a bookshelf, then recoiled at the sight of a mole in spectacles carefully positioned by a copy of *The Wind in the Willows*. If there was a rat and a toad around here too, I didn't want to meet them.

"Don't be silly." Cherry was frowning, and she didn't stop a moment later when Phil and the Worryingly Reverend Greg reappeared, looking oddly furtive. "*There* you are."

Greg beamed at her. "We were in the study. Phillip expressed a desire to see my badger."

I blinked. Even Cherry seemed a bit taken aback. "Good, was it?" I asked Phil.

He nodded. "Bigger than I was expecting too." Totally straight-faced, the git.

"Yes," Cherry put in. "A lot of people say that, don't they, Gregory?"

Sod the orange juice, I decided. I was going back on the Slivovitz.

CHAPTER FIVE

What felt like several decades later, I took in a deep lungful of fresh air as the front door shut behind us. "Thank God we're out of there. That place gives me the bloody creeps. It's like *Animal Rescue* after the zombie apocalypse in there."

"Seriously? You've found dead bodies—human bodies. And you're creeped out by a few animal skins stretched over wire?" Phil laughed, the git. "Bet my leather jacket gives you the right shivers, then. And don't get me started on your shoes."

I frowned at them, crunching over the short gravel drive and back to Phil's car. "That's different."

"No, it's not. Skin's skin." Phil's automatic central locks *ca-chunked* open, and we got in.

I shuddered. I'd touched dead people too. It wasn't an experience I liked to remember. "Your jacket doesn't look like a dead animal. Anyway, what do you mean, 'wire'? I thought they, you know, stuffed them. With sawdust or something."

"Nah. They make a wire frame, then pull the skin on like a glove."

"Okay, that picture is *not* helping." I was going to have nightmares about people wearing dead animals on their hands like some sick cross between *Dexter* and *The Muppet Show*.

"Remind me not to take you to see any horror movies. You'd probably scream like a girl."

"No, I'd scream like a bloke. It's lower-pitched and more manly."

"You keep telling yourself that." He pulled out through the gateway and onto the cobbles of Cathedral Close.

I was silent until we got out onto the road. "What was all that about Old Deuteronomy, then? Since when have you been all bloody theological?"

"Come off it, you've got to know Leviticus is the one the Bible-bashers quote when they want to justify nailing people to fences."

"Maybe." To be honest, those weren't the sort of stories I liked to dwell on much.

"Thought you went to Sunday School?"

"Yeah, but the lessons there were more about Jesus suffering the little kiddies and setting up his own branch of Subway next to the Sea of Galilee."

"You what?"

"You know. Feeding the five thousand. Anyway, they didn't go into the controversial stuff is what I'm saying." Actually, I was surprised how well I could remember Mrs. Whatshername telling us the stories and giving us sheets to colour in where all the blokes seemed to be wearing dresses. I'd liked Mrs. Whatshername, although now I came to think about it, she'd left Sunday School under a bit of a cloud too. Right about the time Mr. Somebodysdad stopped bringing the kids to church.

No wonder they hadn't wanted to go controversial in the lessons.

"What was up with you and Greg, anyway? Disappearing off like a couple of kids going behind the bike sheds for a snog." I gave Phil a nudge with my elbow. "Did he really show you his badger?"

"Jealous, were you?"

"No, just worried about you. If he tried groping you with hands that size, he might snap something off by mistake."

"You really ought to see someone about that castration complex. No, don't tell your sister this, but he's asked me to work for him."

"You what? Oi, you're not spying on my sister."

"Did I say anything about your sister? It's nothing to do with her. Gregory just doesn't want to worry her."

Huh. Now Phil was calling him Gregory. "Worry her about what?"

"He's been getting these letters. Hate mail."

"Seriously? What, from animal lovers?"

"No. He thinks it's queer-bashers, but they're not that specific."

"What, 'Rot in hell for reasons unknown'?"

"Just Bible verses, mostly. About sinners in general, and false prophets, and people who reject God's teachings. But he's spoken out on gay rights, stuff like getting married in church, and that's the one that gets people's backs up the most."

"What are they like, these letters? Are they done with bits of newspaper, like on the telly?"

"He said they were just printed out on cheap paper—like from a computer."

"'He said'? Didn't you ask to see them?"

Phil huffed. We were on the main road now. It was pretty quiet—I supposed this time of a Saturday night, everyone who was going out had already got where they were going, and everyone else was tucked up on the sofa in their onesies watching Graham Norton. "He burned them. Six letters so far, he thinks, though it could have been one or two more or less, and they've all disappeared up the bloody chimney."

"So there's no proof they ever even existed."

"I wondered if you'd spot that. What do you think of him? Apart from the dead animals."

"Dunno. Not what you'd call normal, is he? Then again, who is?"

"Speak for yourself." Phil was silent for a moment. "He seems fairly harmless, though. And he's got integrity, I'll give him that."

"Yeah? How do you know that? Try it on, did you, and he turned you down?"

"As if." I wasn't sure if Phil meant, *as if* he'd cheat on me, or *as if* anyone would turn him down. "He could have been a bishop by now if he hadn't stuck to his principles. Gay rights, women in the church, immigration—he's got some unpopular opinions, at least according to the Church of England, and he'd get a lot further in his career if he kept quiet about them. Which is what most of them do. Just pretend to toe the party line."

"So it could be the National Front sending him these letters?"

"Doubt it. He reckoned they were all spelled correctly, had good grammar and that."

"So you think everyone who never got their A level English is a racist? Cheers."

"No, but I do think your average racist is pig-fucking ignorant. For Christ's sake, stop being so bloody touchy."

"Oi. Just because I don't happen to agree with every bloody word that drops from your lips doesn't mean I'm sodding *touchy*."

"Then calm down, all right? Jesus. You been taking drama-queen lessons from your mate Gary?"

There was a bit of a tense silence for the rest of the drive.

"You want to come in?" I asked as Phil pulled up in front of my house. It might have come off a bit more uninviting than I'd meant it to.

Then again, maybe not.

"Nah," he said after a pause. "Think I'll get an early night. Got stuff to do tomorrow."

"Yeah, me too. Right. Good night, then."

"Yeah. Night."

I walked in, got a beer out of the fridge, and sat on the sofa with it for a minute or two, feeling sorry for myself while the cats ignored me.

Then I pulled my mobile out and called Gary.

"Darling, everything all right?"

"Yeah, fine. Are you at home?" I couldn't hear any background noise on his end.

"Mmm. Quiet night in." There was something in his voice, but I couldn't tell what it was. "I thought you were out tonight, though?"

"I was. I came back." I took a swig of beer. "Do you think it's weird Phil still wears his wedding ring?"

"Weird? No. Disturbing? Yes. Does he wear it in bed?"

"God, no." I thought about it. "At least, not so's I've noticed."

"Good. You wouldn't want him to be pumping away inside you and all the time thinking about a corpse."

Great. Now I had visions of him doing just that. "Cheers, mate."

"Have you confronted him?" Gary made it sound like it'd be some huge dramatic scene like in a soap opera. Of course, if he was involved, it probably would be.

"Well, he knows I'm not happy about it."

"Good. Ignoring the elephant in the room never went well for my mother. Of course, as I told her at the time, she should never have married him. I told her she should make him pack his trunk." There was the sound of muffled laughter.

I frowned. "Have you been drinking?"

"I am over eighteen, darling."

"Just a bit. Is Darren there with you? No, don't answer that. Tell him congrats from me, and if he jilts you at the altar, I'll cut his balls off and sell them on the market, two for a pound."

The laughter wasn't muffled this time, and I was fairly sure I heard Darren say, "Come on if you think you're hard enough," which was asking for trouble with the innuendo meister in the room with him. The conversation deteriorated pretty rapidly after that, and I hung up with a smile.

It was good to see *someone's* love life finally going all right.

CHAPTER SIX

A few days later, I was on my way to a job in Potters Bar when my phone rang.

It was Phil. We hadn't seen each other since Saturday night. Must have been all this "stuff" we both had to do. I froze for a mo, then pulled over—lucky it was a quiet road—and hit Accept Call. "Yeah?"

His voice sounded a bit hesitant. "You all right?"

"Yeah, I'm good. You?" Being so bloody polite was setting my teeth on edge. "Just ring up for a chat, did you? 'Cause I'm on my way to a job right now."

There was a sigh. Or maybe just a particularly heavy breath. It was hard to tell over the phone. "You busy tomorrow afternoon?"

"What time?"

"Straight after lunch."

I mentally reviewed my schedule. "I've got a job on at eleven, shouldn't take more than an hour or so, then nothing until four. Why?" If he said the reason was we needed to talk, I was going to have to invent an emergency call-out.

"I'm going to see Greg about those notes he's been getting."

"And you want me to hold your hand? Now who's scared of the little furry animals?" There was a silence. "Sorry."

Another sigh. "Yeah."

Yeah, what? Yeah, he was sorry too? Or he was agreeing I ought to be?

"So you want me to come with?" I prompted.

"If you want." Another pause. It was a bloody good thing I hadn't been on the motorway with nowhere to stop the van, or we'd have been in six-o'clock-news territory by now. *Multivehicle pileup on A1(M), the* headline would be. Or, if the *Sun* wrote it, *Poofter Plumber Goes Postal in Potters Bar*. "Greg said he'd show us around the cathedral."

I couldn't help smiling. And not just cos Phil was back to calling him Greg. "Well, if there's a trip round the cathedral in it for me . . ."

"Git. So, you coming?"

"Yeah, I guess so. Wanna meet for lunch first?"

"You going to have time?"

"Well, no, not really, but we could grab a sandwich somewhere. Actually, come to think of it, why don't you come round mine tonight? I might even cook you something."

"Sorry. Can't do tonight." He didn't say why.

My smile evaporated. "Oh. Okay. See you tomorrow, then." I hung up and then realised we hadn't made any arrangements for actually meeting up tomorrow.

Sod it. He'd either ring me again, or he wouldn't.

My eleven o'clock job turned out to be a bit more complicated than I'd expected, which was partly my fault. I fixed the leak in the bathroom (easy job: just the loo inlet pipe seal, which had left a nice tell-tale damp patch on the carpet) and was on my way out when I looked up at the ceiling, which was mottled with those lovely brown stains you get from an upstairs plumbing problem.

Except the leak I'd just fixed was placed wrong to have caused them. Now, I'd be the first to admit that sometimes water moves in mysterious ways, but something was telling me we had another leak here. "How long have those been there?" I asked.

Mrs. C. (plump, midsixties, made a nice cup of coffee but wasn't what you'd call chatty) gave me a look that said she was starting to wonder what they were teaching plumbers these days. "Since the leak started, of course."

"Just going to take another look upstairs, all right? Check everything else is okay."

She followed me up, obviously suspicious I might be about to "discover" another leak with a swift blow of a wrench. I stood on the landing and listened, which probably made her wonder even more.

Got it.

"You had your hot water tank checked lately?" I didn't wait for an answer, just opened up the airing cupboard. Bingo.

She had a load of old towels and bedding stacked on the cupboard floor—obviously the type who didn't throw anything away, in case it came in handy later. Which, as it happened, was just as well in this case.

I turned back to her. "See this?" I prodded the linens. "Absolutely sodden. 'Fraid you're going to need a new hot water tank, love. They get these pinhole leaks in them, and then it's only a matter of time before they go completely."

She closed her eyes briefly, her face falling. "I don't believe it. It never rains but it pours, does it?"

"Look on the bright side. At least we caught it before it started pouring through your ceiling."

When I finally got out of there and looked at my phone, I saw there was a missed call from Phil and a text that just read, *Lnch?*

I called him straight back. "Sorry, job overran. We still on for visiting Greg? Want to go via a drive-through?"

"Not a lot, no. Where are you?"

"Top end of Bricket Wood."

"Right. Hop on the M1 and I'll meet you at the Holiday Inn car park on the A414—you know it? Just past that roundabout with the modern art."

"Those claw things? Give me the creeps, those do. Right. How long?"

"Twenty minutes. I'll bring the food."

I hopped and got there in ten. The van's pretty nippy when she wants to be. I still didn't beat Phil there, so obviously he'd already sorted out lunch before I called him, unless he'd changed his mind about the drive-through. Actually, I quite fancied a burger. The chips are always rubbish at those places, though.

I parked the van and jogged over to Phil's car, my hands in my jacket pockets to keep them warm. Might as well let him drive us over to St. Leonards, seeing as Greg would be paying for his petrol. "You all right, then?"

He nodded. "Get in."

"You know, you're going to have to work on toning down these effusive greetings. People are going to talk."

"Git." But he cracked a smile.

There was a paper bag on the seat, so I picked it up rather than sitting on it, then looked inside because I'm nosy like that. The mingled scent of warm bacon and greasy pastry teased my nose and set my stomach rumbling. "Nice. Not Greggs?"

"Nah, I went to the baker's in Brock's Hollow. Pass us a sausage roll."

"You want to start with the bacon butties. They don't stay hot." I grabbed one out of the bag and took a bite. Lovely. Thick, crispy bacon and fresh, floury white bread, with just enough butter. You don't need anything else for a bacon butty, not if you're doing it right. I glanced at Phil. He was staring at me, his sossie roll forgotten and eyes crinkled up a bit at the corners in that way that makes him look like he's got a headache, but actually means he's trying not to laugh. "What? Have I got flour on my nose or something?"

"Yeah, but I was more bothered about what else that bacon sarnie was doing to you. Should I be getting jealous?"

"Hey, you're the one who brought the butty into this relationship. If you didn't want a threesome, you should have left it at the baker's."

He did laugh then. "God help us all when you get on to the sausage rolls. There's a cup of tea here for you too, by the way." He reached into the back footwell and brought out a cardboard cup holder, with his-and-his cups of tea, the teabag strings swinging jauntily. "Better get a shift on, though. We're due at the Old Deanery at two."

We munched in silence. It was, well, crap word, but it was nice. I've never been one for posh dinner dates, but there's just something about sharing food with your bloke. Phil had parked facing away from the Holiday Inn and towards the green bit at the side. The view out the front windscreen wasn't much, but it was all right, gave us something to look at, and it just felt sort of cosy, sitting there with Phil. I mean, it was pretty nippy outside despite the watery sunshine, and if we'd sat there much longer with the car heater off, my toes would probably have gone numb, but as it was, it was just right.

I was kind of sad when we'd finished. Still, places to go, canons to see. I crumpled up the bag, licked a few bits of flaky pastry off my fingers, and wiped my hands on my jeans. "Ready?"

Phil nodded and switched on the ignition. His hand hovered by the gear stick, then changed track and reached over to grab the back of my neck and pull me in for a kiss. His lips were soft and warm and tasted of flour and bacon. I kissed him back, feeling a weird fluttering in my chest.

Too much greasy food, probably. It can give you indigestion.

When we broke apart again, Phil just looked at me for a long moment. "We ought to do this more often," he said finally, with this funny sort of half smile on his lips.

"What, snog in public?" Not that there was actually anyone around to give a toss.

"Meet up for lunch. Go places together. You know."

I didn't know what to say. That fluttering in my chest was getting stronger, so I flashed him a smile and looked at my watch. "Yeah, okay. 'Bout time we were making a move, though, innit?"

Phil made a grunt of a sound that could have been a laugh or could have just been him agreeing with me. Then he put the car in gear, and we set off.

Traffic was light, and we got to the Old Deanery with five minutes to spare.

Gregory came to the door with a twinkle in his eyes and both large hands outstretched. I was worried for a moment he was going to pick me up or pinch my cheeks or something else I might never recover from, but he settled for clapping me and Phil on opposite shoulders simultaneously, as if he was about to knock our heads together. "Come in, come in," he boomed.

We came in. Then we just stood there in the hallway for a bit while he beamed at us happily and I fought the urge to run.

Phil cleared his throat. "Perhaps we should go and sit down, and you can tell us some more about the letters—"

"Oh, I don't think we should start with such serious matters. Let us adjourn to the cathedral. One moment, while I fetch my coat."

We waited while he shrugged on a large, dark overcoat with an upturned collar that made him look even more sinister, then wound a great long woollen monstrosity around his neck. It was a sort of scarf equivalent of a patchwork quilt—someone had clearly had a lot of bits of wool left over and decided to have a clear-out. And either they were colourblind, or they didn't like Greg very much.

He caught me looking. "Er, nice scarf," I said, hoping Greg's boss wasn't about to strike me dead for bearing false witness.

Greg beamed. "Isn't it marvellous? One of my ladies is something of a *Doctor Who* aficionado. Wait there."

Phil and I waited, exchanging glances. Greg bounded back thirty seconds later wearing an old-fashioned, wide-brimmed hat and a manic expression.

"What do you think? Could I pass for Tom Baker's incarnation of the Doctor?"

"Er, bit before my time," I managed. Although I'd have had to admit, I'd have accepted him as a weirdo alien from another planet, no question.

"Oh, Cherry and I have all the DVDs. You must borrow them."

Cherry was a secret sci-fi geek? I couldn't remember any signs of it when she'd been younger. Now I was wondering if she and Greg had met at a convention somewhere, him kitted out in his *Doctor Who* gear and her dressed up as . . . what? Princess Leia in her bondage bikini? I gave a mental shudder.

It was only a hop, skip, and a jump from the Old Deanery to the cathedral. To give Greg his due, he didn't actually hop, skip, and jump over there, but he did keep the *Doctor Who* fancy dress on. No one we passed batted an eyelid.

From the outside, St. Leonards Cathedral was pretty much your average English cathedral—all chunky solid walls and spiky fiddly bits in greyish stone. It looked a fair bit posher than St. Albans Abbey, which has lots of red brick bits that don't really match the rest. Sort of the masonry equivalent of Greg's scarf, now I came to think about it.

We went in through a side door, away from the main visitor entrance where a smartly dressed old lady was sitting, ready to demand a "voluntary contribution" of five quid from anyone who stuck their head in the door. At this time of year, on a weekday, she didn't have a lot of takers.

Inside, it was surprisingly light and bright, a bit like Phil's attic flat, only several hundred times the size, obviously. Tall, thin pillars held up a high arched ceiling, and the main bit had modern folding chairs instead of dark wooden pews.

"You must let me take you on the roof tour," Greg suggested, his eyebrows doing a good impression of the ceiling arches.

Phil frowned. "That'd involve poky little spiral staircases, wouldn't it? No, thanks. I'm not a fan of small enclosed spaces at the moment."

He'd had a bit of a bad experience in one of those, back during the Brock's Hollow business.

Greg's face fell, but he perked up again almost immediately. "In that case, let me show you the gargoyles. Come, this way." He skipped off ahead of us like a kid in a toyshop, his long coat and scarf flouncing after him.

Phil coughed. It sounded a bit like "birds of a feather."

First stop was a fat naked bloke, carved high up on a stone archway. He had a terrified expression, probably because it looked like he was about to be roughly buggered by a club-wielding devil. "Is that sort of thing really suitable for a church?" I asked, frowning.

Greg laughed. "Oh, you'd be surprised at what you find in our churches and cathedrals. Pagan symbols, petty revenge—the man in this carving is supposed to have been a particularly strict foreman during the cathedral's construction."

"Bet he was chuffed when he saw what they'd done. I thought everyone was supposed to be all God-fearing, back in those days?" Whenever those days were. Middle Ages? Greg hadn't mentioned when the place was built, but we were definitely talking centuries ago.

"You must remember that stonemasons were simply working men. Much as yourself. Salt-of-the-earth types, with an earthy humour."

I'd never thought of myself as particularly salty. Or earthy, come to that. Maybe I should ask Phil. If anyone would know what I tasted like, he ought to.

"These notes you've been getting," Phil butted in. "Do you think those might have been someone's idea of a joke?"

Greg whirled and stared at him intently. I squirmed a bit on Phil's behalf. "Do you know, I think you might be right. After all, in these days of *You've Been Framed!* and *Fool Britannia* . . ."

Phil didn't look all that pleased at Greg's answer. "Have there been any more? Since we last spoke?"

"No. Now, if you come this way, you can see Bishop Anthony playing the bagpipes. Apparently he was something of an old windbag . . ."

The tour went on in the same way, and even I noticed a pattern. Every time Phil tried to bring up the notes, Greg bounded off to show us some new evidence of people making their own entertainment in the days before telly.

Phil started checking his watch every five seconds or so and eventually lost patience. "Look, this is all fascinating, but I came here to talk about those threatening letters. Why don't we go back to yours, and we can—"

"Good gracious," Greg interrupted him. Seriously, does anyone actually say *good gracious* anymore? "Is that the time? You've been very naughty, you know, letting me rattle on like this. I'm afraid I'm going to have to leave you. I'm due at the Women's Institute, and I really can't keep the ladies waiting. Perhaps we could meet again another time?"

The tension around Phil's eyes had absolutely nothing to do with wanting to laugh this time. "I'll give you a call," he ground out.

Greg strode off in his seven-league loafers, one hand on his hat to stop the wind snatching it away and that god-awful scarf billowing madly in his wake. Phil and I walked back to the car more slowly. The air outside tasted fresh and clean after the cathedral's stagnant atmosphere. "Do you think he's actually that dippy, or is he messing us about?"

Phil grunted. "I think he knows exactly what he's doing."

"Yeah, but why's he doing it? What's the point of dragging you all the way out here and then not talking about what he's hired you for?" I grinned. "Think he fancies you? Course, then he wouldn't have invited me too, would he? Unless he wants a threesome."

"You and your bloody threesomes. Any more about that and I'll think you're trying to tell me something. No, I don't know what his game is—yet—but let's see how he feels about playing it when I bill him for my time and expenses. What time are you off tonight?" Phil unlocked the car, and we climbed in.

"Dunno, about five?" Course, it'd be sod's law to have two jobs overrun in one day. "Definitely by six. Want to come over to mine, get a takeaway or something?"

Phil nodded and put the car in gear. I glanced over at his left hand where it rested on the steering wheel at a regulation ten-to-two. No ring. No mark either, and wasn't that tan line just a little bit less obvious than it used to be? I smiled.

"What's so funny?" Phil was giving me the side-eye.

"Nothing. Just looking forward to tonight."

"Oh, yeah? That desperate for a takeaway, are you?"

I grinned. "Yeah. Or something."

CHAPTER SEVEN

"I've got to go over to Cherry's chambers this afternoon," I told Phil over breakfast next day. We'd shared a pretty enjoyable night and an even better morning wake-up call.

Phil raised an eyebrow over his coffee mug. We were eating standing up in the kitchen, to show we meant business about finally getting on with the day. "Cherry's chambers? Sounds like a brand of preteen girls' underwear."

I waved my toast at him. "I was thinking more like a covert pudding society. Sort of fruity freemasons."

"Yeah? Better brush up on your secret handshakes, then. What's this about? More on your auntie's will?"

"Yeah. Got a meeting with Mr. Morangie."

Phil sniggered. "Is his first name Glen?"

I swallowed a marmaladey mouthful. "God, you're full of it today."

He grabbed my arse. "No, but you were, as I recall. Could be again later, if you play your cards right."

"Promises, promises." I took the opportunity to grab his last bit of toast and shove it in my gob.

The name Ver Chambers had me expecting something all olde worlde, with oak-panelled walls and little match girls huddling for warmth in the doorway. I was a bit disappointed when Cherry's chambers turned out to be just your average modern office. It was based in an old town house with the back garden converted into a cramped little car park reached through a narrow alleyway. I was glad

I'd taken the Fiesta; I didn't reckon I could have got the van in there without taking out a wing mirror or two on the walls. And parking on the street would have been a bloody nightmare on market day. Just *driving* on the street was a bloody nightmare on market day, what with all the old grannies doddering along at a heady twenty miles an hour on their way to get their veggies.

A chirpy receptionist buzzed me into the building, and greeted me with a bleached white smile and "You're Cherry's other brother, aren't you?"

"Er, yeah, I guess."

"You don't look much like Richard." I got the impression she thought that was a good thing. At least, judging from the way she was looking at me as if she was a spray-tanned shark that'd just spotted dinner.

"See him a lot, do you?"

"Oh, now and then." She lowered her feathery eyelashes for a moment. Either she was flirting with me, or the weight of all that mascara had just got too much. "So you're the black sheep of the family?"

"Me? Purer than the driven snow." I winked at her, wondering just what Cherry had been saying about me. "Shall I go on through, or is she busy with someone?"

"No, she's free right now." She tucked a few strands of blonde hair behind her ear with her left hand, not so incidentally drawing attention to her bare ring finger. Looked like Cherry hadn't told her much about me. "Down the corridor, third door on the left. I'll let her know you're coming."

"Cheers, love."

I wasn't sure whether to knock on the door or not when I got there. I mean, lawyers, you knock, right? But sisters, not so much. In the end, I gave a short, sharp rap and opened the door straightaway, not waiting for an answer.

Cherry looked up from her desk (large, mahogany, with an honest-to-God blotter on it) and gave me a tight little smile. "Thanks for being punctual."

"No sign of Mr. M. yet?"

"No. I asked him to come at quarter past. I wanted a word with you before he gets here."

"Oh?" There were two chairs this side of Cherry's desk, so I picked one and sat in it. "What about?"

She turned her head to stare out the window for a moment. I followed her gaze, but all I could see was a patch of wall from next door. "I want to know what's going on with Gregory. He's been in contact with Phil Morrison."

Shit. "How do you know?"

"I'm not an *idiot*. And I do occasionally answer the phone at Gregory's house. Your Phil rang him only the other night."

"So? It's a free country, innit?"

Cherry spun to face me. "Well, it's quite obvious he must be consulting him professionally about something. They haven't got the first thing in common."

"Dunno about that," I hedged. "Maybe they've been swapping Bible quotes again. Maybe Phil's getting religion."

"You're being—"

"Wilfully obtuse, I know. Look, Sis, what am I supposed to do here? What if I came in here and asked to know all about one of your clients? You'd just hand me the file and let me in on all the juicy gossip, would you?"

"That's—"

"Different? *Course* it is."

"Oh, for—"

This time, it was the phone that cut her off with one short ring. Cherry picked up, listened, and said, "Thank you." Then she put it down and turned to me. "He's here. We'll have to talk about this later." She glared ominously at me, then stood and walked out, her plain black skirt rustling as she went.

I twiddled my thumbs for a minute or so. (All right, I checked Twitter on my phone. No updates from Phil, but Darren had posted a suggestive picture of two turnips and a marrow.) Then the door opened, and in walked Cherry with Mr. Morangie.

Mr. M. was tall and thin, dressed in muted shades of drab and with wispy white hair clinging to his skull like a half-hearted fungus. He had to be the most colourless person I'd ever met, though I don't mean he was an albino or anything. It was more than skin deep with this bloke. He looked at least sixty, maybe sixty-five, and I couldn't believe Auntie Lol had ever married him, even if it had only lasted six months or so. Maybe he'd faded since then, although from the look of him, it wasn't due to being out in the sun too much. He had the sort of dead-fish complexion you tend to see on a certain type of geeky adolescent boy, although on him, the twitching fingers probably weren't from overindulgence in online gaming. Still, you never knew.

"Do come and sit down." Cherry ushered him across the threshold. "It's really good of you to come. I'm sure you're finding this all a bit of a nuisance."

"Yeah," I muttered. "It was bloody inconsiderate of Auntie Lol to go dying like that, wasn't it?"

"*Tom*," Cherry snapped. Now back behind her desk, she turned to Mr. M. and pasted on a smile. "I realise you'd been estranged for some time, but still, it must have been quite a shock to hear that Laura had passed away."

"Yes, of course," Mr. M. said stolidly.

Cherry soldiered on. "This is my brother, Tom. Tom, Roland Morangie."

I stood to shake hands with him and tried not to cringe too obviously at the moist, warm grip of his wrinkly fingers. We sat down in unison, Cherry in her executive swivel chair behind the desk, and me and Mr. M. in the rigid, more-or-less-comfy chairs on the other side, placed a good three feet away from each other. I wondered if that was to stop divorcing couples coming to blows in her office.

"Would you like a cup of tea? Coffee?" Cherry managed to imply with her tone that he'd be doing her the greatest of favours if he accepted.

Mr. M. was unmoved, but he was willing to indulge her. "Thank you. Tea, I think."

Cherry turned back to me. "Tom?" This time, she managed to imply I'd be doing her the greatest of favours if I choked on it.

Got to hand it to Cherry: she could put a lot of meaning into one short syllable.

"Ta. Milk, no sugar. And a biccie would be nice."

Her eyes narrowed, and when she picked up the phone and gave the order to some minion or other, she unaccountably forgot to mention the biccies.

Oh well. I hadn't really wanted one anyway.

"Were you aware of Laura's rather strange will?" Cherry asked as she sat down again.

"No." He paused a minute, twitching. "Laura and I didn't speak after we parted."

"It must have been difficult for you," Cherry said with warm sympathy. Or at least a pretty good imitation.

He stared at her for a moment with bloodless eyes. "Not particularly. We weren't married long. And it was all well over a decade ago, as you know."

I wondered how many years it took to stop feeling bitter over a failed marriage. How long did it take until you could think of your ex objectively, like they were just an acquaintance or something, just another person you'd lost touch with? I supposed I shouldn't be surprised Phil still had feelings for the Mysterious Mark.

The tea arrived at that point, courtesy of the smiley receptionist, which was probably just as well from Cherry's point of view. I don't think she was impressed with Mr. M.'s failure to keep to the script. "Cheers, love," I said as I was handed a cup with a dimple. "I'm Tom, by the way." I was pretty sure she already knew, but it seemed only friendly.

"Oh, I've heard all about *you*. I'm Jeanette."

Cherry glared at me like I'd just dropped my trousers and taken a piss in her tea. "Thank you, Jeanette. That will be all."

Me and Jeanette shared trying-not-to-laugh faces as she left, her high heels making her hips wiggle in her tight skirt. Conversation was reduced for a minute or so to polite murmurings as we passed the milk and offered the sugar, which was probably just as well.

Jeanette had brought biccies anyway, a plate of Bourbons. I took one just to see Cherry's face when I dunked it in my cuppa.

It was a classic: How Can We Possibly Be Related Death Glare #3. I almost did choke at the sight of it.

Fortunately for her blood pressure, Mr. M. didn't seem to notice.

"Now, according to Mrs. Morangie's will, the codicil detailing Tom's legacy is somewhere in your house. I don't suppose you've been able to locate it?" Cherry didn't sound too hopeful.

"Regrettably, no. I understand she wished your brother to search for it?" His mouth was all twisted up like someone had put salt in his tea instead of sugar.

"Yes." Cherry made a *what can you do?* gesture with her hands. "I know it seems a bizarre idea, but perhaps she'd become rather . . . eccentric as she aged."

"Oi, Aunty Lol still had all her marbles. She wasn't old enough to be going senile, nowhere near."

Mr. M. looked pissed off too, which, seeing as he had to have at least ten years on Auntie Lol, wasn't surprising. Nice one, Sis. Cherry seemed to realise she'd shoved her foot in it, as she turned pink and got very interested in her cup of tea for a moment.

Mr. M. filled the silence. "I'm sure you understand that I'm not keen to have a stranger invading my house. At my time of life," he added, with a daggers glare at Cherry. "I thought perhaps we could avoid all the upheaval if I simply made you an offer to renounce all claims." He named a figure that would have taken a hefty chunk out of the money I owed the mortgage company.

I blinked. Then I frowned. "Hang about. We don't even know if she left me anything worth a fraction of that. I'm not taking your money if it isn't due."

"Nevertheless, it seems to me extremely likely that that is what Laura did. In the circumstances I'm quite happy to—"

"Yeah, but what if I'm not? Happy, I mean." I sat forward, struggling to think how to put it. "Look, it was Auntie Lol's last request, wasn't it? For me to go looking for the . . . what do you call it, Sis? Coda?"

"Codicil." It sounded like a brand name for nasal spray.

"So I'm not happy just saying, 'Fine, give me the money.' It's not right."

Cherry cleared her throat. "Actually, the legal situation—"

"Sod the legal situation. I want to do what Auntie Lol wanted."

"Tom, you're just being difficult. Mr. Morangie is being very generous here."

"Not necessarily. What if she left me the deeds to a diamond mine?"

Cherry's face could have blistered paint. "Oh yes, of course, she always used to regale us with tales of her life in the diamond mines of South Africa."

Me-ow. "I'm sure you used to tell me sarcasm was the lowest form of wit."

Mr. Morangie rattled his teacup loudly in his saucer. Cherry and I turned as one to glare at him, and he leaned back with a worried expression as if he was trying to escape through the back of the chair. "Ah. It's, ah, commendable that you want to follow my late wife's wishes, but really, I have my doubts the codicil will ever be found."

Why? Had he found it already, and chucked it on a fire? I frowned and opened my mouth, but he beat me to it.

"As you can imagine, I've already made a thorough search of the property, and I've been unable to locate it."

"Yeah, well, fresh pair of eyes and all that," I said breezily. I wondered if Cherry would mention my special talent for finding stuff, but apparently my *thing* was still on the list of unmentionables. Fair enough: he probably thought we were weird enough already. And if he didn't expect me to find it, he wouldn't bother getting a shift on with trying to find and destroy the thing before I got there. "So when can I come round? Sooner I start, the sooner I'll finish and get out of your hair."

Mr. M. made a face like he was chewing on a cockroach and was too polite to spit it out. "I'll have to consider the matter. I was given to understand we would be able to come to an arrangement." He put his teacup down on Cherry's desk, as if getting ready to leg it.

Cherry wasn't giving up that easily. "Please wait, Mr. Morangie. Perhaps if I had a private word with my brother—"

"You'd be wasting everyone's time," I interrupted. "Sorry, but I'm not budging. What's the bloody point of leaving a will if everyone's going to flippin' well ignore your final wishes?"

Mr. M. and I stood up at the same time like we'd planned it that way. Which was a bit unfortunate, seeing as we'd have to walk out together now. Maybe we could talk about the weather or the crap state of English football. We might even be able to agree on those subjects, although I doubted it.

"I shall have to consult my solicitor," he said. His tone should have carried a warning for mild threat like you get on kids' films.

"Then I'll look forward to hearing from you," Cherry said politely. "Tom, would you wait a minute, please?" *Her* tone was definitely the sort some small children might find upsetting.

It was a toss-up which was the least-inviting prospect: small talk with a pissed-off Mr. M., or a lecture from a pissed-off Cherry. On the other hand, if I didn't let Cherry vent now, she'd only bend my ear about it later on the phone. I sat back down and, while she ushered Mr. M. out, did the modern equivalent of twiddling my thumbs. Gary had tweeted *Bellringers do it with ropes* and Darren had replied *Market traders do it in public*. I was still trying to think up a really good one for plumbers when Cherry said my name in that annoyed tone of voice people use when they have to repeat themselves.

I put my phone away hurriedly. "Gone, has he?"

"Yes. I don't know why you had to be so obstructive."

"Yeah, you do. So what happens now?"

She sighed. "I'll give him a day or so to cool off and then give him a call. Hopefully *someone* will be willing to be reasonable by then. Anyway, that wasn't what I wanted to talk to you about."

"No?" I tried to think what the hell else she might want to talk to me about, and worry tickled the back of my neck. "Mum and Dad are all right, aren't they?"

"They're fine." I waited. Cherry took a deep breath. "Gregory and I are going to be married."

"Bloody hell, that's a bit fast, innit?" I stared at her. Was it something in the water round here? First Gary, now my sister.

Cherry went pink. "It's not fast at all. Just because *you've* only just met him . . ." Another deep breath. Maybe she should see a doctor about her lungs. "Anyway, we're having a party on Friday."

"What, *this* Friday?"

"You know, you could congratulate me." Her mouth tightened.

"Er, right. Sorry. Congratulations and all that." Bloody hell, I was going to be the only one left on the shelf. "Going to be a church do, then?"

"Well, *obviously*. We're hoping to be married by the bishop," she added, sounding a lot less miffed. "It'll be in the cathedral, in any case. Gregory wants to invite all the regulars to fill up seats."

"Surprised he's not planning to prop up that little 'family' of his in the pews."

She *tsked*. "St. Leonards doesn't *have* pews."

"Course it doesn't. Silly me. Should've remembered."

"Oh? I didn't know you'd been there."

"Er, yeah. Just for a quick visit." Fortunately she didn't ask when that'd been or who'd provided the guided tour.

"So are you coming, then?"

"Well, *yeah*." Did she really think I'd miss my only sister's wedding? "You want me to bring Phil, right?"

There was just the tiniest pause before she answered. "Of course. But, um, just the two of you," she added, going even pinker.

I frowned. "Well, I'm hardly going to turn up with a whole crowd of blokes from the pub, am I? So when is it? You haven't said, yet."

She *huffed*. "Yes, I did. *Friday*. At Gregory's. Starting at seven."

"What?" Surely even Cherry couldn't organise a wedding that fast? I did a quick mental gear change as I finally realised we'd been talking about two different things. "Oh, you mean the *party*. Right, yeah, we'll be there. You sure you've got time to get it set up? Want me to bring anything?"

"Oh, we'll be fine. Gregory's going to get some of the cathedral ladies to do some finger food. And if we left it any later, Gregory would be all caught up in Alpha Courses and Confirmation Classes. He barely has an evening free before Easter."

I nodded. "No rest for the wicked. Bit of a quiet time for me, as it happens—a lot of people put off the nonessential jobs until they've had a chance to recover from the Christmas bills. And the sales spending."

"Oh." She paused, and I was just about to get up again when she spoke. "Is work going okay? Are you, well, all right for money?" She brushed furiously at some biscuit crumbs on her desk. At least I assumed that was what she was doing, although, come to think of it, she hadn't actually had a biccie with her tea.

"Yeah, I'm all right. Can't complain. Er, you?" It was probably a daft question, judging from the wood grain on that desk of hers, but it seemed a bit rude not to ask, seeing as she had.

Cherry looked up sharply. "Oh, yes. Of course. Right, well, that was all I wanted to talk to you about. Unless you, er . . .?"

"Nah, I'm good," I said, standing up. "I'll see myself out." I grinned. "I'm sure if I go wrong, Jeanette'll set me straight."

Cherry actually sort of laughed. Maybe it was more of a snort. "I'm sure she'd be only too happy to *set you straight*, but I always thought it wasn't supposed to work like that."

Bloody hell. That was almost a joke.

Maybe the Irreverently Reverend Greg was actually good for her.

CHAPTER EIGHT

Thursday night, Cherry rang me again. The landline probably thought my mobile had done a runner. I was home on my own—I hadn't seen Phil since the night before last, and even the cats had buggered off somewhere.

Not that I was moping or anything. I made sure my tone was nice and cheery as I said, "Hello?"

"Tom?"

"Yeah, it's me. You all right?"

"Fine."

"Is the do still on for tomorrow?" God, I hoped she hadn't gone and got unengaged in the twenty-four hours since we'd last spoken. I couldn't think of any other reason she'd be ringing me so soon after I'd seen her.

"Of course. Actually, I've spoken to Mr. Morangie again." Oh yes. That reason. There was a frustrating pause. Had Mr. M. taken out a restraining order banning me from getting within five miles of his precious house? Set up barbed wire and a minefield? "He's agreed to allow you into his home. We need to have a serious chat about how you're going to do this."

"Oh. Right. Nice one, Sis—how'd you manage that?"

"I spoke to his solicitor. A Mr. Wood. He was very reasonable about it all, especially when I explained how your, um, *thing* works, and that you wouldn't have to rummage through the whole place. Actually, he said he'd quite like to see you in action."

It was on the tip of my tongue to tell her, *Sorry, only Phil gets to see my* thing *in action these days*, but that might just have been a quip too far for dear old Sis. "Tell you what, why don't we put up a poster and sell tickets? We can donate the proceeds towards Mr. M.'s legal fees. Or buy you a really nice engagement present. Matter of fact, you got any ideas on that? Any fish slices or toasting racks you've got your eye on, or would Greg be just as happy with a nice bit of roadkill? I saw a fox out by Brock's Hollow only this morning, looked in pretty good nick."

There was a pause. God, I hoped she wasn't seriously considering it. It hadn't been in *that* good nick, and I didn't much fancy having it oozing maggoty innards all over the back of my van.

"That's very kind, but we're not having engagement presents. We're asking anyone who feels moved to do so to contribute to the cathedral's mission fund instead. Anyway, you've made me lose track. Mr. Wood suggested a few times that would be convenient for Mr. Morangie." She started to rattle off a list.

"Hang on a sec, let me get my work diary." We eventually settled on a date and time—there were a couple I could have done, but I worked on the principle the sooner the better before he changed his mind again, and plumped for next Monday at 10 a.m. I wondered if the solicitor really would be coming along to spectate, and if I'd be able to stop myself from greeting him with a cheery "Morning, Wood!"

Friday night, Phil came round to mine before Cherry's do so we could share a pizza before we went. There was no telling how much food would be on offer tonight, and I wasn't going to take any chances. If the cathedral ladies were doing the catering, that could mean anything from a couple of cucumber sandwiches with the crusts cut off to several truckloads of homemade quiche.

"Are your mum and dad going to be there tonight?" Phil took a bite of Americano.

"Doubt it. Dad's been feeling his age." Ever since I'd been born, as I recalled, although he'd only been in his late forties then. "Doesn't like parties and stuff. Mum might go on her own, but I doubt it. Richard might be there, though." I chased a bit of coleslaw around my plate.

"That's your brother, right?" The last of his slice of pizza disappeared. I was going to have to get a move on if I wanted to get my fair share.

"Yeah. God, I haven't seen him in ages. He's two years older than Cherry, so we were never exactly close."

"You must have seen him at Christmas."

I put my fork down. "There a law about it or something? No, as it happens. We've never really done the big family get-together thing. Richard and Agatha always go skiing that time of year."

Phil huffed. "Wish I could get out of family Christmases. It's a three-line bloody whip round my mum's house."

"Yeah, you said." Back when I'd finally plucked up the nerve to ask him what he was doing that day. "And I kind of noticed I was eating Christmas dinner on my own." It was the first time I'd admitted it. He'd asked how my Christmas was the next time I'd seen him, I'd said, "Fine," and we hadn't gone into details.

"You were on your own? You should have said." Phil frowned down at his plate. Maybe he was annoyed with it for being empty. "You'd have been welcome to come along with me."

"Jesus, could you have said that with any less conviction? Don't worry, I had Merlin and Arthur to help me eat up the turkey." I sawed viciously at a stubborn bit of pizza crust holding two slices together.

"Christ, you're touchy. I just didn't reckon you'd want to go. *I* didn't want to go. Told you, it's a bloody nightmare. Everyone gets pissed on cheap sherry, and it's not Christmas if no one storms out before the turkey's cold."

"Sounds like an episode of *EastEnders*. Anyone get divorce papers as a Christmas present?"

"No, but that's only because the solicitors all close for Christmas." There was a pause. "Mark always hated it." Phil glanced up and narrowed his eyes. "And don't look at me like that. Of course he bloody went. We were married, weren't we? If I'd turned up without him, Mum would've slammed the door in my face."

"From the way you've been talking, wouldn't that have been a pretty good result?"

He huffed, bulky shoulders moving expansively. "It's family."

Like that was an explanation for anything. Still, he wasn't under any obligation to invite me round to his family get-togethers. After all, it wasn't like I'd ever asked him to come along and meet my family, was it?

Oh. Wait. What were we on our way to?

Still . . .

"Come on, don't we need to get going? Thought this do started at seven?"

When we got to St. Leonards, we had to park halfway down Cathedral Close. The Old Deanery drive was already chocker with cars, and they spilled out onto the cobbles too.

"Looks like the Rev's pretty popular," Phil commented as we got out of the car.

"Either that or one of the cathedral ladies does killer vol-au-vents. Course, they could all be Cherry's mates."

Phil shoved his hands in his pockets. Fair dues, it was a bit nippy out. "No offence, but your sister didn't exactly strike me as the life-and-soul-of-the-party type."

"Nah, you're right. God, for all we know there could be half the Church of England in there."

"Or the Guild of Taxidermists." He coughed. It sounded a lot like "Posers."

I grinned. "Hey, nothing wrong with having a guild. There's a Guild of Master Plumbers, you know."

"You missed out 'and Dunnikindivers.'" The streetlamps cast a warm glow over Phil's face that cooled into menacing shadows as we walked.

"We had to kick the cesspit cleaners out. Couldn't stand the smell."

"Who couldn't? You or them?"

I stuck up a finger and swivelled it in his general direction as we walked through the gateway. We could hear the sounds of the party already, and we soon found out why. There was an open-door policy at the Old Deanery tonight—literally. The heavy front door was wedged open with a proper, old-fashioned wooden wedge. Unlike the last time we'd been here, the hallway was brightly lit, and the door to the front room was wide open.

We trooped inside.

The place was heaving. How many people had Cherry and/or Greg invited to this do? Or had they just rung up Rentamob? All the furniture had been cleared to the sides of the room, and there were tables along the wall nearest the door piled high with food. Greg's ladies had done him and Cherry proud. There were dainty little triangle sandwiches, sausage rolls of every size, wrinkly cocktail sausages next to them looking a bit embarrassed about sitting there with their kit off, and homemade quiches by the dozen with little handwritten flags in to tell you if they were veggie or not. Plus a few more interesting bits someone had clearly sneaked in from Marks & Spencer. I hoped they were properly ashamed of themselves for letting the side down like that.

A separate table held the sweet stuff: mince pies (which I hoped hadn't been hanging around since Christmas, but it was probably safer to leave them anyway), heavy-looking cakes and a huge bowl of grapes shining like someone had polished them individually. Of course, that was probably what passed for entertainment around here. St. Leonards is a nice enough town, but it's not exactly renowned for its nightlife.

Case in point: it looked like half the population of the place had turned up here tonight, although there was a definite bias towards the older end of the demographic. Lots of middling-to-old ladies in frumpy skirts and sensible shoes, and balding blokes in saggy trousers. In fact, from where I was standing I couldn't see a single person under thirty. Presumably the ones with young families had all stayed home so the kiddies wouldn't get nightmares from Greg's glassy-eyed chums—the stuffed animals, I mean, not his actual mates. I'm not one to pass judgement on people till I actually meet them. They must've been cursing their luck at missing the social event of the century.

"Think we should say hi to Greg and Cherry, or just dive in?" I asked, raising my voice so Phil could hear me over the din. I couldn't see Cherry right at the moment, but Greg was over the other side of the room, gesturing wildly in a way that was going to have someone's eye out any minute as he spoke to a couple of equally tall, churchy-looking types. "Reckon the church has a minimum height requirement?" I wondered aloud.

Phil grunted. "Why, fancy yourself in a dog collar, do you?"

"Nah, I never got into all that kinky stuff. No, it's just, how many times have you ever seen a short vicar?"

He glanced over at Greg and his chums. "They're not that tall."

"Depends on the angle you're looking from, doesn't it? Want to check out the sausage rolls?"

He shrugged. "Not that hungry."

"Suit yourself." I wound my way over to the table and grabbed a paper plate.

"Do have some of the quiche, dear," a reedy voice quavered by my elbow. "I made it myself."

I looked around—and down: I could swear they were making little old ladies smaller these days—and smiled at the wrinkled-apple cheeks of the old dear who'd spoken. "Is that the bacon and leek, or the"—I peered at the spidery script—"mushroom and tomato?"

"Oh, the bacon. Young men like you need a bit of meat inside them." If it was a cheeky innuendo, she had the deadpan down pat.

"I'll make sure I remember that. Cheers, love," I said and took a big slice.

When I turned round to ask Phil if he wanted some, he'd disappeared—and when I turned back to old Mrs. Quiche, she'd doddered off to fuss with the sausage rolls.

Brilliant. I was on my own in a roomful of people who all seemed to know each other. At least now I had something to do with my hands. And Mrs. Quiche's bacon and leek was pretty tasty.

I could do with a drink, though. I scanned the room. The drinks table was over in the far corner of the room—and guess what? That was where Phil had disappeared to. I looked at the heaving mass of chattering people, and then back at my plate. No way were both of us going to make it through that crowd unscathed. Ah, well. It seemed a bit disrespectful to scarf down the rest of the quiche in a couple of large bites, but I could always go back for seconds.

Sod's law, by the time I got through the crush to the drinks table, which involved a lot of ducking and weaving and apologising for jarred elbows, Phil had buggered off again. Maybe he was just annoyed there wasn't any beer on offer. I poured myself a glass from an open bottle of plonk and turned to survey the scene, trying to look like a seasoned partygoer considering where next to bestow my wit and charm.

I soon realised standing by the drinks table, I just got in everyone's way. Maybe that was why Phil had disappeared. Frowning, I managed to locate him over in the corner. I moved back into the throng and found myself facing a dapper old bloke in a tweed jacket and violently red corduroy trousers.

"Ridiculously crowded in here," he snapped, looking me up and down. I got the distinct impression that if he'd had his way, riffraff like me would have been turned away at the door.

"Oh, I dunno," I said, raising my glass of wine. "Nice to see a good crowd here."

He sniffed. "More like a mob. I haven't seen *you* at Sunday services," he added pointedly.

"Nah, I'm not local. St. Albans is where I'm based."

He was tall but stooped, with hunched, rounded shoulders, so I found myself getting a sympathetic backache the longer I spoke to him. But at least I didn't get a crick in my neck trying to look him in the eye. "Let me guess," I said and gulped down a mouthful of plonk. "Church warden?"

"Lay reader, actually." He seemed mildly offended, which was a great start. Still, maybe it was just my manners. "And you?"

"Plumber."

He relaxed at that. Clearly the labouring classes couldn't be expected to know any better, so no insult had been intended. He held out a hand, and I was half expecting him to use it to point out that the drains were *that* way, but after a mo I realised I was supposed to shake it, so I did. Probably leaving a whole load of quiche pastry crumbs in his dry, bony grasp, but hey, he started it. "Morgan Everton."

"Tom Paretski. So, is that, like, a full-time job, this lay reading?" What the bloody hell was a lay, anyway? Something to do with minstrels? And how much reading did they need? I wondered if he might have meant ley lines, but he really didn't look the hippy druid type. Then again, neither do I, and I've got this weird finding-things gift. Maybe we could swap psychic stories.

"Oh no, no, no. In my other life, I'm a writer."

A writer as well as a reader? I wondered if he did 'rithmetic as well. "Yeah? What sort of stuff?"

He shrugged, which actually came over as a bit threatening, what with the way his shoulders were all sort of hunched over towards me. "Novels of the human condition. Human frailties, I should say. I'm chairman of the Lea Valley Literati. A local writers' group," he added kindly for the benefit of tradesmen and the otherwise educationally disadvantaged.

"Hey, are you the lot who did that anthology?" I frowned. "What was it called again? Something about angels. I saw a copy in the White Hart—"

"No!" he barked. "We are *not* affiliated with that organisation." You'd have thought I'd just accused him of having been a founding member of the Hitler Youth.

"What, the White Hart?" They had some pretty naff décor—I mean, come off it: suits of armour and red plush thrones? It was like they were expecting the Beckhams to drop in for a pint—and the "haunted" bit gave me the creeps, but it was an okay place for a pint.

"No. That was the *other* St. Albans writers' group." He glared at me. "A ragtag, unschooled bunch of self-published hacks and writers of"—his voice dropped in loathing—"genre fiction."

I decided it was probably just as well I hadn't mentioned I liked a good thriller every now and then.

"Some of them," he added, bending low to breathe sherry fumes right in my face, "write *erotica*." His voice was husky with prurient outrage, and his face had gone as red as his trousers.

"Well, sex is all part of the human condition, innit?" I said breezily, just to see if I could bring on a stroke. "If you're doing it right, that is."

"Sex," Morgan said sternly, "should not be used to titillate."

Nope, I decided. He was *definitely* not doing it right. If he was doing it at all. "Is there a Mrs. Everton?" I asked, just to test my personal theory.

"We are sadly estranged."

"Oh, sorry to hear that." I bet Mrs. E. wasn't, though.

"And yourself?"

"Nah, nobody's liked it enough yet to put a ring on it." Well, not a wedding ring, anyhow. I had a few fond memories of a mildly kinky ex. And a lot more memories of the bastard that weren't fond in the slightest, but that was another story. Talking of which … "So, you had any of these novels of yours published?"

"I'm currently between agents," Morgan said shortly.

I wasn't sure whether to commiserate or congratulate him. Playing it safe, I held up my empty glass. "Right, I'm off for a refill. Get you one?"

He shook his head grumpily and held up his own, full glass. I'd checked before I'd offered—I'm not daft.

"See you around, then." I legged it.

Phil was still over in the corner, holding his sherry glass up in front of him as if to ward off evil spirits and/or evangelists. To be honest, it looked a bit too small to do a proper job on either of them, especially in his meaty paws. When I caught his eye, he made a pissed-off face. I raised both eyebrows, trying to convey *sorry, but you're the one who insisted on coming*. The glare didn't alter, so I reckoned my eyebrow semaphore must need a bit of work.

Either that or he was just determined to be a grumpy old sod. I sighed (quietly, because my mum brought me up to have manners), dumped my empty glass on a side table, and started to weave through the crowd towards him. Not as easy as you might think. If Jesus was looking for another rock to build his church on, he could do worse than some of the little old ladies forming a solid wall across the room like a wrinkled, cardi-wearing version of the Arsenal lineup.

"'Scuse me, coming through," I said to the smallest and therefore hopefully least immovable one, flashing a smile so she wouldn't notice I was basically manhandling her out of the way. Then I stopped, still with both hands on her bony, wool-clad shoulders. "Edie?"

Edith Penrose turned and blinked up at me with her disconcertingly bright eyes. "Hello, Tom. Fancy seeing you here! Did you bring your young man?" She lowered her voice. "Such a dreadful business that was. Murder, in Brock's Hollow!"

I rubbed my arm. "Yeah, not what you move out to the country for, is it?"

"Oh, you wouldn't catch me living in a city. Old people aren't safe there, you know. And I could never leave my Albert."

"Guess not." Clearly she reckoned her Albert wouldn't be up for moving out of Brock's Hollow. I had to agree, seeing as he'd had a steady job pushing up daisies in St. Anthony's Churchyard for the last twenty years now. "Hope he appreciated you when he was alive," I added.

"Oh, he was a lovely man. You'd have liked him. But how's that young man of yours? Is he here too?"

I gestured towards Phil's corner, but he was ignoring us, the sod, in favour of renewing his acquaintance with the Awfully Reverend's badger, liberated from the study in honour of the occasion. He was right. It *was* bigger than you'd expect. He didn't look as pleased as you might think to see it again, though—Phil, I mean. The badger seemed happy enough, although his grin was a bit fixed.

Maybe Phil was thinking about his own dead husband.

"Oh dear. He doesn't look much like he's enjoying himself. Not really one for parties?"

"Not this sort, anyway. So . . ." I tried to think of a way of asking Edie who'd invited her that didn't sound like *what are you doing here?* "You know my sister, do you?"

"Never met her before. I must say, she's not at all what I would have expected. Still, at my age, one rather relishes being surprised. No, I knew Gregory in his first curacy, bless him. Such an intense young man. I always thought he'd go far. He buried my Albert, you know. It was Gregory's first funeral, and he did such a lovely job of it."

"Yeah? Small world, innit? Was he into the taxidermy back then?" Hopefully she didn't think I was asking if she'd had her Albert stuffed.

Edie nodded happily. "He was just starting out in that too. I do feel it's important for a young man to have a hobby. Do you have any hobbies, Tom?"

Er . . . "Well, you know. Going down the pub, watching the footie . . ."

"You need to find an interest, young man." She cocked her head on one side. "Something creative, I think. But perhaps not working with your hands, as you do that in your profession." She nodded, more to herself than me. "No, I can see you with a more intellectual hobby."

She could? I was one hundred percent certain nobody else could. Including, to be fair, me. "Yeah, see, school and me didn't go all that well."

"Oh, school." She flapped her crepey hands as if to shoo away such ridiculous, new-fangled notions. "I think a lot of people don't really flower there, don't you? Such a rigid sort of place."

"Edie, you rebel, you." I grinned. "How about I get you another sherry?" Phil would just have to wait.

"That would be very kind of you. But don't think I don't know you're just changing the subject!"

I winked at her, then headed on over to the drinks table, where I finally bumped into Cherry. Not literally, luckily, as she was holding on, tight-knuckled, to a brimming glass of something that looked a lot stronger than sherry.

"All right, Sis?" I asked. She was looking a bit harassed, to be honest.

She glared at me like I was the one who was doing the harassing. "What were you talking to Morgan about?"

Morgan? Right, no-sex-please-we're-British bloke. "Reading and writing, mostly. Why? Worried I'll tell him all your dirty little secrets?"

"What? No, don't be silly. It's just . . . Honestly, I wasn't expecting him to be here."

"You didn't invite him? Want me and Phil to strong-arm him out?" I didn't mention it'd be Phil doing most of the heavy lifting there, and I was grateful she didn't either.

"No—God, no. The last thing I want is a scene." Her face turned a bit pink. "But it's kind of you to offer," she added without a lot of conviction.

"Mate of Greg's, is he?" Maybe he liked playing with dead furry animals too.

Cherry was starting to resemble her name. "He's—well, he used to be—a friend of both of ours, actually. Well, in a way. We used to be members of the same writers' circle."

My eyebrows shot up. "Yeah? What have you been writing?"

"Oh, nothing you'd be interested in. A book."

"Cheers, Sis." My sister: a card-carrying member of Intellectual Snobs 'R' Us.

"Oh, you know what I mean. Anyway, it doesn't matter—it'll probably never get published. But Morgan and I had a bit of a falling-out, and we—Gregory and I, that is—we left the circle. It was utterly ridiculous—he said I'd accused him of misuse of funds, which I didn't at all."

I could believe that. If anyone knew about slander laws, it'd be my sis. "Maybe he came here to mend some fences, then?"

"Burn them down, more likely." Something caught her eye then, and she glanced over my shoulder. "Oh—Richard's here."

I turned to the door. "Bloody hell, what happened to his hair?" Big Brother, currently folding his trench coat, was balder than a ballcock. Granted, he'd been heading that way last time I'd seen him, but he'd at least had a bit of fluff to keep his ears warm back then. "He hasn't been ill or anything, has he?" You couldn't *catch* cancer, could you?

"Don't be stupid. What did you think was going to happen? Look at Dad."

I couldn't, because he wasn't there, but I took her point. My dad, as far as I could tell from old family photos from before I was born, went bald early. And thoroughly. He didn't mess about with a comb-over or those little fringes of hair that make you look like a monk. No, he was doing ping-pong ball impersonations before he was thirty. Fortunately, I seemed to have inherited Mum's hair, although thankfully not the rigid fifties "do" even she's too young for. In her seventies. "Doesn't always follow, does it? I mean, look at me."

She did. With a funny expression, like she was about to say something—then she sort of shook her head. "I'd better go over and introduce him and Agatha to Gregory."

"I'd leave your drink here, then, if I were you. You know what Agatha's like. You'll end up getting the *evils of binge drinking* sermon if you're not careful."

Cherry looked at her glass as if it was someone else's hands holding on to it for dear life. "Oh. Yes." She handed it to me absently and drifted off. I raised it, trying to look like I was just having a sip, and gave it a sniff. Ye gods, she was on the Slivovitz. Maybe letting Cherry get the binge-drinking lecture would have been a good idea after all.

I put the glass down carefully at the back of the table so no one would pick it up by mistake, then glanced over guiltily at the door.

Agatha, like most people in my family, was taller than me. She also loomed over Richard, but he obviously didn't mind too much, seeing as he'd married her. Maybe he'd been too scared not to. Right now, her hawk-like eyes were scanning the crowd as if for prey. I wondered what Greg would make of her. Probably some kind of taxidermy tableau, with her swooping down for the kill on some innocent partygoer.

I hoped he didn't have me on a short list to play that part.

Deciding it was high time I got back to Edie with her sherry—after all, she wasn't getting any younger, bless her—I started to meander in that direction. When I got halfway there, though, I saw she'd already somehow managed to get hold of one that was considerably larger than the glass I had in my mitt. Maybe Edie had some psychic powers of her own. Or more likely it was just down to the natural affinity between old ladies and sherry.

Feeling a bit wrong-footed, I took advantage of a sudden opening in the crowd to make a beeline over to Phil, which entirely coincidentally took me in the opposite direction from my sister-in-law.

"Sherry?" I offered him the glass.

He gave me a look but took it anyway and drained it in one. "Cheers."

"Just warning you, we've got incoming. My brother and his wife."

"I noticed."

"How? I mean, how did you know it was them?"

"I searched him up on the internet. Richard Paretski, consultant oncologist. Works at the Herts Breast Unit. There's a picture of him up on the website." Phil smirked. "Bet he feels a tit sometimes."

"Okay, this sense of humour you've developed lately? I liked you better without it."

He ignored me. "What does the wife do?"

"You're the private eye who's been stalking my family, you tell me." He glared at me. "She works in the STD clinic, all right?"

"Bloody hell. I bet she reduces infection rates. Probably scares them all into chastity."

"I think she has the same effect on Richard. At least, they've been married six or seven years and still haven't had kids."

"Not everyone wants kids."

There was something in Phil's tone that made me glance at him sharply, but he was wearing Patented Unreadable Look #3 so I let it slide.

It's funny—if you're just mates, or even casual acquaintances with someone, you can ask if they plan on having kids one day. And if you're married, or as good as, well, it's a discussion you probably ought to have sooner rather than later. But if you're just going out and not living together or even close to it, you can't do it. It's like saying, *Do you want to get married?* You can't do it without it sounding like there's a silent *with me* on the end of it.

"Yeah, anyway, you'd better come and meet them." I led him around past the drinks table so we could snag a couple of refills on the way. I reckoned we'd need them. "And you call her Agatha. Not Aggie, or Taggie, or Aggs. She has ways of making you regret that sort of thing."

"And let me guess, your brother doesn't like being a Dick, either?"

"Well, he doesn't like being *called* one. Come on, let's get this over with." I shouldered through the crowd—should have let Phil go first; he had broader shoulders—and fetched up just behind Agatha. I remembered just in time she didn't like people touching her to get her attention, so I settled for waving around the side of her at Richard, although I felt a bit of a prat.

"Hello, Tom." Richard reached out a hand, so I shook it. Did other brothers shake hands? I hadn't exactly made a study of it, but I really didn't think so.

"Richard, this is Phil. My, er, boyfriend." I felt all of thirteen saying it.

Phil stuck out his hand. Richard hesitated for just long enough to make a point.

Or maybe I was just imagining it.

"Yes," Richard said coolly. "Cherry told me about you. The old school . . . acquaintance."

Nope, wasn't imagining it. "Water under the bridge, all right? If I don't mind, I don't see why you should." Especially seeing as brother dear had been perfectly happy leaving me alone to cock up my life however I wanted for the last dozen years.

Agatha huffed. "I hope you boys aren't planning to ruin Cherry's party with a row. There are times and places, and this is neither of them. Hello, Philip. I'm Agatha." She pointedly stuck out a big, bony hand, and Phil shook it while I wondered if she and Greg could possibly be related somehow. "And Tom, it's lovely to see you again." I tried not to cringe as she grabbed my shoulders and yanked me in for an air kiss with an audible *mwah*. "We really should see more of you. My own brothers are always coming round to visit."

They were probably too frightened to decline.

"And Philip," she went on. "We hear you're a private investigator. Why don't you tell us all about your last case?"

That had been the dogging one. I cleared my throat. "Let's get you and Richard some drinks first, all right?"

"God, yes—anyone would think this was a—" Agatha broke off as an enormous hand clapped her on the shoulder. I was too busy jumping a bloody mile from similar treatment to worry too much about what she'd been about to say about Cherry's do.

We spun to see who'd assaulted us like a couple of synchronised swimmers after someone had let a shark in the water. I found myself staring a dog collar in the face while Agatha, being taller, got the full force of the Strenuously Reverend Greg's eyebrows.

"Excellent!" Those eyebrows were outdoing themselves tonight. "The family's all here. Lovely! And look who I found in the hall—do you all know our bell-ringing virtuoso?" He turned so we could see past him to his companion.

I stared. "Gary?"

"Tom, darling." I was treated to a Gary version of the air kiss, which contained a lot of kiss and very little air. I could see Richard edging away out of the corner of my eye. Agatha was just looking at Gary curiously. Probably wondering how he'd taste with a nice Chianti.

She was the first to recover her manners. "Delighted to meet you . . . both."

"*Enchanté*," Gary said in a tone that made it clear he hadn't missed that pause.

Greg gave her a penetrating stare. "You must be Agatha. So glad you could come." They shook hands, which for a moment looked like it was about to turn into an arm-wrestling contest. I thought Greg would probably have won, with the weight advantage and all, but then again, it never paid to underestimate Agatha's ruthless desire to come out on top.

They gave each other cautiously respectful glances as they ended the handshake, like a couple of sumo wrestlers agreeing to call it a draw. "And you're Richard?" Greg asked with a twinkle.

Cherry roused herself. "Yes. Darling, this is my older brother. Richard, my fiancé, Gregory."

There was no pissing contest when Richard shook hands with Greg. Their handshake was the briefest touch, soon dropped. Richard's "Welcome to the family" sounded a bit forced.

Greg beamed as if the undercurrents didn't raise a *ping* on his obliviously reverend radar. "So kind. Although I shan't count myself a true member until I've slipped a wedding ring on this shapely finger." He took Cherry's hand with a gentle, old-fashioned flourish that made her blush to her boots and the rest of us look away, embarrassed.

All except Gary, of course, who was staring at Greg with an adoring expression that, if he'd been here, Darren would've had to take serious exception to. I nudged him in the soft bit below his ribs. "Oi," I whispered.

"What?" Gary turned wide, innocent eyes on me.

Been there, got the T-shirt. "No mooning after my sister's bloke. You've got your own, remember?"

"So? A boy can still admire from afar. It's all right to smell the flowers, so long as you don't actually pluck them."

"Yeah, well, just remember, if you pluck Greg, we're going to have a problem."

"My days of indiscriminate plucking are over. Cross my heart." Gary did, with an extravagant gesture that got everyone looking at us. He beamed, the centre of attention being his favourite holiday spot. "Gregory, darling, I'm parched. Drinkies? If you can tear yourself away from your lovely inamorata."

Cherry looked torn between annoyance at him co-opting her bloke, and surprised pleasure that he'd called her lovely. "This way," she said with an almost-smile. Either she'd decided to go with being pleased, or she was really desperate to get back to her Slivovitz.

Agatha collared Phil and dragged him off after her, throwing an "I'll get you something soft," over her shoulder at Richard. I managed not to make any impotence-related gags. Greg disappeared, presumably either to mingle or to save Cherry from Gary's clutches, and that just left me and big brother facing each other like a couple of exes.

I frantically tried to think of something to say to him that wasn't *So, you went bald, then?* "Work all right?"

He shrugged. "You know."

Er, no, I didn't, really. "Still living at . . .?"

"Yes."

"Got any plans for your holidays?" God, I was getting desperate.

"The usual." I could have screamed. Maybe it showed in my face, as Richard seemed to notice he wasn't exactly doing this conversation any favours. "I suppose you'll be going away with, ah, Phil?"

"Haven't made any plans yet. Maybe. Might be nice to go somewhere hot for a change, maybe Turkey or Portugal . . ." I stopped the babbling with an effort. "Have to see."

Richard nodded. "I suppose it could be worse," he said unexpectedly.

"You what?"

"Your choice of romantic partner. At least he's not *obvious*."

I frowned. "Meaning?"

"Meaning like that god-awful bell ringer. I realise they have to allow all sorts into the church these days, but surely he could tone down his behaviour a little? God knows, I'm not homophobic, but, well, *you* don't feel the need to be so blatant about it, do you? If you can act like a normal person, why can't he?"

My fist clenched so tight my knuckles were hurting. I took a breath, about to make some polite excuse, but then I thought, *Sod it.*

I just turned and walked away.

I was still seething when I reached Phil. The way seemed to clear magically in front of me this time, so maybe it showed.

"What's up with you?" Phil asked.

Yep, it showed. "That bloody git of a brother of mine, that's what. He kept going on about Gary. Wanker. Said he should *tone it down*. Play it straight, only not in so many words."

Phil was silent a moment. "Well, he's got a point."

I stared. I must have misheard him, right? "You *what*?"

"Listen, *I* haven't got a problem with Gary being Gary, but he must know it gets up people's noses sometimes. These things go both ways."

"Yeah, but Gary *doesn't*, so why the bloody hell should he pretend to be someone he's not?"

"Self-preservation? A bit of consideration for people who don't find it so easy to get used to new ideas?"

"A bit of . . . I can't believe I'm hearing this!"

Heads were turning in our direction. *Oh, look, two poofs having a domestic.* Just as I was about to snap at them to find something else to gawp about, they did.

Chapter Nine

One minute we were all chatting away—or all right, having hissy fits, as might be—and the next, there were shrieks of horror and a widening circle around Cherry and Greg. She was lying on the floor with him crouching next to her and trying to lift her up. He had his head down, talking to her in a low, urgent voice, so I couldn't see his face.

I pushed through the crowd with a lot fewer apologies this time and knelt down next to her. She looked awful—all pale and twitchy, her face shining with sweat.

"What happened?" I demanded.

"She just collapsed. I think we should call an ambulance."

"Sure?" What was the best way to phrase this? "I mean, she's not just . . .?" I waved at my midriff, my face getting a bit hot.

The eyebrows shot heavenwards. "Good Lord, no."

"Or, you know?" I made drinking-up gestures, mindful of that well-filled glass she'd had earlier. Which, now I came to think about it, probably should have clued me in she wasn't knowingly pregnant.

Now the eyebrows were little lightning bolts threatening dire retribution, probably with a bit of smiting involved, for this sullying of Cherry's reputation. "*No.* An ambulance. *Now.*"

Cherry added her two-bobs'-worth by convulsing and throwing up on the carpet, narrowly missing Richard, who'd just elbowed his way over. Nice one, Sis. There was a shocked murmur, and the circle around us widened significantly.

I thought it was overkill, honestly, but I fumbled my phone out of my pocket and was about to dial 999 when Phil clapped a hand on my shoulder. "I've called them. They're on their way."

Richard nodded briskly. "Good. Now help me turn her on her side."

Right. Recovery position. The Helplessly Reverend Greg seemed as pleased as I was that someone else was taking charge. Richard and Phil rolled her over gently, arranging her arms to support her. Phil even took off his expensive sweater, rolled it up, and put it under Cherry's head. Maybe if she chucked up on that, she'd have to start being a bit nicer to him.

Then Richard stood up and raised his voice. "We need a bit of air in here, so everyone needs to move to the other room. Now, please." It was weird. Suddenly he was every inch the senior consultant, not just my bald, borderline-bigoted big brother.

There were shocked murmurs. Also pissed-off murmurs, confused murmurs, and even the odd laugh. It'd better bloody well be nerves. I heard Edie's voice ringing out with, "Poor dear, she did seem a little overwrought," and spotted some bloke I hadn't met snagging a bottle of brandy off the drinks table on the way out.

At least they all went, though. Cherry wouldn't want people seeing her like this. I was a bit surprised Richard hadn't just suggested everyone go home. I couldn't see the party carrying on after this. Poor Cherry. She was going to be gutted in a couple of hours when she was feeling better.

Gary cast a worried glance over his shoulder as he shepherded the last few stragglers out of the room.

Richard hitched up his trouser legs and knelt down gingerly, obviously trying to avoid the mess, then did all the doctor-looking stuff like checking her pupils and taking her pulse, which seemed to take a lot longer than it did on the telly. Then again, on the telly, people were usually dead.

When he finally looked up again, he was frowning. "What was she drinking?" he snapped out.

"Spirits, I think," I said, looking around for a dropped glass. It'd rolled under a table. I pushed myself up off my knees and went to pick it up. Maybe she'd just overdone the Dutch courage, despite what Greg had said.

Phil stopped me with a firm hand on my arm. "Might be an idea not to touch that."

"Why?" I frowned. "You don't think there's something funny about it, do you?"

"Your sister have a habit of collapsing at parties?"

"Course not. But it's probably just something she ate."

"Or drank." He sent me a significant glance.

I wasn't buying it. Neither was Agatha, it seemed. "Don't you think you're letting your profession colour your views, here?" She marched over, retrieved the glass and gave it a good sniff. "Hm. Something strong, Richard, but I don't recognise it."

She handed the glass to Richard, who took a whiff and shook his head.

"Here, let me." I grabbed it from him and shoved my nose in. Yeah, Cherry was still on the hard stuff. "It's that Slivovitz, I reckon. Unless there's a half-empty bottle of turpentine around here." I looked up and caught Phil's glare. "What? The doctors'll want to know what she's been drinking. How's she doing, anyway?"

"Not good." I didn't like the clipped, worried way Richard said it. I didn't like it at all. It was the sort of voice I imagined him using to tell a nurse to prepare the patient's relatives for the worst.

"Serious?" I knelt back down beside my sister, a tight knot in my throat. Greg was holding her hand and muttering under his breath.

Richard paused before he spoke, presumably to translate his answer into layman's terms. "Her heart was racing just a minute ago, but now it's slowed right down. And she's having difficulty breathing. Where the *hell* is that ambulance?"

Shit. This could not be good. I grabbed my brother's arm. "She's going to be all right, isn't she?" Greg was still muttering. I hoped he had a good line to Him upstairs and was owed a few favours.

"I don't know." Richard's tone was grim. "I'm not a toxicologist."

"Toxic . . . You think she's been poisoned? How?" Did he mean, like, on purpose? Who the bloody hell would do that?

Richard winced. I realised I was probably leaving bruises on his biceps and let go with a muttered *sorry*. He rubbed his arm, but I reckoned it was probably unconscious rather than him making a point. "The symptoms are suggestive. That's all I'm prepared to say. They'll be able to make a thorough investigation in the hospital."

He'd better bloody well not be talking about a postmortem. I felt a warm hand on my shoulder.

"We've done all we can." Phil's calm voice rumbled above me. Easy for him to stay calm. Cherry wasn't his bloody sister. "The ambulance should be here soon."

"Yeah, but how soon?" Was she getting paler? Sweatier? I'd thought I'd heard sirens a minute or two ago, but they'd disappeared off the face of the planet. Couldn't the NHS afford a bloody satnav? Even as I thought it, I realised I could see flashing blue lights pulsing through the curtains. They were here.

Phil squeezed my shoulder. "I'd better go and meet them at the door."

"No, I'll do it." Agatha strode off briskly.

Pretty soon after that, I had to get out of the way so the paramedics could load Cherry onto a stretcher, an oxygen mask strapped to her marble-white face. "Does one of you want to come with her?" the female one asked.

"Uh . . ." I looked up at Greg. His face was all sunken in. "Greg, mate? You should go. We'll come on after." He nodded, and I turned back to the paramedic. "Which hospital is she going to?"

"Don't worry, I got all the details already." Phil put his arm around my shoulders.

"Right. Okay."

God, I hate hospitals. Spent a bit too much time at the business end of one when I was seventeen, and the fact that, this time, I was only there to wait for news of my sis didn't make things any better. She'd been moved out of A&E and into another set of initials I'd forgotten already, which at least meant we didn't have to sit with all the poor drunk sods with head wounds they wouldn't remember getting in the morning.

The orange plastic chairs in the waiting room, which anywhere else would've been a corridor, seemed like they'd been designed to drum up trade for the physiotherapists, and there was that hideous hospital smell of disinfectant and death.

Well, maybe not *actual* death. I've smelled that before, and it's something you don't forget in a hurry. But sickness, definitely. And despair. Even the lights were getting on my tits. Cold, clinical, and headache-inducing. And although it wasn't all that warm, the air was so bloody stuffy I could hardly breathe. I jumped off my seat and paced around the room for the umpteenth time.

Phil stayed where he was, his legs stretched out in front of him like he was at home in front of the telly, the git. "You know your limp's got worse since we've been in here," he said.

I sent him a silent invitation to swivel on it. He huffed out a sigh and pushed himself to his feet, coming to meet me in the middle of the hallway. "Look, I know it's not easy, but just try and relax, okay? There's nothing we can do except trust the doctors are doing their job."

"Would it bloody kill someone to give us a progress report? Do they even know what's wrong with her? Is it some kind of poison, or was Richard just talking out of his middle-aged-spreading arse? Is she going to be okay?"

Phil grabbed hold of both my wrists, which at least stopped me flapping my arms around like a Muppet on steroids.

"Ow," I said, because I was damned if I was going to make it easy for him.

He didn't let go. "They'll tell you when there's anything to tell, all right?"

"And how come Greg gets to be in with her, anyhow? He's not even family." I was starting to regret having let him go in the ambulance.

"Yeah, well, maybe she asked for him? They just got engaged, remember."

"As long as he doesn't just want to measure her up to see how much wire he's going to need—" I buttoned my lip quick as the man himself came in through the door. He looked like he'd been to hell and back and had forgotten to pack a comb, but he was smiling.

The first thing he said was, "She's going to be all right."

The relief hit me so hard, I think I'd have keeled over if Phil hadn't been holding on to me. "Thank fucking God. Uh, sorry about the, um . . ."

Greg waved it away. I could feel the draught from three feet away. "No, no. Quite understandable, in the circumstances. We all have our own ways of calling upon the Lord."

"Did they say what it was?" Phil asked.

Greg didn't answer for a moment. He'd produced a large white handkerchief from a pocket and was scrubbing it over his face like a flannel. I hoped it was clean. When he'd finished, he folded it carefully back into its original creases and put it away again. "They told me they would have to do some tests. But she's responding well to the treatment, and there shouldn't be any lasting effects."

I frowned. "Yeah, but did they give you any clues about what caused it?"

Greg shook his head. "The doctors asked all kinds of questions, such as whether Cherry was a heavy smoker, or trying to give up, but that was all."

"Cherry? She's never been near a fag in her life. Present company excepted, of course."

"Actually, she used to smoke a little in her university days. But only socially."

"My big sis? Never. How would you know, anyhow? You didn't go to Durham, did you?"

"Heavens, no. She told me, of course." His eyebrows softened. "No doubt she feels you see her as someone to look up to. A role model, if you will. One doesn't like to admit one's little peccadilloes in such circumstances."

I blinked at the idea of me having Cherry as a role model. Couldn't see how he thought that one was working out. He probably had a point about the rest of it, though. I was pretty sure I'd never admitted a peccadillo in my life. I frowned. "So, what, it's a lung thing, is it?"

Phil huffed beside me. "Sounds to me more like they're thinking of nicotine poisoning."

"What?"

"You see it in kids, mostly. Toddlers. From eating mum or dad's cigarettes."

Greg nodded like he knew what Phil was talking about. "And in years gone by, of course, it was used as an insecticide. But I really don't see how anything like that could have affected Cherry. I'm sure

I should have noticed if she'd taken to chewing tobacco." He gave a tired little laugh. "At any rate, they tell me she'll need to be kept in here for a few days. We should probably all go home and get some rest."

"Can't we see her first?" I asked.

Phil took my arm. "She's probably not feeling up to visitors right now. Best to leave it until tomorrow, right, Gregory?"

"Indeed. But your concern is much appreciated." He took out his handkerchief again, looked at it like he'd never seen it before, then put it back in his pocket.

I was glad I hadn't let out my first reaction of *Oi, she's my bloody sister, of course I'm concerned*. Greg looked totally done in.

"Come on, we'll give you a lift home," I said instead.

CHAPTER TEN

We dropped Greg back at the Old Deanery, which seemed silent and forlorn now all the guests had gone home, littered with half-empty glasses and lonely sausage rolls. I didn't much like leaving him there with only the "family" of stuffed animals for company, but he assured us the Lord would be his shepherd, so we said our goodbyes and headed back to St. Albans. I gave Richard a quick ring on the way to let him know what was up.

"Surprised you didn't go along to the hospital yourself," I said at the end.

"Doctors make terrible patients and even worse relatives of patients. I thought it'd be better all round if I let the hospital get on with things without my intervention."

"Yeah, fair enough." Still seemed a bit cold, mind. "You going to see her tomorrow?"

"Oh, yes."

"Right, maybe I'll see you then." I hung up and turned to Phil. "You coming in for a bit when we get back to mine?" I tried not to sound all needy.

"Yeah. God, yeah." Phil rubbed the back of his neck with his gear-changing hand. "I could do with a drink. Thought I might stay over. That all right with you?"

"You'll have to excuse the mess, but yeah."

"Seemed all right earlier."

"Yeah, but a couple of lazy tossers have left pizza boxes all over the shop since then." I leaned back against the headrest and closed my eyes, but all I could see was Cherry on the floor, so I opened them again quick.

We were almost back to mine by then, thank God. After we got in, I grabbed a couple of beers from the fridge, opened them, and handed one to Phil. Merlin yowled at me. "You can shut up, you've already had your tea." He flicked his tail at me and went to rub up against Phil's leg. Traitor. "So what did all that mean, back at the hospital? All that talk about nicotine." I bent down to stroke Arthur, who at least still seemed to know which side his bread was buttered.

Phil leaned on the counter. "It means the police are going to be treating this as attempted murder."

"That's just crazy! Who'd want to hurt Cherry? I mean, I might have felt the odd urge to strangle her myself, sometimes, but God, I didn't bloody *mean* it."

"Coo-ee Bonio?"

I stared at him. "You *what*?" Maybe he shouldn't have had that beer after all. "I haven't got any dog biscuits. Only cat treats."

He had the nerve to look at me like *I* was the mental one. "Cui bono? It's Latin. Who benefits? As in, say, who's first in line to inherit your sister's money? Which it sounds like she's got a fair bit of—lawyer, nice house in Pluck's End—"

"Hey, not everyone in Pluck's End is loaded."

"No, but I bet your sister isn't living on the council estate. Do you know what's in her will?"

"I don't even know if she's got one. *I* haven't bloody got one, and she's not *that* much older than me."

"She's a lawyer. Course she's got a will." Phil took a long swig of beer.

I was about to follow suit, but then I frowned and put my bottle back down. "I dunno. What's the old proverb about cobblers' kids?"

"They come from a long line of old cobblers? I don't know, do I?"

"They're supposed to be the worst shod, aren't they? Like, their dad makes shoes for a living, so he can't be arsed when he comes home."

Phil looked unimpressed. "So on that logic, your bathroom leaks and half your pipes are about to burst?"

"Course not! I keep my plumbing in good nick."

"There you go, then. She'll have a will." He nodded and downed the rest of his beer. Smug git.

"What, because me and Cherry are identical in every bloody respect? Anyway, even if she has done a will, she'll be leaving her stuff to family, won't she? Want to go bug Richard's gaff? Or maybe you should be asking me a few searching questions?"

"Don't be a twat. Maybe she changed her will recently. She just got engaged, remember?"

"A whole *five minutes* before she keeled over."

"So? It's not like she'd have had to wait for an appointment with her lawyer, is it?" Phil shrugged. "Maybe it's something to do with her work. She deals with criminal trials, doesn't she?"

"Yeah, but . . . this is the Home Counties, not bloody mob-era Chicago." I threw my arms out wide in frustration.

"Think nothing ever happens around here? You've got a short memory."

I rubbed my arm. "I remember all right. But this is Cherry we're talking about." She was just too, well, *boring*—sorry, Sis—for all this stuff.

"So? Just because she's your sister doesn't mean she doesn't deal with serious cases." He picked up his empty bottle, frowned at it, and put it back down again. "What sort of cases does she specialise in?"

I paused in opening up the fridge. "Dunno. What? Don't look at me like that. I've hardly seen her since I left home, you know that." And maybe careers had been a subject I hadn't really wanted to bring up, what with hers being all high-flying and mine more involved with drains, but I wasn't going to mention that.

"It'll say on their website. Borrow your laptop?"

"It's in there." I nodded in the direction of the living room, and Phil levered his bulk off the counter and went to find it, Merlin trotting at his heels like an undercover police dog. I grabbed another couple of beers and followed them. Arthur stayed in the kitchen, the ungrateful so-and-so.

Phil was sitting on the sofa, tapping his fingers on his leg while he waited for my laptop to boot up. "Is this thing steam powered?"

I sat down next to him and put his beer on the coffee table. "Nah. Just give it a mo, the valves need to warm up." I leaned back.

He huffed impatiently. "You'd better not have dial-up," he muttered as the screen finally flickered on.

"Works on carrier pigeon. You going to use that thing or just sit there and insult it?" I mean, it wasn't like I was particularly attached to my old laptop, but it'd done me fine the last few years or six.

"Finally," Phil said as the Ver Chambers website loaded. "Right. Cherry Paretski . . . specialism: criminal cases."

I sat up to take a peek. Sure enough, he wasn't telling porkies. "Huh. I always thought she did divorces and speeding tickets and stuff. Think it'll say anything about cases she's handled?"

"Nope. Think about it. If you got done for, say, ripping off the customers, would you want your case used as advertising by your defence lawyer?"

"Depends if she'd got me off. Nah, s'pose not. Are you going to ask her about it?" I yawned, leaning back again.

"Who's my client?"

"What?"

"No, I'm serious. If I'm going to be investigating this, who am I working for here?"

I put my beer bottle down on the coffee table with a *clunk*. Merlin hissed. "So my sister's only important to you if you're getting paid?"

"Oh, for— I'm not after your sodding money, you prat." Phil gave me a patronising look. "But if I haven't got a client, it's just me poking my nose in, and the police are going to be even less happy about that than they usually are."

"Fine. I'll employ you to look into Cherry's . . . case." Saying *attempted murder* made it seem too real. "Payment to be in the sexual favours of your choosing. Happy now?"

"Bloody ecstatic. I'll draw up a contract."

I was fairly sure he was joking. "So *now* are you going to ask her about her clients?"

Phil shut the lid of my laptop. "Nope. *Now* I'm going to relax on the sofa with my boyfriend and drink my beer, because I don't know about you, but I've had one bloody long day."

Too right. I switched on the telly. Sky Sports was showing some Spanish football match. I let the sounds of the crowd chants and the hyperactive commentators wash over me as I tried to wrap my head around the thought of someone deliberately trying to kill my big sis.

I must have dozed off at some point, as I woke up to find the footie was over and Phil was gently manoeuvring his arm out from around me.

"Come on, sleeping beauty. Time for bed."

"Going to wake me up with a kiss in the morning?"

Phil laughed quietly, more a hitch in his breath than anything else. "I can do better than that."

He did too.

Gary was on the phone first thing next morning. Or what he called first thing on a Saturday, which was halfway through the day for anyone who didn't get to work at home in their jammies. Actually, to be fair, I wasn't even sure if Gary worked on Saturdays. I'd always struggled with the idea of Gary buckling down and getting serious work done any day of the week, but I supposed he must do something to keep Julian in raw steak and Bonios.

Phil was long gone by then, off to do whatever private investigators did, and I was crouching under the kitchen sink at Mrs. L.'s in Sandridge with water dripping into my hair. Mrs. L. had popped out to catch her neighbour—ignorance being bliss and all that, I hadn't asked what she wanted to catch her doing—and left me to it, so I took the call, glad of the excuse to unkink my shoulders and legs.

Look, I know maybe it seems a bit heartless, me just going to work as normal with my sister in the hospital, but Cherry was going to be all right, which was more than you could say for Mrs. L.'s carpet tiles after she'd gone away for a week and come back to find the place flooded. And it wasn't like I could have done anything at the hospital, except get on her tits when she wanted some time alone with the Demonstrably Reverend Greg. I'd pop along later this morning, take her some flowers or something.

Probably not grapes, what with the dicky tummy and all.

"How is she?" Gary demanded. That's what I like about Gary: he might seem like a total self-obsessed queen, but deep down he's got his priorities right.

"Fine. Well, not *fine* fine, but she's going to be okay."

"Thank God."

"Yeah, I think Greg's got that bit covered." I had a bit of a root through my toolbox for the sealant I was going to need in a bit. Hmm. Getting low—I'd better remember to stock up.

"Was it a miraculous recovery? Do we suspect divine intervention?"

"More like stomach pumping and activated charcoal, from what I heard."

"Ugh. Poor her." There was a pause. "How does one even activate charcoal?"

"Buggered if I know, but it seemed to do the trick. Anyway, I reckon Greg did some serious God-bothering last night, so maybe you were right on the divine-intervention thing." I've never been totally sure how Gary actually feels about the church. I mean, he's a bell ringer, but that doesn't have to mean serious religion. Far as I know, they don't actually make you get down on your knees and swear allegiance to the Archbishop of Canterbury before they let you up in the tower. Knowing Gary, he probably caught sight of one of those thick, furry sausage things they have on the end of the ropes one day and just couldn't resist giving it a tug.

"Well, if a canon of St. Leonards can't put in a good word for the one he loves, who can?"

A drip of water trickled down my forehead, and I wiped it away with my sleeve. "Isn't that nepotism or something?"

"Ooh, did somebody eat a thesaurus for breakfast?"

"Don't be daft. Even I know those have been extinct for millions of years. Listen, I ought to warn you, you might get the police wanting to talk to you. They were going on about her having been poisoned, last night at the hospital. They were doing tests and stuff. Didn't tell me anything more when I rang up this morning, so it might be nothing, but I thought I'd better give you a heads-up."

"Poisoned? You mean, with malice aforethought? Like Lucrezia Borgia, or Dr. Shipman? Why on earth would anyone want to do that to poor little Cherry?"

"Phil reckoned it might be some pissed-off client. He's looking into it. You know, someone who got banged up and didn't reckon she did a good enough job of defending him."

"Or it could be a victim, distraught at her attacker walking free from jail?" Gary was getting into this, I could tell from his voice.

"Maybe. Anyway, we don't know anything for certain yet." I heard the front door open. "Look, I've got to go. Speak to you later, yeah?"

Mrs. L. faffed around taking her shoes and coat off just long enough for me to get my head back under the sink by the time she padded into the kitchen in her fluffy slippers.

"How's it going, love?" she asked. She was probably around Cherry's age, but apart from that, she was nothing like her. Auntie Lol would have called her "brassy."

I stuck my head out and grinned at her. "Have you sorted in a jiffy. Just need to grab a bit of pipe from the van. Who plumbed this in for you? He made a right pig's ear of it."

She nodded, folding her arms and hitching up her tits on top of them like a couple of perma-tanned grapefruit on a greengrocer's stall. "Bloody typical. Wasn't the only thing he was rubbish at, I can tell you."

"Let me guess. The late, lamented Mr. L.?"

"Lamented, my arse. 'Scuse French. Want a coffee, love?"

"Cheers. White, no sugar, please." I winked at her on my way out to the van, and she smiled as she put the kettle on.

I'd suggested she fill it before I'd turned the water off. I'm not daft.

I got along to the hospital later that day.

Cherry was in a room of her own, which at first made me think she must be paying for it. But the telly on the shelf was about as old as I was, so I guessed it was just one of those perks you occasionally get on the NHS for no apparent reason.

Odd, though. I'd have thought if anyone had private medical insurance, it'd be Cherry. She looked pale and tired, and her hair was a right mess, but she was sitting up in bed, frowning at a John Grisham book.

"Those American barristers not doing it right?" I asked.

She looked up and actually smiled at me. "They're not called barristers over there."

"I do watch telly, you know. How are you feeling?" I handed her the teddy bear I'd bought downstairs—there hadn't been any flowers in the hospital shop. Maybe they were against NHS policies these days. Or had all been eaten by hospital superbugs.

Cherry grimaced at the frankly tacky toy—there hadn't been a lot of choice, okay?—but didn't immediately lob it at the bin. She even tucked it into the crook of her arm. "Horrible. But better. You just missed Mum and Dad, by the way." That would explain the discreet Get Well Soon card peeking out from behind her water jug and was another reason to be glad I'd been at work. I wasn't sure I could have faced one of Mum's guilt trips today. "They've been asking me all sorts of questions."

"What, Mum and Dad?"

"No, idiot. The doctors. They said the police might be coming too. It's just so silly." Cherry sank back on her pillows, and I hurried to take her book from her and put it down on the bedside table. "I mean, you don't think it was anything except an accident, do you?"

"Don't know a right lot about it yet, do I? What did the doctors say?"

"Nicotine poisoning. But why would anyone do that deliberately? It must have been an accident."

"Yeah, but how do you reckon that happened? One of the cathedral ladies had a bit of a senior moment when she was making the sausage rolls?"

"Well, maybe. Some of them are getting on a bit. Maybe one of them got a bit mixed up when she was doing the flowers? Gregory said it was an insecticide."

I frowned. "He said it used to be. Don't know if it still is."

"Oh, you know old people. They keep things *forever*." She closed her eyes.

"Er, do you want me to leave you to have a sleep, then?" I said after a minute or two went by.

Which, of course, was her cue to open her eyes again. I was a bit horrified to see they looked leakier than Mrs. L.'s pipes. "Don't go," she said in a little-girl voice, reaching out for me.

I wanted to run screaming for the hills, but what I actually did was sit down on the bed and take hold of her hand. Should I pat it?

Would she think I was taking the piss? "Is Greg coming over again?" I asked. "Soon?"

"I think so," she said moistly. "I'm just really glad we got back in touch. We shouldn't have drifted apart like that." She squeezed my hand. "Promise me we won't do that again? Families should stay together. No matter . . ." She trailed off.

"Yeah, promise," I said and cleared my throat.

We sat there like that so long, Cherry cuddling Tacky Teddy and me holding her hand, I got painfully aware of the tension in my shoulders. My fingers felt like they were about to cramp up any minute too, and my back was aching from this morning. Must be old age creeping up, I thought, because what this moment really needed was another reminder of mortality.

I was just wondering how the hell I'd ever get out without upsetting her when she started to snore.

Thank God. I eased my hand out of hers and legged it.

CHAPTER ELEVEN

When I got out of the hospital, I saw I'd missed a call from my old mate Dave. Or DI Southgate, I should say, seeing as he'd had his Old Bill hat jammed firmly on over his bald patch when he'd rung. He'd left a message politely requesting I call him back. Well, sort of. What he'd actually said was, "Get your head out of that bloody toilet and give me a bell, all right? I don't want to have to send the boys round—you'd bloody enjoy it too much. Call me. You know what it's about."

I did. I called him.

Upshot was, I had thirty minutes to shove a sandwich in my gob and get round to his office, otherwise known as the nick. I tried ringing Phil to let him know, but he wasn't picking up. I texted him, *Gon 2 see Dave. If not back by tonite, bake cake with file*, and set off.

I was ushered in by a woman PC with a face like granite and, by the look of her, muscles to match. "Cheers, love," I said as she turned to go.

I probably imagined her snarling.

Dave was on his feet by the window, blocking out most of the light. He turned when I came in. "Bloody hell, I can't leave you alone for five minutes, can I?"

I glared at him. "Thought you lot had sensitivity training these days?"

He subsided, huffing, into his chair. "So? *I* thought *you* hadn't spoken to your sister for years. Go on, sit down, don't just stand there giving me a crick in the neck."

I sat. "Yeah, well. Just because we weren't speaking, doesn't mean we weren't *speaking*." I frowned at that myself. "You know what I mean. Anyway, that was before. We're speaking now. She invited me to her party, didn't she?"

Dave raised an eyebrow, then nodded.

"What, you thought I'd crashed it? Trust me, if I'd wanted to crash a party, I'd have picked a better one."

"Yeah, sherry with the vicar's not exactly your style, is it? So you're getting on all right these days, you and her?" His gaze got a bit more focussed. "What does she think about that bloke of yours?"

"What, Phil?"

I gave myself a mental kick up the bum as Dave went for the predictable response. "Why, how many you got?"

"Just the one. Nah, she doesn't like him much." I shrugged. "Came over all big sister, only thirteen years too late."

"Feeling's mutual, is it?" His chair creaked as he leaned his not-inconsiderable weight back.

"If you're trying to pin this on Phil, you can bugger off. He's on your side, remember? Solves crimes, doesn't do them."

"On our side? Pull the other one. You try telling that to anyone else in the force. Now me, I'm open-minded—"

As a bloody clam, I carefully didn't say. Mostly because I knew it wasn't actually fair. At least, I knew I knew it when I was thinking straight which, now, not so much.

"—but to your average copper on the beat, private investigators are just one step above ambulance chasers. And cockroaches."

"Yeah, Phil sends his love to you and all."

"You can give him this little billy doo from me." Dave stuck up a finger. "How's it going with him, anyway? In general terms, please."

"Fine." Oops. Said it a bit quick. If you do that, people tend to hear an invisible *Not* in front of it. "I mean, you know. Fine. How about you and Jen?"

His eyes went worryingly misty. "Good. Really good. We're trying for a kid, you know?"

"Hey, that's great." I meant it. He'd been a right saddo when she'd left him last year.

"It's harder work than you'd think, though," Dave said with a mock sigh that wasn't fooling anyone. "Since she hit forty, her fertility's gone right down, she reckons. The number of times she's rung me up at work to come home for a quickie 'cause she's ovulating—"

"Yeah, all right, got the picture, thanks," I said quickly. Nothing against Mrs. Dave, but middle-aged married couples shagging isn't an image I really want in my head.

Dave coughed and adjusted himself. "Right. Anyway, I've got to ask, has your sister got any enemies? Anyone you can think of who'd want to hurt her?"

"Not really. I s'pose I've been assuming it's to do with her work? You know, the court stuff? Maybe she didn't get someone off—in the legal sense, obviously—when she was supposed to? Or did, when she wasn't?"

Dave nodded again. "Yeah, we're looking into it. What do you know about Gregory Titmus?"

He's a creepy sod with strangler's hands? "Um, he seems like a decent bloke. And, you know, there's the whole man-of-God thing. I only just met him."

"What, at the party?"

"Well, no. Me and Phil went round to his for drinks a week or so ago. With Cherry, obviously."

"So you saw him and your sister together before the party? How did they seem?"

I shrugged. "Pretty loved-up. Before and during. And after, come to that. You don't seriously reckon he did it, do you? What was the point of proposing if he was going to try and off her afterwards?"

"Buyer's remorse?"

"Oi, that's my sister you're talking about, not some bit of tat off eBay."

"Sorry." He didn't sound it. "Partners are always the obvious suspect, though. And most of the time, it's the obvious suspect who's guilty."

"So if I pop my clogs in a suspicious manner, you'll be banging down Phil's door?"

"Too bloody right." Dave rubbed his neck. "Okay. Let's leave the Right Reverend—"

"Nah, that's bishops." I'd looked it up on the internet. "Greg's just an ordinary Reverend. Not even a Very."

"Since when are you such a bloody expert on the clergy? Forget about him, anyway. Did anyone else at the party give the impression of not being too keen on your sister?"

"Well . . . There was this bloke from her old writing group. Fuck, what was his name? Tall old bloke, bit round-shouldered. Looked like he liked a drink or six. Morgan, that was it. Morgan Everleigh or Everton or something. But don't get me wrong, it wasn't anything *he* said. It was just Cherry. She didn't seem all that chuffed he'd turned up. Said they'd had a few words about something he'd said she'd done, but she said she hadn't. Done the thing he said she had, I mean, not had a few words."

"God, I hope I never have a case that rests on getting you into the witness box. So this thing, what was it? And without all the he-said-she-saids."

"Fiddling the funds, though God knows how much a writers' circle has in the kitty. Couple of quid and an IOU, I'd reckon. He thought—that all right?—she'd accused him of it. She said she hadn't." I shrugged. "He seemed a bit, I dunno, high-strung?"

Dave laughed. "That's rich, coming from you. In what way?"

I ignored the dig at my masculinity. "Well, you know. Just getting a bit hot under the collar when he was talking about stuff. Like it was all a personal insult." I was starting to feel a bit queasy. "Shit, do you think he did it?"

There was something pretty horrifying about having a cosy chat with someone who ten minutes later tried to kill your sister.

"I don't think anything right now. Except that when we've finished this little chat, I want you to go and write down everything you can remember about this EverReady bloke." He sighed. "This would all have been so much easier if we'd been called in straightaway. We don't even know half the people who were at that bloody party."

"Hang on, Cherry and Greg must know who they invited."

"Must know, my arse. We're only looking at the whole bloody diocese of St. Leonards. Your Averagely Reverend chum put a sodding notice up in the bloody cathedral inviting all comers. And then Facebooked it. He was lucky he didn't have a couple of hundred teenagers roll up and turn it into a rave."

"Shit. I thought it was a bit packed. Well, that's a bugger."

He smirked. "Takes one to know one."

"Eff off." I paused. "Off the record, have you got anything to go on?"

"Officially, I'm not allowed to tell you anything about an ongoing investigation. Unofficially, bugger all. Although we did get a great set of prints off your sister's glass."

"Yeah?"

"Yeah. Belonged to one Thomas Paretski. Haven't you ever watched any cop shows on the telly? Even kids of five know you don't bloody touch anything at a crime scene."

"Oh. Sorry about that." I thought about it. "Hang about, I didn't bloody know it was a crime scene then, did I? And they'd have been on there anyway. I held her drink for her when she went to say hi to Richard and Agatha."

"That's your brother and the missus, right?"

I nodded.

"Get on all right with your sister, do they?" There was a steely glint in Dave's eye. "Their prints were on there too."

"Come on, you can't think they did it. Bloody hell, am I a suspect too?" I held out my hands, wrists together. "It's a fair cop, guv. You got me bang to rights. Me and Richard were in on it together, and Agatha's an accessory after the whatsit. That's the last time she'll cheat us at Monopoly."

"Don't be daft." Dave looked out the window, and I got a nasty feeling in the pit of my stomach. I was about to say something, when he turned back to me. "Tell me more about this drink, then. You were holding it. Put it down anywhere?"

I thought back. "Well, yeah. I left it on the table when I went over to grab Phil and take him to meet my brother. Shit. Is that when someone poisoned it?"

"Never said it was the drink, did I?"

"Well, was it?"

"Maybe." He sighed. "Didn't your mother ever tell you not to leave drinks unattended?"

"If we'd been in a pub, I wouldn't have, all right? The place was full of bloody church types. I wasn't expecting anyone to get roofied." My guts twisted painfully. I wished I hadn't shoved that bloody sandwich down so fast.

Dave shook his head wisely. "Shouldn't make assumptions. Some of these so-called God-fearing Christians have pretty dark pasts."

"Yeah, yeah. Been there, bought the T-shirt." I stood up. "Right. Why don't you get one of your lot to show me to where I get to write this bloody essay for you? *What I did on my night out.*"

"Long as it's only stuff that's pertinent to the enquiry. I don't want to hear about the rest of your Friday night."

"Oi, there wasn't any of that, not after my sister nearly died."

"Yeah, bit of a passion-killer, I expect. So he was with you all evening, was he? Morrison, I mean. Looked after you all right?"

"I'm not a kid. I've been looking after myself for quite a few years now." I resisted the urge to roll my eyes.

Dave showed no such restraint. "Says the bloke who managed to get himself shot in bloody Hertfordshire not so long ago."

I'm not sure if Phil was at the station the same time I was or not. If he was, Dave didn't let on. Sneaky sod. Anyway, when I got out, there was a message on my mobile from Phil saying they'd put him through the wringer too, and we ought to compare notes.

I hoped Dave's boys weren't monitoring our phone calls. Something like that probably sounded as guilty as hell.

We met up in the foyer of the Merchants Café in St. Albans. It was a big place, as they went in St. Albans, but cosy, with lots of little round tables and dark wood everywhere. In the summer, they'd have ceiling fans going, or you could sit outside in the market square on the rare occasions the sun actually shone.

This time of year, with everyone bundled up in thick coats, there was hardly room to move inside, but it was worth it for the smell of the place—rich, dark coffee with just a hint of chocolate. I almost didn't bother getting a drink—I could have got my caffeine fix just by breathing in deep.

Then again, I'd have had nothing to dunk my biscotti in. I got a cappuccino and a smile from the blonde barista as she gave me extra chocolate sprinkles.

Phil got an Americano. And no smile. Then again, he was looking a bit grim. We sat down at a table in the middle of a row. Even though we were banging elbows with the neighbours, the din of chatter in the place gave us all the privacy we needed to talk. We could probably have discussed our sex life at full volume and no one would have batted an eyelid.

Then again, after what Phil had told me about his dogging case, I was beginning to think me and him weren't trying all that hard with our sex life.

"Did you tell the police about Greg hiring you?" I asked. "I mean, I didn't. Wasn't sure it was relevant or whether it was one of these professional confidentiality things, so I thought I'd leave it to you."

Phil sipped his coffee. "I told them. You don't know what's going to be relevant in a case like this." Voice of experience, here. Phil was a copper himself, once upon a time.

"Yeah, but it'd be stretching it a bit, wouldn't it? I mean, someone doesn't like Greg, so he—or she—poisons my sister? Why not cut out the middle man? Or woman, rather."

"You don't know what's going on in these people's heads. Maybe they thought if his fiancée died, Greg would turn away from his evil ways and repent? You think they were just out to hurt him, but these religious nutters usually aren't that straightforward. They reckon they're doing the right thing. Saving his soul. Maybe they think if someone has to die, that's worth it."

"What, so Greg's soul is worth more than my sister's life?"

"Maybe. To someone like that."

I hoped they'd burn in hell. If, you know, it existed.

Phil carried on. "Or maybe your sister wasn't the intended victim, have you thought of that?"

"That'd make more sense. If they thought it was Greg they were poisoning."

"Or you."

I choked on my cappuccino. Must be the biscotti crumbs. "You what? Why'd anyone want to kill me?"

Phil didn't say, *Because they've met you?* which I was grateful for. "Why does anyone kill anyone?" he asked instead.

"You want to get all philosophical about it? I don't know. Money, sex . . . Uh, maybe they were being blackmailed? They *weren't* being blackmailed, by the way. At least, not by me. *If* I was supposed to be the victim."

"Were you having sex with them?" He smirked at me over the rim of his mug.

"Well, Dave did say you'd be suspect number one if I ever kick the bucket in dodgy circs, so maybe."

Phil nodded. "Yeah, that's why I'd never poison you."

"Thank God for small mercies."

"I'd push you off a ladder or booby-trap your toaster. Make it look like an accident. Safest way."

A woman on the next table shrieked with laughter, but I was fairly sure it was at something her friend had said, not the thought of Phil getting domestically violent with me.

"Glad to hear you've got my untimely death all planned out. Oi, you didn't tell Dave about this theory of yours, did you? They'll be on you like a bloody rash if you did." The last thing we needed was a bunch of flatfooted policemen poking their noses into our relationship.

"Course not. I'm not daft." He paused. "Might be an idea if I move in with you for a bit, though. Just in case."

"See, now, if you *were* trying to off me, that's just what you'd do, innit? All those opportunities to shove me down stairs and say I tripped over the cat." I wasn't sure how I felt about him moving in. Yeah, it was nice waking up to him in my bed, and all right, I liked the cosy evenings and, yeah, the shagging, but did I really want him there all the time? Wasn't that how the magic went out of a relationship? Plus, I'd have to start keeping the place tidy *all the time*. Phil's flat was always immaculate, since he'd got rid of the last of the boxes from moving in.

Course, now I came to think about it, I'd never dropped round unannounced. Too much of a faff to find he wasn't even in, so I always called first. Maybe he was a closet slob. Anyway, I decided to deal with his moving-in suggestion by the fiendishly cunning and mature method of ignoring it completely. "Right, assuming it's *not* you, what does that leave? Money? I wish. Nah, can't be me. Not unless Mum, Dad, Cherry, and Richard all ganged up to get their hands on my two-bed semi in Fleetville. Which, I might add, is still mostly owned by the mortgage company."

"What about your auntie's legacy?"

"Seriously? You reckon Mr. M.'s tried to off me to stop me getting my hands on a half share in his des res in Mill Hill? We don't even know that's what the legacy is—and anyway, wouldn't it just go to my family?"

"Not necessarily. Some wills have a clause in saying the beneficiary has to outlive the deceased by at least thirty days. Look, I'm not saying you *were* the intended victim. I'm just saying it's possible, all right? You were holding that drink for a while; they could have thought it was yours. It's more likely than they thought it was Greg's, anyway."

"Shit." My cappuccino curdled in my stomach.

"What is it?"

"I nearly drank some of it. I mean, I was wondering what Cherry was drinking, so I picked it up to have a sniff, but I didn't want to make it obvious, so I pretended I was having a sip. I mean, I nearly *did* drink some."

Phil frowned. "You'd have been fine. Cherry must have drunk more of it than that, and she's going to be okay." He still didn't look happy about it, which was fine by me. *I* certainly wasn't happy about it. "Has it ever occurred to you this whole legacy thing is a bit iffy? I mean, I get how your auntie wanted to have a last laugh with you about your hidden talents, but why hide something in her ex-husband's house? Come to that, how did she even manage to do it?"

I shrugged. "Maybe he hasn't changed the locks in the last fifteen years? I don't know."

"So what, you reckon your terminally ill auntie hopped onto the train from Scotland and came all this way, turning up fortuitously right when her ex happened to be out—which at his age probably only happens once every other month; you know what old people are like—nipped into the old place and stashed her will under the floorboards? Why not hide it in her own house? Or at least in her own bloody country?"

I shuffled my bum on my seat. When he put it like that, it did seem a bit daft. "Maybe she got someone to do it for her?"

"Who do you know that she's kept in touch with down here?"

"Well, no one, apart from me. That I know of, I mean. It doesn't mean she *didn't*."

"Even if she did have help, it's a lot of bother. So why did she bother?"

"I don't know!" I glanced around the place. The people at the next table had been replaced by a fat bloke with his iPad, and I hadn't even noticed. "Maybe she was worried I wouldn't go for it if it was too far away?"

"So why's it so important to her you go along with it?" Phil leaned forward, pointing his teaspoon at my chest. "Maybe her will isn't the only thing hidden in that house. Maybe that's what she really wants you to find. 'Cause once you get in there, you'll start getting vibes, or whatever, from anything hidden, won't you?"

"Well, yeah. What do you reckon it is, though?"

"Maybe she murdered his first wife and buried the body under the patio? And now she's dead, she wants the truth to be known?"

"Oi, Auntie Lol wasn't a murderess." I thought about it. "Mr. M. could have done it, though. Maybe he's got a whole bloody harem of wives buried under there. Like Bluebeard. Oh, bloody hell." My gut twisted.

"What?"

"I just realised. That'd be a motive, wouldn't it? For him to try and kill me. To stop me finding the bodies." Was it me, or was it bloody chilly in here all of a sudden?

"Right. Well, you're the one who's met this Morangie bloke. Was he at the party?"

All at once, it warmed up again. "Oh. No, he wasn't. I mean, I didn't see him. And I think I would've noticed him, if he'd been there." I gazed moodily into the dregs of my cappuccino, feeling like a muppet. Then I looked up. "Hang on, he's got a son, hasn't he? Maybe he sent him to do the dirty work?"

"So if your dad just gave you a call and said, 'Listen, son, I want you to go to a party and poison someone you've never met,' you'd just up and do it, would you?"

"Well, no. But we're not that close. Never have been."

Phil raised an eyebrow. "We're pretty close, you and me. Certainly were this morning, as I recall. If *I* asked you to go to a party and poison someone, would you do it then?"

"*No*! Fuck it, I'm not a murderer." I might have said it a bit loud. The bloke on the table next to us shot me a startled look, quickly followed by a nervous smile. Which was daft, getting all worked up about it, seeing as I'd just said I *wasn't* a murderer.

"See? That's how most people would react. Still, might be worth looking into. How old's this son supposed to be?"

"Dunno. Twenties? Thirties? Must be somewhere around there."

Phil nodded. "I'll see what I can turn up about him. You done there?"

I nodded, and we stood up, pulled on our jackets, and headed out to brave the cold and the market-day crowds.

"I'm supposed to be going to Mr. M.'s house in a couple of days," I remembered. "Cherry set it up."

"What day?"

"Monday. In the morning. Why?"

"Want me to come with?"

"Why?"

"How about to make sure you don't drink any nicotine cocktails?"

"If he starts offering cocktails at ten o'clock in the morning and I don't twig there's something funny going on, I probably deserve to get poisoned."

"Right. Because he'd never think of putting it in a cup of coffee."

"I'm not totally daft, you know. Look, just hang a sign round my neck that says *Nil by mouth*, all right?"

Phil looked like he was seriously considering it. Then he glanced along the road at the market stalls. "Are we going to say hello to Darren while we're here?"

Phil had met Darren when I'd taken him up the Devil's Dyke a while back. They got on disturbingly well, God knows why. Phil and my mate Gary, Darren's bloke, still hadn't really taken to each other. I'd have liked to think it was loyalty on Gary's part and him reckoning Phil wasn't really good enough for me, what with all our history and all. But basically I was fairly sure they just got on each other's tits.

Darren and Phil, though, they got on like a house on fire. And I had a feeling I was the one who was going to end up with third-degree burns. "Well, I said hi to him only the other day . . ."

"So? I didn't, did I?"

"Yeah, I s'pose." We couldn't be more than fifty yards away from Darren's pitch, so there was no excuse not to drop in on him really. We wandered down the street, Phil's shoulders taking up way too much room in the narrow gap between stalls and shop fronts. Past the sock stall, past the silver jewellery, past the hat stall, past the ladies' undies, and there we were at Darren's fruit-and-veg emporium. We heard him before we saw him, of course. He was in full voice, extolling the virtues of seasonal produce.

"Git your brussels sprouts—they're not just for Christmas. Come on, ladies, fresh cauli, pahnd a—" He broke off mid-spiel to flash a grin at Phil so wide you could see his gold tooth. "Well, if it ain't Dirk Gently. How yer doing, mate?"

Phil smiled back. "Not too bad. Yourself?"

"'Dirk Gently'?" I interrupted. "If that's your porn-star name, it needs a bit of work. *Stab Ruggedly*, maybe, or *Shaft Vigorously*?"

Phil rolled his eyes. "Prick. Dirk Gently is a fictional private detective. Haven't you ever heard of Douglas Adams? *Hitchhiker's Guide to the Galaxy*?"

"Hey, I *heard* of the film. I just never got around to seeing it, that's all."

"Tragic," Darren put in. "Bet he doesn't have a bloody clue where his towel is."

Phil sniggered.

See, this was why I hadn't been keen on dropping by the stall. "Oi, this better not be some gag about those sanitary things women wear."

Both of them cracked up.

An old lady in a coat that looked like she'd knitted it herself thirty years ago took pity on my obvious terminal bewilderment. "It's a quote, dear. The radio show was very popular in its day. It's supposed to be a good idea to always know where your towel is. Of course, at my age, I always feel I'm doing well if I can remember where my house is."

I winked at her. "Nah, you look like you've got plenty of marbles left."

"Trouble is, I've forgotten where I put them." Her wrinkly cheeks dimpled.

"Oi, Phil," Darren's voice cut in. "Better watch out. Looks like pint-size has got himself a girlfriend."

She wagged a mitten at him. "You're a cheeky young man, and I hope you're ashamed of yourself. Now, I'd like some stewing vegetables, please."

"Coming right up, so no getting saucy with Tom Thumb there while you're waiting." Darren tipped a couple of bowls into a carrier bag and held it ready to hand over. "That'll be fifty pee." He waited patiently while she counted out her coins with bloodless fingers. "Cheers, love. You enjoy your supper."

"Shouldn't that have been two pounds?" I asked when she'd doddered out of sight.

"Who are you, chancellor of the bleedin' exchequer? Ain't you heard? Bottom's dropped right out of the root veg market. It's all these Waitrose shoppers demanding baby courgettes and premature bloody pea sprouts." Darren shrugged and rearranged a couple of cabbages. "She ain't got much. Used to be a nurse, and the pension's bugger all. When it's summer, she comes round at packing-up time when I'm selling stuff off cheap, but she don't like being out after dark."

"Darren," I said sincerely. "You give me faith for the future of humanity."

"Oi, give over. It's only a couple of turnips, not the national debt of Ethi-bloody-opia. No need to go having a moment over it."

"Wedding plans going okay?" Phil asked abruptly. He must have been just as uncomfortable with all the genuine emotion and spirit of charity flying around as the rest of us.

"Yeah, great. Few hitches—Gary was all set on releasing a flock of doves, bless his fluffy little heart, but I told him, last thing you want when you're in your dry-clean-only gear is a load of birds shitting everywhere. And no one wants crap on the cake. So we got that sorted, but now we're looking at menus. We're trying to decide between a buffet and a sit-down. What did you have at yours?"

Phil at least had the decency to shoot me an uncomfortable glance. "Sit-down. Wasn't a big do, though."

"No? How many did you have?"

"Couple of dozen."

"Bloody hell, that's tiny. That's like the bloody Paretski of weddings." Har sodding har. "What were you—Billy-no-mates, a Barnardo's boy, or both?"

Phil grunted. "None of my family went."

Something wasn't right there. "Hang on," I butted in. "What about all those family Christmases you told me about where you *and* the Mys—I mean, Mark had to turn up or get disowned?"

He didn't answer for a moment. "That was after my dad died."

Oh. I supposed that explained a couple of things. I wasn't sure *which* couple, mind, but I was pretty sure this must have been a significant factor in making up the six-foot-one, emotionally constipated private eye currently squiring me about town. "Um, how'd he die?" I asked weakly.

"Heart attack." Phil huffed without humour. "Docs told him years before he ought to cut down on the booze and the fried stuff, but he wasn't having any of it."

I didn't know what to say. Phil still looked cut up about it. Maybe they hadn't been talking when he'd died? I tried to imagine how I'd feel if my dad popped off after we'd had a row, but to be honest, he's never really *done* rows. He's always been more into disappointed looks or, in extreme cases, disappearing into the garden shed for the rest of the day.

Darren nodded sadly. "I'm always telling people they should eat more veg."

"Chance would be a flippin' fine thing," a sharp female voice cut in. "I've been standing here half an hour while you lot tell each other your life stories. Any chance I might actually get served today?" She was around my age, her face pinched with cold. Or maybe it was just the Essex up-do giving her a migraine.

Either way, it didn't seem like a good idea to piss her off anymore. Plus Darren had a living to make. Phil and me said quick goodbyes and legged it.

CHAPTER TWELVE

Phil and me had gone our separate ways after we'd talked to Darren. He'd said he had stuff to do, but he would see me later for a curry. When I opened the door to him that evening, he was lugging a smart leather holdall and a laptop bag.

I raised an eyebrow. "Guess you were serious about moving in, then." Luckily, I'd had stuff to do that afternoon too, and it'd involved a bit of a blitz on the pigsty that was my house.

"Just for the weekend. If that's all right." He hovered, stony-faced, on the doormat for a mo instead of barging past me like he usually did. Shit, was he nervous?

Now *I* was nervous too. "Er, yeah. Course. Come in." Bloody hell, any minute now I'd offer to shake hands. But it felt weird, this. A bit, well, significant. Despite the fact he'd stayed over here plenty of nights. But those had just happened. He'd never brought luggage before.

"Thought it'd make sense. In the circumstances," he muttered, looking at his feet as he wiped them carefully.

"You mean, in case Mr. M. pops round and tries to poison me? I thought we'd decided he couldn't have had anything to do with it, though?" I could have kicked myself the moment I'd said it. Did I *want* him to bugger off again? "Course, better to be safe than sorry and all that bollocks."

He gave a quick nod. "There were a lot of people in that place. There's no guarantee you saw everyone who was there—especially someone you'd only met once, and who was trying to avoid you."

"He'd have had to be trying bloody hard. Not the sort of looks you forget." Nice one, Paretski. Go on, shoot yourself in the *other* foot now.

Phil raised an eyebrow. "Fancy him, did you?"

I shuddered. "Not so much, no. Are you coming in, or were you planning on camping out on the doormat all night?"

He smirked. "Going to make it worth my while?"

"Oh yeah." I leered at him. "I ordered poppadoms and everything."

"Think I'm easy, do you? One poppadom and I'm anyone's?"

"Reckon I've got a jar of mango chutney in the cupboard," I said and licked my lips for good measure.

"Well, in that case, you're on." Phil lumbered past me and dumped his bag in the hall. "Kinky sod."

After an early night that didn't involve a whole lot of sleep, we had a lazy, shagged-out Sunday morning on the sofa with the papers. Well, I did anyway. Phil had been slouched at the other end of the sofa, Merlin on his lap, making eyes at his phone for the last ten minutes. I had a strong suspicion he was doing some work.

"I want you to go along and take a look at this lot," he said just as I was about to tell him he might as well stop pretending and get his bloody laptop out. "Says here they meet on Monday nights."

I folded the sports pages to keep my place for later. There's a lot to get through on a Sunday. "What lot?"

"The Lea Valley Literati." He held out his phone and flashed the screen at me. Seeing as the website he was looking at apparently didn't have a mobile version, all I could read was *ley Lite*, which sounded like something lay readers cut their teeth on when they were just starting out.

"Oh, them." Morgan Everton's crew. "Oi, why's it got to be me? I don't know the first bloody thing about writing." Or private investigating, to tell the truth, although I had got a bit of an introduction to the art since Phil had unexpectedly popped back into my life in Brock's Hollow.

"Doesn't matter. Look, I knew someone who used to go along to one of these circles."

Not, *I had a mate who* or *someone I used to work with*. Which didn't *necessarily* mean it was the Mysterious Mark, obviously.

But I knew what my money was on.

"Anyway," Phil was saying, "he said it was just a bunch of old women sitting around drinking tea and writing stories about their cats." He stroked Merlin's head and got a toothy yawn for his trouble.

"So?"

"So you'd be a natural. Wow them with a few reminiscences about your Auntie Lol, tell them how Arthur once maimed a burglar, that sort of stuff."

"In his dreams, maybe." I cast a glance around for the cat in question and spotted him fast asleep on a chair, tail twitching. Maybe he was dreaming about maiming small furry animals. "Anyway, I don't think this lot are like that. I can't see Morgan Everton writing stories about cats, can you? And he's the wrong sex."

"Like you'd get anything out of him anyway. It's the rest of them you need to talk to." His eyes narrowed. "Just give them a bit of the Paretski charm. You'll have them eating out of your hand."

I flashed him a flirty smile. "I can think of someone else I'd rather have eating out of my hand. Or, you know, other places."

"Focus."

"Killjoy. Anyway, I still don't see why you can't do it."

"You've got the connection with Everton. I haven't."

I leaned my head back on the sofa and stared up at the ceiling. "We talked for five minutes. I wouldn't call that a bloody connection."

"You don't have to have sucked his dick to have a connection."

"Great, make me lose my appetite, why don't you?" I had moussaka in the oven for a late Sunday lunch. I'd be well pissed off if he put me off eating that, after all the faffing around with the sauce.

"Anyway, if I go, it'll be a whole different ball game. Some stranger turns up out of the blue directly after an ex-member gets poisoned? He'll know—they'll all know—I'm there to dig up the dirt about their relationships with Cherry."

"S'pose." He had a point. Plus there was the whole thing where Phil still looked and sounded like a copper, particularly when he was on the hunt for information. Like Gary once said, Phil had this way of asking "Tea or coffee?" that made you worry your answer might be taken down and used in evidence against you.

"If you go," Phil went on, "they'll be more willing to buy into the idea you might actually be serious about writing."

"Yeah, maybe. Until they actually ask me to, you know, *write* something."

"You don't go to these things to write. You go there to talk crap about writing." He smirked. "So like I said, you'll be a natural."

"What, at talking crap? Love you too, you bastard." There was a catch in my chest as I realised a split second too late that I'd never really said it, not properly. Neither of us had, come to that. The l-word, I mean, not called him a bastard. I'd done that plenty of times.

I glanced at Phil. He was looking at me funny. Or maybe he just had wind. Then he sort of shook himself. He didn't say anything.

"Right," I said, standing up. "Better go check on the moussaka."

True to his word, Phil buggered off Monday morning, taking his posh holdall with him. Apparently he reckoned murderers had day jobs just like anyone else. Either that or sixty hours straight was as much as he could take of my company, which was fair enough. The place felt a lot bigger without him in it, and Merlin slunk around the kitchen with his belly to the ground as if his best friend had died. Arthur and I left him to it and stretched out on the sofa with the laptop. Well, I stretched. Arthur just curled up into the usual solid, furry lump.

The Lea Valley Literati website, when I finally got it up and running, was so bloody clunky I expected it to carry ads for flypaper and crinolines. Or, you know, my old laptop. But at least it gave me a number to ring to find out where they actually met. This information was clearly too sensitive to be trusted to the World Wide Web.

I punched the number into my phone and waited.

A dozen rings later—I can be a persistent sod when I want to be—the phone was answered with a brusque, "Yes?"

"Is that Margaret Pierce?"

"Whatever it is, I'm not interested. Goodbye."

She slammed the phone down. Seemed the so-called Paretski charm was getting past its sell-by date.

I sighed and pressed redial. This time, it only took three rings before she picked up and drew in a breath, presumably about to demand to know what I was selling and why I was harassing her like this. "I'm calling about the Lea Valley Literati," I said quickly, before she could get a word out.

"Yes?"

I'd been hoping for a more encouraging response. "Er, yeah. You're the contact name on the website? I was thinking of joining."

"I see. Well, you'd be very welcome to come along to a meeting." Her tone called her a liar. I felt about as welcome as syphilis.

"Great! Er, so when and where?" It'd said on the website that they met on Monday evenings, so there ought to be a meeting tonight, but it'd been a bit short on any other helpful information.

"We meet at the chairman's house." That, if I wasn't mistaken, was my old friend Morgan E. "Half past seven. Don't be late."

"I'll set my alarm. So where's that, then?"

"You do understand this is a *literary* society?" She reeled off the address—one of the posh places in Redbourn. Nice if you can get it. I'd done some work up that way not so long ago. Friendly lady, always happy to chat and served up M&S choccy biccies with the morning cuppa. Terrible taste in carpets, though. She went for these fluffy cream ones that showed a speck of dirt at five hundred yards. I mean, I always took my boots off when I went inside, but that place made me worry even my socks weren't clean enough.

"I'll see you tonight, then. Cheers." I managed to stop myself calling her "love." I had a feeling she wouldn't have been impressed.

I'd almost forgotten about going to see Auntie Lol's ex. If Cherry hadn't rung from her sick bed to remind me, I'd have ended up blowing him off. As it was, I didn't much fancy going round there—seemed a bit, I don't know, disrespectful, messing about with gag gifts from beyond the grave when Cherry had just come close to joining Auntie Lol in the afterlife.

Not that I believe in the afterlife, really.

Well, probably not.

I mean, who knows?

Anyway, I thought seeing as Cherry had bothered to ring and remind me, I should probably bother to go, and it wasn't like I had any jobs on, seeing as I'd blanked out the space in my diary. So I bombed down the A1(M) in the van to the sounds of an animated discussion on Radio 5 about violence on the football pitch. Just as I reckoned they were about to come to blows in the studio, I hit Mill Hill. The satnav perked up at finally having some work to do, so I had to switch off the radio and listen to Sean Connery doing James Bond as he told me to turn left at the lightsh.

The roads got posher as I neared my destination. Shame I hadn't brought any leaflets to bung in letterboxes. There's a lot of money in Mill Hill, although it's got its grotty side too. Morangie Manor (not that it was actually called that, mind) was very definitely at the posh end, near the old village centre rather than the modern bit around Mill Hill Broadway. This is commuter country, same as St. Albans, only more so, seeing as it's that bit farther down the line towards London. Lots of high-powered jobs in the City funding all the big houses and professionally tended gardens.

I wondered if Mr. M. had a high-powered job. Mind you, he was what, in his sixties now? So he could be retired. Maybe he'd be glad to get rid of the big house and move somewhere smaller.

Or maybe he'd be horrified at the thought of moving after living in the same house so long. God, I felt like a home wrecker, or some heartless bastard of an absentee landlord turfing old folks out of their homes so Tesco could build their six-millionth store.

I gave a low whistle as I pulled up outside Mr. M.'s place. Suddenly, his offer didn't look anything like as generous, if we really were talking half the house. Half of this place wouldn't just take a chunk out of my mortgage, it'd pay the lot off with change to spare. I wondered what I'd do with the money, if I got it. Develop a cocaine habit? Buy a wardrobe of cashmere sweaters to match Phil's?

No point counting those chickens, I thought. I got out of the van, walked up the short brick drive, and rang the doorbell.

"Morning," I said cheerily as Mr. M. opened the door.

His sour expression didn't alter. "At least you're punctual." He stood back, leaving the door open, so I took that as all the invitation

I was going to get and stepped into the house. It was weird—once I was in there, I could actually really imagine Auntie Lol living there. She was into all this sort of stuff: solid, chunky furniture that had had a few knocks in life and looked like it could take plenty more, and bright, cheery fabrics. The sofa and chairs were covered with the sort of scatter cushions posh women on the telly show you how to make yourself for only three times the price you could buy them in a shop, and the walls were cheerfully accessorised with haphazardly arranged pictures showing animals and landscapes.

"Nice house you've got here." I cringed inside. Shit, did that sound like I was looking forward to kicking him out of it? He didn't reply. "No Mr. Wood?" I tried again.

"He's been detained."

I hoped that just meant he'd been held up, not that he'd been arrested or anything. Still, it wasn't like he was my solicitor, so no skin off my nose either way. "So, should I just get started?"

Mr. M. glared at me. "Tea?" he said abruptly.

"Ta. White, no sugar, please. Actually, second thoughts, I'll drink it black." I was betting any tea served in this house would be more watery than the River Lea.

Mr. M. stomped off to make it, and too late, I remembered I wasn't supposed to be accepting any offers of refreshments. Still, it'd be okay if I watched him make it, wouldn't it? I hesitated, then followed him into the kitchen. It had honest-to-God gingham blinds and tiles with hens on. Had Auntie Lol married him for his house?

Then I remembered they'd bought it together. Maybe she'd decorated, and he hadn't bothered to change anything since she'd left? I wasn't sure I'd be too happy living in a house that had my ex stamped all over it.

"So, er, how's things?" I went on awkwardly as Mr. M. fussed with his state-of-the-art electric kettle. Auntie Lol had had an antique stovetop one that even whistled, like the ones in the battered old Enid Blyton books she used to lend me. I remembered being fascinated by it as a kid. I wondered if it was still around here somewhere, shoved in a cupboard after she'd left. Maybe that was what she'd left me in her will. "Family okay? Cherry said you had a son—what is he, about my age? He doesn't still live here, does he?"

His face went purple, and he turned on me. He was still holding his box of Waitrose Ceylon teabags, and I winced a bit as it crumpled in his hand. "I've changed my mind. I no longer wish to allow this imposition. You can leave, now."

"What?" Seriously, what? "Sorry if I said something to upset you—"

"Do you want me to call the police? Get out!"

"All right, I'm going!"

I scuttled back to the van with my head in a whirl. How the hell had I buggered that up so badly? Not to mention so bloody quickly. I'd barely been in the place five minutes.

I was *not* looking forward to letting Cherry know about this little fiasco.

CHAPTER THIRTEEN

After the wasted morning at Mr. M.'s, I had a pretty busy afternoon, work-wise. What with getting home, having a shower, feeding the cats and even grabbing a bite myself, it was well on the way to seven o'clock before I knew it. I thought about ringing Phil and telling him I was off to see the literary crowd, but it seemed a bit, well, unnecessary. I might be a short-arse with a dodgy hip, but I can take care of myself. I shoved my phone back on the table.

Then I remembered what'd happened to six-foot, able-bodied Phil when he'd turned up to a suspect's house on his tod back in Brock's Hollow, and decided it wouldn't be a bad idea to text him the address at least. I picked my phone back up again.

Secure in the knowledge that if Morgan Everton battered me to death with a typewriter tonight, Phil would at least be able to find the body, I set off for the lit fest just after seven. I wanted to make sure I could find the place all right. Yeah, I know I could've just borrowed the satnav from the van, but I don't like relying on it all the time, 'specially when I'm going somewhere local. Anyway, I've got GPS on my phone if it all goes tits-up.

Actually, I'm pretty sure Gary thinks I've got GPS implanted in my brain. He's never really *got* how my finding-things talent works.

As it happened, I found the place with no trouble and got there with ten minutes to spare. So I sent Phil another text—*was nice knowing you, pls look after cats*—and got one back saying *wankr*. Then another that said *call me when ur out*.

It wasn't quite *I love you*, but it showed he cared, right? Anyway, time to get out of the car.

Morgan's place was big, but there was something about it I didn't much like. It was right on the edge of Redbourn village, and I'd passed a lot of nice houses on the way—I couldn't see them very well, as it was pitch-black right now, and the place had the sort of street lighting you get in the countryside, meaning practically none, but I knew they were there. I'd been a bit disappointed to pull up outside this mock Tudor monstrosity, tall and austere looking, with square, unfriendly pillars holding up the porch. A security light flashed on when I got out of the Fiesta and nearly blinded me as I crunched up the drive to the front door.

There was one of these big brass knockers on the door, which was probably supposed to look grand and imposing but just made me think of Mrs. L. in Sandridge. I would've knocked, but despite all the coloured blobs floating in my vision courtesy of that bloody security light, I could just about see that the front door was ajar. Talk about sending out mixed messages. After a moment's dithering on the doorstep I walked straight in, trying not to look like an opportunistic burglar. The hallway was in darkness, which didn't help one bit.

If I'd got the wrong house, this was going to be really embarrassing.

Thankfully, I could hear voices down the other end of the hall, coming from another door that was open just a crack to let the treacly glow of a low-wattage bulb spill out.

I was under strict instructions from Phil to use any opportunity to have a nose around the place, and I wondered if now would be a good time. Trouble was, I hadn't expected Morgan to make life easy for nosey parkers, so if I took time out now, I'd be late. Margaret would probably stab me with a fountain pen for that even if I didn't manage to get caught sneaking about. I had a feeling it wouldn't make a great first impression with the group.

I walked down the hallway, wincing a bit as my boots clattered on the tiles and trying to tread more lightly. No wonder Morgan felt safe leaving his front door open. His whole bloody hallway was an early-warning system. Just as well I hadn't tried any sneaking.

I knocked lightly on the door at the end and poked my head into what turned out to be a large sitting room, the dim light seeming to soak straight into the antique furniture. Perched uncomfortably on various hard-looking chairs and horsehair-stuffed sofas were a motley bunch I guessed must be the writers' circle. There were five of them in the room, which to my mind made a pentagon, not a circle.

It also made me wonder if there were any Satanic rites about to be performed—no, hang on, that was pentagrams, wasn't it?

I still wouldn't have put it past this lot.

Morgan Everton was in the far corner, head-down over a wodge of dog-eared papers with a skinny young Asian bloke. Neither of them glanced up when I spoke, but three faces turned my way with varying degrees of welcome.

"Hi, I'm looking for the Literati?"

"Yes?" The woman who spoke was in her fifties, thin and beaky, and I had a feeling I'd seen her before somewhere. At Cherry's do? Maybe. Or maybe she just reminded me of one of Greg's cathedral ladies. I tried to picture her with a plate of sausage rolls but came up blank. If she'd seen me before, apparently she hadn't enjoyed the experience.

"So is that you lot?" I prompted when nothing else was forthcoming.

"Oh yes." The breathless voice came from a washed-out fortysomething woman draped in fifty shades of grey. I was betting it wasn't ironic. "Are you here to join us?"

"That was the plan. Hi, I'm Tom."

"Hannah." Grey-Lady turned a bit pink as she took my outstretched hand in her warm, plump little mitt. "And this is Margaret, and Peter."

"Margaret, hi! We spoke on the phone? I'm Tom." Beaky looked down her considerable nose at me and gave me a damp, bony handshake.

"You found us all right, then?" She sounded disappointed.

I flashed her a winning smile, as if to suggest it was all down to her address-quoting skills. "Yeah, thanks. No problem."

She sniffed.

Peter, although younger, was as grey looking as Hannah. But where she was soft, he was hard as ice. He had a sharp, ferrety face, and a jerky way of moving as if he'd been filmed in stop-motion like a cut-price knockoff of Wallace and Gromit. He didn't take my hand, just nodded, the stuck-up sod.

"And over there are Morgan and Raz. Raz is a poet," she added in awestruck tones.

"Yeah, me and Morgan have met. It's how I heard about you lot."

Finally, they deigned to notice me. Morgan's eyes were shifty, like he wasn't too keen on owning up to the acquaintance. I imagined Margaret flashing him a look of triumph behind my back, in an "Ah, so he's *your* fault" sort of way.

"Ah, yes," he admitted finally, under the weight of their collective stare. "Tom. Good to see you again."

He didn't ask how Cherry was, which might have been an important clue but more likely just meant he was a thoughtless bastard. I thought about shouting out a progress report on her to annoy him, but I was supposed to be in stealth mode and that probably wouldn't have been very stealthy. "Yeah, cheers for telling me about this group."

Morgan glared literary daggers at me. "I didn't know *you* wrote."

"Oh, it's a new thing. See, I was talking to this lady—Edie Penrose, she's a lovely old girl—and she reckoned I ought to get a hobby. Something intellectual. So I thought I'd give writing a go." Not bad, I thought, for a total bit of improv. Maybe I'd fit in better here than I'd thought—I seemed to be a natural at making stuff up.

"And what do you write?" Margaret demanded. I snapped out of the self-congratulations and general musing. With a nose that sharp, she'd stab me if I didn't stay on my toes.

Excrement, meet air-moving device. "Gay literature," I said with a smile, and braced myself for the outrage.

It didn't happen. All around the room, heads were nodding in, dare I say it, approval.

"Oh, excellent. Such a rich vein of tragedy," Margaret murmured with a suitably mournful expression.

What?

"I take it you are, yourself, of that persuasion?" she carried on.

"Er, yeah."

A sort of collective sigh went around the place. With a kind, almost motherly look on her face, she took my arm. "Do come and sit down."

She led me to a seat next to Hannah, who gave me a sad smile. "You must have a great deal of tragedy in your own life to draw upon," she said in a barely audible voice.

"Er, yeah? Still, mustn't grumble." They were all so bloody sombre and sympathetic, I felt I had to be extra bright and breezy to compensate.

"Do you write poetry too?" Raz asked, pushing his glasses back up his nose and staring at me with big, earnest eyes. He had the sort of beard that looked like it had started out as designer stubble and still wasn't sure it hadn't preferred it that way.

"Does the odd naughty limerick count?"

They all laughed politely, despite the fact I hadn't been joking. "So tell us about your novel, Tom," Morgan demanded.

Bugger. I hadn't expected anyone to actually want to know more about gay literature. "Well, it's about this plumber, see," I began. They always said you should write what you know, didn't they? So that probably applied to making up stuff on the spur of the moment. "He shows up at this bloke's house to fix the washer, and of course, the bloke's not got any clean clothes because his washer's kaput, so he's just wearing a tea towel . . ." Too late, I realised I was reproducing the plot of one of Darren's pornos. *The Plumber Always Comes Twice*, if I recalled correctly.

Luckily, it didn't look like anyone here had seen it. They were still nodding along in unison like a row of those dogs you see in the backs of people's cars. Half of them even had the jowls to complete the illusion. I breathed a sigh of relief.

"And what's the central theme?" Margaret asked, jabbing her beaky nose in my direction.

Theme? I thought fast. "It's, um, about the shallow, empty nature of casual relationships?"

"I imagine the washing machine is just a metaphor, then?" Hannah suggested timidly.

"I like that," Raz threw in while I was still struggling with that one. "Like life, it goes in cycles. And you could go one of two ways with it. Either the machine gets fixed, or it doesn't. Whichever you choose, it's a strong statement."

"No, no." This was Morgan Everton, butting in with an air of authority. "The machine has to be fixed. Otherwise it's just too obvious. And I think the tragedy is more poignant that way."

Nods all round. Even from Raz.

"So," Hannah asked hesitantly. "Do we ever find out what's wrong with the machine?"

"I'm still working on that bit," I said firmly. "So what's everyone else writing?"

Everyone else, I discovered, was writing literature. Funny how nobody could actually define it for me. There was a lot of woolly bollocks about themes and allegories. Oh, and none of their books had made it into Waterstones yet, although some of them had had some really encouraging rejections.

I was still trying to wrap my head around this last concept when Margaret announced it was time to break for a cuppa and some biccies. Not that she put it that way, obviously, but that was what "refreshments" turned out to mean. Morgan's tea, I noticed as he took hold of my arm, had a bit of a funny smell, as if he'd somehow managed to slosh some rum in on the sly. He certainly didn't offer any to the rest of us.

"I wonder if I might have a word?" Morgan murmured in my shell-like. Or, to be more accurate, seeing as he was so much taller and stooped with it, he murmured it into the top of my head.

"Course," I said, although I'd been hoping to nip out for a bit of snooping around. Not a lot of chance with old Morgan's iron grip on my sleeve.

He steered me to a corner, presumably so he could loom over me more effectively. Then he coughed. "I felt it would be better not to advertise your connection with Cherry. The other members of the group are . . . unaware of the circumstances of her departure from our circle."

"Right . . ." I wasn't sure what he was getting at. Or why, for that matter.

"I thought it best you weren't plagued with questions that would only serve to embarrass your sister. What's done is done, and I don't believe in giving a dog a bad name and hanging him. Or her, as it might be."

Had he just called my sis a dog? I frowned.

Morgan straightened his cuffs. Even in his own house, he was wearing the tweed jacket. I wondered if he had little tweed jim-jams he changed into for bed. "We've always kept to first-name terms within the group, and I feel that's a tradition that should continue."

"Fine by me, Morgan," I told him breezily.

His eyes got a bit of a pinched look, like he was wondering what the world was coming to when oiks like me called him by his first name. Maybe I'd try shortening it to Morgs next time. "Excellent. Well, I must move on."

"Yeah, don't let me keep you," I agreed. I stayed in the corner a minute, watching him. Both Margaret and Hannah seemed to want to speak to him, but he blew them off and headed back to Raz, who was apparently the golden boy right now. Margaret had to make do with Peter, and they bent their heads together, muttering occasional words to each other I didn't catch and wasn't sure I wanted to.

Hannah, for her sins, got me. "You been coming here long?" I asked as she stirred three sugars into an anaemic cup of tea. I thought she must be pretty new, judging from how scared she seemed to raise her voice. Although mind you, there was something about the dimly lit room we were in that seemed to muffle conversation. Sort of like a thick tweed blanket.

"A couple of years," she whispered. "I tried another circle first, but I couldn't get on with it. Too much banging."

"Er, what?" I had brief visions of highly educated orgies, everyone quoting Shakespeare as they shagged.

"It was the chairman. He was a little overenthusiastic with his gavel. It used to give me terrible headaches."

"Ah. Right. Well, you'll be fine here, love. Old Morgan doesn't believe in banging."

The pink tint to her cheeks came back in full force. "He's very good, isn't he? He's going to be the next Kazuo Ishiguro."

"Bless you. Kaz who?"

She giggled, then clapped a hand to her mouth and glanced around nervously. No one was looking at us, though, and she relaxed. "I'm so glad you've joined the Literati." Her voice lowered so far I had to strain to hear her. "It's been so flat here, since . . . You won't believe it, but sometimes I think we get just a little bit pretentious here."

"Never," I said with a wink, and she choked on her rich tea biscuit.

I didn't get a chance to ask to use Morgan's loo before he was coughing politely but firmly, signalling the break was over. Maybe he wanted to stop us eating all his biccies. Sod it. I knew I should have had a poke around at the start.

We had to sit through a few of Raz's poems after that. I've never been a big fan of poetry, not since they made us learn it at school, but I tried to keep an open mind. I soon realised he wasn't likely to win me over. None of his stuff even rhymed, and he was a bit too fond of the word *shards* for my liking. Still, give him his due, he was obviously pretty passionate about his subject. Only trouble was, by the time he sat down, I still wasn't sure what the subject actually was. Unless it was shards.

Margaret's voice cut into my thoughts like a viciously sharpened paper knife. Or, as might be, some shards. "Tom, perhaps you'd like to read us something now?"

My stomach hit the Axminster. "Er, sorry, didn't bring anything with me. Next time, maybe?" Shit. I hoped Phil wasn't going to want there to be a next time. Maybe I'd better pull my finger out with the investigating. "Actually, mind if I use the loo?"

Morgan shot me a look like I'd just crawled out of it. "Down the hall, to your left."

"Ta." I got up and legged it out of the room.

I realised as soon as I reached the hall I was in trouble. Bloody echoing floor tiles. Sod it. I clattered down the hall as quietly as I could, paused outside the loo, opened up my spidey-senses and *listened*.

Jesus. There was hidden stuff here, no question about it. The air was thick with it. It left a foul, bitter taste in my mouth. Trying to work out what sort of thing it was, I got the impression of some horrible greasy stew of concealment. It was nasty.

Except . . . I didn't get the feeling of anything serious. It was all petty stuff. Spiteful, not vicious. What Greg might have called a peccadillo—see, I know how to use a dictionary. (All right, I looked it up online.) And the tug from it was coming from upstairs, not down here.

Just as I was wondering if I could possibly get away with following the trail, Margaret's pointy nose poked out from behind the living room door. "Are you all right? You've been taking rather a long time."

"My mum always taught me to wash my hands thoroughly after I'd been," I said, hoping I didn't sound as rattled as I felt. That had been a close call. "Have I missed much?"

"We've finished."

Oh.

Bugger. Phil was going to kill me. I made a mental note not to climb any ladders in his vicinity for the foreseeable. And to stop eating toast for breakfast.

When I followed her back into the sitting room, sure enough, it was now a standing room. Everyone was gathering papers and coats—all except Hannah, who was being talked at by Peter and looking like she wished her clothes would hurry up and finish the job of making her fade into the background so she could escape.

Ah well, at least I could accomplish something while I was here. I headed over. "Great evening, wasn't it?" I said loudly over whatever Peter was ranting on about. "I really enjoyed it. Are we going to get treated to some of your stuff next time, Hannah?" I didn't bother mentioning I wasn't planning on turning up.

She'd already turned to me, and now she gave me a mousy smile. "Oh, I'm not sure about that. But perhaps you could read us something?"

"Yeah, maybe. So have you got far to go?"

Peter, who'd been lurking around like an angry customer trying to make a complaint, seemed to realise we weren't going to be letting him back into the conversation anytime soon, and stomped off with a final glare in my direction.

"No, I'm quite local really. Um, I hope you don't mind my asking, but I, well, I've got this dripping tap—it's not a big thing, really, so it's not urgent, but..."

I gave her one of my cards. "Here you go, love. You get any more drips bothering you"—I gave a sly nod in Peter's direction—"just give me a call."

She glanced at the card, which had *Paretski Plumbing* on it in a pretty nifty font, and her face froze. My card fluttered to Morgan Everton's Axminster carpet. "P-Paretski? Like Cherry?"

Oops. Or maybe not oops. "Yeah, she's my sister." I kept it light, but she still looked like the bottom had dropped out of her cosy little world. Her face had gone as grey as her cardi.

I picked up my card, seeing as she wasn't making any move to do so. She took it again and shoved it blindly into a shapeless handbag so vast I was pretty sure it'd never see the light of day again.

"Is she . . . I mean, she was ill, wasn't she? I mean, I heard she was." Hannah wasn't looking at me; her gaze went right over my left shoulder. Guilty conscience? Or was she just distracted?

"Yeah, but she's going to be fine. Morgan told you about it then? The party?"

"I— Yes. I mean . . . Yes." I followed her fixed stare, and found myself face-to-face with Morgan.

He looked bloody furious. What the hell was that all about?

"I've got to go," Hannah said and scurried out, her head down.

"Well, cheers for the evening," I said with a wave in Morgan's direction. "Maybe I'll see you next week." I clomped back down the hall and let myself out.

I was just about to get into my car when I looked up and saw a shape outlined in the security light. I blinked at it, startled. I hadn't heard anyone behind me either on the tiles or the gravel.

"You may think no one's on to you, but you're wrong," it said. Raz. It was his voice, although I couldn't make out his expression. He was entirely in shadow.

I swallowed. "Come again?"

"I'd suggest you don't," was all he said before turning and walking back to Morgan's house as silently as he'd come out.

Bloody hell.

"So basically," I concluded my sorry little tale of the evening's activities back at Phil's flat, "I found out bugger all."

Phil didn't look too obviously murderous. Mind, it was sometimes hard to tell with him. He had the mean, moody, and magnificent look down to a T. "I wouldn't say that. You found out Everton didn't want people asking you questions about your sister—that bit about not wanting to embarrass her was bollocks. And you found out this Hannah woman heard about Cherry being taken ill. So Morgan must have told her, which means *he* doesn't mind talking about your sister—he just doesn't want *you* doing it."

"Yeah, but why not? What's he afraid of?"

"Something she told you about him? Or something he thinks she told you? And then there's Hannah. From what you said, that was a bit of a funny reaction when she found out whose brother you were."

"Or maybe just when she realised Morgan could see her fraternizing with the enemy."

"Maybe." He was silent for a moment. I leaned back on the sofa and pondered the ceiling. It was white, like the walls. Bit too clinical for my tastes, but it takes all sorts. And Phil hadn't lived here long. For all I knew, he was planning to paint it rainbow colours as soon as he got a mo.

I wasn't holding my breath, mind.

Phil leaned back too and made a move with his legs that looked like he was about to put his feet up on the coffee table but remembered his manners in time. He crossed one ankle over his knee instead. "Reckon she was there Friday night?"

"What, at Cherry's party?" I frowned, thinking about it. "Don't think so, but I couldn't swear she wasn't. I mean, she's not that, well, memorable. And everyone and his bloody dog was at that party."

"Yeah, but the dog's stuffed, so we're not counting him. What about the rest of them?"

"I don't think Margaret was. Again, can't be certain—she might have been in the other room all the time we were there, mightn't she? It wasn't like I was taking a lot of notice of anyone after Cherry keeled over anyway. And Peter—I can barely remember what he looks like now, to be honest. Bit of a type—just your average thirtyish office worker. Tell you one thing, though, Raz wasn't there. At least, not in the same room as us at any time. That crowd was so bloody white you could use them to advertise washing powder."

"Yeah, it'd have to take a lot of nerve for the one nonwhite bloke at a party to try and kill someone. He'd have to bank on people noticing him more."

"So what do you reckon that tender little goodbye of his was all about?" It might just possibly have had something to do with me heading straight over to Phil's place after I'd left Redbourn, instead of going back to mine. Actually, it had been the first thing I'd asked Phil about, but him being him, he'd insisted on me going right back to the beginning before he'd condescend to offer an opinion on anything. Git.

That coffee table was looking well inviting. I thought, *Sod it*, and put my feet up. Hey, I took my boots off first. I wasn't born in a barn. Phil gave my only slightly holey socks a sidelong look, but all he said was, "Maybe he's just watched more porn than the rest of them? Got a bit upset about you taking the piss?"

"Yeah, but he seemed to take it seriously at the time. I mean, if he saw through me, why not out me to the rest of them right at the start?"

"You reckon he heard you giving Hannah your name?"

I tapped my fingers on my leg, thinking about it. "Maybe. Not sure. I mean, I didn't really notice where he was at the time. And other people were talking and stuff—it wasn't like everyone in the room would have been able to hear us. 'Specially the way Hannah talks, like she'd really rather nobody heard her."

"Hm. Think someone in the group's intimidating her?"

"I think the whole bloody world intimidates her. Anyway—Raz?"

"Maybe you fooled him to start with, but he'd had time to think about it by the end of the meeting and was pissed off because you made him feel like a twat?" Phil grinned. "Couldn't you at least have ripped off Charles Dickens or Jane Austen or someone, not some bloody bargain-basement porno?"

"Hey, you try thinking of a novel plot on the fly. It's sodding difficult. Anyway, they're all into that literary stuff, aren't they? They'd have recognised that sort of thing straight off."

Phil's feet joined mine on the table. Score one for being a bad influence. His socks had little embroidered polo players and didn't have any holes in at all. "You'd be surprised. I read somewhere there's only seven basic plots. How hard can it be? Money for old rope, that writing lark."

"Yeah. They've got to be a bit weird and all. Writers, I mean. Who spends all day sitting in a room on their tod making up stories? It's not like living in the real world." Which would be the one where I waltzed around pretending to be someone I wasn't so my boyfriend could find out who tried to kill my sister.

Phil nodded. "You got a busy day tomorrow?"

"Too bloody right. New bathroom in Sandridge, and an emergency kitchen sink in Marshalswick I was too soft to say I hadn't got time for."

"Better get an early night, then." One of his feet nudged mine. It tickled a bit, but luckily I'm too manly to giggle.

I gave Phil a look. "Are you trying to kick me out?"

He grinned. "Nope. I'm just trying to get your arse off my sofa and into my bed."

"Oh yeah? What's in it for me?"

"I'll tell you what's going to be *in it* in a minute." He grabbed me. I grabbed him back, and we had a brief tussle for the upper hand.

I lost.

Sometimes it's more fun that way.

CHAPTER FOURTEEN

Of course, sod's law, having moaned on to Phil about how busy I was going to be next morning, I had not one but two jobs cancel on me. I'd barely had time to get back to mine from Phil's and feed the cats before the phone started ringing. First up was the emergency sink, cancelled because Mrs. C. got an unexpected lunch invitation. Emergency, my arse.

I put a black *X* in the address book next to Mrs. C.'s name, but I let Mrs. V. in Sandridge off when she rang ten minutes later. I reckoned she probably hadn't meant to go into labour three weeks early, although God knew when she'd be up for having her new bathroom fitted now. Sometime around when the new twins started school, probably.

What with all this free time, I was about to toss a coin between cleaning the van and sorting out the cardboard box I hand over to my accountant when it's time to do the tax return. Luckily, Greg rang.

"Ah, Tom. You're well?"

I held the phone a little farther away from my ear. "Yeah, fine, ta. Nothing wrong with Cherry, is there?"

"No, no. She's well on the way to recovery, thank the Lord. She's come out of hospital now and gone to recuperate with Barbara and Gerald."

"She's at Mum and Dad's? She never said." Not that I was narked about getting my family news second hand or anything.

"I'm sure she'll be ringing you soon. In the meantime, I wondered if I might tempt you with a tour of the cathedral roof?"

And how the hell did he know my schedule had suddenly freed up? I sent a brief, suspicious glance skywards. Well, ceiling-wards, seeing as I was still in the house. All I saw was the light fitting and a couple of dusty cobwebs. Not a whisper of a divine confession of meddling in my private life.

"Yeah, all right." Poor bastard could probably do with the company. "Um, you didn't mean to invite Phil, did you? Seeing as he's got this claustrophobia thing."

"No, no. Just the two of us, I thought. A good opportunity to get to know one another better, in view of our impending connection." He made it sound like he was planning on slotting us together with a bell and spigot joint. "When would suit you? This morning?"

"Yeah, okay. I can be there in about an hour, if you like."

"Perfect."

I was getting pretty used to the drive over to St. Leonards, I reflected as I tootled along the A41, the fields to either side cold and brown, and bare trees looming like frosted veggie skeletons. I turned the Fiesta's heater up a notch—it was being a bit slow to warm up this morning.

Although now I came to think of it, this was the first time I'd actually driven over to see Greg myself. I frowned a bit at that thought, but it wasn't like Phil *insisted* on driving whenever we went out. He just sort of ended up doing it most of the time.

Maybe I should tell him we were taking my car next time we went somewhere? But then Phil would just moan about the Fiesta having no leg room, like it was my fault he was so bloody tall. And he'd mock the furry dice. Which, fair enough, they were supposed to be ironic, but still. I had half a mind to see if they still made those car sun strips with names on, and get one done that said *Tom* on the driver's side and *Phil* on the other, and then he'd really have something to complain about. But even in these so-called enlightened times, you could probably count the days on the fingers of one hand before someone chucked a brick through it, so it didn't seem worth the hassle just to make a point.

Cathedral Close, when I got to St. Leonards, was emptier than a Sally Army collection box at a Pride festival, and the cobbles were slippery with frost. Getting out of the Fiesta's warm cocoon and into the freezing-cold air of a Hertfordshire winter morning was a bit of a shock to the system. I could feel my hip seizing up with every cautious step I took over to the Old Deanery's front door.

Either Greg had been looking out for me or the bloke upstairs had tipped him a nod again, as the door was flung open before I could even knock. Greg stood there, beaming. He'd left off the *Doctor Who* accessories today and was looking like an advert for Clergy Casuals in his tailored wool trousers, dark-grey dog-collar shirt and matching sweater. It looked suspiciously soft, like he'd been shopping for cashmere with Phil. Maybe Cherry had bought it for him, like an engagement pressie or something—I might be wrong, but I'd always thought church salaries weren't exactly at the luxury end of the market.

He advanced on me, both hands outstretched. "Tom! Marvellous to see you."

I managed to hold my ground, even when he grabbed me by the shoulders. "Er, right. You too. Am I coming in, or are we going straight over?" I'd actually been thinking longingly of a cup of something warm on the way over, but now I'd got here, the thought of getting any cosier with the Touchy-Feely Reverend Greg was putting me right off my coffee.

"If you're ready, I thought we'd commence with the cathedral. One moment." He gazed at his shiny black shoes briefly, then turned to me with manic eyebrows. "Onwards and upwards!"

"'Faster, Higher, Stronger,' and all that?" I was quite proud of myself for remembering the Olympic motto.

Greg twinkled. "I've always been rather partial to 'You'll Never Walk Alone.'"

I might have known he'd be a Liverpool fan. I opened my mouth to tell him Man U were going to have their arses in the FA Cup this year, only probably not in so many words, him being a man of God and all that, but he beat me to it.

"And how is your dear Philip?"

I'd never described him as *my dear* in my life. "He's good."

"Excellent. And his family?"

"Dunno. Haven't met them." Well, not since school, and then not to talk to or anything. I just had a vague memory of a couple of

Phil-shaped lads who must have been his brothers, and wasn't there a sister too? "His dad died a few years ago, I know that."

"He hasn't taken you to meet them?" The eyebrows drew together in concern.

"Yeah, well, I was going to see them at Christmas, but you know how it is. Busy and all that." I tensed, waiting for the bloke upstairs to do a bit of smiting for bearing false witness to a man of the cloth. "We'll sort something out soon," I added a bit more truthfully.

"I do hope it'll go well," Greg said as we reached the cathedral door. "I find it fascinating, the differences in background between us all, but these things can be a little hard to overcome. Still, we're all equal in the eyes of the Lord, as you know."

I was pretty sure we weren't equally baffled by what he'd just said. At least, I hoped he at least knew what he was talking about. "I s'pose you do a lot of sermons in your line of work," I said, struck by the image of Greg in the pulpit, rambling on to a cathedral full of bemused God-botherers.

"Oh, absolutely. Preaching is one of the things we are called to do. Although one tries not to proselytise, of course. It's rather out of fashion these days."

I'd take his word on that one. "Yeah, last thing you want is the Church of England being accused of being out of touch."

Greg guffawed. I tried not to cringe as the sound boomed out and echoed around the huge, empty space. Seriously, didn't he know we were in a church? I shot an embarrassed glance at the donations lady, still sitting at her desk, but with a different hat on today. She just dimpled fondly and shrugged in a *what can you do* sort of way.

"Now, to the stairs." Greg led me over to an arched doorway, just past the stack of tea lights waiting to be lit by the faithful to carry their prayers up to heaven on a waft of greasy smoke. He had to duck his head to go through. I didn't. I immediately wished I hadn't just wrecked my night vision by looking at the candles—it was blacker than a septic tank in that narrow spiral staircase. It wasn't too bad going up, but I wasn't looking forward to coming down again. My hip twinged in agreement.

Several hundred steps later (all right, I wasn't counting, but that was what it felt like) there was finally a glimmer of light, and Greg's reverend bum gave way to a bit of open space in my field of vision. "And here we are," he said, although I'd sort of guessed that.

The cathedral roof was . . . surprisingly like any old attic anywhere, although there was a fair bit more headroom. It had the same dry, dusty smell, and was filled with centuries' worth of dead flies and old bits of junk. The roof itself was way up above us, fifteen feet or more, and this attic space stretched out in front of me for around twice that. If Phil could manage to survive the staircase, he'd be fine when he got up here, claustrophobia and all. I raised an eyebrow at one of the beams, which was basically a massive curved tree branch they'd built around, rather than cut into shape. The staircase, I saw when I turned round, had come up right by a big, circular window, taller than me.

"That's the Rose Window," Greg pointed out helpfully.

It wasn't rose-coloured, or flowery, or anything. Just round. "They've got one of those in York Minster, haven't they?" I vaguely remembered a trip there with my parents when I was a kid. I'd been into photography at the time and had taken endless fuzzy, overexposed shots of brightly coloured stained glass windows with light shining through them.

"I'm afraid ours is altogether more modest. But it does have its own charm. Look closely at the panes."

I peered at them. They were all six inches across at most, separated by enough lead to have a scrap merchant praising God. "Hang on, is that graffiti?" There were names scratched onto them, in varying wobbly handwriting. "'Edmund Wallis, Verger, 1918,'" I read out. "'Charles Glover, Canon, 1936.' Were they allowed to do this?" I imagined generations of clergy sneaking up into the roof to rebel, maybe having a crafty smoke while they were up here—or maybe not, seeing as setting a Cathedral alight with a carelessly dropped match would probably get you sent straight to hell with no time off for good behaviour.

"Oh, it's all above board. I've left my own mark here too—look." I tried not to cringe as he loomed over me from behind. An orangutan-like hand and arm (minus the orange fuzz) appeared in my field of vision and pointed up to a pane on the top right. I squinted and could make out *Gregory Titmus, Canon* in noticeably firmer engraving than the average.

I wondered what'd happen if I waited until Greg's back was turned and scratched out *Tom Paretski, Plumber*, and added my mobile number. Probably a bolt of lightning from Him On High. If you believed in such things, of course.

"And over here," Greg was saying, his voice suddenly far away, "we have the treadwheel. It's rather unique."

I turned. Greg was stepping into a man-sized, wooden hamster wheel at the other end of the roof. How the bloody hell had he managed to get all the way over there without me hearing him? Boards creaked under my feet as I went to join him—not in the wheel, it was only big enough for one and anyway, not really my thing. I've never understood why hamsters seem to think it's so much fun, running around and getting nowhere. "Uh, what's this for?"

Greg smiled in that weirdly demonic, slightly crazed way of his. "Oh, nothing Wildean, don't worry."

Uh?

"It was built for raising building supplies," he carried on, starting to walk. Ancient timbers didn't so much groan as purr. "Ah. You might want to avoid stepping too far to your right."

I twisted to look. He wasn't wrong. There was a circular section of the floor, maybe four feet across, that had lifted a few inches and was now swinging slowly from side to side, attached by chains to a pulley in the roof. It looked a bit like one of the pans on a set of old-fashioned jeweller's scales, only on a much bigger, hah, scale. It was still rising. When it was a couple of feet higher, I could see the underside was plastered and painted, with one of the gold ceiling bosses I'd noticed from downstairs.

I could see right down into the cathedral. The black and white floor tiles God knew how many feet below looked like a chessboard, with people as the pieces moving on them, apparently unaware that anything was happening up above their heads. Even if they looked up, would they be able to tell from this distance that a bit of ceiling had moved?

"Is this safe?" I asked, crouching down to peer through the hole. I could lob something down right on someone's head. If I was that sort of bloke, obviously. I wondered if I had any odd bits of paper in my pockets.

"Oh, don't worry. We never allow anyone up here unaccompanied."

"Good idea," I said, still hypnotised by the view. The chairs looked tiny from up here, and so did the font, like you'd never fit a real baby in it. "Just imagine a bunch of schoolkids up here. You'd have 'em crowding round the hole, pushing and shoving and— *Jesus fucking Christ*!"

I don't know what had made me look round—maybe my subconscious had noticed the wheel wasn't turning anymore?—but when I turned my head, he was right there. In my face. With one hand outstretched and the eyebrows doing their Satanic worst. I reared back in shock and lost my balance. I teetered queasily on my toes, my arms flailing. Oh God. I was going to end up one big, messy splat on the cathedral floor.

If you die in a cathedral, do you go straight to heaven? Or is it the other place, for disturbing God's peace?

Then the Hand of God grabbed me roughly by the shoulder and pulled me back to safety. I sprawled on my arse on the wooden floorboards, my pulse hammering and visions of headlines like *Plumber in Death Plummet* dancing through my head. "Jesus... What the bloody hell?" Glancing warily at Greg, I scuttled, crablike, back to a safe distance, making sure the ecclesiastical death trap was between me and him.

Greg's eyes were wide, and he was breathing almost as fast as I was. I was glad to see he wasn't totally calm about almost having fucking *killed* me. "I do apologise for startling you," he said, his voice a bit shaky. Good. "I was about to suggest you move back a bit from the aperture."

Either that or shove me through. "Right. Well. Think I'd like to get my feet back on solid ground, if it's all the same to you." I levered myself up on said feet and told my knees to stop shaking. They weren't listening. I narrowed my eyes as I looked at Greg. "You can go first." Spiral staircases could be perilous bastards, and I wasn't taking any more chances.

Apparently he could read my mind. "I assure you, I approached you with no malicious intent." He took a step towards me, and I took one back before remembering that was a pretty risky manoeuvre up here. Greg folded his hands in front of him and looked at me sorrowfully, in a "You have made little baby Jesus cry" sort of way. I recognised that look from my old Sunday School teachers. "Tom, be reasonable. What possible grounds could I have for wishing you harm? After all, we're soon to be family."

Maybe. If I—or Cherry for that matter—lived that long.

Then again, hadn't Dave Southgate told me most people were murdered by their nearest and dearest?

I've never been so glad in my life to see the bottom of a bloody staircase. I stepped out, blinking, into the flickering light of the cathedral and wondered if I should be thanking God for a lucky escape or making an official complaint about His staff. My hip was hurting like a bastard.

"Did you enjoy the tour?" Donations Lady asked with a smile that faltered when she got a good look at my face.

I flinched as the Dangerously Reverend Greg clapped a hand on my shoulder and answered for me. "I'm afraid Tom discovered a hitherto unsuspected dislike of heights."

"Heights are fine," I said shortly. "It's just the hundred-foot drops I'm not so bl—not so keen on. Here you go, love." I handed over a crumpled fiver. Not that she'd asked or anything, but I just felt like it. "Right. Better get going."

"You'll come over to the Old Deanery for a coffee first, of course?" Greg said, his big hands scuttling over one another like baby gorillas having a play fight.

Over my dead body, I thought but didn't say, seeing there was a worrying chance he might have taken me literally. "Er, thanks, but I'd better be off. Work," I added vaguely. He couldn't argue with that one. Well, I might not have any jobs booked in, but there was always stuff I could be doing. Sorting out paperwork. Cleaning out the van. Putting an ad in the Yellow Pages—not because anyone ever reads it these days, but just for nostalgia value. Changing the cats' litter. Okay, maybe not *technically* part of my job, but you try telling the cats that.

I stalked off back to the car and maybe slammed the door a bit harder than I needed to.

CHAPTER FIFTEEN

Of course, halfway home, with some idiot babbling away on the radio about how Rooney hadn't been playing half so well since the latest cosmetic touch-up, I started to feel a bit daft. Not to mention embarrassed. Cherry was going to kill me—although not literally, I hoped—when she found out I'd all but accused her bit of reverend rough of trying to off me in a house of God.

And seriously, what had he actually done? Given me a bit of a fright and then saved me from splatting myself on the cathedral floor. If he'd wanted me dead, why bother grabbing me back from the brink?

Course, it was probably easier offing someone if they weren't staring at you in abject horror. Maybe he just couldn't do it, when push—*hah*—came to shove.

But I kept coming up against the question: *why?* What on earth had I ever done to the dubiously reverend Greg? I could just about see him trying to off Cherry in a crime of passion—although it was a stretch: *passion* wasn't exactly the word that came to mind when I thought of her. Then again, that was probably just as well, her being my sister and all. But me? It just didn't make sense.

I wasn't sure whether to tell Phil about it or not. I felt a bit of a prat, to be honest. Either Phil was going to think I was being a total drama queen, or he'd go totally the other way and get in a huff with me for going up in the bloody roof with a possible murderer in the first place. Nah, it was better to play this one down. Keep mum about it for now, then laugh it off the next time we were all together.

Then again, I thought as I reached the outskirts of St. Albans, seeing as I didn't have a right lot else to do today, I might as well pop in and see if Phil had worked out who was trying to do my sister in yet. I was *not* just running off to see my bloke because I'd had a bit of a scare. This was practical stuff, all right? He might have had something he wanted me to check out. Or something. And anyway, this time of day, he'd be in his office, if he wasn't out investigating, and it was on my way home.

I swung the Fiesta down Hatfield Road. Parking's a bastard in town—all vouchers and permits and traffic wardens who'll have your nads if you stay one second over time—but the big advantage of Phil's little shoebox is it's got a tiny car park out back of the building, with two designated spaces for Alban Investigations Ltd. Not, to be honest, that I couldn't have parked at my house and walked here—Hatfield Road runs right through Fleetville, and Phil's office was halfway back up towards St. Albans centre, up above a gang of ambulance chasers. Well, lawyers who specialised in compensation claims. I wasn't sure if they actually did any ambulance chasing. Probably couldn't afford to, what with the price of petrol these days.

I parked next to Phil's VW Golf, my little Fiesta looking a bit dingy next to its gleaming silver perfection. Still, at least my car's got character. I rang the bell, and Phil buzzed me straight up to his office. It was at the top of a steep flight of stairs carpeted in dusty pink— that was the colour, I mean, not that Phil had been a bit lax with the hoovering lately. He probably had a cleaning service to do that anyway.

Phil looked up from his desk when I walked in. It was wood, like Cherry's mahogany monstrosity, but a lot more modern looking. Also smaller, but he probably wouldn't appreciate me saying so. He had it in the big bay window at the front, which had to be deliberate. It meant the client or whoever got all the light right in their face, and Phil was just a sort of looming shadow. "Thought you were busy today?"

"So did I. Bloody customers." I flopped down into one of the client chairs and set it swivelling lazily.

Phil rolled his eyes and looked back at his computer screen. "Most people get playing with the chairs out of their system in their first year of work."

"Never worked in an office, have I? Does it get on your tits when your clients do it? I mean, all that nervous energy's got to go somewhere."

He smirked. "Why do you think I bought them?"

"What, so you're sizing up your clients by the way they swivel?" I grinned. "Sounds a bit kinky."

"Yeah, you got me. Modern investigations, it's all about the orgies in the office. So what, you come to drag me out to lunch? Bit early, innit?"

I looked at my watch. It wasn't *that* early. "Maybe. Nah, just came to see how you were getting on with things. You know. Found any skeletons in Literati closets?"

Phil leaned back in his chair and looked at me. "One or two. Hannah Mudge had a breakdown a year or so ago. Peter Grissom took voluntary redundancy from his last job and hasn't worked since. And the word is, it wasn't half as voluntary as he likes to make out. Haven't got anything on the others yet, but I'm working on it."

"And Raz? Seeing as he's the one who actually threatened me?"

"Told you. Working on it."

I swivelled a bit more. "Hey, how come you know all their surnames? I only know Morgan Everton and Margaret Pierce. Knew. Whatever."

"Trade secret."

"What, worried I'm going to set up in competition? Actually, yeah, Paretski Investigations, that's got a bit of a ring to it. Way more interesting than Alban Investigations."

"Maybe, but it's wasted if no one ever sees it. Most people, when they're looking for a tradesman, company, whatever, don't bother to look down past the first few listings. Why do you think there's all these businesses called A1 This and Aardvark bloody That?"

"Oi. Paretski Plumbing does all right."

"Yeah, but that's word of mouth. You'd be amazed how many of my clients *don't* go around telling all their mates they hired me to stalk their cheating wife stroke husband stroke significant other."

"That's a lot of stroking going on there. I can see why you went into this job."

Phil held up a finger. "See this? Why don't you swivel on that for a change?"

"Tempting, but what if a client comes in? So how did you find out those surnames, anyway?"

"I asked Everton."

"Hang on a mo, I thought the idea was to not let them know you're looking into them?"

"Well, when I say *I* asked, I actually meant Paul Morton, reporter for the *Herts Herald*, asked. He's doing a feature on up-and-coming authors in the county."

"Is he now? Let me guess, he did the interview by phone?"

"Well, one wouldn't want to waste Mr. Everton's valuable time, would one?" Phil's accent did such a rapid social climb during that sentence I was surprised his ears didn't pop.

"Indeed one would not." Shame I hadn't got a cup of tea—I could have stuck my little finger out with the best of them. "So where are we getting this lunch we're doing, then?"

"Who's buying?"

"Don't you usually charge it to the client?"

Phil smirked. "That'd be you in this case."

"Nah, we could talk about Greg a bit and then you could charge it to him."

"And you'd be happy to freeload off your sister's fiancé?"

"Too right. He owes me after this morning." Oops. Hadn't meant to bring that up.

Phil leaned forward, his eyes narrowed. I swear his bloody nostrils were flared as well. "What happened this morning?"

Shit. "I went to see him, all right? I mean, he invited me. To go see that bloody cathedral roof."

"And?"

"And nothing. I just had a bit of a dodgy turn, that's all."

"Right. Because you're well-known for your fainting fits. So how come you reckon he owes you?"

"God, you're like a bloody terrier, aren't you?"

Phil smiled. "No. You're the terrier. I'm a rottweiler. Stop trying to change the subject."

"There's no subject. Seriously. I just got a bit of vertigo, that's all." I stood up. "Are we having lunch? Some of us have got work to do this afternoon."

"Right. Better go somewhere local, then. Want to give the Cock a go? And no, that isn't a come-on."

"Shame. All right, then."

The Cock and Hens (or, as Gary likes to call it, the Cock and Bollocks) is a small pub on the edges of Fleetville not noted for being particularly gay friendly, but I reckoned we'd be safe going in for a bit of pub grub at lunchtime. Let's face it, if you were feeling a bit bored and looking for a couple of queers to bash, you wouldn't pick on the six foot one of solid muscle and surliness that's the face my so-called better half presents to the world. Not without calling up half a dozen of your mates, and with a bit of luck, they'd all be off shoplifting from Lidl or signing on for benefits before toddling off for a bit of housebreaking, this time of day.

At any rate, we managed to walk in without the whole place falling silent like that scene in *American Werewolf.* And trust me, I've been in pubs where that's really happened. Here, it was pretty quiet already, just a few old blokes—no women—nursing lonely pints, and nobody even glanced up at our entrance.

I decided I probably wasn't going to make this my new local.

"What do you fancy?" Phil asked.

I left that innuendo well alone and took a glance at the specials board. It didn't look all that special to me. "Dunno. Fish and chips? Not a lot they can do to that, is there?" I added in a lower voice.

"You'd be surprised," Phil muttered back. But he ordered it for both of us, plus a couple of pints.

The bloke behind the bar took his money without a smile, and we went and sat at a table by the window, not that you could see out or anything. It was that sort of bottle glass you get in basement skylights.

"So, you come here often?" I asked, still keeping my voice down.

Phil grunted, possibly in amusement. "Never been in before. Christ, this place is depressing."

He wasn't wrong. The main theme in the decor seemed to be dark, drab colours that wouldn't show it if someone spilled their pint—or a bit of blood—on them. The brightest thing in the place was the worn patches on the faded velour seats where an off-white lining was showing through.

"On the bright side, you're going to be pretty keen to get back to your work." I grinned. "You take me to all the best places."

"You spend half your working life with your head stuck down a drain. Don't tell me you're getting all high maintenance now."

"Nah, I'm strictly low rent, me." My stomach rumbling, I glanced hopefully up at the bar, even though it was way too early for the food to be on its way. I frowned at what I saw. "Not acting too gay, am I?"

"You what?"

"There's a bloke who's just come in. He's over by the bar. Staring at us."

Phil tensed but didn't look round. "Describe him."

"Big—as in, muscles, not fat—probably about your height, sort of dark-blond hair shaved short at the back and sides, bit scruffy, *Daily Mail* under one arm. Sort who'd probably leap at the chance to glass a couple of poofters." Phil turned to look. And oh shit, I'd just realised why the bloke had looked familiar.

Bar-bloke lumbered over. "All right, Phil? Didn't know you drank here. Who's this, then?"

"Jase, this is Tom. Tom, Jase. My brother." I stood up to offer him a hand. He shook it, but only for a moment and not before giving it a wary glance, as if he was wondering what I'd been doing with it and if I'd washed it since.

I was tempted to give his hand a little extra squeeze just to mess with his head, but I was worried he might retaliate by messing with mine all too literally.

"You're the new one, are you?"

I didn't ask, *New what?* I had a fair idea I wouldn't like the way he worded the answer. "Tom Paretski. Plumber," I added out of habit, not because I was really expecting him to put any work my way.

He nodded. "Jason Morrison. Deliveries. Pay's crap, but the work's a piece of piss."

I nodded back. We sat down, Jase pulling up a stool to our table. Wasn't this cosy?

Phil stirred himself to ask a question. "You eating?"

"Yeah." Jase leaned back in his chair, his legs spread wide. He'd worn a hole in the crotch of his jeans and a flash of bright-red underwear was showing through. I looked away quick before he could catch me staring at his meat and two veg. "Hot food's crap here, but the baguettes are all right. What you having?"

"Fish and chips," I confessed.

Jase laughed. "Don't worry, it won't kill you. Probably."

Funny how your appetite can just disappear. Jase yawned and unfolded his paper to the sports pages. Nice of him to come over so he could ignore us from close quarters. I glanced at Phil, but he was staring stonily into the middle distance. Not a lot of brotherly love flying around right now, I guessed.

I stifled a sigh. "Bloody outrageous what they paid for Rooney, innit?" I piped up, referring to one of the articles on the *Mail*'s back page.

Jase lowered the paper. "You what? All right, maybe his form's been off this season, but it ain't his fault. Should shoot the bloody manager, if you ask me. See, that last match against Chelsea, he switched from a 4-3-3 to a bloody 4-2-3-1, the wanker . . ." And he was off. We spent the rest of our lunchtime discussing the finer points of the Premiership, Jase and I did, while Phil munched on his fish and chips and threw in the occasional grunt.

The fish and chips was fine, by the way. Jase didn't know what he was talking about. Fish or football.

At the end of the meal, Jase downed the rest of his pint, scratched his balls, and stood up. "He's all right, this one," he said over my head to Phil. "You should've brung him round for Christmas. Better than that posh tosser." He slouched away, secure in his place in the world.

"You all right?" I asked when Jase had finally buggered off. "That was out of order, what he said about your Mark."

Phil shrugged, but the tense lines were easing from around his eyes. "That's family for you. Didn't know he came in this pub. Might have known you'd get along okay with him," he added, looking away.

It didn't sound like a compliment. "Got to be able to get along with anyone, my line of work. He's a bit . . ." Exactly like I remembered Phil being, back when we'd been at school together. Except somehow Phil had got out of the council estate, got an education, and upgraded his accent, and developed a very expensive taste in sweaters. Oh, and ditched the Neanderthal attitudes.

"Yeah, he is," Phil agreed, despite the fact I hadn't finished the sentence. "You ready?"

"Depends what for." I flashed him a smile.

Phil's gaze turned dark. "That."

"Right." I swallowed. "Mine?"

He nodded.

We barely made it inside my front door before he was on me, shoving up my shirt and tearing at my jeans. "Need to fuck you," he grunted, one hand pinching a nipple and the other groping my arse while his rock-hard dick tried to bore a hole in my stomach.

"God, yeah." I'd have been happy with anything, so long as he did it with this intensity of focus. He kissed me, openmouthed, all teeth and tongue.

"Upstairs. Stuff," I managed. Phil gave my arse a vicious squeeze—not that I was complaining—and let me drag him up to the bedroom. Merlin passed us on the way, took one look, and then bombed down the stairs like someone had lit a firework under his bum.

My jeans were hanging at half-mast, and I nearly tripped over the bloody things before we got to the bedroom and I could finally kick them, and my underwear, all the way off. I tried to get my shirt off too but was still fumbling with buttons when Phil tackled me to the bed. "Christ, you want to warn a bloke?" I gasped when I'd got my breath back.

"Shut up," he growled and kissed me again, his stubble rasping against my skin, making it tingle. He tasted of salt and beer and the lemon he'd squeezed on his fish. I pulled his hips down against me, and he groaned into my mouth, then pushed up away from me on shaking arms.

His face . . . God, his face. His eyes looked more black than blue, and he had the sort of expression you see on blokes just before they swing for you, although in Phil's case I was pretty certain he had sex on his mind, not violence.

Fuck, that was a turn-on. "Get your clothes off," I said, my voice sounding like I'd been gargling with gravel.

He stared at me for a moment, like it was taking a while to work out what the words meant, then he pulled his posh sweater and shirt over his head together and flung them on the floor. I reached out to help him with his trousers, but he batted my hand away and ripped them off himself.

Okay, now I was feeling overdressed. I undid the rest of the buttons on my shirt and struggled up onto my elbows to shrug it off, but he pushed me back down to the bed with a shove from one of his great big mitts in the middle of my chest.

"Oi, I'm trying to get naked here."

"Leave it on. I like it."

He did? I'd gone back to the plaid this morning, having run out of other options. Maybe Phil had a pocket lumberjack fetish. "Suit yourself. So are you going to fuck me, or wait until I die of old age?"

"Wanker. Get your legs in the air."

I pulled them up obligingly, my hands behind my knees. Phil stared down at me so long I started to get self-conscious. "What? Going to tell me I need to get my arse bleached or something?"

"You're fucking gorgeous, and you know it." Strong fingers wrapped around my dick and pumped a few times, sending electric currents through my balls and making my eyes roll back in my head.

Then he stopped, the bastard. I opened my eyes again, but seeing he was putting a condom on his prick, I decided not to complain after all. Clearly there was nothing wrong with his priorities. He'd got the lube out too while I wasn't looking, and he put that to good use, then shoved two slick fingers up my bum.

"Impatient bastard," I gasped, squirming at the rapid stretch. I could take it, though.

"Too fucking right." He crooked his fingers and smirked at the involuntary noise I made. "Going to fuck you so fucking hard."

Any more of this and he was going to be beating his chest and making ape noises. My dick twitched at the thought. "I know your sort," I panted as he pumped his fingers in and out of me. "All mouth and no bloody trousers."

"I'll show you fucking trousers." He pulled out his fingers with a *pop*, lined up his dick, and plunged it inside me.

Jesus. Christ, I felt that. I was glad he stilled for a bit once he was balls-deep in me. What with the rapid prep and all, he felt fucking massive inside me. For a couple of minutes, there was nothing but our breathing, harsh and ragged, then he drew in a deep breath and looked me in the eye. "Shit. You okay?"

"I'm not made of bloody china. Fuck me already."

"Fucking tosser." He shifted up so he was firmly on his knees, then he grabbed hold of my hips with both hands. "You asked for it," he warned, before pulling out and slamming straight back in, his balls slapping against my arse and his dick hitting my gland like a ten-ton truck.

"*Jesus.*" I couldn't find the breath to tell him to do that again, but that was all right because he did it anyway, over and over. I grabbed on to the headboard to stop my head going right through it as jolts of sensation shot up my spine.

When he let go of my arse and wrapped a hand around my dick, I nearly lost it there and then. Never thought I'd be so grateful for thoughts of Morgan Everton dropping into my head while I was in the middle of a shag, but I was desperate to hold off a bit longer. Phil had to be close now, the way he was going, sweat dripping off his forehead and splashing on my belly to mingle with the pre-come I'd left there myself.

"Gonna come," Phil grunted, sending a shiver right through me. I grabbed hold of the hand he had on my dick and tugged it along faster, harder. God, I loved this. Loved him.

Then he got the angle just fucking perfect, and with his last, desperate thrust, I was over the edge and falling.

I knew Phil would catch me.

We lay in bed for a long time afterwards, not talking, just holding each other. It got a bit hot, to be honest, under the duvet with fifteen stone of muscle wrapped around me like an overprotective teddy bear. Not that I was in any hurry to cool down.

"Know what I like about you?" Phil rumbled in my ear.

"Based on recent experience, I'd say my arse comes pretty high on the list."

He chuckled. "You don't judge. And you get on with people. Ever meet anyone you couldn't charm?"

"Plenty. I just murder them and hide the bodies."

"Yeah, you'd know all the good hiding places, wouldn't you? What did you think of Jase? *Really* think."

"I think I like his brother better."

"Don't dodge."

"Well . . . Are you going to get offended on his behalf?"

"Just answer the question. No."

"I think he's just pretty happy thinking like he's always thought, doing what he's always done, and he doesn't see the point of making any effort to change or see anyone else's point of view." I shrugged, which isn't easy when you're on your back in bed with the world's biggest limpet. "Some people are just like that. Doesn't make him a bad person."

"Yeah, it does."

"Well, maybe, but we're not talking on the scale of mass murderers or traffic wardens."

Phil breathed a laugh into my neck. "They're all like that. Mum too. Mark hated them. They weren't too keen on him, either."

It was getting a bit too hot and sweaty to stay under the covers, so I shouldered out of Phil's arms. "Going to take a quick shower."

When I came out of the bathroom, Phil was already dressed. "I'm going to head off. Need to get some work done, seeing as this afternoon was a write-off." He paused. "You all right?"

"Fine. Why wouldn't I be?"

He looked like he was about to say something, but then he just nodded and buggered off.

I mooched downstairs and threw myself onto the sofa. Arthur hissed at me as his cushion bounced in sympathy.

So the Mysterious Mark had been a posh tosser. And hadn't got on with Phil's family.

I guessed I really was the bit of rough.

CHAPTER SIXTEEN

I rang Dave Southgate that evening, after I'd rustled up a quick plate of pasta and fought off the cats when they tried to nick the tuna I was having with it. "Fancy a pint?"

"What, so you can pump me for information on your sister's case?"

There was an obvious answer to that one, but if I tried it on Dave, he'd run a mile. And fair dues, the thought of any innuendo involving Dave and "pumping" was putting me right off my beer anyhow. "Can't I just want a drink with a mate? So are you coming, then? Or has the missus got you on a tight rein these days?" All right, that was a dirty dig. Got results, though.

"Fine. I'll see you at the White Hart at eight. Or thereabouts."

I got there early, but Dave was there before me, staring moodily at the football on the telly and picking at a bowl of chips. After I'd got myself a pint and one for him, I slid onto the bench beside him and nabbed a chip.

"Bugger off and get your own, Paretski."

"Nah, I already ate." I swiped another, then felt guilty when he pushed the whole bowl in my direction. "You all right?"

"Yeah, fine." Dave gave a heavy sigh. "I'm not supposed to be eating this stuff anyway. Or drinking, for that matter."

"You what?" My chest prickled uneasily. "You had a health scare?"

"Nah, it's the wife. Says I've got overweight sperm or something. Little bastards are too fat to swim. That's her theory, anyway."

"Still no luck with getting her up the duff?"

"No, and I'll tell you something straight, you might think it's a bloody dream come true to have her wanting sex all the time, but it takes all the fun out of it. And that's even before she starts criticising the little wrigglers."

"Tell her to stand on her head after sex and let gravity do the work for them."

"Not the point, is it? She's convinced if I don't lose a bit of weight before we conceive, our kid's going to be the sad fat bastard who never gets picked for games." Dave stared gloomily at his pint. I wondered if he'd been a sad fat bastard when he was at school. He was definitely a bit on the podgy and pessimistic side these days.

"But she's still demanding sex at all hours?" Judging by the dark circles under Dave's eyes, that wasn't an exaggeration.

"Yeah, says we've got to take all the chances we can, at our age. Women, eh?" Dave took a long swig of his pint. "Times like this I start wondering if your lot have got the right idea."

"We'll have you marching in the Pride parade yet," I said, toasting him with my pint.

We talked about football for a bit, as you do, and I polished off Dave's chips. I could always have a salad tomorrow or something. I was just wondering how I could turn the conversation round to my sister without being about as unsubtle as Dave's wife with her hormones in a tizzy, when he saved me the trouble by bringing her up himself. Cherry, I mean, not his wife and her hormones. Again.

"How's your sister doing?"

"She's good. Out of hospital and staying with Mum and Dad, so if she's got any sense, she'll be back on her feet in no time. Reckon you're any nearer catching the bastard who poisoned her?"

"In a word: chance'd be a fine thing. The Church of England's worse than the bloody freemasons for closing ranks under pressure."

"So you've been working the Greg angle?" That prickle in my chest was back. Maybe it was just indigestion from eating too many of Dave's chips.

"We've been working all of 'em." He shrugged at my sharp look. "Some bright spark came up with a jealousy theory—after all, up-and-coming young canon, he's got to be a bit of a catch in clergy terms, right? So we started checking out if he had any ex-girlfriends. Turns out—at least as far as we can find out—your reverend chum had less action than the pope before your sister came along." Dave took another long swig of his pint. "You sure he's not one of your lot?"

"Pretty sure. I could ask my mate Gary, if you like. He always knows."

"He bloody would."

"What about clients? Cherry's, I mean." I thought I might as well save Phil the bother of looking into it if Dave had already been there, done that.

"She says not."

"What, none who'd want to murder her, or none of them at the party?"

"Both. Come on, Tom, she's not daft. She'd have noticed any old clients with a grudge turning up at her private do."

"S'pose. Although that Slivovitz she was drinking was pretty strong stuff."

"Yeah." Dave looked at me significantly.

I huffed. "What?"

"Drinks a lot, does she, your sister?"

"*No.*" Then I thought about it. "Don't know, to be honest. You know I haven't seen that much of her lately. But I don't see what that's got to do with anything, anyhow."

"Look, I'm not saying this is what happened, but it's not unknown for people to do themselves harm—" I slammed down my pint and braced my arms on the table, about to get up. "Just listen, all right?"

I subsided.

Dave gave a quick nod. "See, sometimes if they're a bit, well, emotionally unstable, people do stuff they wouldn't dream of, normally. Like a cry for attention."

"You're saying my sister's unstable?"

"I'm not saying anything. Just talking generally, all right?" Generally, my arse. "But she's at a difficult age, right? About to turn forty, not married, no kids. Take it from me, mate, that's a dangerous time for a woman."

"Yeah, but she was engaged. *Is* engaged. And she could still have kids, easy. My mum was forty-six when I was born."

"It's like they say—ninety percent of accidents happen in the home."

"There'll be an *accident* happening in this pub if you don't watch out. And you can cross the self-harming theory off your list, all right? Cherry would never do anything like that. What about the Literati? Seem like a right suspicious bunch if you ask me." I crossed my fingers he wouldn't have heard about my little visit to them last night.

"What, that bunch of old has-beens, wannabes, and windbags? Think they've spent so long cooking up plots for their books it's sent them barmy and they've tried to act one out for real?"

"Don't think they go for mysteries, actually."

"Got all that from your little natter with the chairman at the party, did you?"

"Er, well . . ."

"Or could it be down to the fact that the Literati's latest member is one Thomas Paretski? Funny how that name keeps cropping up, innit?" Dave shook his head. "Wish I'd never called you in on that Melanie Porter case. Might've known it'd come back to bite me on the arse. What am I, a dating agency for nosey bloody parkers?"

"Well, if you want a testimonial for your website . . ."

"Fuck off. So what's your bloke got, then? Seeing as we're sharing information here."

"You know, you could ring him and ask him yourself."

"Yeah, and he'd tell me to piss off. Come on, give."

I sighed. "Fine. But you're buying me a pint first."

It took a couple more pints before I'd finished filling him in on what Phil and I had learned. Well, that, and somehow I got talking about my Auntie Lol and her weird bequest.

"Bit of a coincidence, innit?" Dave leaned back in his seat and belched. "Your auntie asks you to go poking around her ex-husband's house, and five minutes later, people start keeling over from poison. Makes you wonder. You were holding that drink for a bit, weren't you? Wouldn't be beyond the realms of possibility for some people to have thought it was yours, now would it?"

I shivered. Must be a draught in here. "God, not you and all."

"What's that supposed to mean?"

I took a swig of beer. "Ah, Phil had this daft idea it might have been meant for me too. It's bollocks, though. What would he—Mr. Morangie, I mean—what would he have been doing at Cherry's do?"

"What, besides trying to get away with murder?"

I laughed. "Well, there's that. Don't you reckon me or Cherry would've noticed him, though?"

"Maybe he turned up in drag."

"Yeah, right. That's about as likely as him getting Morangie junior to do the deed."

"Who?"

"Cherry reckoned he's got a son. Dunno how old he'd be. The old bloke's, what, in his sixties now? The son could be anything between twenty and forty." I did some sums in my head. "Couldn't be younger than mid-teens, seeing as he was already in the picture when Auntie Lol married his dad. And while I'm on the subject, what the bloody hell was all that about?"

"Just because he doesn't float your boat doesn't mean he didn't sweep your auntie off her feet all those years ago." Dave scratched his armpit. "There's no accounting for women, I'll tell you that straight. All the tosspots and no-hopers I see on the job, they've all got some female at home crying over 'em. And it's not just your daft teenage girls who don't know any better. It's like they've got a blind spot. You can tell 'em till you're blue in the face he's not going to change, this bloke what's been knocking 'em about or doing over houses since he was in short bloody trousers, and they just smile and they nod, and they tell you no one knows 'im like they do. No one believes his lies like they do, more like. What is it about the adult male that makes the other fifty percent of the population—more, with your lot—turn into a self-deluding, hormonal wreck? I tell you what, mate, if I was a woman, I'd be a bloody lesbian."

We clinked glasses. "To lesbians."

We sort of got a bit off-topic after that, although I might just possibly have said a few embarrassingly mushy things about Phil and how he wasn't like all the other blokes as we shared a taxi home.

Hopefully Dave was drunk enough that he'd have forgotten them by tomorrow morning. Or would at least have the decency to pretend he had.

CHAPTER SEVENTEEN

I was out at work all day Wednesday—couple of easy pipework jobs, then a new washing machine down in Fishpool Street that turned out to be a bloody nightmare. It was one of those houses that were built way back when the mangle was considered dangerously advanced technology, and the owner, a camp old queen in his seventies or maybe even eighties, was way more fussed about *preserving the period ambiance* than he was about plumbing logistics. I swear, I was *this* close to suggesting he just use the bloody Laundromat.

By the time I'd finished, I had a painful bump on the back of my head (don't ask), an invitation to *drop round any time—day or night* from the customer (really, really don't ask), and I'd missed a call from Phil.

I rang him back from the van. "What's up?"

"Your literary mates ever mention the last chairman? Bloke called David Evans."

"Nope. Why, did he leave under a cloud too, like Cherry? Morgan Everton topple him with a military coup?"

"He died. Guess how?"

"I dunno, do I? Someone bash his head in with his own gavel? No, hang on, that was Hannah's other group. The gavel, I mean. Not the head bashing. What, then?"

"Gastroenteritis. At least, that's what was on the death certificate." Phil left a significant pause. "He was in his eighties, dodgy heart, so no one was that surprised it killed him."

"But you reckon it might have been poison? Like Cherry?" Shit.

"I reckon it's a bit of a coincidence, two members of the same literary group having a life-threatening attack of Delhi Belly on two separate occasions. I think we need to have a little chat with the Literati. All of 'em. And Tom?"

"Yeah?"

"That includes Greg Titmus. So no more going to see him on your own, all right?"

Shit. I'd almost forgotten Greg had been a member of the Literati with Cherry—in fact, maybe he'd been the first one to join? I couldn't remember if she'd said or not. "Hang on, we can't stop Cherry seeing him."

"She ought to be safe enough at your parents'. Are you done for the day?"

"Yeah. Want to get a takeaway?"

"What happened to home cooking?"

"Too bloody knackered. Last job was a total bastard."

There was another pause. "I could probably throw together a curry."

Phil sounded a bit uncertain, so I thought I'd better encourage him. "If it helps, I'll definitely put out after."

"Bit rash making promises like that. You haven't tasted my cooking yet."

"Long as you remember to leave out the nicotine, we're good. So I'll come round to yours, yeah?"

"How about I cook at yours? Unless you've got a thing about other people touching your pots and pans?"

"Baby, you can touch anything of mine you want." I gave it a mock-sexy growl. "Want me to get anything on the way home?"

"No. I'll bring everything. See you in an hour or so."

That gave me plenty of time to get home, feed the cats, have a shower, put on a clean shirt, and think about why it gave me a warm fuzzy feeling to have Phil coming over to cook for me. All right, part of it was the cooking and the promise I'd made for afters, but not all of it. Did Phil like my house better than he liked his flat? Or did he just realise I felt more at ease in my own, comfortably messy house than in his sterile white flat?

"Course, it could just be you two," I said to Arthur, who was purring away on my lap. He purred harder and kneaded my leg with his paws. "Oi, no claws."

Merlin butted up against my knee, as if to say, *See, I should be your favourite.*

The doorbell went. "Sorry, mate," I said as I tipped Arthur off my lap. He dug in a claw to register his protest and then dropped heavily to the floor, flicking his tail at me as he stalked off.

Maybe I should give Phil a key? I'd never done that before. With a bloke, I mean. Mrs. E. next door had one in case I did something daft like lock myself out or walk under a bus and leave the cats unfed. Although, knowing them, they'd be off out the cat flap and finding themselves new people to freeload off of before I was cold in my grave. It'd be a bit more significant giving a key to Phil.

Maybe he wouldn't want me to give him a key? What if I handed it over and he ran a mile? Nah, it was way too soon. Best leave it. I opened the door. Phil was standing there, bags of groceries in both hands. There was a stiffish breeze whipping down the street, and it just ruffled his short blond hair on top. He looked solid and warm and fucking gorgeous in his blue cashmere sweater.

"Do you want a key?" I blurted out.

His eyes—same colour as the sweater—widened. "What?"

Shit. "Nah, it's daft. Forget it."

"You're offering me a key to your house?"

"Well, you know. Seems a bit weird you having to ring the doorbell. Number of times you've slept over, and all. And if we were going to meet up here, and I got held up . . . Just thought it'd be convenient. That's all."

"Okay."

"Right. Good." That was it? No *Are you sure?* Or *Hang on, this is a big step, we've only known each other five minutes?*

Phil gave me a flicker of a smile. "You going to let me in, now? I'm not sure how long these carrier bags are going to hold together."

"Right! Yeah, sorry." Feeling like a right muppet, I stood back to let him come in the front door. "I'll get some pans out."

"This is pretty good," I said half an hour later as we sat in front of the telly with our plates on our laps. I mopped up some spicy sauce with a bit of naan bread and shoved it in my gob with relish.

Phil shrugged, one-shouldered, and forked up some more of his lamb jalfrezi. "The sauce is just out of a jar."

"So? If I wanted gourmet food cooked from scratch, I'd be shagging Gordon Ramsay."

"And there's a picture I didn't need in my head while I'm eating."

I shuddered. "Me either. Or at any other time, for that matter. Seriously, that bloke is a dire warning of what getting all het up over your job can do to you. He's got more wrinkles than a bloody Sharpie."

"Shar-pei."

"Whatever. Hey, do you ever think about getting a pet? Dunno why, but I've always thought of you as a dog person." Course, I wasn't sure how well that'd work in his top-floor flat.

"Yeah, well. The cats are growing on me." He stroked the nearest furry head, which happened to belong to Merlin, sucking up as usual.

"What, even Arthur?"

Phil smiled, put his mostly empty plate on the coffee table, and leaned back. "It's a work in progress. I still like his owner better, don't worry."

"Well, I should hope so. There's laws against that sort of thing. Plus I've had him seen to, so I think you'd be in for a bit of a disappointment anyway." I slid my plate underneath Phil's, seeing as I'd practically licked it clean. "So what's for pudding?"

"Even you can't still be hungry after that lot."

I gave him a saucy smile. "Oh, I can always manage a bit more."

"Yeah? Bit of what?"

"What are you offering?"

Phil let his legs fall open. "See something you like?"

"Mmm, think I'm going to have to get closer to see for sure." I knelt down between his legs and ran my hands slowly up his thighs, loving the feel of all that muscle under the fabric of his trousers. When I got to his hips, Phil shifted a bit, giving me plenty of access to what I was after. I traced the outline of his balls and his rapidly hardening cock with one finger, deliberately teasing.

Phil wasn't amused. "Are you going to suck it or just tickle it to death?"

"Any more sarcasm from you and it'll be neither." But I took pity on him and undid his zip. Phil's dick, still covered in stretchy cotton, erupted from his flies like a slo-mo version of Alien bursting out of whatshisname's chest. I raised an eyebrow. "Someone's in a hurry."

"*Someone's* a fucking prick-tease." But his hand stroked my face as he said it.

I carefully peeled away Phil's underwear to free his cock. The tip was glistening, and my mouth watered instinctively. I licked all the way up his erection, then circled the head with just the tip of my tongue. Phil shuddered. I teased him some more, then plunged my mouth over his cock.

Spreading his legs even wider, Phil groaned and grabbed hold of my head with one hand, which ordinarily I'd be fine about. Unfortunately, he managed to zero in on that lump on the back of my head with painful accuracy. I let out a muffled yelp.

Phil pulled out and frowned at me in concern. At least, I thought that was his expression. I kept getting distracted by his dick still bobbing in my face. "What's wrong?"

"Nothing. Well, bit of a bruise on the back of my head, that's all."

Phil's fingers were probing under my hair, and I sucked in a breath as he found the sore bit again. "Christ, there's a lump here. When did this happen?"

"This afternoon. Job on Fishpool Street." Phil junior was looking a lot less perky, I noticed sadly.

"What, fall off the pavement on the way there, did you?"

"Har, har." Fishpool Street is one of those streets in St. Albans where the pavement is set a bit more than your average three inches higher than the road. But not by *that* much. "Nah, I was plumbing in a washing machine. You want to hear the story, or you want to get your dick sucked?"

Phil zipped up his flies and pulled me back up onto the sofa.

Flippin' marvellous.

"You daft . . . Why didn't you tell me? I thought you'd just had a bad day, not got a bloody concussion."

"I haven't got a bloody concussion! And oi, get your fingers out of my eyes."

"Just checking. You got a headache?"

"Only a bit. Getting worse now," I added pointedly. "I hear sexual frustration can do that."

"Dizziness? Nausea?"

"No, and no. I'm fine, all right?"

"So what happened?" God, he was a persistent bastard.

"I was on my hands and knees under the work surface in the kitchen, having a look at the pipes, and something startled me, all right? So I jumped, and bashed my head on the bottom of the worktop."

"See a spider, did you?"

"Saw two of 'em, actually." I held up the appropriate two fingers.

"Come on, then, what was it?"

I rolled my eyes, then wished I hadn't. That headache really was getting worse. "It was the customer, all right? Copping a feel."

"You what?"

"You heard me. And before you tear down to Fishpool Street to put the fear of God into him, the bloke's eighty if he's a day. It was probably the most action he's had since the original Summer of Love. And oi, stop laughing. What happened to being all worried about me?"

"God, I can't trust you anywhere, can I? Every time I look round, you're charming the pants off someone."

"Mr. C.'s pants stayed very firmly *on*, thank God. And so did mine. God, now I've got wrinkly arses in thermal long johns stuck in my head, fuck you very much for that."

"Better than having wrinkly bits stuck anywhere else."

"Are you seriously trying to put me off sex for life? Because you're doing a pretty good job."

"Bloody diva." Phil slung his arm around me and pulled me in close. "Come on, let's just watch the telly."

I sighed and cuddled into his side. Bloody cock-blocking head wounds.

CHAPTER EIGHTEEN

Next morning, we had a lazy breakfast and then a confab about the Literati so Phil could fill me in on all the dirt he'd managed to dig up on them.

Which, frankly, wasn't a lot. I supposed all would-be murderers didn't come with handy criminal records so you could point to them and say, *That's a bad'un*, but I'd been hoping for *something*.

Phil had found out a bit more about David Evans, the late Literati chairman. He'd been eighty-four when he'd died, so it hadn't exactly been a life cut tragically short in its prime—then again, it seemed he'd still been pretty fit, heart troubles notwithstanding: playing bowls regularly at a local club, doing the garden. At any rate, he'd still had all his marbles, and I bet if you'd asked him, he'd have said he wasn't ready to go just yet.

He'd been a retired bank manager, but nobody's perfect.

"So did anyone cry foul when he tottered off to the big bowling lawn in the sky?" I asked, lolling on the sofa.

"Nope." Phil scrolled through his notes on his laptop. "Good turnout for the funeral, apparently, although the neighbour I spoke to reckoned he—Evans—wouldn't have approved."

"Why not?" I grinned. "When I go, I want the works—horse-drawn hearse with black feathers, weeping women, pomp and bloody circumstance. If you've got to go, you might as well do it in style."

"I'll bear that in mind."

"What, for when you off me with the toaster?"

"Something like that. They had a big church service for Evans, the vicar going on about how he'd been a pillar of the parish. Thing is, according to this neighbour, she knew him pretty well, and he hadn't been to church for close on five years. Lost his faith when his wife died, she said."

"Poor sod."

Phil looked up from his laptop screen. "Didn't reckon you were into religion."

I shrugged. "I'm not. Just, it's a comfort, innit? For old folks. Believing it's not the end when they pop their little orthopaedic clogs, and they'll see their loved ones again when they get to the other side. Just seems a shame, if he had that all his life, to lose it when he really needed it." Phil was still staring at me. I picked up my mug. "Want another coffee?"

"If you're making." He handed me his mug, and I took them into the kitchen, Merlin trotting hopefully at my heels.

"So what did old Evans leave in the way of family?" I called back to Phil as I got the coffee out.

"Couple of grown-up daughters. One married, one divorced, both with kids in university."

"Huh. I've heard those fees can be a right bastard these days."

"Suggesting they did him in for his money?" Phil's voice sounded close, and I looked up from the cafetière to see him leaning on the doorframe. With his arms folded like that, he looked like an advert for cashmere sweaters. And gym subscriptions. And sex. Giving up on me, Merlin padded over to rub his cheek on Phil's leg adoringly.

"I'm just saying, a bit of money from Gramps'd probably come in handy. Course, we don't know yet that anyone killed him, do we?" I poured in the hot water and put the lid on the cafetière. "And I s'pose it'd be a bit of a funny coincidence, both him and Cherry getting poisoned. If it wasn't the same poisoner, I mean." I leaned back on the counter. "So why do writers kill other writers? Apart from wanting to prove the pen really is deadlier than the sword?"

"Mightier."

"What?"

"It's *mightier* than the sword. Same reasons anyone kills anyone. Money. Sex. Love. Jealousy. Revenge. Fear." He nodded, presumably to himself, seeing as I hadn't said anything. "The interesting question is, why does a writer try to kill *two* other writers? Assuming the old chairman was murdered."

I frowned. "Well, I can see Morgan offing someone to get the top job. And he never did like Cherry. And him and Margaret are pretty tight. Maybe she helped?"

"Unlikely. Think about it—if you want to kill someone, are you going to take a chance on trying to bring someone else in on it? Chances are they'd be horrified, and then there's no chance you'd get away with it, 'cause they'd shop you if you did it." He stared at the wall for a moment. "What about her doing it off her own bat? Just *how* tight are her and Morgan?"

"You mean, are they shagging?" I thought about it. Then I wished I hadn't. "Dunno. He's a bit of a puritan, old Morgan. I s'pose it doesn't necessarily mean she wouldn't have killed for him, either way. Actually, there's Hannah too, in that camp. She seemed to have a bit of hero-worship going. Called him the next someone-or-other. Come to that, him and Raz had their heads together a lot at that meeting I went to. And Raz was definitely unfriendly to me."

"What about Peter?"

"Yeah, what about him? Bit of a dark horse, that one. Although he looked more like a rat. A dark rat."

"Don't let him bite you, then. I hear bubonic plague can be nasty. So who's he in with, in the circle?"

"Not sure. No one, particularly, far as I could tell from one meeting. Oh, and I'm pretty sure Morgan's a drinker. His tea smelled funny."

"Sure it wasn't some herbal stuff? Maybe he had a dodgy heart, got told to stay off the caffeine."

"Positive. It reeked of rum. And Tetley's."

The coffee had to have brewed by now, so I pushed down the plunger and poured it into our mugs, taking a deep, coffee-scented breath as I did so. Lovely. It's got texture, proper coffee has. Even filter coffee isn't the same—too watery. Give me a rich, thick cup of cafetière coffee any day.

Phil made a noise, sort of halfway between a grunt and a huff. I looked up. "What?"

"You want to drink that coffee or shag it?"

I grinned. "Both."

"Well, don't blame me when you get third-degree burns on your dick."

"Wanker." I passed him his mug, and we took them through to the living room.

We were halfway through our coffee when Phil's phone rang, and he stood up from the sofa to answer it. As one-sided conversations went, it wasn't all that thrilling to listen in to. "Yeah? Right. Right. Yeah. I owe you."

"Well?" I said as he put his phone away.

"Interesting." Phil sat down again.

"I'll reserve judgement on that until you tell me what the bloody hell it was all about."

"Morangie junior. I asked a mate to do some digging for me. It's a girl. Elizabeth."

"Congratulations. I'm very happy for you both."

"Piss off." He only said it half-heartedly, too busy staring out of the window. I didn't reckon it was because he thought the view was interesting, because, trust me, it wasn't. Plus I could practically hear the cogs going round in his brain.

"Old Mr. M. went a bit over the top about it then, didn't he? I mean, me getting the sex of his kid wrong. Assuming that's why he chucked me out of the house."

Phil turned to look at me, still thoughtful. "Maybe he was just looking for an excuse—any excuse? Trying to buy time by seeming to agree, but still not letting you search the place? Did you get anything from there? Anything at all?"

"Well, no. Didn't have time, did I? I mean, I thought I was going to have all the time I wanted, so I didn't bother getting a shift on."

Phil huffed. "We need to get you back in that house."

"Maybe. I'd be more chuffed about the prospect if I was certain he wasn't trying to kill me. Still, I suppose if I find what he's hiding, he won't have a reason anymore, will he?"

"You've got a short memory. That list of motives for murder I gave you? Revenge was in the top five. No, if you go back in that house, I'm going too."

I grinned at him. "Watch it. People are going to start thinking you care about me."

"Wanker." He gave me a shove, and my coffee sloshed in my mug but didn't splash onto my lap. "I do, all right? Care."

"Yeah, well," I muttered to my knees. "Me too."

By the time we'd finished our coffee—and all right, a fair bit of slobbing around on the sofa talking the case round in circles—it was late morning, so we decided to have an early lunch and go interview the Literati after that.

First up was Margaret. She actually lived in St. Leonards, it turned out, which must be nice and handy for murder attempts in the Old Deanery. We probably should have rung before we went, but based on my last experience of phoning her, I thought we'd be better off surprising her. Of course, she might not be in, but in that case, we could go and have another chat with Greg.

Bit of a lose-lose situation, that.

Margaret's house was small and cottagey, but there was something very *Margaret* about the way the box hedge had been trimmed with the aid of a spirit level and all weeds ruthlessly exterminated from her brick driveway.

Nicotine was a weed killer, wasn't it? Or a pesticide or something? I was sure someone had said so.

"Nice little house," Phil commented. "Must be worth a bit."

I might have known he'd like it. I rang the doorbell and cringed as an ear-piercing, high-pitched buzz sawed jaggedly through the midmorning peace. I half expected neighbours' heads to pop up over the hedge and go, *Do you* mind? Still, at least you knew you'd rung it. I hate it when you ring a doorbell and you can't hear it from outside. Do you press it again and risk pissing them off? Sod's law, if you don't, you'll end up standing on the doorstep like a lemon for the next ten minutes, until the neighbours or the postman or, if you're very lucky, the householder him or herself happens by and lets you know the doorbell hasn't worked for months.

Margaret kept us waiting long enough for me to worry she was out or, more likely, had spotted who it was through the window and was lying low. Eventually, though, the door was opened a crack, chain kept firmly on. "Yes?"

"Hi, Margaret. It's Tom. From the Literati? I wondered if we could ask you a few questions."

Suspicious eyes glared at us through the crack. "What about?"

Phil got there first. "Can we come in? It's not really a suitable subject for the doorstep."

He'd got Margaret's number, all right. She shot a worried glance over at the neighbouring cottage, then opened the door fully, her mouth tight. "Come in," she said curtly, the *I suppose you'd better* understood.

I got a weird case of déjà vu walking the short distance down Margaret's hallway to her sitting room. It took me a mo to realise both rooms were done up like Morgan's, only on a smaller scale. I wondered who'd copied the other—or did they plan their home decor together? There were the same echoey tiles on the hallway floor and the same horsehair furniture in the front room. Even the colours were similar: brown mud and green sludge. A sort of septic-tank chic. Although unlike at Morgan's, here and there I could see splashes of rose pink attempting to enliven the mix. It didn't.

The whole place had that over-sweet, fake flowery smell you get from air fresheners. It was getting right up my nose. The sofa was predictably hard, and if we'd been hoping for a cup of tea, it looked like we were going to be disappointed. Then again, seeing as she was a suspect in a poisoning case, maybe that should be "relieved."

I thought I'd better follow Phil's lead, seeing as this was his area. Since he was apparently going for the intimidating-silence tactic, this meant we all just sat there like a whole bloody crate of lemons for several minutes.

Margaret cracked first. "Well? I thought you had some questions you wanted to ask?"

Phil nodded. "Did you go to the party at the Old Deanery?"

"Naturally. Although the short notice was most inconvenient. I barely had time to get the baking done."

The baking? "Hang about," I burst in. "*You're* one of Greg's cathedral ladies?"

She looked at me frostily. "I'm a sidesperson at services, yes."

"Which means?" Phil looked a bit uncomfortable at confessing his ignorance. He ought to leave that sort of stuff to me.

The ignorance, I mean. Definitely not the church stuff.

"I greet the congregation as it arrives and welcome them to the service," Margaret explained impatiently.

Bloody hell. No wonder church attendances were declining.

Margaret sniffed. "Why don't you ask Hannah what *she* was doing at the party?"

What? I sat forward. "Hang on, Hannah was there?"

"Of course she was. You think she'd miss any opportunity to see Gregory?"

This was doing my head in. "You mean she was sweet on him? Bit masochistic going to his engagement party, then, wasn't it?" *If* she'd been there. I wasn't sure I trusted Margaret as far as I could throw her, and I'd always been pretty crap at javelin.

Course, with a nose that pointy, she'd probably stick in the ground all right . . . Oops. She was glaring at me. "Sorry, did you say something?"

"I *said*, she probably hoped to change his mind." She sniffed again.

Should I offer her a handkerchief? Course, mine wasn't all that clean. She'd probably faint with shock at the sight of my manky hanky . . . I just about managed to turn a snigger into a cough. "Sorry. Still, a bit desperate, innit?"

"She's the sort of person who *would* read too much into the invitation."

Phil coughed. Possibly to remind both of us he was still here. "When you say invitation . . ."

"Gregory telephoned us. At least, he telephoned me and said he would be doing the same to the rest of the circle, although I told him not to bother calling Morgan, as he would be coming with me. I believe he—Gregory, that is—had some romantic notion of letting bygones be bygones, and having Cherry make her peace with us all. Well, we all saw how that turned out."

Was she saying what I thought she was saying? "You mean, you think one of the Literati poisoned her?"

Margaret's cheeks flushed livid, and she stood up abruptly. I stood too, automatically, then took a step back before that beaky nose could take an eye out. I heard Phil cursing under his breath as he heaved himself off the sofa to join us.

"How dare you?" Margaret snapped. "I said nothing of the kind. I might have known you'd be cut from the same cloth as your sister. This interview is at an end."

Shit. "Wait— Sorry, all right? I misunderstood. Benefits of a crap education. Look, just tell me what you *did* mean? Please?"

"I *meant*, that disgraceful exhibition of hers. Turning to drink, and then to dramatics. Gregory will come to regret tying himself to her, you mark my words."

Anger shot through me, sharp and hot. "You know what? You were right. This bloody interview *is* at a sodding end."

There was an exasperated rumble in my ear. "Tom . . ."

"You want to stay here while she insults my sister? Fine. You can do it on your own." I stomped out of the room and was at the front door before I realized I was alone. Bastard. I hadn't meant him to take me literally.

Slamming the front door behind me would have been childish and petty. Also unsatisfying, as it was ringed all round with foamy draught excluders. Planning to take my frustrations out on the car door instead, I developed a few more when I remembered we'd come in Phil's car and he was the one with the keys.

I slouched by the hedge with my arms folded, wishing Margaret had had the decency to provide a proper wall for me to lean on.

After five minutes or so, I started feeling like a bit of a prat, so unfolded my arms and got out my phone. I was just getting interested in a Twitter discussion of footballers' salaries fuelling celebrity culture when Phil emerged from the house and ambled down the garden path. "Cooled down a bit, have we?" He unlocked the car.

"Eff off." I glared at him, then rolled my eyes and got in the passenger seat. "Get anything more out of her?"

"You mean apart from a rant about the disgraceful manners of the younger generation? Not really. Although she confirmed all the Literati were at the party. They were hanging out in the 'family' room while we were there, most of them."

"Talking to Mrs. Tiggywinkle?"

"Something like that. I got the impression most of 'em felt a bit uncomfortable with all the High Church lot. Raz especially, she reckoned, although that might just be her prejudices."

"So . . . if they were all together the whole time, they're each other's alibis?"

"Nah. There was a lot of to-ing and fro-ing, she reckoned. Going for drinks and eats. Making sure no one was treading pastry crumbs into the Old Deanery carpets—that was Margaret."

I nodded. "And Morgan was in the other room at least some of the time. Talking to me. So any of them could have nipped in and slipped the nicotine into Cherry's glass while we were distracted by Richard and Agatha?" I tried again to think if I'd seen any of them, but to be honest, it was all a bit of a blur now. All I could really remember clearly was the stuff after Cherry collapsed.

"Yeah. It's interesting, though."

I waited, but he didn't say *what* was interesting. Just tapped his fingers on the steering wheel and stared out through the windscreen. "Well, come on. Big secret, is it?"

"Greg invited the Literati to the party. He made a *point* of inviting them."

Shit. "You think he did it as some sort of smokescreen? You think *he's* the one who poisoned Cherry?"

"Not necessarily. But if it *was* him, he'd have to think it wouldn't hurt to have a few more suspects in the place."

I scrubbed my hands over my face. "Oh, bloody hell. Cherry's going to be gutted if it turns out to be him."

"Hey, I'm not saying it was him. Could still have been one of the Literati, making the most of the opportunity. And don't forget, Margaret Pierce had more notice than the rest of them. More time to make plans."

"Except she probably got straight on the phone to old Morgan, so we can't rule him out."

"Not ruling any of 'em out. Then there's the Morangies."

I turned to stare at him. "You don't seriously reckon it could have been Morangie junior, do you?"

"Why not? At least there's a motive there. If it was you the poison was meant for, that is."

"Yeah, but it was Cherry's party, not mine. They wouldn't even have known for sure I'd be there."

"Come on, you're her brother. Course you'd be there. And with an open invitation like that, it was too good a chance to miss."

"*If* they knew about it. Don't you reckon Cherry might have noticed if she was friends with someone called Morangie? It's not exactly a common name."

Phil nodded. "And it's not like anyone ever changes their name or lies about it or anything."

"Git. Nah, I'm not buying it. It'd have to be taking the *premeditated* thing a bit far, wouldn't it? How would they know they'd have to hide who they were all that far in advance?"

"Just because you didn't know about the will or your auntie being ill doesn't mean nobody else did." Phil tapped his fingers on the steering wheel. "Maybe Morangie's been playing you and your sister all along. Maybe he's already found the will. It'd fit with him making you that offer, wouldn't it? And then when you didn't accept, he knew he'd have to go a bit further."

"Yeah, but . . . All this, for a house? *Half* a house, even. I mean, it's a nice house, but it's in Mill Hill, not bloody Mayfair."

"You don't know she's left you half a house. Could be a fortune in bling for all we know."

"Or it could be tuppence ha'penny. Sod it. Let's go talk to Greg."

"Hmm." The steering wheel got another tapping while Phil's gaze bored a hole in the windscreen.

I got fed up waiting for him to say something. "Hmm, what? I don't speak Morse code."

Phil turned to look at me, brow furrowed. "What?" Then he shook his head. "I think we'll leave Greg for now."

"But we're right here. He's only, what, three streets away? Might as well cross him off our list."

"No, I want to talk to your sister again first. Is she still at your mum and dad's?"

"Dunno. I'll give her a bell. We could get her to meet us somewhere, anyhow. She must be feeling all right by now."

He gave me a look. "Worried about taking me home to meet your parents?"

It wasn't exactly that I was *worried* about taking Phil to meet Mum and Dad. Well, not on their end, anyhow. I mean, they'd met Gary, so after that anyone I could think of to take round would probably come as a relief to them. Well, except maybe Darren. But Phil, well . . .

I wasn't sure what I was worried about, really. He'd probably get on better with them than I did.

I frowned.

"Penny for them?"

"What?"

"These deep thoughts you're having instead of phoning your sister."

"Oh. Right. Yeah, I'll just give her a call." I pulled out my phone and scrolled through my contacts before realising I didn't actually have her number. Shit. I really needed to get myself organised. I dialled Mum's number instead.

The phone (landline, obviously) rang eleven times before she picked up and told me the number I'd just rung, in case I'd forgotten during the long wait for the answer. I've never quite worked out why she doesn't just say "Hello" like everyone else.

"Mum? It's me. Tom."

"Oh? I didn't recognise the number." She sounded suspicious.

I wondered if I was about to be asked for the name of my childhood pet. (It was a goldfish called Chips, if you're wondering, and I won him at the fair. I was thrilled; Mum and Dad less so, seeing as they had to fork out for a tank for him to live in. Given the number of times he somehow managed to leap out of his new home and land, flapping, on the carpet, I suspect he wasn't too thrilled about it either.) "Yeah, calling on my mobile. You all right?"

"Well, you know. The usual."

"Dad?"

"He's been having some trouble with his knees, and I'm not sure the cortisone injections are really doing what they should . . ." There was another ten minutes or so in this vein, then a bit about the weather before she finally got round to, "Did you want to speak to him?"

"Er, actually I was ringing to talk to Cherry."

"She's gone home. I thought you'd have known."

Triffic. "Thanks. I'll try her there. Um. Can you give me the number?"

Mum reeled it off painfully slowly, waiting for me to say yes after every digit. "Ta. I'll, um, give you a call when I've got more time to chat, all right?"

She ignored me. "I suppose Cherry told you about Laura?"

"Auntie Lol? Yeah. I was gutted. I mean, she was no age to go, was she?"

"No." There was a pause. "Did you go to the funeral?"

"No—didn't find out about it until it was all over." I tried not to sound too bitter.

"Well, you know how busy Cherry is, with her career." Mum's tone was a bit vague, so maybe I'd succeeded.

"Yeah. Listen, I'd better go—"

Just as I was about to say goodbye, she sneak attacked. "Cherry told me you're seeing someone."

"Er, yeah."

"She said it's that awful boy from the council estate who put you in hospital. Although she didn't quite put it like that."

She didn't? There was hope for Cherry yet. "Phil's changed, Mum. And it wasn't really his fault, the accident. You know it wasn't."

"All I know is that he chased you down the street, and then I got a phone call saying my youngest son had been hit by a car and was in intensive care." I heard her take a deep breath. "They told us to be prepared for brain damage."

Ouch. Way to wring the guilt muscles. "Mum . . . It was a long time ago. Water under the bridge."

"Is this a serious thing?"

"Um. Sort of."

"And are we going to meet him?"

"Uh . . . Look, I really need to give Cherry a call. We'll sort something out, okay? You take care of yourself, and I'll speak to you again soon. Love to Dad."

I hung up and called Cherry quick before Phil could grill me about the conversation with Mum. Cherry answered on the first ring. She seemed keen enough for us to come over, so she must have been well bored. I supposed Greg was busy ministering to the flock. Or maybe shoving it off the cathedral roof and then stuffing it.

CHAPTER NINETEEN

Cherry's house was in the old part of Pluck's End, near enough to the church that the bell ringers must give her a right ear-bashing in the summer. It was smaller than I expected and, well, cosier. You could probably get away with calling it a cottage if you were willing to be fairly elastic with the definition. There was no thatched roof and no roses round the door, but there was ivy climbing up the walls, and the front gate had a roof over it like they do in churchyards. I've never quite understood the point of that, but it always looks sort of quaint and rustic. Maybe that *is* the point.

The small front garden was well tended, but there were a trowel and a pair of gardening gloves in a discreet corner of the porch that suggested she did it all herself rather than pay someone to keep it nice. The porch itself was enclosed and had potted plants in it on shelves, including a healthy-looking variegated ivy that hung down and tickled the back of my neck as I rang the doorbell. Presumably she'd be moving out to go and live in the Old Deanery with Greg when they tied the knot. I wondered if she'd miss the place.

Cherry opened the door in a big, hairy man's sweater—the sweater was hairy, I mean; I couldn't vouch for the man—and, ye gods, leggings. The outfit took ten years off her, compared to her buttoned-up workwear.

"All right, Sis? You're looking better."

She gave a faint smile. "I should hope so. Come in. Phil, it's lovely to see you again."

"You didn't last long at Mum and Dad's," I said as we wiped our feet.

Cherry rolled her eyes. "Couldn't stand it any longer. I swear they have the thermostat turned up to thirty degrees. And the television's always at full volume, because Dad won't admit he needs a hearing aid. I've got loads of paperwork to catch up on, and it really wasn't helping."

The house was a little on the cool side, but when she ushered us into the living room, it was cosy enough. There was a real log fire laid in the hearth, and although it wasn't lit, it gave the impression it could be, if you know what I mean. The furniture was a bit old-fashioned for my liking, but the fabrics were all in warm reds and golds, and the sofa, when I parked my arse on it, was way more comfortable than Morgan's had been.

Plus, of course, it had the added advantage of Phil taking up space at the other end. Cherry took one of the armchairs and swung her legs up onto the seat beside her, like she used to do when I was little. I had a sudden flashback to her in a pink leotard and tights, back home from ballet class and with her hair up in a bun. She'd looked impossibly grown-up to my preschool eyes, but she must only have been in her early teens.

I blinked the memory away and waved at a gift basket of toiletries sitting on the hearth. It was all cellophane and curly ribbons, and even from a few feet away, the pungent smell of fruity bubble bath and body lotion and God knows what else was threatening to send me into a sneezing fit. "Greg been sending you welcome-home pressies?"

"Actually, it's from the Literati." She smiled, looking genuinely touched. "They clubbed together to get it. It was so kind of them, but the trouble is, I can't use any of it." She caught my look. "Allergies, remember? That's why I've never been able to wear makeup. I was going to give it to Mum next time I go over there."

Phil frowned. "I'd hold off on that if I were you. Better make sure none of it's been tampered with."

We stared at him in unison. "I don't think Mum's planning on drinking any of this stuff," I said at last. "I mean, she may be getting on a bit, but last I checked she hadn't gone completely gaga."

"Doesn't matter. Nicotine can be absorbed topically as well as by ingestion. How else did you think those nicotine patches smokers wear work? There was even a woman back in the forties who offed her husband by mixing the stuff with his aftershave."

"Oh." Cherry and I said it at the same time. It was a bit creepy, to be honest.

"Oh my God," Cherry went on. "I could have killed Mum!"

"Look, we're being a bit hasty here, aren't we?" Voice of reason, me. "We don't *know* there's anything wrong with it."

Phil frowned. "No, but we don't know there isn't, so until we do, no one touches anything in that basket. Who gave it to you?"

"Well, the card said it was from all of them. I found it in the porch when I got home."

"Still got the card?"

"It's up on the mantelpiece. The one in the middle, tucked behind the clock."

We looked. There were half a dozen or so Get Well cards up there, mostly floral but with a couple of jokey-looking cartoon hospital scenes. Phil strode over, grabbed the one in the middle, and opened it up. He grunted and held it up for the rest of us to see.

It was written in block capitals with a thick black pen, and all it said was *GET WELL SOON FROM THE LITERATI.*

"That's not a lot of help." I glanced at Cherry. "Unless you recognize the writing?"

She shrugged. "I'm not sure I've ever seen their handwriting. Everyone uses a word processor."

I turned back to Phil. "What about the card?"

"Just your bog-standard card from M&S." Phil shoved it back behind the clock, leaving them both a bit wonky.

I slumped back in the sofa and blew out a frustrated puff of air. "So how are we going to get this stuff checked out?"

"Well, there's private labs. Easiest would be to have a word with your mate DI Southgate."

I nodded. "Fair enough."

"Wait a minute," Cherry burst out. "Why on earth would the Literati want to, well, hurt me?" She looked upset, which I guessed wasn't all that surprising. I'd be pretty miffed if a bunch of people clubbed together to try to off me, although I supposed the chances were it was just one person acting alone and trying to spread the guilt. A murder shared is a murder halved, that sort of thing.

"We were coming to that." Phil was in business mode, all stern and efficient. "What do you know about David Evans?"

"The old chairman? In what sense?"

"Specifically, the way he died."

"Well, he was ill, poor man, wasn't he? Heart disease, and then..." Her face paled. "You don't think he was poisoned, do you?"

"Didn't get any gift baskets the week before he died, did he?"

"No—I mean, I can't believe it. He was such a lovely old man. He was writing a murder mystery, you know? It was really very good. Terrific plot, terribly ingenious. He asked me about a few things—court procedure, that kind of stuff. He made me promise not to tell the other members of the group—you know what Morgan's like about genre fiction. Plus, there had just been all this hoo-ha about plagiarism within writing groups, and David said while of course he trusted all the Literati, he didn't want to risk being disillusioned at his age. He was rather sweet about it."

She hugged herself, which was so un-Cherry-like I felt awkward watching her. Sort of like I was failing in my brotherly duties by not going over and giving her a hug myself, but God, this was Cherry. She'd probably be horrified. It'd been different, somehow, when she'd been in hospital.

"You know," she continued, staring at the unlit fire, "the circle was so much more fun with him as chairman. Morgan and I never did really get on. Meetings got a lot, well, stuffier after he took over."

"How did they decide who got to be the new chairman?" I threw in. "Draw straws, hold a vote, or was it just no one else wanted to do it?"

Cherry frowned. "You know, I really don't know. I think, actually, he just stepped in, and of course, nobody protested. I mean, we could hardly have made a big fuss about leadership when poor David had just *died*. We were all really upset, and it just wouldn't have been, well, the thing." Her eyes widened. "Oh God. I've just realized—I haven't even offered you a cup of tea. You'd like one, wouldn't you? Milk? Sugar?" She jumped up and scurried into the kitchen without even waiting for an answer.

I exchanged glances with Phil and followed her in there. She'd taken the kettle over to the sink to fill it.

"I'll do that—" I started.

Cherry jumped a mile, turned the tap on too full, and water spurted everywhere. "Oh . . . *Bugger.*"

I reached past her to turn the tap off, and Cherry just stood, staring at the puddle on the floor. "Sorry. Didn't mean to make you jump." I patted her awkwardly on the nearest woolly shoulder. The whole front of her sweater (Greg's sweater?) was wet, so I handed her a tea towel. "Should have left that to me. You know water's my area."

Cherry managed a wobbly smile as she mopped herself up, but it didn't last. "It's all just so . . . so bloody horrible. To think someone hates me so much. And I don't even know who it *is*. Or why." She sniffled. "I'm going to be expecting bricks through the window. And razor blades in the post."

"Nah, you'll be all right. You're coming back to mine." I hadn't really thought about it, but well, it made sense, didn't it? "That way, you won't be on your own at night. And my neighbours are a lot closer." And nosier, probably, come to that. "Go on, go and pack a bag."

"You don't have to . . . I mean, Gregory's got plenty of spare rooms in the Old Deanery."

I gave her a look. "What, and you and him only engaged? Are you trying to cause a scandal in the church? Those old ladies who do the flowers would probably keel over in horror."

She huffed. "*Fine.* I'll get my things. Can you sort the floor out? There's a mop behind the door."

"Oi, what did your last slave die of?" I went and grabbed the mop anyway. I was just about to start when I noticed she hadn't gone yet. "Cherry?"

She took a deep breath. "It wasn't Gregory, you know. He'd never hurt anyone."

"Hey, did I say it was him?" I said it gently, and she smiled that brittle smile again and left.

I had the floor sorted in a jiffy. When I got back in the living room, Phil was busy wearing a track in the carpet. "Tea's off," I told him. "Cherry's packing a bag, and she's coming back to mine."

He nodded. "Good."

There was a short silence.

"Oh—before I forget . . ." I held out my spare house key.

Phil looked at it.

"It's a key. To my place. We talked about this, remember?"

"Yeah, but . . ."

"But what? You don't want it? Fine." I shoved the bloody thing back in my pocket so hard I felt the stitches in the lining go.

Phil slipped his arms around my waist. "Wanker. I just meant I wasn't going to hold you to anything you said yesterday, that's all. What with the head and all."

Oh. "Yeah, well. I told you I hadn't got a concussion, didn't I? So do you want it or not?"

"Oh, I want it all right." He pulled me closer, then stepped back with a sigh. "But what about your sister?"

Oh. Shit. Cherry was going to need a key, wasn't she? "I'll get another one cut, all right?"

Phil smirked. "What makes you think it was the key I wanted?"

"Prick. Right. I'll give Dave a ring while we're waiting. Unless you've changed your mind about it?"

"What, about having you in your sister's living room?"

I held up the appropriate finger and, with my other hand, got out my phone and made the call.

"Southgate." Dave's voice sounded a bit rough.

"All right?"

"Peachy. If you're ringing about another trip to the pub, you're going to be on your own. I caught a right earful from Jen when I got home the other night."

I managed not to snigger down the phone. "Drunk too much to rise to the occasion, had you?"

"And then some. I'm not as young as I used to be, you know."

"If you ever were. Nah, it's just, Cherry's got this gift basket from the Literati. Least, that was what was on the card. They left it on the doorstep, though, so . . ."

"Has she eaten anything from it?" Dave's tone turned businesslike.

"Not that kind of gifts. Bath stuff, body lotion, that kind of thing. And nicotine's—"

"Easily absorbed through the skin, yes, thank you, we're not total morons here. Has she used any of it?"

"No."

"Good. Make sure it stays that way, and tell your sister I'll send someone round for it in the next hour or so. And for God's sake, don't go leaving your grubby fingerprints all over the evidence this time, all right?"

"I haven't even touched it."

"Surprised you haven't sampled half the bloody products."

"Yeah, right." We hung up, and I turned to Phil, who'd been doing that looking-at-bookshelves thing you do when someone's on the phone and you want to pretend you can't hear their conversation. "Dave's sending one of his minions to pick up that basket."

"Good. So what are we going to do with your sister while we talk to Nair?"

"Who?"

"Your literati chum. Only not so much. Raz Nair."

"Oh, him. He's on the way back to mine, is he?"

Phil nodded. "He lives the other end of the village."

Raz lived in Pluck's End too? "S'pose that's a point in his favour. I mean, what's the point of going all the way to St. Leonards to try and murder someone when you can do it in the village and support the local economy? So to speak."

"Maybe that *is* the point—if she'd been poisoned in Pluck's End, he'd be the obvious suspect, wouldn't he?"

"You mean, apart from Greg?"

"Obviously. Anyway, we can't drag your sister along when we go and see him."

"Point." I looked at my watch. "He ought to be back home from work by now. I'll tell Cherry we'll pick her up after we've seen him. It'll give her more time to pack stuff, anyway. Actually, come to think of it, someone needs to stay here for a bit anyhow, for when the boys in blue get here."

I went upstairs to update Cherry on the change of plans and caught her just as she was taking Tacky Teddy off her pillow and putting him in her bag. She went pink, so I cleared my throat and pretended I hadn't noticed.

"Phil and me are going to head off for a bit, give you some space, and we'll see you in an hour or so, all right? Make sure you've got everything you need, and don't open the door to anyone. Unless it's the police, obviously. They're coming round to pick up that gift basket."

She nodded. "You really think they'll find something?"

"Dunno," I said as lightly as I could. "Better safe than sorry, though, innit? And like you said, it's not like you could use the stuff. I'll see you in a bit, okay?"

I ran back downstairs again, and Phil and I grabbed our coats and headed off for Raz's place.

We walked, seeing as it wasn't far according to the map Phil had pulled up on his phone. There were a few people out and about, most of them walking dogs, their breath fogging in the light from the streetlamps. The people, that was. Actually, no, when I looked properly, it was the dogs as well. I huddled into my jacket and wished I'd brought a scarf.

"Think you'll ever get a dog?" I asked idly as a couple of Westies snuffled past in a cloud of white fluff, stubby little tails wagging.

"What, some kind of bloodhound or something?" Phil smirked. "Got you for that, haven't I?"

"Any more of that and I'll pee on your leg."

"Marking your territory?"

I gave him my best suggestive leer. "If I was doing that, it wouldn't be your leg I'd be marking."

CHAPTER TWENTY

The high street was long, narrow, and winding, built in the days when you were lucky to see two wheeled vehicles all day, let alone have them needing to pass each other in the street. I cast wistful glances at the pubs we passed, although, to be honest, it was a bit early for a pint anyway. Maybe I could drag Phil down the Rats when we got back to St. Albans . . .

Right. Because Cherry would be so chuffed to either join us or be left on her tod. I could see this was going to take a bit of adjusting to.

Raz didn't have a house—just a flat above the village hair salon, tucked down the far end of the high street. Still, he was young, yet. Probably. I wasn't quite sure how old he was, actually, but I was guessing early to midtwenties. He opened the door in a shirt and tie, and I guessed he'd only just got back in from work and hadn't had time to relax yet. He didn't look too pleased to be interrupted in the process. "What do you want?"

"Can we come in?" I asked.

Raz's eyes narrowed. "Both of you?"

No, I'd thought we'd leave Phil on the doorstep. "Yeah, if that's okay."

Phil butted in. "We just wanted to ask you a few questions about the Lea Valley Literati."

"Why? Who are you? Police?"

"I'm a detective investigating the attempted murder of Cherry Paretski," Phil said in an official-sounding voice. Nice, I thought. Make Raz think Phil was police without actually saying it.

Raz folded his arms. "Then you can show me some identification."

Well, I guess it couldn't work every time.

Phil wasn't ruffled. "I'm not with the police. I'm a private investigator."

"Then I don't have to talk to you." He started to shut the door.

"Hey, hang on a minute," I said, putting my boot in. In the door, that was, not Raz's face, although I won't say I wasn't tempted. "What if whoever it was tries again? You want my sister's death on your conscience?"

His eyes opened wide. "Your sister? *You're* Cherry's brother?" Raz looked away, his mouth tight, like he was fighting against himself. Finally, he took a deep breath and turned back to me. "I didn't know. Look, you can come in if you want. But not him."

"Why not?" I was baffled.

"I don't have to give a reason." The arms were folded again. I could see the outline of a sleeveless T-shirt under his formal shirt. I guessed either he felt the cold a lot, or he was one of those blokes who are surprisingly hairy under their clothes and get a bit self-conscious about it.

Odd, though. Raz's beard was thin enough that if it hadn't been jet black, he'd never have got away with it, and he had a sort of softness about him, a bit like puppy fat. Then again, so did Gary, and he was older than me. I found myself wondering if Raz was gay. I'd have to ask Phil later, seeing as his gaydar was way more reliable than mine. Or, as he put it, I couldn't find a fag in a Marlboro factory.

Raz wasn't a big bloke, I realised. No taller than me, although he looked it from a distance because he was so bloody skinny. Maybe that was why he didn't want Phil in his flat? Raz was dark-skinned, and although I'd heard things were a lot better these days than they used to be, it wouldn't be totally off the wall to speculate he'd had a bad experience with six-foot-plus policemen, ex or otherwise.

"Fine," I said, and flashed a glance at Phil.

He didn't look like he reckoned it was fine. He looked like he'd just bit into a lemon.

"I'll see you back at Cherry's, yeah?" I added quickly. "In about half an hour or so?"

Phil glanced between me and Raz, presumably trying to decide if I'd be able to take the bloke in a fight. The process went on a little longer than I found entirely flattering. "Half an hour. And don't forget what I told you," he growled and stomped back down the stairs, leaving me with Raz.

Who was staring at me in a bit of a creepy way. Fan-bloody-tastic. "Come in, then," he said at last.

The flat was small but neat. There wasn't a lot of colour in the place, and it could have done with a cat or two, but it looked comfortable enough. Remembering my theory, I cast my eyes around for signs of Raz being gay, but unless you counted the arty black-and-white photos of suspiciously tall skyscrapers (symbolic, much?) there weren't any.

"I'd offer you a coffee, but I don't suppose you'd take a drink from a suspect in a poisoning case," Raz said, angrily straightening a cushion that'd already looked pretty straight to me.

"Hey, who said you're a suspect?" I bluffed, thinking *Right, that's what Phil was just on about.*

Raz raised an eyebrow. "I'm not an idiot. And I've had dealings with the police before."

That was interesting. "Phil's not police."

"Maybe not now. You hired him?"

"Uh, yeah." I rubbed the back of my neck. "But he's, well. We're together."

I got a sharp look. "Oh? You mean you work with him?"

"No." I wasn't about to come right out and say, *No, I sleep with him,* but Raz seemed to get the message. He nodded, anyway.

"You should sit down." We sat, him perched on the edge of the leather sofa and me lounging on the leather recliner, both of which were way too big for the flat. Did he have a bit of a leather fetish, our Raz? Or just size issues? "What did you want to ask about?"

I thought I'd leave the *Did you try and kill my sister?* for later. "Your old chairman. The one before Morgan."

His brow creased up, and his glasses slipped down his nose. He pushed them back up with an impatient finger. "David? Why?"

"He died, didn't he?" I tried to listen in to the vibes from Raz's place while we were talking, but it was hard to concentrate on both. Maybe if I was more relaxed? I leaned back a bit.

"Yes, but it was due to illness."

"Yeah, gastroenteritis, from what I heard. Bit like food poisoning, that, innit?" I leaned back a bit farther, then sat up hastily as the recliner showed signs of slipping into full-on bed mode. Bugger. That was my concentration shot right to hell.

Raz looked distressed. "Are you suggesting he was murdered? That's terrible. He was such a gentleman."

"Can you think of any reason why someone in the circle might have wanted him out of the way?"

Raz got up. He must have realised he didn't have enough floor space for proper pacing, so he just stood there in front of the sofa, looking like he was about to bolt for freedom any minute. I stood up too, with a bit of difficulty seeing as the recliner seemed to be having a few abandonment issues. Although whether it was so I could catch him or just to keep him company, I wasn't sure.

I took the opportunity to let the spidey-senses roam free. There was something there, all right—but the vibes were weird. Sort of defiant rather than ashamed, at least I thought so. It was hard to tell.

"I can't," Raz said at last, shaking his head at the carpet. "I can't think of a single reason. This is all very upsetting. I— Can you leave me your phone number? If I come up with anything, I'll call you. I need a drink, and I haven't eaten yet. I can't think." He glanced up at me. "Tell Cherry I'm sorry, please."

Sod it. I only needed a few more minutes. Probably. "Can I just ask you a couple more questions? Then I'll leave you alone, swear to God."

"No. I can't do this now. I'll call you." He'd shepherded me halfway to the door before I'd realised what was happening. I should have stayed in that bloody chair; he'd have had to prise me out with a crowbar. When we reached the door, Raz hesitated, and I thought for a moment he'd changed his mind. But all he said was, "We should stay in touch. When . . . when this is all settled. We can talk about things."

"Yeah, sure." I flashed him a smile, but he just kept staring at me with those big, earnest eyes of his.

"And come to the reading," he added. "Tomorrow night, at the library here. Eight o'clock."

I blinked, surprised. "Thought you didn't want me coming to any more of your 'do's."

"Oh . . . that was when I thought you were just there to make fun of us. I didn't realise, then. But you should come." He urged me out of the door and shut it firmly behind me.

Mixed messages, much?

CHAPTER TWENTY-ONE

I caught up with Phil on the village high street. He was staring at the ads in an estate agent's window. "Fancy moving out to the country, do you?"

Phil turned to face me. "That was quick."

"Yeah. Apparently, he can't answer questions on an empty stomach. Maybe I should have made him a sandwich."

"So what did he tell you?"

"Not a lot. Can't think why anyone would want to off the old chairman and didn't like to think about it either." I shoved my hands in my coat pockets and stared at a *stunning Grade II listed period home of immense charm and character, 5 beds, 4 bathrooms, 7 receptions—* seven? Really? Why the hell would you want that many? That was more than one each for the people living in the bedrooms, although maybe some of them would double up—*Price on Request.* "He said to tell Cherry he was sorry."

"What for?"

"Didn't say. Maybe he's just generally regretful. On the plus side, though, I reckon I've pulled. He was very keen on keeping in touch, and he made me promise to go to his poetry reading tomorrow night."

Phil scowled. "Jesus."

"Oi, I can't help it if people are drawn in by my natural charm." From the look on his face, it'd probably be in my best interests to change the subject right now. "So what sort of place you looking for?"

"I'm not."

"Just enjoying the pretty pictures?"

"Something like that. Pipe dreams. No, if I was really looking for a house it'd be more like your place."

"Got a thing for poky little semis in the scruffy part of St. Albans?"

"Got a thing for places I can actually afford."

I shrugged. "If they kick you out of your flat 'cause you can't make the rent, you can always move in with me."

There was a silence. Shit, this was like the kids thing, wasn't it? As in, Phil was the one person I couldn't just casually toss that sort of thing into the conversation with. "I mean," I said quickly, "just till you get sorted, obviously. Wouldn't want to think of you kipping on a bench in Verulamium Park."

"Right," Phil said after a pause that was just a little too long.

"Let's see if Cherry's ready to go, yeah?"

If I'd known my sister was going to be coming to stay, I'd have tidied up the spare room a bit. Actually, sod that, I'd have hired a bloody skip. The room wasn't exactly big to start with, and I'd managed to fill it up with all kinds of crap over the five or so years I'd been living here. When I opened the door and reminded myself of the state it was in, I seriously considered just giving Cherry my room and kipping on the sofa.

Trouble was, she might look under the bed and discover my stash of porn. Not to mention one or two specialised articles I mostly hadn't even got around to using with Phil yet. Given the choice between clearing a load of junk and clearing a load of sex toys and probably getting caught red-handed before I'd had a chance to work out a new place to hide them, I thought, *Sod it, I'll clear the junk.*

"Can I help?"

I looked up from the pile of fashion disasters, boxes of invoices, and other guff that was hopefully going to reveal a bed underneath when I'd finished excavating. "Nah, it's okay. Shouldn't take too long. Put your feet up and watch the telly. Actually, tell you what, are you hungry?" I'd forgotten about dinner, I realised with a bit of a shock.

Phil would be calling a doctor. If, that was, he hadn't buggered off back to his place already. Not that I was feeling resentful, or anything. Still, maybe this whole thing with the key was a sign. Maybe him and me moving in together wasn't meant to be.

"I'm starving," Cherry was saying. "Have you got anything in?"

I frowned, trying to visualise the contents of my cupboards. I'd been a bit busy to go shopping in the last few days, despite the nearest supermarket being only yards away. "Well, there's eggs." There's always eggs in my fridge. They're handy to have around. And Phil likes them. "Bacon and bread too, probably. Fancy a fry-up?"

Cherry made a face. I was guessing that meant no. "How about I pop down the road and get something?"

Now I wasn't sure. "You okay about going out on your own?"

"Do you honestly think someone's going to try and run me down with a Morrisons shopping trolley?" She might have been going for sarcastic, but it came out a bit too wobbly for that.

I tried to lighten the atmosphere with a smile. "You can joke all you want, but some of those old ladies in there are lethal. 'Specially if you get between them and the going-out-of-date bargain bin. Tell you what, why don't we get a takeaway? There's loads—"

Cherry cut me off. "Why don't we go out for dinner? Look, you're putting me up and doing all this . . ." She waved a hand at the explosion-in-an-Oxfam-shop theme I currently had going in my spare room. "I'll pay."

"Well . . . you paid last time." God, that lunch in Carluccio's seemed like it'd been years ago now.

"Yes, but I must earn considerably more than you." She said it offhand, like male pride was something she'd heard of once but immediately dismissed as an urban legend.

"You've got a wedding to save up for." I thought about it. "Or are you getting Dad to pay? That's traditional, innit?"

"It may be traditional, but I'm not going to ask him to spend his pension on my wedding when I'm earning perfectly good money myself. So are we going out?"

Well, if she was *that* desperate to splash the cash . . . "Go for it. Got a place in mind?"

"Not really. I don't eat in St. Albans a lot."

"What, not even with the people from your office?"

She shrugged. "Not really. I don't really like that kind of thing. Everyone getting drunk and embarrassing themselves, and then you have to work with them next day or next week, or whenever. It's silly."

I didn't really feel I could comment. I've never worked in an office. The closest I've ever been to a works do was buying my accountant a pint. "All right, what sort of food do you fancy?"

We ended up heading for a newish place, just down the road from Jamie Oliver's overpriced Italian. It promised fusion food. I hoped that didn't mean we'd end up glowing in the dark after eating it. I took the Fiesta—parking's not so bad in the evenings, when the shops have shut.

"Oh, Waterstones is having a book launch on Sunday," Cherry said as we tootled down St. Peter's Street, stopping for the traffic lights every ten yards or so.

I kept my eyes on the road. "Yeah? Anyone famous?"

"Not sure. The name didn't really ring a bell. Hayden Mead. Still, I don't suppose you'd have heard of him anyway. Or her. I suppose it could be either."

"Cheers, Sis. I have heard of a few authors, you know."

"All right, name some, then."

Er... "Whatsisface who did the da Vinci ones, um... Oh, I know. Salman Rushdie. There you go."

She *tsked*. "It was Dan Brown who wrote *The Da Vinci Code*. And you've only heard of Salman Rushdie because of the death threats."

I winced. That probably hadn't been the best name to pull out of the hat.

Cherry was silent a moment. "I used to feel sorry for him—but annoyed too, because he brought it on himself. I never thought I'd know what it was like myself. It's just so horrible."

"Yeah, but at least you've only got one person after you, probably. Not a whole crowd of religious fundamentalists."

"Is that supposed to be comforting?"

Er, yeah? I thanked the gods of parking that allowed me to avoid answering in favour of pulling in, not ten yards from the restaurant. "Here we are, then," I said. "Got your bag?"

"I'm not a child."

"Oi, never said you were. But it's my car's going to get broken into if someone sees a bag in it."

"What, this old thing? I'm sure even car thieves have *some* standards." She rolled her eyes at me. "Oh, for heaven's sake, I'm only teasing. You're so touchy."

Had she been talking to Phil? "Restaurant's that way," I said firmly and got out of the car.

We got a table straightaway. I hoped it didn't mean the food was a bit dodgy. Still, the place was more than half-full, so the chances were we'd just been lucky.

"Oh, Raz said he's sorry, by the way," I said over the top of the menu.

"Oh? What for?"

"Dunno. Hopefully not for poisoning you. Actually, hang about, if he did poison you, and he's sorry, that's good, right? Means he won't do it again. Probably."

She gave me a weak smile. "He's probably referring to the unpleasantness with Morgan. It must have been very awkward for him. I'm sure he's been avoiding me in the village ever since."

"What, because him and Morgan are like that?" I held up two fingers pressed together.

"Mm. And because he was the one who introduced me to the group, of course."

"He was?" I got distracted then, as the waitress came over to take our order. She was short and pretty, with red hair in bunches, and she went pink every time I spoke to her.

"Do you have to flirt with every woman you meet?" Cherry said snippily once Little Red was out of earshot. "It's not like you're even going to follow through."

"I wasn't flirting!" Bloody hell, she was as bad as Phil. "There's nothing wrong with a bit of banter to brighten up the day."

"As long as she doesn't start expecting you to brighten up her nights as well."

"Come off it. I asked her for the specials, not her bloody front-door key. Anyway, weren't you going to tell me about you and Raz?"

"Oh, that. Well, nothing to tell, really. We just got talking one day in the post office. I think he commented on my name—asked if I was Polish, you know how people do."

"Just a bit," I agreed with a grimace.

Cherry took a sip from her water glass. "Well, after that, we carried on saying hello. And one day he mentioned he wrote poetry, so of course I mentioned that Gregory was a writer too, and he suggested I tell him about the group."

"So Greg joined the Literati, and then after a bit, you started wondering what you were missing?"

"Well, it wasn't *exactly* like that. I've always thought about becoming a writer."

"Oh yeah?"

"Just because I didn't go on and on about it . . . Oh, here's the food. Thank you."

"Cheers, love," I said with a wink, and Red went all pink again.

We managed to spend the rest of the meal talking about non-deadly stuff, and it actually went all right. Cherry was picking at a fruit salad while I wolfed down a ginger cheesecake when I made the mistake of mentioning our old house in London in between mouthfuls.

Cherry scooped up a lychee. God knows why—they've always looked the opposite of appetising to me. Like tiny bleached brains. "I hated you for that, you know," she said in a conversational tone and popped it in her mouth.

"What?" I stared at her.

She chewed and swallowed. "You know. When you found that girl in the park, and Mum got all upset about it and insisted on moving out here. You *ruined* my social life—I hardly ever saw my friends after that, and it wasn't easy making more. I'd finished school, so it was really hard to meet people. Not to mention Martin."

"Martin?"

"My boyfriend." She went pink. "I'd have thought you'd remember *him*. There was such a row after you found that test."

Ah. Come to think of it, that did ring a bell. "The pregnancy test?"

She rolled her eyes. "No, a history test. What do you think?"

"Bet it taught you to be more careful, though, didn't it?"

"I didn't have much choice, did I? Not after the house move effectively split us up. He started going out with my best friend after that."

"Sorry." What else could I say?

There was a flicker of a smile. "It was more than twenty years ago. I think I'm over it now. But it wasn't easy for Dad either, suddenly having a much longer commute." Cherry put her spoon down. "Are you finished? I don't think I want to stay for a coffee."

I nodded. "Nah, I've got to finish clearing your room yet. I'll get the bill."

"I'm paying, remember."

While Cherry was faffing around with credit cards, I checked my phone in case I'd missed any calls. Not that I was expecting Phil to call or anything.

He hadn't, but there was a text.

"Shit," I muttered when I read it.

Cherry, of course, heard me over the chatter in the restaurant. "Is something wrong?"

I showed her the message: *the worst has hapnd!!! come to dyke at once!!!*

Her eyebrows nearly hit the ceiling. "Who on earth is that from?"

"Well, you remember a couple of Christmases ago . . ."

"Oh God. Not that awful man you brought round to Mum's."

"Oi, Gary's a good mate. And yeah, it's him."

"So what do you think has happened?" Cherry, bless her, held off from adding the eye roll and *Did he break a nail?* But I had a fair idea it was a close-run thing.

"Not sure. It might just be a case of the amateur dramatics, but . . ." I screwed up my face, trying to think how to put it. "See, Gary's not had a lot of luck with blokes, and this new one, Darren, Gary thinks the sun shines out of his bum. They just got engaged. It's going to kill the poor bloke if this one's gone sour too. I'd better give him a call."

I dialled, but it went straight to voice mail.

"Shit," I said again. Gary *never* turns his phone off—can't stand the thought of the world keeping on turning without him being in the know. "He's not answering. Look, do you mind if we just drop in on the way back? He means the Devil's Dyke pub in Brock's Hollow."

"It's not exactly on the way." She sighed. "Of course not."

She didn't suggest I drop her off at mine and leave her there, which was good, because I wasn't planning to. That'd be a fine way to keep an eye on her.

Also, she might terrorise the cats. "It shouldn't take too long," I reassured her. "If he's in a really bad way, we'll just bring him back with us."

On second thoughts, judging by her expression, she didn't find that all that reassuring.

CHAPTER TWENTY-TWO

When we got to the Dyke, it was easy to see this wasn't just one of Gary's storm-in-a-teacup, everyday crises. He was moping in the far corner, being comforted by the Devil's Dyke herself. Harry, the frankly terrifying landlady of the pub, was patting him on the shoulder with a battle-scarred hand that rivalled Greg's for size, and Flossie, the pub dog, had her head on the knee not already being drooled on by Julian, Gary's Saint Bernard.

I headed straight on over to him. "What's happened? Er, you remember my sister, Cherry, right?"

Gary looked up with red-rimmed eyes and sniffled in acknowledgement.

"I'll get some drinks," Cherry said quickly.

"Cheers. Pint for me, vodka martini for Gary, and . . ." I looked questioningly at Harry.

"I'll get 'em," she said gruffly, unfolding her sizeable frame from the chair. "You take care of your mate."

"I'll go and, um, help carry," Cherry said and followed Harry before anyone could say anything else that might threaten her escape.

I put an arm around Gary. "Come on, tell me all about it. What's the bastard done?"

He hiccupped. "We had a row."

"About?"

"About the wedding, what else? He won't even *consider* us both wearing white."

Huh. Maybe it wasn't quite as serious as it'd looked. "Is it really that big a thing?"

It was a clear sign of how upset Gary was that he heard that line and did absolutely nothing with it. "I gave in to him over the doves, and now I'm worried I'll just give and give, and there'll be nothing *left* of me!" Gary made an extravagant gesture that narrowly missed sending his drink flying.

Okay, so now I was beginning to see where he was coming from. It gave me an uncomfortable feeling. "Bit of a control freak, is he? I don't know. Maybe it's better to find that out now?"

Gary gave a large sniff and downed the rest of his martini, which, as answers went, was less than helpful.

"Has he done this before? You know, tried to make you change stuff?" A thought hit me, and I flushed. "When you go out, does he always insist on driving?"

There was a smaller sniff. "Not really."

Huh. "Maybe he's just got a thing about white? You know, doves, clothes . . ."

"You really think so?"

"Have you actually talked about it?" I gave him a pointed look. "Or have you just been hiding in here with your phone switched off?"

Cherry came over with our drinks at that point. Gary thanked her in a pathetically small voice, and she almost smiled at him. "I'll be over at the bar if you need me," she said as I reached to pull her out a chair.

"Oh. Okay. Cheers, Sis."

Gary watched her go. "I always thought she hated me," he said, cradling his martini glass.

"What? Cherry? Nah, never," I said and took a long swig of my pint so my face wouldn't give me away.

I almost had Gary talked round to giving Darren a call, when there was a commotion at the door.

Darren. Bloody hell, he had guts, turning up here. He strode into the pub like he owned the place, all four foot six of him, and stood glowering at me and Gary, his hands on his hips. Out of the corner of my eye I saw Harry pause in wiping down the bar. Like any good landlady, she had an eye for potential trouble, and I knew she wouldn't hesitate to sling Darren, quite literally, out on his arse if the situation called for it.

Darren stomped over to our corner. I was expecting him to come out with something belligerent like *Hands off my bloke, pint-size*, but his face softened and what he actually said was, "You all right, muffin?"

Gary sniffed and said "Fine," in classic *No-I'm-not* tones.

"Sweetheart, if it's that important to you, I'll get married in fairy wings and a fucking sparkly thong, all right?"

God, I hoped Gary wasn't going to take him up on that. He'd already asked me to be his best man, and there was only so much my eyes could take.

"Really?" Gary asked, in a tiny, hopeful voice. Julian whined in sympathy.

Darren nodded. "Really. Nothing's more important to me than my sugar muffin's happiness, you got that?"

Harry's posture relaxed, and she went back to wiping the bar as Gary stood and embraced his fiancé. There was a smattering of applause and a couple of wolf whistles from the regulars—all of whom know Gary well—and I might even have felt a slight prickling at the corner of my eye.

It was probably Darren's aftershave, mind.

As the kiss carried on, someone yelled, "Get a room!" and I fully expected our two turtledoves to follow the suggestion and disappear off home for some make-up sex. But instead, when they finally separated, Darren announced the drinks were on him and swaggered off to the bar.

Gary excused himself to splash a bit of cold water on his face. Well, he *actually* said he was going to powder his nose, but I was fairly sure he didn't mean that literally. I hoped.

"Well, all's well that ends well," Cherry said brightly, coming back over with her drink and mine. I could see she was itching to leave but was too polite with the large glass of Shiraz Darren had bought her in her hand.

"I bloody wish," Darren grumbled. He carefully positioned Gary's martini dead centre on a beer mat and sat down at the table, pint in hand.

"Sore loser?" I said with a wink to show I was only teasing.

"Something like that." Darren took a long swallow of his pint. "See, you've gotta know where I'm coming from, right? God knows I love my pumpkin—worship the bloody ground he walks on—but the plain fact is, he's not going to look his best in a white suit. You think he's going to be happy when he gets the wedding video back and he's got an arse on 'im that could sink the bleedin' *Titanic*?"

I pursed my lips and thought about the arse in question. It looked okay, more or less, in relaxed-fit black denim, but yeah, now I came to actually picture it in tailored white trousers . . . "Fair dues, you've got a point. Trouble is, how are you going to convince him without actually coming out and saying it?"

"Buggered if I know. Nah, I'm stuck with it now. Can't risk upsetting him again over the same bloody issue. Maybe I can delete the file before he sees it. At least the photos will all be from the front."

It was a practical solution, but I could see a major flaw there. "Yeah, but Gary's going to be gutted not to be able to watch himself starring in a movie with you."

Darren shrugged. "Ain't like it's the first one."

"Bet it's the first one he could show to his mum, though."

"Well, she's pretty broad-minded . . . Nah, you're right. Bugger."

Cherry stood up abruptly. "I'll see you in a minute." She took her glass with her, and seconds later, cut Gary off at the pass and manoeuvred him to the bar.

Darren looked at me. "What the bleedin' hell's that all about?"

"Don't ask me." I shrugged. "Maybe she wants to apologise for the last time she met him. They didn't get on all that well."

"You reckon? Nah, don't believe it. I mean, look at 'im."

I looked. Cherry and Gary were at the bar, her perching on a barstool and him standing, hip cocked and wrist limp, in a parody of a pose I reckoned he must have bought at Queens'R'Us.

"See that?" Darren went on. "Who could look at that and not love 'im?"

I took a sidelong glance at Darren. He'd gone a bit misty about the eyes, and there was a smile on his face that made me embarrassed to look at it.

Maybe he wasn't so bad, after all.

Cherry and Gary were back with us in ten minutes, just as Darren was really getting into one of his porn-filming anecdotes, this one involving a stepladder, a unicycle, and a python. Still, it was worth the interruption to see Gary looking so happy, bless his little designer socks.

"Cherry's come up with the most marvellous idea," he gushed. "Midnight-blue tuxedos, just like James Bond, but with crimson bow ties, not black. Dashing *and* sexy. What do you think, sweetie pie?"

Darren got down from his stool and adjusted his trousers. "I think, pumpkin, I'm going to take you home right now and ravish the fucking pants off you."

"But darling," Gary cooed with a fluttery gesture. "We're not even married yet. What will people say?"

"They can say it to my arse, 'cos my face ain't fucking listening. Cheers, Tom." He grinned at Cherry. "And you can get down the market and buy yourself a hat, love, 'cos you're coming to our wedding. No argument."

Cherry, bless her, just smiled and sat down next to me.

"What the hell did you say to Gary?" I asked in amazement when the lovebirds had left.

"Oh, I just pointed out that with Darren's past career, there might be people—cruel, heartless people—who would say the white was wholly inappropriate, and did he really want to expose his fiancé to that sort of unkind gossip?" She smiled smugly. "I said I thought Darren was far more sensitive than people give him credit for, and Gary wouldn't want to ruin their special day for his loved one, would he? I might also have mentioned *Fantasy Island* reruns, and how they were perhaps not the best source of style advice. And then I just went on about how suave Darren would look in darker colours."

Thank God I'd filled her in on a few details about Darren on the way over. "You're a marvel, Sis. I owe you for that. Well, technically Gary and Darren owe you, but they're mates, so . . ."

"Don't be silly. I just like to help." She frowned. "Oh, and the lady at the bar asked me for my phone number. I gave it to her, obviously, but do you think it was legal advice she wanted or, well . . ."

We both glanced over at Harry's granite features. She gave us a nod that didn't give anything away.

"Nah," I said. "Legal advice. Bound to be. You're not her type."

Cherry still looked dubious.

"I'll make sure I mention you're engaged, next time I'm in," I promised.

By the time we finally got back home, I don't think either Cherry or me had a lot of enthusiasm left for clearing the spare room out. But it didn't take too long in the end to shift a manageable amount of junk and put fresh sheets on the bed. Once we were done, I sat down on the sofa for the more important job of keeping Arthur happy while Cherry got herself settled in.

I was just beginning to regret not having made sure the TV remote was in reach before he'd plonked his furry ton-and-a-half on my lap, when Cherry walked into the living room. Arthur's ears twitched, but other than that, he remained unmoved by her presence. Merlin was still sulking somewhere. Bloody diva. "Pass us the remote, will you?" I asked with a winning smile that faded when I saw Cherry was carrying her phone.

Cherry flushed when she saw my look. "I gave Gregory a ring," she said, all defensive before I'd even got around to saying anything. "Just to let him know I was here. He'd be expecting me to be at home, and I didn't want him turning up there and worrying." She shoved her phone back into her handbag, avoiding my gaze.

I'd paused midstroke. Arthur's ears pricked, and he kneaded my lap with his paws, probably to remind me he had claws in there and wasn't afraid to use them. "Right . . . Are you sure it was a good idea to tell anyone you're here?"

"Gregory's not just *anyone*. You can't possibly think he had anything to do with the poisoning."

"Um."

"Don't be absurd. He's a *clergyman*."

"What, and you've never seen one of them in the dock, in your line of work?"

"Well, yes, but this is *Gregory*. He has a vocation. And he's the gentlest man you could ever meet."

Oh, sod it. "Listen, there's something I ought to tell you. I went to see Greg on my own, while you were in hospital—no, wait, it was after you'd gone to Mum and Dad's. Whatever. Anyway . . ." I took a deep breath. "He took me up in that cathedral roof, and I bloody near came down the quick way. I'm not saying he tried to kill me, mind," I said quickly as she paled. "Just, well, that's two of us who've nearly died while in old Greg's company. Bit of a coincidence, innit?"

"I can't believe you're even *suggesting* he could have tried to hurt either of us. Why on earth would he do that?"

"Just . . . How much do you really know about him? Have you met his family?"

"He hasn't got any close family," Cherry said shortly. "His parents are dead."

That was convenient. Say, if there was the odd skeleton in your closet you didn't want anyone to know about. "And how did you two even meet?"

"You're being ridiculous. I'm going to have a bath." Cherry stormed out without even answering my question.

Or passing me the bloody remote, either. Bloody marvellous. I tried to stretch out a socked foot far enough to reach it, but all I managed to do was nudge it off the other side of the coffee table. Meanwhile, Arthur, deciding my lap had become worryingly unstable, anchored himself more firmly by digging his claws into my legs.

Sod it. I shovelled him off my lap, earning myself a furious yowl and a couple more puncture wounds, grabbed the remote from the floor, and sat back down, flicking on the telly with a sigh of relief. There was a *Mock the Week* on satellite I'd only seen about half a dozen times, so I let the controlled anarchy and carefully scripted ad-libs wash over me for a bit.

Then I remembered I'd used up the last of the milk and there'd be none for breakfast if I didn't shift my arse out to the shops.

Bugger it. "Cherry?" I yelled up the stairs. "Just popping out for some milk."

I didn't hear an answer, so either she was sulking or she hadn't heard me over the running water. Still, I'd only be ten minutes, tops. I shoved my feet into my trainers, pulled on a jacket, dithered over a scarf but decided not to be such a bloody wuss, checked I had a couple of quid in my pocket, and opened the front door.

And almost walked into the Terrifyingly Reverend Greg, looming there on my doorstep.

CHAPTER TWENTY-THREE

"**B**loody fuck!" I stepped back instinctively and almost tripped over Merlin, who'd come to see what all the fuss was about.

Greg's devilish grin faltered a little. "Ah, Tom," he said, as if he hadn't expected to see me here in my own sodding house. "Cherry told me she was staying here, and I happened to be in the vicinity. May I?"

No, I thought, you bloody well may not. Not with Cherry in the bath and me not there to protect her. How easy would it be for him to hold her down and drown her with those massive hands of his? "I was just on my way out, actually. Fancy a walk?"

The eyebrows drew together, a couple of disapproving hairy caterpillars cosying up like grannies having a grumble. "Are you sure it's wise to leave Cherry on her own?"

"Positive," I said, stepping through the door and closing it behind me. As Greg didn't give an inch, this put us uncomfortably close together on my doormat. The height difference seemed a lot more pronounced. I wished I couldn't vaguely remember horror movies where unspecified demonic creatures gained power and size after dark. "Shops are this way," I said, trying to nudge him along without actually touching him.

"Shops?"

"Yeah. Just need to get some milk." Weren't there some supernatural beings that liked drinking milk? Elves, maybe? Or was I just thinking of hedgehogs?

"Oh, of course. Lead on." Despite his words, Greg strode off down the street towards the bright lights of Fleetville without waiting for me. I ended up scurrying along to catch up.

"And how is your dear sister bearing up? She seemed somewhat agitated on the telephone."

"She's okay." I wondered if I'd missed obvious signs of agitation from Cherry while we were out for dinner. She'd certainly *seemed* okay in the restaurant and when we'd got back to mine.

Except she'd sneaked off to call her bloke first chance she'd got. Maybe she was feeling more vulnerable than she wanted to let on. What if she got out of the bath and found herself all alone when she wasn't expecting it? We needed to get a shift on. I scurried a bit faster and managed to jolt my hip with an unwary step. The sudden pain made me draw in a hissing breath.

"Are you all right, Tom?" Greg loomed over me, his eyebrows quivering with concern.

"Yeah. Fine. Just trod a bit awkward, that's all."

"Is it much farther to go? Can you manage?"

Blooming marvellous. Now I was a bloody cripple who couldn't make it down the road without help. "It's here," I said shortly, opening the door to Vik's convenience store and off licence that never seems to shut. I picked up a couple of litres of milk and some chocolate for Cherry, then decided a bottle of Merlot might be nearer the mark and grabbed that as well.

"All right, Tom?" Vik (short for Vikram, but only his mother calls him that) rang up the total on a till so old-fashioned he actually had to put the numbers in by hand. "Cold enough for you?"

"And then some." I fumbled in my pocket with numb fingers, realising a bit belatedly I'd come out with *literally* only a couple of quid in my pocket. "Bugger. I'm a bit short, Vik, I'll have to leave the wine."

"Nah, pay me tomorrow." He grinned and cast a quick glance over my shoulder at Greg hovering behind me. "Don't want to ruin your first evening in with the new bloke."

I don't know what my face looked like, but Vik cracked up at the sight of it.

"Right. Home," I said firmly to a blessedly oblivious Greg.

Cherry was still in the bath when we got back, so at least she hadn't found herself home alone and thrown a wobbly. That was the only plus point I could see, though. It left me and Greg sitting in the living room glaring balefully at each other. Well, all right. Maybe Greg was smiling genially. Then again, he hadn't been the one having a near-death experience last time we'd met. I offered to open the wine; Greg declined. I offered to put the kettle on; he protested he didn't want to put me to any bother.

I was ready to scream by the time Merlin poked his furry little nose around the doorframe.

Greg beamed. "Ah! You have pets." Like he hadn't noticed the cat hair already making pretty patterns on his smart black trousers. "Wonderful. As you know, I have a great fondness for animals."

Dead ones, maybe. If he came anywhere near my cats with the glint of taxidermy in his eye, we were going to have serious words. Luckily, Merlin caught him watching, spooked, and voted with his paws, running out of there like he'd seen the skinning knives. Hah. My pets weren't stupid.

Then Arthur prowled in, gave a disdainful sniff in my direction, and jumped straight onto Greg's lap.

Typical.

There was the noise of a door opening and closing upstairs, then Cherry appeared, towel round her head and wearing my dressing gown, her face pink and shiny. "Tom, I need to borrow a— Gregory!"

I couldn't help smiling at her double take. "You want to borrow him, it's Arthur you need to speak to."

"I meant a hairdryer . . . Gregory, what are you doing here?"

Greg stood, having picked up Arthur and deposited him carefully and without protest on the floor (no clawed legs for a man of the cloth, apparently). He went to meet her, taking her hands in an old-fashioned gesture. "I had to make sure you were all right, my dear."

"I'm fine, darling," Cherry simpered. Oh God. Were they going to kiss?

Yep.

I tried looking away, but that just left my imagination free to run riot, which was even worse. I coughed loudly. "I'll put the kettle on, all right?"

I didn't wait for an answer.

An hour later, our cups of tea had long since been drained and Greg still hadn't bloody gone. I yawned loudly, hoping he'd take a hint.

Cherry glanced over. "Tom, if you want to go to bed, we won't be offended."

"Nah, I'm good," I lied.

She smiled. "Lovely! I'll open that bottle of wine, then."

We each had a glass while they carried on billing and cooing and having animated discussions over exactly which of the cathedral ladies simply had to be asked to do the flowers for their wedding, and which should, under no circumstances, be allowed to decorate.

I nearly melted in relief when Cherry offered top-ups and Greg held a large hand over his glass. "No more for me, I'm afraid. Indeed, I should really be getting back home."

"Why don't you stay here?" Cherry said. "It's far too late for you to drive all the way back to St. Leonards tonight."

What? "Nah, he'll be fine," I said quickly. "Roads'll be empty this time of night."

"But they could be icy." She topped up Greg's glass without waiting for either of us to chip in.

Course, she wouldn't have been able to do so if he hadn't moved his hand away first.

"Really," he fake-protested even as he raised his glass to his lips. "I shouldn't like to put Tom to any trouble."

Cherry gave him a girlish smile. "Don't be silly. It isn't any trouble, is it, Tom?"

I coughed. "You do know I've only got one spare room, don't you?" And the bed was pretty bloody narrow, even setting aside any qualms I might have about her seducing God's representative on earth into rumpy-pumpy out of wedlock.

Greg patted the sofa as if he'd stuffed it himself. "This will do admirably."

Cherry looked almost as horrified as I was feeling. "You can't sleep down here. You'll ruin your back. You can share with Tom."

What? "Hang on a minute . . ."

"He's got a lovely big bed," she continued, talking over me.

Shit. I had to nip this one right in the bud. "Sis, most straight blokes wouldn't be too happy about sharing a bed with a poof."

"You shouldn't use that word. And Gregory knows perfectly well you're not going to molest him in his sleep."

That was more than I knew. What if I rolled over and my subconscious thought he was Phil? It didn't bear thinking about.

"I'm sure my virtue is safe in your hands," Greg agreed genially and took another slurp of wine.

Bloody brilliant. "I snore," I blurted out as a last-ditch attempt to save myself.

"Oh, you won't wake me. I've spent most of my adult life sleeping close by church bells and clock towers. I sleep like the dead."

And he'd know, wouldn't he? If he was a bloody *murderer*. Shit. There was about a glass of wine left in the bottle. Sod politeness—I tipped it into my glass and downed it in one.

It only got worse after that. Obviously, Greg hadn't brought his pyjamas with him, and equally obviously, there was no way anything of mine was going to fit the bloke, so he stripped down to his ecclesiastical undies to go to bed. Apparently, the church favoured white cotton Y fronts these days. I'd have been a lot happier to see him in a full set of thermals, or maybe some of those old-fashioned one-piece combinations they used to sew kids into for the winter back in the Dark Ages. I dug out my thickest set of PJs—some that Mum bought me one Christmas and I'd never worn—from the bottom of the wardrobe and changed, miserably, in the bathroom.

When I got back into the bedroom, Greg was stretched out in bed, taking up a good two-thirds of it. His hairy chest peeked over the top of the duvet like a badly trained pet dog, and his welcoming smile was weirding me out big-time.

Not that I've got anything against hairy chests. Or smiling blokes in my bed, for that matter. But Christ, not this one.

"Just as well I never gave Phil a key, innit," I joked weakly as I climbed in beside Greg. "He'd have a fit if he turned up unexpected and found me in bed with another bloke."

Greg rolled onto his side, propped himself up on one elbow and loomed over me with earnest eyes. "I'm quite certain he trusts you implicitly. It's heartwarming to see the two of you with such a loving, committed relationship."

"Er, thanks." I wasn't sure what to say. Were we committed? I mean, I hoped Phil didn't want to break up with me, and I was bloody sure I didn't want to break up with him. But we'd never talked about, well, commitment and stuff. Still, it was early days yet, wasn't it?

I wondered how long Phil had been with Mark before they'd decided to get married.

Shit.

"I hope you don't mind," Greg was saying, "but I'd like to say a short prayer before we retire. Perhaps you could join me in the Lord's prayer?"

"Right. Yeah." God, I hoped I could remember the words. It'd been a long time since Sunday School. Feeling about five, I put my hands together and closed my eyes, and waited for him to start *Our-Fathering*.

"Before we begin," he said instead, startling me so I opened my eyes again. Greg's face filled my blurry vision, and I flinched. He ignored it. "I have a little confession to make."

Despite the PJs, an icy chill ran over me. "Yeah?" I said weakly. "How little?"

"Ah, there is only one true Judge of our sins. But I trust that He will see my intentions were pure." Greg beamed.

Was there a manic edge to his smile? Shit, was I in bed with a murdering religious nutter? "Er, yeah, that's His job, innit?" I said, trying to edge away unobtrusively.

"*Nevertheless*," Greg barked, freezing me in my tracks. "I feel a certain amount of remorse."

"So, er, maybe you should just 'go and sin no more'?" I'd have given myself a mental pat on the back for the sudden inspiration if I hadn't still been in terror for my sodding life.

"Excellent!" A massive hand clapped me on the shoulder. "I can see we're going to get on splendidly, Tom. Now, to prayer."

"Hang on a mo," I blurted out before my better judgement could kick in. "What about the confession?" *Christ, Paretski, have you never heard the phrase* least said soonest NOT murdered in your own bloody bed?

"Oh, indeed. Thank you for reminding me. Yes, well." The hand massaged my shoulder. I wondered if its owner was aware of it. "I realise it's a great deal to ask, and I wouldn't want you to go against your conscience, but if you could perhaps see your way to not mentioning this to Cherry?"

"Y-yeah, no problem." I cleared my throat and hoped he hadn't noticed the stutter. "Silent as the grave, that's me." God, not literally, I hoped.

"You're too kind. I'm afraid I have been a trifle mendacious. The notes, I must tell you. A mere figment."

"The . . . What?"

"The threatening letters. I'm afraid they never existed. Cherry was so worried about you, you see—or should I say, she was worried about your relationship with Philip. I decided it would be good to arrange an opportunity of observing him more closely." The eyebrows softened. "I'm happy to say that my impressions have been entirely favourable."

"Right." I cleared my throat again. Must be an allergy or something. "So you were just checking out my bloke. In the, um, non-gay way, obviously."

"Indeed!"

"But Cherry didn't know."

"I didn't want to give her cause for more concern."

"Course not."

"But can you forgive me?" Big, worried eyes peered at me from way too close for comfort.

"Er, yeah. Course."

He beamed. "Excellent. Now, as I said, to prayer."

"Yeah. Fine. Um. Do you think you could . . .?" I shrugged the shoulder he was still crushing with his massive mitt. Or tried to, at any rate. It only moved about a millimetre, but Greg finally got the hint and let go of me.

I felt weirdly lopsided as Greg composed himself for prayer, which seemed to consist of taking a deep breath, letting it out slowly, and smiling briefly to himself. Or, you know, the bloke upstairs. "Our Father . . ." he began.

Funny how you remember stuff. I managed to follow along with Greg pretty well, although we had the odd disagreement between *sins* and *trespasses*. It was easily the most bizarre thing I'd ever done in bed. Darren would be so disappointed in me, I thought, and only just managed not to snigger.

God duly bothered, I switched off the light.

I lay there for hours while Greg snored away like a buzz saw. Every time I dozed off, I dreamed of being smothered by enormous hands—all right, one time it was the chest hair—and startled awake, panting. Greg, true to his word, didn't stir.

In the end, I decided that even if he was planning to wake up and murder me and Cherry in our beds, I was too bloody knackered to fight back or even, for that matter, care. I grabbed a blanket and staggered down to the sofa, where I finally managed to get a couple of hours' kip.

CHAPTER Twenty-Four

Friday morning, my phone rang while I was still rubbing sleep out of my eyes. Not that it was all that early, I realised when my vision cleared enough to see the clock. Good thing I didn't have any jobs on this morning. Next week was going to be a bugger, catching up with it all.

I lurched into the kitchen, where I'd left my phone on charge, and, wonder of wonders, managed to pick up before the caller rang off. Must be some persistent bastard.

Phil?

Nope. It was Dave, the other persistent bastard in my life.

"All right?" I asked, yawning.

Apparently he wasn't in the mood for small talk. "You heard from your sister lately?"

"Not since last night. Why?" I blinked at the kettle. Coffee, that was what I needed.

"We've been trying to get in touch with her. She's not answering her phone, and there's no one at the house either."

"Yeah, there is," I said, puzzled. "Both of us."

"What, you're at hers now?"

"No, she's at mine. Has been since yesterday." The cafetière hadn't been cleaned out since last night. I managed to open the jar of instant one-handed and spooned some into a mug. Merlin tangled round my legs in his usual *feed me* dance, and Arthur gave a pointed meow.

"And for fuck's sake, it didn't occur to *either* of you to bloody well let us know? Brains run in the family, do they? Jesus. Can I speak to her?"

"Well, she's still asleep. I think. Told you I hadn't seen her since last night. Why, you arrested someone?" Could I fill the kettle and still hear Dave speak? Probably not. Might as well feed the cats before they went feral and started munching on me.

"Not even close. But you were right about that bloody basket. I pulled some strings, and the lab just got back to me. The body lotion's lethal. Nicotine again."

My stomach dropped. "Jesus. Any signs of who sent it?" I stood there for a moment, then, remembering what I'd been in the middle of doing, I opened the cupboard and got out a pouch of Fisherman's Choice. The audience went wild.

"Not as yet. Whoever's doing this knows their stuff. Christ, what the bloody hell are you doing to those cats? Skinning them alive?"

Fair dues, the caterwauling had got a bit out of hand. If Greg and Cherry hadn't been awake already, I was betting they would be now. "Feeding them."

"What, to the lions? Listen, while we're on, I had 'em check out Little Miss Morangie."

"Yeah?" I tried to remember exactly what I'd told Dave about her, while ripping open the cat food and squeezing it out into the cats' bowls.

Heads down, tails up. The sudden silence was deafening.

"You weren't so far wrong about it being a son. Elizabeth Morangie changed her name when she hit eighteen. Along with her sex."

"Bloody hell. I guess Daddy wasn't too chuffed about that. I mean, judging by the way he reacted. When I went to his house," I explained, not sure if I'd told him this already or not.

"You were at this bloke's house?" From his tone, apparently this was the first he'd heard about it. Course, he'd been pretty trollied by the end of that night in the pub. Maybe he'd forgotten.

"Well, yeah. I was supposed to be looking for that bloody will thing, wasn't I? But then I asked about his son, and he threw me out."

"Could have just been the natural effect of your charming personality, of course."

"Piss off. Nah, I mean, it wasn't like he was overjoyed to have me there anyway, but it was as if this was the last straw. He even threatened to call your lot in if I didn't scarper. So what's he calling himself now, then? Morangie junior, I mean."

"Funny you should ask. Reckon you were right about there not being too much love lost between Morangie and the kid—she, sorry, *he* took Mum's maiden name. Nair. Mum being of the Asian persuasion."

Even in my sleep-deprived state, this was ringing more bells than Gary and his mates at a royal wedding. "What, like *Raz* Nair? From the Literati?"

"Exactly like. Bit of a coincidence, innit? Which, by the way, I don't believe in. Right. You look after your sister, and don't let her do anything daft. Don't let her hang around with the fiancé either. There's something funny about that bloke."

He hung up while I was still wondering how I was supposed to bloody well stop her. But at least it saved me having to explain how I'd had him in my bed last night.

I shuddered. Not a good choice of wording, that. I hoped to God I never slipped and described it to Phil that way. Speaking of which . . . I dialled Phil's number. He answered immediately, sounding brisk and professional.

I stifled another yawn. "Dave just rang. There was nicotine in the body lotion."

"Right."

"Right? That's all you've got to say? Cherry could have bloody *died*. Again."

There was a silence. "Yeah. But you couldn't."

Oh. Right. I felt a weird mix of emotions: touched, because his first thought was of me; still a bit miffed on Cherry's behalf; and daft, because that hadn't actually occurred to me. "I suppose it doesn't matter about Morangie junior, then."

"What about her?"

"Him. He's trans. Dave just told me. And get this: it's Raz Nair."

"Bloody hell. I *knew* it."

"That's more than I sodding well did, then. So that means . . . Actually, what does that mean? Really?"

"Buggered if I know. Not a lot, I suppose, now we know it's not you they're after. Unless of course someone's doing a really callous bit of misdirection. How'd your sister take the news about the basket?"

I sighed. "Haven't told her yet." I heard a sound and looked around nervously in case Cherry had crept up on me and was listening in, but it was only Arthur, nudging his now-empty food bowl across the floor towards me in a pointed gesture. Greedy bastard. I shook my head firmly, and he stalked out of the room, his tail giving me the finger. Merlin had already disappeared somewhere. "Think I should?"

"Well, put it this way, if anyone ever tries to top me, you'd better bloody not keep quiet about it."

"Yeah, you're right. It's just . . . she's already in a bit of a state."

"She's a big girl. She can handle it. Listen, I'm going to talk to Hannah Mudge today. You coming along?"

I hesitated. "Nah, I'd better stay with Cherry. Think she might be feeling a bit fragile after I tell her the news."

I hung up and wandered back into the living room to eat my toast in front of the telly. I nearly dropped my plate when I saw Cherry curled up on the sofa with the cats. Had she been taking lessons from Merlin on sneaking downstairs? I wondered how much she'd heard of me talking on the phone.

She glanced up at me, her eyes red and her face longer than a bank holiday tailback on the M25. "Morning." It came out with a shrug and a sigh. Her hair was loose, for once, and it hid her expression as she bent her head and focussed on Arthur's twitching ears, but I was betting it wasn't exactly chirpy. She had yesterday's clothes on—well, the same baggy sweater; I couldn't have sworn to the leggings. They all look alike, don't they? Especially with a generous coating of cat hair.

I'd meant to tell her about the gift basket, but I just couldn't do it. Not when she was miserable already. It could wait. At least until after I'd had my coffee. "Er, yeah. Morning. Greg up yet?" I asked, expecting a no.

"Oh, yes. He left to go back home about an hour ago." Cherry looked even glummer now. She fished out a hanky from somewhere under the sweater and blew her nose.

I wasn't too happy myself at the thought I'd slept right through him getting up, saying goodbye to my sister, and leaving. Some bloody watch dog I was. "Want some breakfast?" I said, hoping to cheer her up a bit.

She blinked at my plate of toast and marmalade, then smiled faintly and held out a hand. "Thanks."

Good thing I hadn't already taken a bite. I handed it over, then realised with an unpleasant jolt I'd have to give her my coffee as well. I considered hanging on to it, but she'd be bound to realise then I hadn't made the toast for her either.

Cherry took the mug, then made a face. "I have tea in the morning."

"No problem." I snatched it back, pleased. And maybe a bit insulted on my coffee's behalf. Okay, it might have been instant, but it wasn't like it was Morrisons own brand or anything. "I'll go and make you a cuppa."

I found myself whistling as I boiled the kettle—probably a subconscious memory of Auntie Lol. I stopped whistling when I realised there was only enough marmalade left for half a slice of toast.

To add insult to injury, when I got back into the living room with Cherry's tea and my toast, I saw she'd left most of the original plateful uneaten.

Maybe she caught my glance. "I'm just not very hungry. Sorry."

"Hey, who do you think I am? Mum? You don't want to eat it, you don't eat it, all right?"

"You can have it if you want," she suggested, and I was on that like, well, marmalade on toast.

It was a bit on the lukewarm side, but I've had worse. I munched away happily, only looking up when I felt Cherry's critical gaze on me. "What? I get hungry in the mornings, all right?"

"Oh, it's not your eating habits. Although now you come to mention it . . . No, I was just looking at those pyjamas. You look about fifty in them. Actually, no, you look like you're from the *nineteen* fifties." She smirked. "I hope you don't wear them in bed with Phil."

"Nope. I keep 'em for when I go to bed with *your* boyfriend, all right?" I smirked right back at her, glad she'd cheered up a bit. "Wanna borrow them sometime?"

I gave Phil a ring later in the day. Cherry had disappeared into the bathroom after lunch, although what she was doing in there I wasn't sure, given that she was apparently allergic to all bath products. Also, who has a bath after lunch? "There's something I forgot to mention earlier," I opened with. "You'll never guess what Greg confessed to me last night."

"His undying love?"

I shuddered. "No, thank God. Those letters you're looking into for him? You can stop, 'cause they never existed."

"Figures. So what was his game?"

"Vetting you. You'll be pleased to hear you've got the Gregory Titmus seal of approval."

"Ecstatic." His tone was so dry I felt an urge to pour myself a drink.

"Hey, it's only one step below canonisation, that." I frowned. "Actually, that's a bit weird, innit?"

"What is?"

I wandered into the kitchen. Yep, there was a good half cup left in the cafetière from after lunch. I tipped it carefully into my mug. A bit sludgy but still good. "Well, if you call it canonisation when you make someone a saint, what do you call it when you make them a canon?"

"Iron foundry."

I blinked. "Oi. You thought I wasn't going to get that, didn't you?"

"Guilty as charged." I swear I could hear the smirk. "So what are you and your sister up to today?"

"Sorting out the van, mostly. Me, I mean. You wouldn't believe the stuff I found in there—"

"I'll believe anything. I've seen inside the back of your van—it's like a black hole that's swallowed a scrap yard. Let me guess, enough spare parts to plumb out an entire house, and a couple of old lovers?"

"Yeah. I'd been wondering where they'd got to."

"Remind me never to accept any invitations to get kinky in the back of your van." Not that he ever would, anyway. Phil, risk snagging one of his expensive sweaters on an off-cut of pipe? "What about your sister?"

"Cherry? Well, she's not going into the office. Think she just wants to slob around and watch daytime telly. Help her empathise with her clients, that sort of thing. Oh, and there's Raz's thing this evening."

"Christ, with you around, I'm spoilt for innuendo. Go on—tell me about Raz's *thing*."

"It's poetry in motion, Raz's thing. Well, close, anyway. It's poetry in the library. In Pluck's End—didn't I tell you?"

"Yeah, you told me. A poetry reading. And you're going because?"

"Well . . . he's Auntie Lol's stepson. I just thought we could talk and stuff." Realisation hit me like a sock in the jaw. "Shit, he knows, doesn't he? I mean, he's got to."

"What, that you and him have got the Auntie Lol connection? Course he knows."

"Were you ever going to mention this to me, or do you just enjoy keeping me in the dark?"

Phil huffed. "I thought you'd already realised, you twat."

All right, maybe it was a bit obvious. "Yeah, well. Put it down to lingering concussion from the Fishpool Street fondler. So how long do you reckon . . . That must have been what he was on about on his doorstep. Why he let me in and all."

"Yeah. What interests me is how long he's known him and Cherry had the connection."

I took a sip of sludge to fortify my brain. Jesus, it had a kick like a mule. "I reckon he must have known all along. Auntie Lol must have told him about her, and then when they met in the post office, he realised who she was from the name. Wonder why he didn't say anything? I mean, apart from asking if she was Polish."

"Does he strike you as the sort to trust anyone as far as he can throw them? Anyway, you can ask him tonight, can't you?"

"Yeah, guess so. You want to come?"

"All right. Be interesting to see who else turns up."

"What, like the Literati? Hey, how'd it go with Hannah this morning?" I'd forgotten he was going to interview her today.

"It didn't. She left me a voice mail cancelling the appointment."

"Suspicious."

"You'd be amazed how many people blow me off when I'm working," he said, deadpan.

"Right. I hope by *blow you off* you mean *stand you up*, not *give you head*."

"Jealous?" There was a grin in that voice. I grinned back at it.

"You wish. So what time am I seeing you tonight?"

"Depends if you're offering me dinner first, doesn't it?"

"Beans on toast do?"

"Beans on toast? What happened to home cooking? Something tells me the magic's gone out of this relationship."

"Nah, we've just reached the cosy, comfortable stage where neither of us has to pretend to be something he's not. I'll see you around six, all right? Got to leave time to get there."

"See you then." He hung up.

I slurped down the rest of my sludge and bunged my trainers on to go shopping. Phil knew I wouldn't *really* serve him up beans on toast.

He did know that, didn't he?

Right?

In the end, Cherry and me between us managed to put together a fairly decent risotto.

Cherry stirred the pan with a doubtful look on her face. "I'm not really all that keen on home-cooked risotto. Does it *need* four kinds of mushroom?"

"Well, yeah, if you don't want it to taste like boring mushy crap." I peered over her shoulder. "You can add a bit more stock now. Just half a cup."

"Can't we put it in all at once? That's what I always do."

"Which would be why you don't like home-cooked risotto. That's a no, by the way. And keep stirring."

She tutted, but just added half a cup. And kept stirring. I felt safe enough to go back to grating the parmesan.

Phil turned up right on time, just as the rice was getting to the al dente stage. I dished up the risotto with a couple of chicken drumsticks on the side, for the benefit of muscle-bound hulks who might be worried about losing an ounce if they didn't eat meat at least twice a day.

"It's good, this," he said, showing his approval by helping himself to seconds of risotto. I grabbed a bit more myself before he could scoff the lot.

"Thank you," Cherry said, as if it'd been all her own work. Then she gave me a look. "It's not an eating competition, you know."

"Oi, I've got a fast metabolism," I defended myself.

"Hollow legs, more like," Phil muttered. "Are you coming to the reading tonight?"

Cherry shook her head. "I really don't think I can face it. I'm just going to have a quiet evening in."

"What, on your own?" It was Phil's turn to give me a sharp look.

I swallowed my mouthful indignantly. "*No*. Gary's coming round."

"Gary?" Now Phil was looking like he was worried for my sanity.

Cherry stabbed a few leaves of rocket, oblivious to the undercurrents. "Yes. Tom *insists* I need a babysitter, and unfortunately, Gregory's got a meeting tonight." Or fortunately, depending on your point of view. I still didn't trust that bloke, with his murderer's mitts and evil eyebrows. "Anyway, Gary wanted an opinion on the wedding invitations. I know he and I didn't get off to a good start, but he's rather sweet, once you get to know him."

Phil frowned at me. "Just how much wine did you put in the risotto?"

"None. It was brandy. Nah, it's okay. We met up with Gary in the Dyke last night, Cherry and me, and they got on great."

"Do your mum and dad know you're such a corrupting influence on your sister?"

"Probably," I admitted.

Cherry tutted. "I'm thirty-nine, you know. Not thirteen."

I smiled at her. "And it's just lovely the way you've kept your childlike innocence all this time."

I don't think Cherry quite knew what to say to that.

CHAPTER TWENTY-FIVE

"**F**eels a bit weird, this," I said as Phil and me walked into Pluck's End library for Raz's reading. "Last time I came to a library for a reading, I was in short trousers, and we all had to sit cross-legged on the floor. And no, it wasn't just last week."

Phil grunted. "If you're hoping he's going to hold the book up to show you the pictures tonight, I think you're in for a disappointment."

We'd left Cherry in the hopefully capable hands of Gary, who'd brought round a shed-load of wedding magazines and left Darren at home with Julian, thank God. I'm all for people having their minds broadened, but an evening with Darren would have left Cherry with her mind so bloody broad her brains would be dribbling out of her ears.

Libraries had changed a bit since last time I'd been in one. It was all electronic scanners now instead of little date stamps with purple ink, and there were notices up on the wall about their range of audiobooks and ebooks.

"How do you borrow an ebook?" I wondered aloud.

"Just download it, like if you were buying it." My Phil, expert on everything.

I frowned. "How do you bring it back, then? Does it self-destruct after two weeks?"

"I don't know, do I? Never tried." All right, maybe not expert on *everything*.

One thing hadn't changed—the librarians still looked motherly. Maybe taking care of books was like looking after children? Keeping them in order, making sure their jackets were clean, letting them go home with random members of the public . . . Okay, maybe the analogy wasn't perfect.

This particular librarian was tall and well-built but round-shouldered like she spent a lot of time bending down to talk to kids. She was in her thirties, wearing trendy glasses and a name badge reading *Bridget*. "Are you here for the reading?" she asked brightly.

I smiled back at her. "Yeah—Raz Nair, right?" Just in case we'd got the wrong library or something.

"It's this way. Are you both poets too?"

"Nah, we're just, er, friends of Raz. Do you have a lot of these readings?"

"We do like to support our local authors wherever possible." Bridget led us around the shelves to a corner, where about forty plastic chairs had been laid out in optimistic rows. "You can sit anywhere. It'll be about ten minutes or so before the start."

"Cheers, love," I said with a wink. Bridget pursed her lips and gave me an over-the-glasses look and a smile as she went back to the desk. Raz wasn't there yet, and neither was anyone else, much, although in amongst a gaggle of old grannies clearly up for all the free entertainment Pluck's End could provide, I spotted one or two familiar faces. I nudged Phil. "That's Peter Grissom," I said, nodding to the bloke in question. "And Morgan," I added. "Next to Margaret."

"Literati's out in force, then."

"'Cept Hannah," I said and then jumped a mile when I heard her voice right in my ear.

"Hello, Tom. I wasn't expecting to see you here."

I spun. "Hannah. Er, yeah. Well, you know. Got to support local authors, and all that. You're looking . . ." Grey. She was looking grey, in a shapeless cardi over a frumpy dress over clunky shoes. I racked my brains for something more acceptable to say. ". . . well."

She peered at me, her brow furrowed. "You look a bit tired. Have you not been sleeping well?"

"Few too many late nights, that's all. And, you know, worrying about my sister. It was a really nice gesture, you sending that gift basket to Cherry," I added as innocently as I could.

Hannah frowned. "Um, thanks, but I didn't send anything. And I wouldn't really have thought it was appropriate, sending fruit to someone who's had an upset tummy."

Had an upset tummy? That was a new euphemism for *been poisoned and nearly died.* "It was signed from all the Literati. I assumed you'd all had a whip-round."

The frown cleared. "Oh, it was probably Margaret, then." Hannah smiled. "She's really quite sweet, once you get to know her."

I followed her gaze over to where Margaret was in furious confab with Morgan. She glanced up at me and glared daggers. Probably poisoned ones.

Sweet? Yeah, right. Like a bloody python.

Speaking of unpleasant animals, Peter Grissom was heading our way. He didn't smile as he came to stand next to Hannah, a faint air of *are these men bothering you?* about him. "Surprised to see you showing your face here," was his version of a friendly greeting.

"Er, Raz invited me."

"Oh? Now that I find hard to believe."

Phil stepped forward. "Why's that?"

Peter sent him a suspicious glare. "Who are you?"

"Poetry lover," Phil said, straight-faced. Was it just my imagination, or had he just straightened his shoulders to add a bit more menace to his loom?

"Really? Or did you just come to mock, like *him*?" Peter definitely did a bit of chest-puffing before sneering in my direction.

Oops. Rumbled. "I didn't go along to the Literati to mock anyone," I protested.

"Raz had your number. Said you played us all for a bunch of idiots." Our dark rat's sneer was turning into a snarl. I wondered how painful it'd be if he bit me, and tried to think how long it'd been since I'd last had a tetanus shot.

Hannah made a distressed little noise and grabbed hold of Peter's arm. "I never believed that. You wouldn't do that to us, would you, Tom?"

"Course not! It was all a misunderstanding, that's all. I spoke to Raz yesterday, and we're good mates now." I gave them my best innocent smile. "Like I said, he even asked me to come along to this do."

"Really." Peter's chest deflated.

"You see?" Hannah said brightly. "I knew it couldn't be true."

"I'd suggest you watch your back," Peter muttered. "He may say one thing to your face, but it's another matter when you're not around. You can't trust people like that. That book he's reading from tonight? It's not even properly published. *Self-published.*" He said it like it was the literary equivalent of having a wank in public. "It's just vanity."

I shifted on my feet, a twinge of unease making me restless. *Was* Raz that sort of bloke? All sweetness and light until you turned your back on them and they stuck a knife in it?

"When *I* get published," Hannah put in, her tones smug as she looked up at Peter, still hanging on to his arm like a fainting Victorian maiden. "I'm holding out for a proper contract with a major publishing house. And a five-figure advance."

"Of course you are. There's no point, otherwise. It's not like there's even any money in self-publishing. Just think about it—unless you spend a fortune on advertising, how is anyone even going to know your book exists?"

"Quite right. Why don't we go and sit down?" Hannah suggested and steered him off to a couple of seats in the front row.

"You were quiet during all that," I said to Phil in a low voice. "Menacing but quiet. Aren't you going have another go at talking to Hannah?"

"Not while she's with him, I'm not. She wouldn't say anything she didn't think he'd want to hear."

"Yeah, I got that impression too. Funny, I thought at the meeting it was Morgan she was all starry-eyed over, not Peter. Want me to try and grab him later, and you can corner her?"

"Maybe. See how things go." He paused. "What do you reckon to what he was saying about Raz?"

"Dunno." I looked away. An elderly couple were doddering among the chairs, trying to sort out each other's walking sticks. She sat down with an audible huff, and he eased himself down beside her slowly, as if half his joints had rusted up. Then they shared a smile that seemed to say *We made it, and we're not dead yet. Good for us.* "I'd like to know exactly what he said about me. And whether he's still saying it when I'm not around."

"Good luck on that one. Course, you could always ask him."

I followed his gaze. Sure enough, Raz had just walked in the door. He gave a jerky little smile that lasted all of half a second when he saw me looking at him. I took a step towards him, meaning to go and say hi, but he blanked me and started weaving his way through the chairs to the front.

"Huh. Maybe Peter was right about old Raz blowing hot and cold," I muttered as Phil and me took a couple of seats near the back.

"It's nothing personal. Look at him. He's wound up tighter than a bishop's balls in a brothel."

"Get that one from Greg, did you?" I followed his gaze. Sure enough, the slim book in Raz's hands was trembling as he stood up there in front of a mostly empty rank of chairs, all on his lonesome. "Bloody hell, the poor sod's got a bad case of stage fright."

"Either that, or he's just found out what they're putting in the tea at halftime. Any rate, we'd better sit down. I think it's about to kick off."

Bridget came up to the front and said a few words about Raz, and then we were up and running.

Not literally, unfortunately. God, it was dry. Raz had only been reading for about two minutes before I remembered just why I never go to poetry readings. It was so far over my head it was practically stratospheric. Plus, I was having flashbacks to English classes at school, and Mrs. Mertle singling me out of the class and demanding to know exactly what whoever-it-was meant when he wrote the words *vegetable love*.

I got a two-hour detention that day. *And* she never told me what the right answer was.

"*Oof.*" I glared at Phil, who'd just elbowed me in the ribs.

"For Christ's sake, don't go to sleep," he hissed.

"I wasn't!" I hissed back.

Raz faltered in his reading, and both of us sat up straighter, trying to look like we were paying really close attention and absolutely not talking in class.

By the time he finally closed his book, my bum was totally numb and my legs felt stiff from sitting down so long. We joined the smattering of polite applause. Raz, I was relieved to see, was smiling properly now. "Is it over now?" I whispered to Phil. "Or is it just the interval?"

"It's over."

"I'm gutted. You promised me a halftime. With poisoned tea." We stood up, along with everyone else. "Are you going to nab Hannah now?"

"Yeah. You going to talk to Raz?"

I nodded, but by the time we'd threaded our way out of the chairs, Morgan was standing in our path, flanked by a tight-lipped Margaret.

"This is disgraceful. Must you hound us everywhere we go? I've a good mind to call the police and complain about this harassment."

"Hey, hold on a mo." I held up my hands. "We're just here to listen to Raz's poems, that's all. No harassment. Honest to God."

Morgan's eyes narrowed. "Really? Then perhaps you'd like to give an opinion on them."

Shit. "Er . . . Very heartfelt, I thought." That was a safe comment, wasn't it? "I really liked the one about the shards."

Morgan's looming menace didn't soften. "He didn't read that one tonight."

Oops. "Yeah. Shame, that. Still, the others were good too. What did you reckon, Phil?"

All right. I was being a bit of a bastard, dropping him in it like that. But it was his job, this sort of stuff, wasn't it?

Phil paused before he answered. "I thought it was pretty brave stuff. Putting so much of himself out there like that."

Christ. Morgan was actually nodding. Then he frowned at Phil. "Your voice sounds familiar. Have we met?"

"We spoke briefly at Cherry's party," Phil said smoothly.

I gave him a sidelong look, caught myself, and stared guiltily at my feet, hoping I hadn't given the game away. When I looked up again, though, Margaret's beady eyes were piercing right through me.

"Really?" Morgan was saying. "I'm afraid I don't remember your name."

"Phil Morrison. Good to see you again. You'll have to excuse me, though. There's someone I wanted to—"

He didn't get to finish. Raz bounced up to us, still hyped up on nervous energy. "What did you think?"

He was looking straight at me, which I was pleased to see confused the hell out of Morgan and Margaret.

"Great." What had Phil said? "Really brave."

Raz looked like I'd given him a puppy. "Thank you. It's not easy, standing up and baring your soul in front of people like that."

Now I felt like a total shit about the whispering in the back row. Mind you, Phil had started it. "Tell you what, have you got any more copies of that book of yours?" Maybe if I sat down and spent a couple of hours reading the thing, I'd work out what it was all about.

"I have, yes. Would you like one?" Raz was already opening up his backpack and pulling out a copy of *Splintered Soul*. He'd brought a whole stack of the things along, but obviously not quite got up the nerve to actually get them out and encourage people to buy them. "Would you like me to sign it?"

"Yeah, that'd be great. How much is it?" I dug in my pocket for my wallet and managed not to wince when he named his price. But seriously, *how* much? The book only had about twenty pages. I handed over my tenner with a smile, though, and he signed the book with a flourish.

"We're going for a drink now," Raz said as he passed it to me. "Would you and Phil like to come along?"

I looked up to find the rest of the Literati ranged around us, staring with varying degrees of bemusement at me and Raz being BFFs. Drinks with this lot didn't sound like my idea of a fun night out, and there was no way I was going to talk to Raz about Auntie Lol in front of everyone. But maybe Phil would want to go along and observe the Literati in their unnatural habitat? I glanced up at him, and he shook his head minutely.

"Thanks," I said. "But we'd better get back and make sure Cherry's okay. Some other time, maybe?"

"Oh dear." Hannah made a concerned face. "She hasn't been ill again, has she?" She was still standing close to Peter but not hanging off his arm anymore.

"Nah, she's fine. Just don't like leaving her alone for too long, that's all."

"Oh, are you staying at her house?"

"Er, something like that." I didn't want to go handing out Cherry's current location to any murderers who might be in the vicinity. "You ready, Phil? Right. You enjoy your drinks, Raz, and I'll give you a bell, okay?"

We turned and walked briskly to the door, me cursing myself under my breath. "I shouldn't have said that about Cherry. What if one of them's the murderer and they work it out?"

Phil gripped my shoulder reassuringly. "Look, we're doing okay. We're not leaving her there on her own, and anyway, it's not like she's being stalked by a bloody axe-murderer. Whoever's poisoning stuff is using that method to avoid confrontations. They're not likely to turn up on your doorstep with the carving knives."

"Yeah, yeah. Just wish I'd thought more before I opened my gob, that's all."

Phil just squeezed my shoulder again.

"Thought you might have wanted to go to the pub with them and see if alcohol loosened a few tongues," I said as we got back in his car.

"No point. Not with them all closing ranks like that." Phil buckled on his seat belt and started the engine.

"Yeah, but you still might have learned something."

"What, like how you've apparently got a death wish, wanting to go for drinks with a bunch of poisoners?"

"Bloody hell, you think they're all in on it?" I grinned. "Wouldn't have put you down for a conspiracy theorist. But seriously, I thought we'd agreed it was Cherry they were after?"

"Yeah, well. Excuse me for not wanting to take any chances with my boyfriend's life."

"Careful. You keep saying stuff like that, I might start thinking you care."

"Course I bleeding care."

"Yeah, well. Me too and all," I muttered to my boots.

Then I switched on the radio so we could listen to the sports news and avoid any more awkward talk about feelings.

"Think Cherry and Gary are still speaking to each other?" I asked as I opened my front door.

They weren't. They were sprawling on the sofa, giggling helplessly. Cherry even had tears in her eyes. When we walked in, they both looked up, tried to straighten their faces, then fell about laughing again.

Bloody hell, just what had they been talking about? There was a half-full bottle of Pinot Grigio on the coffee table, and—yep—an empty one hiding coyly underneath it. "Oi, Gary, have you got my sister pissed?"

"It's all right," she said solemnly. "He hasn't tried to have his wicked way with me."

Then they both cracked up again. Seriously, I wasn't sure who was in more danger of wetting themself.

"Looks like you've got your hands full with these two," Phil muttered.

"Yeah. And it looks like Gary's not going to be driving home tonight. You all right giving him a lift back to Brock's Hollow?"

"No problem."

"Coming back after?"

"Think I'll call it a night after that. Got to go talk to Peter Grissom first thing." He yawned.

Come to think of it, I was feeling pretty tired myself. Exhausting stuff, this poetry. "Right. I'll see you, then. Come on Gary, time for all good little boys and girls to go home to bed."

Gary held out a plaintive hand, so I grabbed it and heaved him to his feet, not without a bit of difficulty, seeing as he weighs half as much again as I do.

Predictably, he did a fake stumble and landed in my arms. Drunk Gary is the cuddly sort. And then some. "Whoopsadaisy!"

I backed away from the fifty-proof breath. "Christ, Gary, you stink like an alkie. Darren's going to think we're a corrupting influence on you."

"You've never let me corrupt you in your life. Ooh, is that an invitation?"

"Gary, you're engaged. And my boyfriend is *right here*."

He pouted. "Spoilsport. I'm sure Darren wouldn't mind if it was you. Or Phil. He *likes* Phil."

I had horrible visions of us being invited to make up a foursome. "C'mon, Gary, just let Phil take you home. And try really hard not to open your mouth on the way, yeah?"

He sniggered. "Are you worried something might fall into it?"

"Nope. Not worried at all." I glanced at Phil. "Sure you're okay with this? I could give Darren a call and let him sleep it off on the sofa."

He shook his head, smiling. "Come on, Gary. I'll take care of you."

"Promises, promises!"

When the door had finally shut behind them and we only had the lingering smell of alcohol to remember Gary by, I turned to my sister. "Right. You, young lady, are drinking a pint of water, and then you're going to bed."

She giggled.

"Did I say something funny?"

"No." She giggled again. "'Something might fall into it,'" she quoted, and spluttered with laughter. "He meant Phil's penis, didn't he?"

I winced. Maybe, just maybe, if I drank the rest of the wine, I'd be able to blot out the memory of my straitlaced big sister saying the words *Phil's penis* and then cackling like a witch.

I wasn't holding my breath, mind.

CHAPTER TWENTY-SIX

Saturday morning, I'd just finished getting dressed when my phone rang. I didn't recognise the number, but then again, I'd been handing my number out pretty freely over the last couple of days. Maybe it was Dave, borrowing someone else's phone to tell us they'd caught the poisoner and we could all sleep easy in our beds from here on in.

It wasn't.

"It's Hannah. From the Literati. I've got a bit of a plumbing emergency. I hope you don't mind me calling you—but you *did* give me your card . . ."

"Yeah, don't worry about it. So what's the problem?"

"It's . . . it's one of the pipes in the bathroom. I'm really scared the ceiling's going to fall in." Her voice was breathless enough I could easily believe she was as worried as she said.

"I'll be right out. What's the address?"

Now, I'm not daft. Despite what some people seem to think. And it *did* cross my mind to be a bit wary of Hannah, seeing as she was a member of the same lot who'd apparently sent Cherry a poisoned pressie. Then again, just because it was signed *from the Literati* that didn't mean it really *was* from one of them. Plus, it'd be a first-class opportunity to ask her some questions and maybe even have a snoop around her house. I'd just have to remember to say no if she offered me a cup of tea, that was all.

Should I ring Phil first? Probably, if I knew what was good for me. Overprotective so-and-so. I dialled his number, but there was no answer and it went to voice mail. I left a brief message, then went to knock on the door of the spare room, where I'd left Cherry with a large mug of tea, some dry toast, and a couple of headache pills.

She hadn't made a lot of headway on the toast, but she'd got out of bed and pulled on some clothes, so she couldn't be feeling *that* bad. Then again, she'd been drinking wine, not Slivovitz.

"Sorry, Sis, I've got to go out for a bit. Your mate Hannah from the Literati—she's got water coming through her ceiling."

Cherry looked up, her face tired. "Poor her. Fine. I need to sort out my emails anyway. I can't believe how it's all mounted up in just a few days."

She didn't seem in any hurry to get on with it, though. I hesitated—but Hannah's problem had seemed a bit urgent, and anyway, Cherry had the cats to look after her. "Shouldn't take long. She's only up in Sandridge. I'll see you in a bit," I said and left.

Hannah was in a right state when she let me in her house, despite the fact I got there only around ten or fifteen minutes after she'd called. Her round face was shiny and her hands all twitchy. "It's upstairs. I've put towels down to catch the water—I've no idea where it's coming from."

She wasn't joking. The whole, sizeable bathroom was carpeted in a thick layer of sodden towels. "Don't worry, love. If there's one thing I'm good at, it's finding leaks."

Hannah gave me a jerky nod. "Good. I'll leave you to it—I just need to pop out to the shop in the village. I'll be back soon."

She might have offered to put the kettle on first. "See you later, then," I called out to the sound of the front door closing behind her.

I set to work.

Ten minutes later, I was starting to get a bad feeling about this. I wasn't just boasting when I said I was good at finding leaks. It's what I do—why I became a plumber. That's what the spidey-senses are good for. Finding hidden things. And water.

But I was getting *nothing* from Hannah's pipes. Not a dicky-bird. I was getting a strong sense of déjà vu instead, going back to a job a few months previously when a lady thought she had a leak, but it turned out to be her little tot playing a bit too vigorously with water. Now, judging by the lack of toys cluttering the floor and childish scribbles stuck up on the fridge, Hannah didn't have a daughter—but what if she'd been doing a bit of playing with water herself?

Unease fluttered in my stomach like the ghost of a late-night curry. I grabbed all the soggy towels off the bathroom floor and threw them out of the room just in case they were messing up the readings, then listened as hard as I could.

Nothing. Well, nothing of the leak variety, that was. I was getting a whole lot of background noise, though, and it wasn't pretty. Hannah had hidden secrets, all right, and they were sending out some really nasty vibes.

My blood went cold. I couldn't stop to follow the trail. There was only one possible reason Hannah would drag me out on a wild-goose chase—Cherry. Currently all on her tod in my house.

Shit.

I ran out of Hannah's house, trying to simultaneously watch where I was going and dial up Cherry's number. It went straight to voice mail. Shit. I tried Phil next. I was back in the van by the time the ringing stopped and it went to voice mail too—for Christ's sake, what did these people think they were playing at?—so I held the phone with one hand and started the engine with the other, hoping to God I wasn't about to have an accident or get arrested. Or both.

"Phil? It's Tom," I said, switching hands so I could put the van in gear. "If you get this in the next ten minutes or so, get over to my place. I think Hannah's the murderer, and she's there alone with Cherry." Probably. Possibly. Shit, was I just jumping to conclusions? "Also, where the bloody hell are you?" I flung the phone on the passenger seat and screeched around a corner, only to nearly rear-end a bloody milk float, trundling along so sodding slowly it was practically going backwards.

My hands clenched on the steering wheel with the effort of not honking my horn. Normally, I'm all for doorstep deliveries—after all, many an old dear's been found collapsed in her home in the nick of time when the milkman noticed she hadn't put out the empties—but Christ, right then I was wishing they'd just learn to use the bloody shops. If only I had a big blue flashy light and a siren like the cops . . . *Dave.* I could call Dave and get him to send the boys in blue round.

I fumbled for my phone. Managed to knock it off the passenger seat and into the footwell.

Oh, *bloody* hell. Sod it. Chances were all the patrol cars were miles off anyhow. I left my phone where it lay and concentrated on driving. There was a gap in the traffic, and I edged out to the middle of the road, hoping to overtake the milk float. Then ducked back in sharpish to avoid the oncoming bus.

Finally we got to the wide bit at the start of the forty-mile-an-hour zone, and I floored the accelerator to zoom round Mr. Milko and tear up the hill like a proverbial out of a whatsit.

And got caught in the queue for the bloody traffic lights. I thumped the steering wheel in frustration and honked the horn by accident. The bloke in front gave me a stern glare in his rearview mirror, and his passenger looked round pointedly. Her eyes widened when she saw my face, and she tapped the driver on the shoulder. Dunno what she said to him, but when the lights changed, he didn't hang about, and he turned off the road a minute later.

I reckon I must have aged several decades in the ten minutes or so—by the clock, at least—it took me from leaving Hannah's to when I pulled up in front of mine with a screech of brakes. It was a wonder I wasn't too bloody decrepit to burst into the house at Mach seven.

Hannah was there, all right. Sitting on the bloody sofa with Cherry. Stroking Merlin—the traitor—and drinking a cup of coffee.

Cherry had a mug in her hand too.

"Put the bloody coffee down!" I yelled. All right, maybe it came out as more of a shriek.

Both women—and the cat—stared at me.

Neither of them put the bloody coffee down.

"Tom?" Cherry said, her eyebrows halfway up to her hairline.

"She—she could be here to kill you, okay? Jesus, don't drink that!"

Cherry looked at the mug she'd been about to take a sip from, clearly decided that yes, I was worked up enough to lunge over and knock it out of her hand if she carried on, and put it down on the coffee table. "It's all right, Tom. *I* made the coffee. And seriously, you can't really believe that Hannah—"

"She's a Literati, isn't she?" Or a Literatus, or whatever the bloody singular was, not that I gave a shit.

"So? We've absolutely no evidence one of them was involved."

"The gift basket," I blurted out. "It was poisoned. Dave rang yesterday."

Cherry's face went white. "And you didn't *tell* me?"

"I was going to," I protested. "But you've got to see—"

"That gift tag means absolutely nothing. *Anyone* could have written it. You've got no grounds whatsoever for accusing Hannah like that."

"But there wasn't a leak!"

Hannah, who'd been politely pretending to search for something in her handbag so we'd think she wasn't listening—or maybe really searching for something; I've gone away for a week with smaller luggage—looked up and frowned at me. "How could you possibly know that in such a short time?"

"Oh, he's got this *thing*." Cherry made a dismissive gesture. Then she frowned at me as well. "Are you sure it was working properly this time? Maybe you should go back and check."

"My *thing* is working fine, thanks so much, Sis. And I'm not leaving you here with her." I sat down on the arm of the chair opposite them and folded my arms.

"Tom, you're being incredibly rude. Hannah's done absolutely nothing wrong. She just popped round to cheer me up."

"So why did she tell me she was just going to the village shop?"

"I *did* go to the village shop," Hannah piped up, sounding annoyingly reasonable. "Then I suddenly thought about Cherry, left here all on her own while you were fixing my bathroom. So I thought I'd surprise her."

"See?" Cherry said. "You're just being ridiculous." She picked up her mug again.

"Oi. You're not drinking that."

Hannah heaved an obviously fake sigh. "Why don't you pass me your mug, Cherry?" She took it, held it up to her lips, then swallowed. It didn't *look* like she was faking it. "Happy now?" she asked me. "I can't believe you actually thought I'd come here to poison poor Cherry. Why on earth did you think I'd want to do that?"

I threw up my hands. "Well, somebody bloody does! Sod it. I'm going to make some coffee. Proper stuff." Not the instant Cherry had made for Hannah, which was possibly a subtle hint she hadn't been all that welcome, but more likely just a sign Cherry couldn't be arsed with the cafetière.

God, I'd have felt a right muppet if Phil had turned up, guns blazing. I wondered if there was any way I could somehow delete that last voice mail before he heard it. At least I'd be able to offer him a coffee, I thought as I spooned it out, breathing in the rich, dark fumes and feeling the tension unravel.

I'd calmed down a bit by the time I got back in the living room. "It's brewing," I said shortly.

Hannah got up. I hoped she was leaving, but no such luck. "Can I use your loo?"

"Yeah. Down the hall, first on the left."

She swept out in a cloud of floaty drab layers, the charms hanging off her overstuffed brown handbag jangling as she walked.

Neither of us said anything for a minute.

"Why *do* women always take their bags to the loo with them?" I asked, mainly to break the awkward silence. "I mean, it's not like they're generally going to pass the shops on the way."

Cherry glared at me. "Maybe she was worried you'd rifle through it if she left it behind."

"Maybe . . ." I'd had a nasty thought. What if Hannah had turned right, not left? "I'm going to check on that coffee."

I made it to the kitchen just in time to see Hannah, bizarrely clad in the "glamour" washing up gloves Gary bought me last Christmas, tipping something from a plastic mineral water bottle into the cafetière.

I was betting it wasn't full of vulcanicity.

"Oi," I started and took a step forwards.

Hannah turned and, with a shriek of "You *cunt*!" that shocked me rigid coming from her, threw the contents of the bottle at my face.

CHAPTER TWENTY-SEVEN

I threw up an arm just in time to shield my eyes, thank God, and scrunched them tight shut, but the stuff went in my hair and was dripping down over my face. *Shit.* I didn't dare open my eyes, but what the hell was she doing now? Creeping up to finish the job with one of the kitchen knives?

"Cherry! Don't come in the kitchen!" I yelled—all right, squawked.

I was hyperconscious of the wetness on my skin and soaking through my sleeve and shirt front. Christ, just how bloody quickly did this stuff work?

I was just imagining the burning, right?

Right?

There was a barrage of loud banging that I realised had to be coming from the front door. Had Cherry called the police already? No, it couldn't be them. Not this soon.

"Oh my God!" Cherry's voice was high-pitched, panicked—and right by my bloody ear. "Tom, are you all right?"

"Jesus, I told you not to come in here! What's that—Hannah doing now? Don't go near her, she's fucking mental. Throwing stuff. I can't open my eyes. And you've got to get the door. For fuck's sake, just get out of here." The knocking was getting louder.

"But I can't leave you!" Oh God, she'd completely lost the plot.

There was a humongous *crash* followed by the sound of glass breaking. "Tom?"

Thank God. It was Phil.

"Kitchen," I yelled. "But watch out, she's chucking stuff. Cherry, get out of here, okay?"

Someone grabbed my shoulder and spun me round. I braced myself for another attack, but instead of stabbing me in the gut, all they did was whisper "Jesus Christ" and mop me up with a tea towel or something. I was pretty sure even with my eyes still closed it was Phil, not Hannah.

I was even more certain when I heard him snap out, "Sit down there and don't bloody move, got it? No, not you, Tom. You just get your clothes off."

"Is now really the time?" I squeaked.

"*Yes.* Shower. Now. We need to get this stuff off you. Quickly."

Right. I knew that. I yanked my shirt over my head and threw it on the floor. I kicked my trainers off and started to unbutton my jeans, but sod it, I wasn't in the mood to give free strip shows to bloody murderers. The jeans could wait till I got in the bathroom. I started to feel my way to the stairs, still not daring to open my eyes in case some of the stuff got in. I just hoped the cats wouldn't take it into their heads that now would be a fun time to play trip-the-human.

"Cherry, can you watch her? And call the police." Phil took my arm and started to lead—or more like, manhandle—me along.

I wasn't bloody having this. "You can't leave my sister down here with a murderer."

"We need to get you sorted *now*," Phil snapped.

"I'll go up with Tom and make sure he's all right in the shower," Cherry said in a subdued voice by my ear. I bet she was feeling guilty now for as good as calling me a drama queen over my suspicions of Hannah.

Then I realised what she'd said. "Oi, you're not watching me shower."

"I used to bathe you when you were a baby, you know." I swear I could hear the eye roll in her voice as she dragged me over to the stairs. "Steps here. *And* change your nappies. I've seen it all before."

"So you don't need to see it again, do you?"

"Jesus," Phil huffed. "Stop bloody bickering and get it in the sodding shower, will you?"

He probably had a point.

Cherry grabbed my wrist with a surprisingly strong grip—I guessed years of lugging legal briefs around must be good for building up muscle—and dragged me upstairs. She shoved me into the shower without even waiting for me to get my jeans off and turned on the taps full blast.

"*Bloody hell!*" The water hitting my head and chest was sodding *freezing*. I groped numbly for the temperature control, only for Cherry to slap my hand away.

"Hot water will open up your pores," she yelled over the rushing water. "Make the poison work faster. I read it on the internet."

"Won't have to worry about that," I said through chattering teeth. "Hypothermia'll do the job instead."

"Stop being a baby. And get those jeans off." It was my turn to bat away hands as she fumbled at my jeans buttons.

"Oi! I can do that myself."

"Well, get on with it, then."

Figuring it was safe now to risk opening my eyes, I blinked into the deluge of ice-cold water and realised Cherry was actually in the shower with me, still fully dressed, her hair in rats' tails and her sweater hanging soggily by her knees. "Bloody hell, Sis, go and get dry. I'm fine, okay?" I desperately wanted to ask her to go back down to make sure Phil was all right, but if anything had happened to her, I'd never forgive myself.

But if anything happened to Phil . . . Nope. Best not to go there.

Cherry nodded and left me to get on with the task of getting soaking-wet jeans off my shivering self with numb fingers.

Thank God I was wearing my work jeans, not my impressing-Phil-with-the-shape-of-my-arse jeans. I'd have been there all bloody year trying to get them off.

Fifteen minutes later, scrubbed to within an inch of my life—by my own fair hands, not my big sister's, thank God—I sat blinking at my would-be murderess through shampoo-reddened eyes. We were in the living room, Phil having survived unscathed and confiscated Hannah's handbag of horrors. I had a large glass of (unadulterated) water in my somewhat unsteady hand, courtesy of Cherry—apparently you were supposed to drink loads if you'd been poisoned. Well, she should know.

There was a manic, twitchy air about Hannah, but fair dues, she was waiting for the police to come and take her away.

I wished they'd get a bloody move on. Still, while she was here . . . "So was it me you were after? Or was it Cherry?" I asked. "And, you know, why?"

Hannah sent me a withering look. "I never cared about you. I just wanted to *do* something. Achieve something."

I stared at her. "What, like an impressive kill count?"

She ignored me and turned on Cherry, who was curled up on the sofa in a fresh baggy sweater and identikit leggings, with a towel wrapped around her hair. Cherry shrank back at the sight of Hannah's snarling face. Christ, she looked bloody well feral all of a sudden. "It's all right for you, with your high-flying legal career and your tall, dark, and handsome fiancé."

Hannah thought Greg was handsome? Really? Still, I suppose it takes all sorts.

"How do you think *I* feel? You just waltz into the Literati, just *playing* at writing, and everyone thinks you're so bloody marvellous. *I* was the one David turned to for advice before you joined us. He trusted me. He said Morgan and the others wouldn't understand him writing genre fiction, but he trusted me. Trusted my opinion."

Again: really?

"And suddenly it's all *Cherry* this, and *Cherry* that. Even Raz . . ." She was crying now, I noticed with horror.

Cherry protested faintly at that. "But I was new, it's hardly surprising they—"

"*Shut up.*" Me and Cherry both jumped a mile at Hannah's shrill voice. Phil took a step forward, his face dark, but he halted when she stayed in her chair.

"Have you any idea what it's like for me? No one notices me. No one's *ever* noticed me, and it's only got worse as I've got older. David was the only one, and you *took* him from me."

"Hang on a minute," I said, not liking where this was going. "Are you accusing Cherry of—"

"God, you're so *stupid*."

I frowned, a bit hurt. Then I caught myself. Caring what a psycho murderess thought of me? Really?

Hannah was still speaking. "Her, kill someone? She wouldn't have the nerve."

"It was the book, wasn't it?" Cherry said suddenly. "You stole his book. And . . . and you killed him, didn't you? So you could publish it under your name. Well. Hayden Mead's name. That's you, isn't it?"

Jesus. All this over a *book*?

"That was your fault. He was dying anyway. I could have waited. But then he said he was going to show it to you, so I had to do something."

Cherry nodded. "But you were too late. So then you had to kill me." There was a slight stutter over the *k*, and she hugged herself, her knees drawn up in her chair. "Why did you wait so long?"

"Because you left, of course. After everything I went through, you just got bored and *left*. As if the whole thing meant *nothing* to you."

Right. She hadn't known about Cherry's little tiff with Morgan. Made me wonder if he'd suspected something fishy was going on and wanted to get Cherry out of harm's way. Although it was probably more likely he was just a puffed-up, self-righteous git.

Phil cleared his throat. "Then you got the invite to the party. Must have seemed like fate."

"Yes!" She turned to him eagerly. "I'd been so worried . . . but then the invitation came, and I knew what I had to do. It was so easy—I told you, nobody notices me. I did get a bit worried when I saw you"—she turned to me—"with Cherry's drink, but it all went as I'd planned in the end. But then *she* didn't drink enough."

Bad Cherry, I thought. Not cooperating in your own murder.

Phil was glowering at Hannah. "And what about Tom? Just a bit of collateral damage?"

She shrank a little under his glare. "I'd have felt bad about him, of course. But anyway, he's fine, isn't he? Everybody's fine. Except me." She started sobbing as the sound of sirens rang through the air.

Chapter Twenty-Eight

The police didn't bother knocking when they got here. Then again, Phil had pretty much done a number on the front door, so I suppose they decided we might think they were taking the piss. Dave Southgate lumbered into my living room with a couple of uniforms. "Bloody hell, Paretski, get ram-raided, did you?"

I grinned. "Something like that."

As Dave was taking her away in handcuffs, Hannah raised her head. "I still win, you know. I'll be famous now. Everyone's going to buy my book."

"*David's* book. Not yours." Cherry fairly spat it out. "I should have known what was going on as soon as I saw the notice about the book launch."

I thought she was stretching it a bit there. *Hayden Mead* doesn't sound that much like *Hannah Mudge*.

"You, with a book deal?" Cherry went on. "You haven't got the imagination." Her lip curled up. It really wasn't an attractive look, so it was probably just as well Greg wasn't here right now. "You couldn't even come up with more than one way to kill someone."

Ouch. "Well done, Sis," I said, patting her shoulder as Hannah disappeared. "Harsh but fair."

She collapsed onto the sofa. "God, I need a drink."

I joined her, running a hand through my still-damp hair. "You're not the only one."

Phil's meaty mitt dropped onto my shoulder. "The only thing you're drinking is water until we know you're all right."

"Killjoy."

Cherry raised her head, her eyes tired. "Can we not use the k-word right now, please?"

"You know, there's one thing I don't get," Phil said, looking thoughtful. "How the hell did she even find out you were here?"

"My fault, remember?" I grimaced. "Telling them all at Raz's do that I was going back to see Cherry. She must have worked it out from that."

Phil squeezed my shoulder. "Bit of a leap of faith to set up the whole plumbing emergency based on a guess like that."

"Or maybe . . ." Cherry trailed off, avoiding Phil's gaze.

"Maybe what?"

"Well, it's possible she asked Angela at number 22. My next-door neighbour. I mean, I had to tell her where I was going when I went round to ask her to look after the plants again."

Phil pinched the bridge of his nose. "And it didn't occur to you to tell her not to let on to anyone?"

"Well, of course not. She'd have thought there was something funny going on."

"*Something funny* . . .? Believe me, Sis, nobody's laughing."

"You don't know what it's like in Pluck's End. Any excuse to gossip. The old lady who runs the post office keeps tabs on everyone, and it's got so I can't even have Gregory round in the evening without people watching to see if he stays the night. *And* everyone keeps demanding to know how we met, as if that's any of their business."

I blinked at her. "Now you come to mention it, how did you meet? You never said."

Cherry went bright red. "Why does everyone *insist* on knowing that?"

"Probably because you're making such a big secret of it?"

"Oh, for heaven's sake!" Cherry looked down at her lap. It was catless, so no distraction there. She muttered something.

"What was that?"

"Clergy Dating, if you really *must* know."

"What?"

"Clergy Dating. It's a website. For people who like, well, clergymen. And women, obviously."

"Seriously, that even exists? And oi, how does Greg feel about all this?" I grinned. "You're just objectifying him, aren't you? Anything in a cassock."

"Shut up. I wish I'd never told you. And if you breathe a word about it to anyone else—*especially* Richard and Agatha—I'll . . ." She trailed off, apparently unable to think of anything bad enough.

It was probably the release in tension from the near-death experience making me laugh at her. Probably. "Do you get all hot and bothered when he quotes the Bible? Hey, if you ask nicely, does he come to bed in nothing but his dog coll— *Oi!*"

For the first time I could remember, *ever*, she'd thrown a cushion at me.

Phil—not to mention Cherry and Dave—had insisted on me getting checked out by a doctor, even though I kept telling everyone I felt fine. Phil wasn't happy until he got official confirmation and a promise from me that if I started feeling a bit iffy, I'd get him to drive me straight back to hospital. Then we had to go and make our statements down the police station. It was weird—even after everything Hannah had done, I still felt bad about the thought of her going to prison on my evidence.

Then I asked myself how I'd have felt going to my sister's funeral—or my own, for that matter—and felt a lot less guilty about it all. Besides, she'd been caught bang to rights with a bottle of poison. The lab results hadn't come back yet to confirm it, but Dave told me Hannah had confessed that what she'd chucked over me was a concentrated solution of nicotine. Just like she'd used in Cherry's gift basket. I guessed Sis had been right about her not having much imagination.

I got a chippy I know who owed me a favour to come over and sort out the front door while we were out, and while it wasn't exactly good as new when we got back, at least we could close it, lock it, and feel fairly secure. Barring any more acts of Phil.

"So what took you so bloody long getting to my place?" I asked when we were sitting on my sofa, just the two of us, pretending to watch some reality rubbish on the telly. Cherry had gone back to Pluck's End with her light o' love, who'd been predictably horrified at the day's proceedings. And ever so slightly smug at having been fully exonerated.

Phil yawned. "Went to interview Peter Grissom, didn't I? Your dark rat."

Oh yeah. Now I remembered him mentioning it. "He's not my anything. Did he tell you anything interesting?"

"Oh, he *told* me plenty. Not a lot of it was interesting, though. Although he did mention David Evans owned a lot of books on toxicology. Wonder who might have borrowed a few?" He chuckled. "Grissom had a theory the old bloke was writing a crime novel on the QT."

"Imagine that. Did you tell him he was right?"

"I'm in the business of getting information, not giving it away." He pulled me in closer to his side, which was fine by me. "Speaking of which . . ."

I braced myself to meet the sexual innuendo and return it with interest, but all Phil did was reach into his trouser pocket and pull out a key. "Thought I should give you this. And I'll have that key Cherry left behind, if it's still on offer."

"She never even used it," I said, staring at the key in my hand. "Could have given it to you days ago." Dunno why, but I'd never thought about Phil giving me a key to his place. In a lot of ways, he was very private. Hah. It was in his job title and everything. The key was still warm from where it'd been in his pocket. The heat seemed to spread right through me.

Was I being daft, reading too much into it? Sometimes a key is just a key.

Then again, sometimes it isn't.

"Would have saved your front door a world of pain," Phil went on, apparently not noticing we were having a moment here. "Not to mention my shoulder."

Shit, I hadn't even thought about that. "Oi, are you all right?" I twisted around to look at him in concern. I'd have pulled at the neck of his sweater to try to get a peek at his shoulder too, but the thought of a hundred cashmere goats in tears at the mistreatment of their wool restrained me.

"I'll live." Phil's smile faded. "Christ, when I finally got in and saw you dripping wet with that stuff . . ." He closed his eyes briefly.

"I'll get the key," I said, scrambling into the kitchen where the spare key lived, when it wasn't stuffed uselessly into the bottom of my sister's handbag. I pulled it out of the drawer, then stood there for a moment, staring at it. Was it just a key? Just a practical solution to life's little problems, like being locked in the house with a murderess?

I was still staring at it when strong arms slipped around my waist from behind. "Look, if you don't want me to have it, that's fine."

"What?" I twisted in his arms until I could see his face. "That's not— It's just, I dunno."

"That was eloquent. Ever considered taking up writing?"

"Piss off."

He smiled and ruffled my hair. I hate that. "You know I love you, don't you?" he said, like it was nothing out of the ordinary.

I swear my heart stopped. I did? I mean, *he* did? I started to say something—buggered if I knew what, but it didn't matter anyway because my throat caught.

Phil just carried on smiling. And then he kissed me.

We popped along to Waterstones next day, Cherry and me, after she'd driven back over from Pluck's End. I half expected her to bring Greg along from hers, but apparently he'd dropped her off home, then spent the night at the Old Deanery. Which seemed a bit weird to me, but hey, it was their relationship, not mine. I wasn't surprised she'd become a bit more careful about sleeping with blokes after the teenage pregnancy scare, but come off it, that was decades ago. Then again, it being Sunday, he was presumably up in a pulpit somewhere, preaching to the faithful, so maybe he hadn't wanted to chance a bit of fornication the night before.

No one had told the bookstore staff about Hannah yet, so the books were still on sale, although the manager kept looking nervously at the door, probably wondering when his author was going to turn up for her book launch. I picked up a copy of the book. Like a blood-soaked newspaper, it was black and white and red all over, the title in hard-hitting capitals.

It was from a publisher even I recognised the name of, so I guessed it was one of the "major" ones she'd been talking about at Raz's do. No wonder she'd sounded smug back then. I wondered if she'd had the five-figure advance too. With a bit of luck, they'd make her pay it back.

It went against the grain a bit, handing over money for something that'd nearly got Cherry—and me—killed, but I had to admit I was curious to see what all the fuss was about.

Cherry was flicking through the book before I'd even got my change. "Yes. I recognise this. It's changed very little since I first saw it. David was a fantastic writer, poor man. Have you got a pen?"

I patted my pockets. "Sorry, no. What did you—"

Cherry was already striding back up to the sales counter. "Can I borrow that, please?" She grabbed hold of a marker pen without waiting for an answer—and with vicious strokes, scribbled out Hayden Mead's name on the cover of the book I'd just bought. "There. That's better." She handed the pen back to the bemused sales assistant. "Oh, and she won't be turning up this morning. She's been arrested for murder and attempted murder. Come on, Tom, let's go get a coffee."

I let her grab my arm and march me out of there and over the road to the Merchants Café.

"I spoke to Mr. Morangie again, by the way," she said over a couple of skinny lattes. "He's willing to let you have another look in his house."

"Oh. Right. Him." I'd almost forgotten about Auntie Lol's legacy. Again. I was frankly amazed Cherry had managed to find the time and energy to deal with it what with everything else going on, but maybe she'd wanted the distraction.

"You can go over there tomorrow. Do you want me to come with you? In case there's any more . . . difficulty?"

"Nah, don't be daft. You've had enough of all this confrontational stuff lately." Not to mention, I'd feel a right wuss turning up chaperoned by my big sister. "Why don't you spend some time with Greg? Argue about the flowers for the wedding, that sort of stuff?"

"Actually, I really need to get back to work. If you're sure, that is?"

"I'll be fine. Trust me," I added with a wink.

She didn't look reassured.

CHAPTER Twenty-Nine

"**W**e're taking my car." I folded my arms, determined to assert my manly independence no matter what argument Phil might come up with.

Phil just shrugged. "Fine."

"You sure?" I blurted out and could have kicked myself.

Phil was giving me a funny look. "Yeah, why not? Unless you reckon we're going to need boot space for whatever your auntie's left you. In fact, tell you what, why don't we take the van?"

"You're a bit optimistic, aren't you? It's probably just an envelope with a tenner in. If that. Probably an out-of-date book token. Or a packet of those choccy biccies she always used to keep in the house."

"Whatever. It's your call."

We took the van.

"Want me to come in?" Phil asked as I pulled up outside Morangie Mansion.

"Nah, best not. Don't want to give the old bloke anything else to complain about."

I was about to open the door, but he put his hand on my arm. "You sure? Bad things tend to happen when I let you out of my sight."

I smiled—and then pulled him in for a kiss for good measure. "I'll be fine. Trust me."

"Do I look like I was born yesterday? Go on, then. And try not to take all day. Some of us have got livings to earn, and my last client never even paid me, the bastard."

"Oi, payment to be in sexual favours, remember? And there were plenty of those flying around last night as I recall."

Phil squeezed my leg. "That was just the retainer. You still owe me for hours worked and expenses. Now piss off, before I start demanding an instalment."

"Promises, promises." I winked at him and got out of the car.

I knocked on Mr. M.'s door and waited. I was starting to get a bit, well, nervous. Excited, I suppose. I wasn't sure what I was hoping for here. If she'd left me something big, I wasn't sure how I'd feel about it. I mean, it wasn't like we were related. She didn't owe me anything— the other way around, more like. But if it was only something little, it'd be a hell of an anticlimax after all this fuss.

Footsteps sounded in the hallway, and I took a deep breath. When the door opened, the wrinkly face that looked out at me wasn't the one I was expecting. "Mr. Paretski?" this one said. "I'm Mr. Wood, Mr. Morangie's lawyer."

Seemed he'd been let out of detention. Clearly, he wasn't all that much of a danger to society in general. I just hoped that also held true for yours truly in particular. And weren't we all formal this morning? I wasn't sure whether to shake his hand or drop him a curtsey. Seeing as I'd probably have fallen on my face on the doormat if I'd tried anything that daft, I shook his hand. It was like grasping a paper bag full of twigs. I was paranoid I'd snap one of them, and let go probably a bit sooner than was polite.

"Mr. Morangie wishes to apologise for his conduct to you the last time you were here," he continued.

Personally, I thought if he was that keen to apologise to me, he'd have come out and done it, not left it to the lawyer. Still, gift horses, mouths, don't peek. "Yeah, no problem. I'm just sorry I hit on a sensitive subject."

Mr. Wood nodded. Woodenly. "Mr. Morangie would like me to reiterate that he is quite prepared to make you an offer pertaining—"

"Nope." I cut him off before he could get into full-on legalese. "This isn't about money, all right? It's about what Auntie Lol wanted."

He recoiled. "You're referring to the second Mrs. Morangie, I take it?"

"Yeah, about that. What happened to the first Mrs. Morangie?"

"She died." Could his expression get any more disapproving?

"How?"

Apparently it could. "I *really* don't believe that's any of your concern. Now, if you wouldn't mind . . .?"

Okay, so that wasn't suspicious at all, was it?

Mr. Wood (or "Morning" as I liked to think of him) led me to the cosy little sitting room I'd seen on my last visit. And then stood there, watching me.

"Any chance you could leave me to get on with it?" I asked without a lot of hope.

"I don't think that would be appropriate, Mr. Paretski. You may start in here."

"Right. Fine. Just need a mo to think about it."

As I stood there, psychically limbering up—all right, just gathering the nerve to get on with it and finally find out what all the fuss was about—I wished I'd asked Dave to check up on the first Mrs. M. But he'd been a bit busy lately, what with arresting and charging the St. Leonards Poisoner, as the papers had dubbed her.

I hoped I wasn't about to meet Raz's mum. Still, if I was in for an unpleasant discovery, it wasn't going to get any better for pratting around for half an hour first. I took a deep breath and listened.

I found the trail almost immediately. Oh, there was some background noise, always is—but the main thread was loud and bright. There was a sense of . . . mischief. Of fun. I suddenly found myself missing Auntie Lol like mad—which was daft, because I hadn't seen her in years before she died. I suppose it just made me remember what she'd been like when I was a kid. Although weirdly, there was something masculine about it too.

Of course, we'd speculated that Auntie Lol might have had some help hiding stuff here. I wondered who the bloke was—Raz? It'd make sense; he was still on the spot, even if he wasn't exactly welcome at the old homestead.

I was definitely going to give him a call after we were done here. I had a feeling we had a lot to talk about.

"Are you planning to start searching sometime soon?" Wood's voice jolted me right out of my train of thought.

I turned on him. "Do you *mind*?"

There was actually a flicker of discomfort on that crepe-paper face. "Ah. My apologies. Please proceed."

I felt a bit guilty myself, so I just nodded and mumbled, "Thank you."

It took me a mo to catch the thread again, but this time, when I had it, I followed it. Out of the living room, across the hall, and into the kitchen. Huh. If only I'd known—I'd been right in the room with it last time I'd been here.

Once I'd got in there, I stood for a moment in the middle of the room, spinning around slowly. Listening.

There. I looked up.

Someone had clearly been having a laugh, because the trail was leading to the top of the kitchen units. They were fake olde-worlde, pine-fronted ones that finished about six inches under the ceiling and went nicely with the chickens on the tiles, in a feminine, twee sort of way. A tall bloke—like, say, Phil—could probably reach up and over the lip that jutted up at the edge. Me, not so much. I cast my eye around for something to stand on and caught old Wood watching me. "Need a leg up," I explained, grabbing a chair from around the kitchen table.

He nodded and carried on playing the hawk to my wood pigeon as I climbed up on top of the chair and felt carefully over the top of the cupboard. The first thing I noticed was that Mr. M. was definitely of the "out of sight, out of mind" persuasion when it came to dusting. I hoped I wasn't going to run into a wasp's graveyard up here. Those bastards can still sting you even when they're dead.

The second thing I noticed was the corner of something that shifted when I touched it—but not before I got the telltale tingles all up my arm confirming this was what I was after. I fumbled for the corner, grabbed it, and brought the thing down in a cloud of dust.

It was an envelope, one of those ones a bit bigger than a normal letter, but not big enough to hold an A4 sheet without folding it. I could feel there was stuff inside, and it had neatly typed on it, *Codicil to the Last Will and Testament of Laura Morangie, née Fernside*. But it was what was handwritten underneath that made me stare. It said, *Keep Looking.*

Yep, definitely someone having a laugh here.

I stared at it for a moment longer, then waved it at Wood too fast for him to see it properly. "Just a clue," I said breezily, then rolled it up and shoved it in my back pocket. "It says to keep looking."

He raised an eyebrow, causing ripples in the forehead wrinkles. "Impressive. Although, of course, you could have known already that would be the place to look."

I just shrugged. No skin off my nose if he didn't believe in my "thing," as Cherry put it.

"And where will you look next?" he persisted.

"Gotta think about that one. If you don't mind?"

"Oh, of course." He folded his hands together and pretended to look out of the window. There was even the faintest sound of whistling.

I was starting to like old Morning.

The vibes now were fainter. Older. Whatever I was supposed to keep looking for—assuming that was what I was picking up, of course—had been hidden here a long time ago. Years. Lots of them. And unlike the codicil, there hadn't been a lot of fun involved. Regret. Anxiety. And . . . maybe just a whiff of annoyance?

At least it probably wasn't a body, then. Not that I'm an expert on the subject, but when you imagine how a murderer must be feeling when they stash away a corpse, the phrase "a bit miffed" doesn't exactly spring to mind. Maybe it should, I dunno. I suppose it depends on whether you believe we're all potential murderers, given enough provocation, or whether you're of the opinion anyone who could kill another person has got something seriously wrong with their head.

You can probably tell which view I subscribe to. I was pretty sure I was on the right track, though. There were other trails, yeah, there always are—but this one was much brighter, even though it was older. All the rest, I was betting, were just the usual sort of hidden stuff: that letter from Auntie Mary you knew you should have answered five years ago and which now makes you feel guilty every time you look at it; the paperwork for a nice wodge of income that completely slipped your mind when you filled in that year's tax return (not that I'd have any personal experience of this one. Seriously. I pay my dues); the trashy books and magazines you wouldn't be seen dead reading by anyone you knew. That sort of thing. Petty stuff.

Anyway, this one was leading me upwards. I jogged up the stairs, hearing old Wood's slower footsteps behind me, and stopped.

It still wanted me to go upwards. I stared up at the hatch in the ceiling leading to the attic. "Got a ladder somewhere?"

For the first time, I missed Mr. M. being around, but we eventually tracked one down in the garage, which gave me a chance to check that place out too. Clean as a whistle; no dirty secrets hidden among the dirty rags and oil cans.

"Mr. Morangie looked up there, you know," Wood chided me as I set up the ladder under the attic hatch and checked it was firm. "He told me there's nothing there but old clothes, furniture, and letters."

Well, that could be promising. Maybe Auntie Lol had left me an antique clock. Or some vintage Prada. I smothered a grin at the thought of Auntie Lol in Prada. Not really her thing—she was more into long, flouncy skirts and market-stall finds. "A second pair of eyes can't hurt," I told him and climbed up the ladder. I'd found a torch in the garage too and flicked it on. The first thing I saw was a light bulb swinging from the rafters, and a bit of hunting about found me the switch.

The attic was . . . sad. I mean, not in and of itself, obviously, but when you knew about the bitter old bloke who owned it who couldn't even stand to have anyone mention his only kid to him: yeah, sad. There was a sturdy-looking wooden cot, in pieces, neatly stacked, and storage bags and boxes labelled *blankets, newborn baby clothes*, and *6-12m*. Saddest of all: *baby toys*. Maybe they'd thought they'd have another, Mr. M. and the first missus, and kept everything in readiness.

I wondered what had happened first: her popping her clogs, or them giving up hope. Maybe Mr. M. had thought Auntie Lol was his second chance. It hadn't happened; was that why the marriage didn't work out? Funny things, marriages. You find that one person you want to spend the rest of your life with, just the two of you, then next thing you know, you're not going to be happy until someone else comes along to—

"Have you found anything yet?" Old Morning's reedy voice quavered up through the attic door, reminding me I had a job to do and wasn't just here to get all philosophical.

"Not yet," I yelled back and got my arse in gear.

I found it under some bags of clothes. Women's clothes. I couldn't tell, from just a brief glance, if they'd belonged to Auntie Lol or to the first Mrs. M, and it seemed a bit disrespectful to get them out and have a good look. Not that it mattered anyway. I'd got what Auntie Lol had wanted me to find.

It was an old biscuit tin, one of those family assortment ones I remembered from when I was a kid that never had enough of the chocolate fingers in. Probably because Richard and Cherry always got there first. The lid was spotted with rust. It'd been sealed up with Sellotape that was now all brittle with age and peeled away practically with a look.

The contents had stayed dry.

It wasn't like in the movies, where you find a bundle of love letters all tied up with ribbon, scented with lavender. These were just shoved inside a brown paper bag, and they smelled a bit musty.

They really were love letters, though. Well, there were a couple of them in there. One or two postcards that had been written and never posted. Maybe they'd been brought back and delivered by hand? All were from some bloke called Mike and addressed to "Sweetheart." And there were photographs. Not many, but they all showed the same two people. A dark-haired bloke, not over-tall, who looked a bit familiar. And my mum, looking younger than I'd ever known her—but still older than the pictures I'd seen of her when Cherry and Richard were little.

I sat back on my heels, my head hurting and my chest tight. I didn't get it. I wasn't sure I wanted to either. Why would Auntie Lol have done this? Why set this all up, make a game of it, almost—just so's I could find out Mum had cheated on Dad? Why would *anyone* do that? Let alone someone I always thought had, well, loved me?

Then I worked it out.

Christ.

I felt it physically, like a punch in the gut. Or maybe to the heart. Whatever it was, it left me sickened, and my hands shook as I put the letters back in the bag and then levered myself to my feet.

Don't know what I said to old Wood. Probably just something like, "Found it," and waved the paper bag at him. I don't think I even remembered to close up the attic, take down the ladder, or shut the front door on the way out, for that matter. I should probably give him a ring and apologise for that, I thought, as I climbed into the driver's seat of my van and sat down. Cherry probably had his number.

Or should I ring Mr. M.? He was the one who'd have to clear stuff up after me. Probably. Christ, did I leave the attic light on? That was bad. Old people got uptight about stuff like that. I should definitely apologise. Maybe to both of them, just to make sure.

My heart was still racing, but at least the cold air outside had helped with the queasiness. Wasn't sure I was really up for driving yet, though.

"You got it, then?" Phil asked. I could feel him staring at me.

I waved the codi-thingy at him, then leaned back in the seat and closed my eyes. "I'm a bastard," I said bleakly.

"Why? What've you done?" Phil sounded startled.

I opened my eyes. Yeah, he had an expression to match. "Not that kind of bastard. I mean, my dad's not my dad. Probably."

"What, your mum was playing away from home? *Your* mum?"

"Yeah." I laughed. It wasn't a good sound. "She was what, early forties? It's like Dave says, I guess. Dangerous age for a woman."

Phil laid a hand on my thigh and gave it a quick squeeze. "You got evidence for this?"

I handed over the paper bag. Phil took his time. I wondered if I should feel bad, letting him read my mum's old love letters, but sod it, she was the one who'd started all this.

"Dates are right," he said at last, his tone neutral. "And the bloke in the pictures looks like you. Doesn't prove anything."

"No." I scrubbed my hands over my face. "Think I should ask my dad for some DNA?"

"Probably not. But you could ask your mum for an explanation."

"I can't just ask my mum about her sex life!" I cringed at the thought. "God, it's bad enough I read her bloody letters. I let *you* read her letters."

"It's ancient history now. Not like she got them last week." Phil hesitated. "He seems like an all right bloke, this Mike. You know, from his letters and the photos."

"You mean, apart from the bit where he was messing around with a married woman?"

"Well, there's that." Phil's hand was rubbing my thigh, moving rhythmically up and down, up and down. Any other time, I'd have been wanting to take things somewhere more private, but right now it was just a warm, solid comfort. "What I don't get is, how come your Auntie Lol had these letters? Why not your mum? There any clue in the codicil?"

"I haven't even looked at that." Funny, after I'd been getting butterflies over it earlier. Didn't seem half so important now.

"You what? Come on, hand it over, then."

"Bugger off. We can read it together, all right?" I pulled out the envelope and hesitated, my brain finally juddering back into action. "Do you think we need to do this in front of a solicitor or something? I mean, is it legal if we just open it?"

"Don't see why not. But if you're worried, we can take it round to your sister's. She's the executor, so she's going to have to see it anyway."

"Ah, sod that. I'm opening it." I stuck a finger under the flap and tore it open.

There were two smaller envelopes inside. One of them had written on it, *Read this first.* I had half a mind to stick a metaphorical two fingers up and open the other, but I decided to be a good boy.

It was a letter from Auntie Lol, of course.

Dear Tom,

So funny to write this now and not know when you'll get it. I'd like to think it'll be a long time from now, but I have to be realistic. By now you should have found your mother's letters. As you've probably guessed, she gave them to me for safe keeping, as she couldn't bear to destroy them. Perhaps I should have taken them with me, when Raz and I left, but there was only so much we could carry. But I'm so sorry you had to find out about your father this way.

I looked up. "Shit. So it is true."

Phil gave my thigh another squeeze. "Keep reading."

I've kept trying, through the years since you grew up, to persuade your mother to tell you herself. And you mustn't blame her for not telling you—she's just as convinced it's the right thing to do as I am that it isn't. She made me promise, all those years ago, not to tell you, so I never did. But I think we should face uncomfortable truths. I have to face the fact that this cancer is almost certainly going to kill me. And I think that makes me stronger. Far better to face my death and meet it on my terms. I like to think the Tom I knew would feel the same.

I'm so sorry I haven't seen you these last years. I'm afraid your mother's secret came between us, in the end. But from your cards and the photos you've sent me, I think you've grown up, as my Heather used to say, a fine, bonny young man. I hope you find someone to love you as you deserve. Don't be afraid to use your talents.

If I can ask one last thing of you (and I know you may be feeling I've got a bit of a cheek!) could you, perhaps, keep in touch with Raz? He's had a difficult journey, and if you could make sure he's all right, that would ease my mind. You've probably guessed he's who I've asked to hide this for me.

I think you two could be friends, you know.

With love,

Auntie Lol

That was it.

Phil pursed his lips. "Why don't you open the other envelope?"

"You're bloody desperate to find out what this legacy is, aren't you?" It didn't seem all that important to me anymore. It was just . . . stuff.

"Might as well."

I rolled my eyes. "Fine. Let's find out what this codicil's got to say for itself." I ripped open the second envelope.

There were a lot of long words, *aforementioneds* and other legalese. But the upshot of it was, as far as I could gather, that she'd left me a bequest of £500 and my mother's letters. Her part of the house had been left to her stepson, Raz Nair. She'd even put in all the details of his former name, just to dot all the i's and cross all the t's.

I huffed out a breath. "That's going to put the cat among the pigeons, innit? Him owning half of his dad's house. Think she meant it as a final *screw you* to the old bloke?"

"Well, you knew her best."

I thought about it, staring out through the windscreen. Down the road, a mum was pushing triplets in one of those modern stacker-system buggies, and an old lady walking two Yorkshire Terriers stopped to coo over the cuteness. To be honest, it was a relief to think about something other than what was in those letters.

"Nah," I said in the end. "She wasn't like that. She'd have just wanted him to have what he was due. Raz, I mean. His dad might have cut him off, but she wasn't going to stand for it. You never know, she might even have thought it'd get them speaking again."

Was that what she'd wanted to happen by telling me about my real dad? Me and him getting to know each other? I wondered what he was like, this Mike bloke. Was he even still alive after all this time?

"Right. Because arguments over property are well-known for leading to reconciliations." Phil was obviously still thinking about Raz.

"Yeah, well, hope over experience and all that bollocks. You know, I can't believe I never realised he was trans. I just thought he was gay."

"He still might be. Doesn't matter, does it?" Phil grabbed my thigh, hard. "You're taken, and don't you forget it, all right?"

"So now would probably be a bad time to mention I had Greg in my bed the other night? Not in the biblical sense, obviously," I added quickly as the storm clouds gathered on Phil's brow. Obviously, me sleeping with other blokes wasn't something he had much of a sense of humour about.

"Right." The weather forecast still wasn't looking all that sunny. Oops.

"We just shared a bed 'cos Cherry insisted on him staying. *I* didn't want him in there. And it's not like I even slept." Too late, I realised that last bit wasn't exactly helping my case. "He snores. Like a bloody foghorn."

"Does he." There was a long silence. "It's okay," Phil said at last, "I trust you. Sometimes wonder why I put up with you, mind." But there was a fond twist to his mouth, and his hand was stroking up and down my thigh in a way that promised . . . Well, I wasn't sure exactly what it was promising, but I was looking forward to finding out when I got him home.

"Love you too," I said, and this time, I meant it.

Explore more of *The Plumber's Mate Mysteries*:
riptidepublishing.com/titles/series/plumbers-mate-
mysteries

Dear Reader,

Thank you for reading JL Merrow's *Relief Valve*!

We know your time is precious and you have many, many entertainment options, so it means a lot that you've chosen to spend your time reading. We really hope you enjoyed it.

We'd be honored if you'd consider posting a review—good or bad—on sites like **Amazon, Barnes & Noble, Kobo, Goodreads, Twitter, Facebook**, **Tumblr,** and your blog or website. We'd also be honored if you told your friends and family about this book. Word of mouth is a book's lifeblood!

For more information on upcoming releases, author interviews, blog tours, contests, giveaways, and more, please sign up for our weekly, spam-free newsletter and visit us around the web:

Newsletter: tinyurl.com/RiptideSignup
Twitter: twitter.com/RiptideBooks
Facebook: facebook.com/RiptidePublishing
Goodreads: tinyurl.com/RiptideOnGoodreads
Tumblr: riptidepublishing.tumblr.com

Thank you so much for Reading the Rainbow!

RiptidePublishing.com

ALSO BY JL MERROW

The Plumber's Mate Mysteries
Pressure Head
Heat Trap
Blow Down
Lock Nut (coming May 2018)

Porthkennack
Wake Up Call
One Under (coming March 2018)

The Shamwell Tales
Caught!
Played!
Out!
Spun!

The Midwinter Manor Series
Poacher's Fall
Keeper's Pledge

Southampton Stories
Pricks and Pragmatism
Hard Tail

Lovers Leap
It's All Geek to Me
Damned If You Do
Camwolf
Muscling Through
Wight Mischief
Midnight in Berlin
Slam!
Fall Hard
Raising the Rent
To Love a Traitor
Trick of Time
Snared
A Flirty Dozen

ABOUT THE AUTHOR

JL Merrow is that rare beast, an English person who refuses to drink tea. She read Natural Sciences at Cambridge, where she learned many things, chief amongst which was that she never wanted to see the inside of a lab ever again. Her one regret is that she never mastered the ability of punting one-handed whilst holding a glass of champagne.

She writes across genres, with a preference for contemporary gay romance and mysteries, and is frequently accused of humour. Her novel *Slam!* won the 2013 Rainbow Award for Best LGBT Romantic Comedy, and her novella *Muscling Through* and novel *Relief Valve* were both EPIC Awards finalists.

JL Merrow is a member of the Romantic Novelists' Association, International Thriller Writers, Verulam Writers and the UK GLBTQ Fiction Meet organising team.

Find JL Merrow on Twitter as @jlmerrow, and on Facebook at facebook.com/jl.merrow

For a full list of books available, see: jlmerrow.com/ or JL Merrow's Amazon author page: viewauthor.at/JLMerrow

Enjoy more stories like
Relief Valve
at RiptidePublishing.com!

The Best Corpse for the Job
ISBN: 978-1-62649-192-2

The Two Gentlemen of Altona
ISBN: 978-1-62649-219-6

Earn Bonus Bucks!
Earn 1 Bonus Buck for each dollar you spend. Find out how at
RiptidePublishing.com/news/bonus-bucks.

Win Free Ebooks for a Year!
Pre-order coming soon titles directly through our site and you'll
receive one entry into a drawing for a chance to win free books for
a year! Get the details at RiptidePublishing.com/contests.

9 781626 497221